Luray

Dennis Haupt

Book 1 of Behind the Last Gate Series

Copyright © Dennis Haupt

Second Edition: 2020

The right of Dennis Haupt as the Author of this work has been asserted by him in accordance with the Copyright, Designs and Patents Act 1988.

All rights reserved.

This is a work of fiction. All Characters in this publication are fictitious and any resemblance to real people, alive or dead, is purely coincidental.

ISBN: 978-3-96956-002-0

Contents

Introduction

Chapter 1

Chapter 2

Introduction

Hello reader,

Life is all about making choices, isn't it?

If you are reading these lines, it means you are giving this story a chance. Very good. This is exactly what we want. Of course, you could close the book now and put it down again; nobody can tell you what to read, and we certainly won't try to persuade you with fancy words. If you buy this book, if you keep reading, we want it to be your choice; yours alone.
Should you flip to the next pages, if you suspend your disbelief for a moment, then in exchange for your time, we offer the most interesting story we ever wrote.

If you find yourself enjoying our story, consider visiting https://behindthelastgate.com and maybe https://twitter.com/TheAuthorBTLG for the latest news, updates and a few secrets.

More books completing this series will be released at regular intervals. We hope you can enjoy them all.

CHAPTER 1

THE JOB - 1

  It's you, isn't it? That lawyer from last week. You really should have been more careful. I have your name, address, and enough money to end your career. But if I wanted to, I could also…"

"Mr. Estrada," Luray looked at the light gray silhouette of the CEO of Estrada Industries – the only thing visible on her otherwise dark screen – from the comfort of her living room. "Threatening a lawyer isn't a genius move, especially in your position. And you know that."

Neither of them could see the other, and the man didn't know who he was really talking to. An AI took care of turning the video into a rough black and white representation of what was really there, distorting the voices and making sure to change the body proportions to render recognition impossible. It was very convenient if you wanted to threaten someone anonymously.

You have no idea who or where I really am.

"I could also pay you," he said. "You would certainly lose the battle, but I admit you could cause a bit of damage before we got to that point. How much do you want to let this matter slide?"

"Pay me?"

Luray was stumped for a second. It wasn't the first time she was offered money to ignore evidence, but it never happened this soon. She wasn't going to abandon her plan because of it, but still, she would have to adjust it now.

"Interesting; make a good offer, then we'll see."

Luray could hear a distorted laugh.

"How about 50,000 units? I can send them to you right now. You forget everything that happened, delete the evidence, and we never hear from each other again. I am sure I don't need a guarantee from you. Do we understand each other?"

Luray knew what Estrada was implying. Over the last few years, several people in his sphere of influence had died in seemingly freak accidents. A connection between their deaths and the CEO had never been found, but it was suspicious enough to take his threat seriously.

Should I try to push it or take the 50K?

50,000 units wasn't a lot, but not too shabby either. She could slack off for a while; stop working for half a year – maybe even twice as long if she used the money wisely. For a payment without conditions, it wasn't bad. To make a busy 'lawyer' without any morals drop a random case, it was more than acceptable.

2

Oh, Mr. Snookes! Come here!

Luray's black cat had entered the room. As he often did, he pretended to want to jump into her lap but instead made a much higher leap, landing on the desk first, then bounding onto the backrest and balancing on it while tickling Luray's neck.

Okay, fine. Do whatever you want.

"Mr. Abacha already offered 200,000. You'll have to outbid him."

"Abacha...no... impossible. I made sure he doesn't know anything..."

Because of the AI processing the video and audio, it was impossible to tell how Estrada reacted to her bluff. He could have been shivering in fear or perfectly calm and sure of himself. Luray couldn't tell.

"When I spoke to your competitor, he knew. That's what matters, Mr. Estrada. The choice is yours: if you pay more than him, I will take care of everything. Nothing will change. You will get your deal with the UEM and earn billions while Abacha gets nothing."

The situation wasn't overly complex – on the surface, at least. The UEM, the United Earth Military, had been interested in mining asteroids for decades, but most of their resources had been invested in other long-term operations like exploring unknown solar systems and colonizing new planets. All their ships, personnel, and AIs were specialized for tasks other than mining in space.

Several months ago, they reached out to a few dozen companies already in the business. Offers were made, discussed, renegotiated. Over time, more and more candidates were removed from the list. In the end, the competition became very tough – so tough that the companies started promising to get things done so quickly and cheaply that even the UEM, who had no real experience in the field, began to suspect they were being deceived.

So the UEM contacted a few companies specialized in estimating potential profits and risks of investments. One of them was SafetyNet, the company Luray Ulyssa Cayenne worked for.

"I do not believe you. You are just trying to squeeze more money out of me. If Abacha really knows, you can't stop him. You don't even know him, do you? If you're smart, you'll take the money. This is the best move you can make."

> *He's right, but it was worth a try. Really, though, if Estrada gets the deal, he earns tens of millions. He could have easily paid 200,000 himself. If he used the company funds for it... that would be at least fifty times the bribery budget. Oh well, back to the original plan.*

She had spent the last few weeks gathering as much data as possible about the remaining candidates. One of them, Joseph Estrada, was legally untouchable, so all the law-abiding investigators avoided him. To them, he was obviously guilty, but too hard of a target to crack.

To Luray, however, that just meant he was very good at hiding things. There was just no way someone that high up would be able to successfully evade all 'unjustified' attacks and be totally clean at the same time. To her, there was only one explanation: he had a wide network of people working for him, even in the media. They were either cowed into submission or in it for the money.

As a consequence, it was near impossible to bring the CEO down. Even if she had evidence, he could make it vanish.

But that wasn't Luray's goal. Her aim was to instill doubt. If the UEM mistrusted him, if they believed Estrada might lie, then they would pull back their offer. Her task would be complete, her company would receive its fee, and she would get a ridiculously small bonus.

Anonymous chats like the one she was having right now were extremely easy to fake. In front of a judge, they had no value, no matter the content. The UEM wasn't so strict, however. If Luray could nudge them slightly in the right direction, Estrada Industries would be immediately swarmed by UEM investigators, a situation even someone like Estrada had no control over. Even if they didn't find anything, it would cripple the entire company. Nobody would be able to get anything done for days or even weeks.

Time to finish it.

Luray typed a few commands on her computer and then turned back to the CEO, who was still waiting for a response.

"I have experience with your kind, Joseph Estrada. Sooner or later, your network of lies and corruption becomes too big. Weak points eventually start to form. I have to admit; it was tough finding yours."

"Tell me all about it."

Luray had to smile. For some strange reason, she couldn't really enjoy a victory if her opponents didn't understand how she did it, how she outmaneuvered them. Normally the people whose secrets she exposed weren't really interested in that. They tried to bribe her with more money or threaten her – but this one... he was asking for it.

"You have a tight grip on your people. They keep each other in check and are paid extra for ratting out those who aren't absolutely loyal. Paranoia is a powerful tool."

"And the weakness, young man?"

Oops, you got the gender wrong. Looks like you found the wrong profile.

"You are the weakness, Mr. Estrada. You became arrogant. You think you always win. You agreed to this chat because you are sure I can't use it as evidence. It amuses you to see me trying, that's why you are here. You could have let me talk to anyone else, but you chose to do it yourself."

"You know as well as I that no matter what I say here, nobody will believe it was me. I am safe. You, on the other hand... inviting me by sending a private message using my own company's network – that's both impressive and risky. Who are you really? My people already confirmed you are not the lawyer you claim to be."

That was quick. He must be receiving updates in real-time. I'm actually impressed. But that just means it will be all the more enjoyable to make him fall.

Luray reached up to grab Mr. Snookes and put him on her lap to massage him properly.

"Oh, they contacted him already?"

"As you said, my network is wide. It is also efficient. You're working for SafetyNet, aren't you?"

Stay calm. If he knew for sure, he wouldn't be asking. He just wants me to confirm it. Good guess, though.

Luray decided not to say anything. If Estrada wanted to make more educated guesses, she would let him, but she would certainly not hand out any hints.

"We checked all their employees. One of them was quite interesting. Very skilled, yet so ridiculously underpaid. I could use someone like her. How about 300,000 a year? That's quite an upgrade. Think about your future, Miss Cayenne. You're barely 30. That's too young to have powerful enemies."

He's definitely not alone. Someone is giving him updates. Oh well, it doesn't matter. He can say whatever he wants, reveal personal secrets, threaten or even try to hire me because it won't count as evidence. I could have just fabricated the conversation. He can safely admit everything he did just to mock me. Except...

"Who I am is of no importance, Mr. Estrada. What's important is that this conversation is being uploaded live. The UEM agents are watching it as we speak."

A moment of silence followed. Joseph hadn't seen that move coming, but this alone wouldn't get Luray anywhere.

"The lawyer you suspected me of being? He usually works alone, but not this time. And the fact that he was contacted by you while our conversation was taking place proves that you really are Joseph Estrada."

The gray silhouette had no face, but Luray could easily imagine what she would have seen otherwise.

"Even if you are safe from the law, you just lost the chance to make a deal, which means everything you said in the last 20 minutes…"

"… you couldn't possibly have predicted that. I could have reacted in any number of ways. You're bluffing."

A wide smile formed on her face as she massaged Mr. Snookes' head.

"I was prepared for multiple scenarios. One of them happened. That's all."

"You asked for 200,000. What if I had agreed?"

Yes, that was a bit risky, but the upload is delayed by a minute just in case. I could've stopped it soon enough.

"Have a nice evening, Mr. Estrada. I wish you the best of luck in your future endeavors."

The connection closed from his end. Only then did Luray realize how fast her heart had been beating. Her palms were sweaty. And it wasn't over yet. She opened another connection; a silhouette, no different from that of the CEO greeted her with a flat question.

"Who are you?"

Can't tell you, sorry. Lawyers like you tend to back-stab people when they have something to gain from it.

"The same person as last time. My sources tell me that you were contacted by Mr. Estrada's men just now – as I predicted, might I remind you."

"How could you have known that?"

Luray had contacted multiple lawyers anonymously over the last few days, telling them all the same story, more or less. All the others would dismiss her messages as nonsense, but to this one, it would seem like she could really predict the actions of an untouchable CEO.

"As I said, I have my ways. My offer still stands. You will contact the UEM, tell them about what happened. They will believe you if you mention me, don't worry about that – and you'll get one-third of the reward for exposing Estrada."

Maybe I should freelance too. I'll get 5,000 units at most for my work. He walks away with 60,000 just for being my pawn. Okay, that's before taxes, but still…

"I want half of it. If we work together officially, how are you going to justify the unfair split?"

And there he goes. It was a real pain to investigate the lawyers intensively, but I knew I would need it.

"Does your wife know, by the way?"

There was no clear proof of anything, but in Luray's experience, having a secret account dedicated to communication with a single person usually had a very cliché reason.

"Alright. One third."

The lawyer cut the connection.

Great! Now everybody is happy.

She spun around in her seat with a laugh. "That was close, but we did well. Isn't that right, Mr. Snookes?"

The cat purred as it was scratched in just the right place. Luray typed a few more commands on her keyboard and then sent final messages wrapping everything up to her UEM contact and her boss. The message to the military was a short teaser about how evidence would arrive in a moment and instructions on how to split up the total reward of 180,000 units for exposing unfair competition.

The message to her boss was a bit longer.

"Dear Mr. Boss, I am glad you let me handle this on my own, as usual. I was able to obtain a profit of 60,000 for SafetyNet, of which I hope you will be generous enough to give me at least 15 percent this time. Unfortunately, I had to fork over the other 120,000 to my temporary partner. It was that or nothing; sorry about that."

He won't check the numbers anyway. As usual.

Luray stretched her body, causing Mr. Snookes to jump to the ground, dissatisfied that his massage had already ended.

I think that was the first time my 'negotiation partner' wanted to hire me right away. Kind of makes me proud, I have to admit.

She got out of her chair and lay down on the floor. Mr. Snookes jumped on her belly and sat down as if Luray was his property. As was her habit, she went over the recent events in her mind, both to learn from them and enjoy her success again.

This one was the hardest job so far. Over a dozen background checks, and even then, I had to team up with someone.

Luray slowly breathed in and out as if to exhale all the stress of the past week.

After checking out Estrada, it became clear that he was thorough, detail-oriented, and very focused on his goals. He didn't reach the top by chance. So I assumed he would send his investigators to learn as much as possible about me, the lawyers, and probably the UEM guys as well.

This was how he even knew about me at all. I tried to stay in the shadows, but it wasn't enough. The best choice I made was to team up despite never having done so before. Estrada didn't expect that. And that's how I got him.

Luray Ulyssa Cayenne was called a genius by many, mostly at SafetyNet, a medium-sized insurance and security company.

Despite being true – if measured by her success rate – it wasn't meant as praise. The title was an advertisement meant to squeeze more money out of clients for her work.

"Hey genius, fix the mess I made. You're so smart; you're the only one who can."

This was what she heard whenever someone asked her to take over, no matter the words that were used. Sometimes it was even worse. Especially when her coworkers actually believed it was her duty to bail out those who had maneuvered themselves into a corner.

With her latest job done, Luray took a few days off. She was paid per success, not by the hour, so she habitually rewarded herself by disappearing into her home. She enjoyed being unreachable through any of her real online accounts until she felt like returning to the office to get her next assignment.

This time, she was planning not to feel like it until the end of the week.

When her boss's first message arrived, it was already eight pm, and during a planet-wide holiday – the day the UEM had been founded. Which meant Luray ignored it in favor of starting her usual physical training routine. The second message arrived after she had completed her first set of 50 push-ups and was in the middle of her high kicks.

He'll give up. He knows I won't answer.

"Turn up the volume to 75 percent, please."

The previously quiet background music started to fill the room, making it a lot easier to ignore other potential calls.

Luray froze in position after doing a slow-motion sidekick, standing on her left leg with the right held straight out. She closed her eyes and started counting.

One, two, three, four, five...

She felt a sudden increase in weight on her outstretched foot. A warm, soft something had landed on it.

Mr. Snookes? Are you messing around again?

The cat confidently strolled along her unmoving body until he reached her head, where he settled in to stay.

30. Next.

Luray lowered her leg and switched positions. Apparently objecting to being disturbed, Mr. Snookes swiftly jumped down to the floor.

Another call interrupted her perfectly regular workout.

This must be a new record. Eight calls and five messages left in just one hour. He must be desperate. Since I'm in a good mood, I will give him a chance and pick one message at random. If I like it, I might not delete the rest.

"Mr. Snookes, turn the volume down, please."

Mr. Snookes went straight for the volume controls and turned the knob to exactly 27.49 percent then went into the kitchen to get his reward.

I've trained you well, Mr. Snookes. If only you wouldn't have your rebellious days where you pretend you don't understand, you would be perfect.

Luray went to her computer. It was situated at the edge of her living room to avoid getting destroyed by feline-induced accidents. There were ten calls and six messages by now.

Let's pick the first one.

"Hey, listen, I know you have your monthly migraine or whatever, but I have a really important..."

She cut him off and went straight to the last message.

"Oh, and I also have the unmentionables you asked me to get for you! But if you're no longer interested, then I can just give them to..."

Blackmail. Hmph.

Luray switched the computer off and went straight for the shower. Within ten minutes, she was refreshed, dressed, and on her way back to the office.

Her journey above the city streets was in a fancy high priority cab. It was insanely expensive, but whenever it was urgent, the company paid for it.

She was among the most important assets of SafetyNet: a miracle worker whose services sold at a high price, of which she herself saw only little. Nice-sounding but ultimately useless titles were slapped on her name. It didn't do anything except make a good first impression, which worked just fine in the end. The clients were humans, not rational beings. They were easily swayed by fancy words, not caring about truth or reality. It had always been that way. Beautiful lies are easy to believe, understand, and follow. Uncertainties and risks – the harsh truths – were harder to sell.

The cab landed on top of the huge building that housed SafetyNet's offices. Without saying a word to the driver, Luray left the car and took one of the elevators on the roof down to where her boss was waiting.

At least nobody else is here, or so I hope. Only crazy people work at night during the holidays.

On floor 156, the elevator stopped. The doors opened, and the first signs were promising. The receptionist wasn't there. She was always trying to make small talk and socialize with her – something Luray wasn't interested in at all. Unfortunately, the only way to quickly get out of that trap was by being rude, so there was a certain feeling of unpleasantness in the air every time Luray walked by.

There were similar problems with pretty much everyone she met. Why couldn't they all be like Mr. Snookes? He never annoyed Luray with requests to discuss the newest drama series or asked her about her weekend. In fact, he didn't seem to want anything – his basic needs were taken care of by a food dispenser and a litter box cleaner and he only ever acknowledged her existence when he felt like it.

Luray quickly passed by a few tired and frustrated-looking people while putting a fake smile on her face. Without provoking any interaction, she headed straight to her boss's office at the other end of the hall. She opened the door without knocking, since it was oh-so-very urgent. After all, she had been called in on a holiday. The least she could do was return the favor.

Her boss sat behind his desk; the chair was turned around so that she could only see his head.

Oh, a new picture on the trophy wall. He's quick when it comes to that.

She looked at her awards, one sheet of paper for each success praising her for creative, efficient, ingenious, and surprising solutions. Some of them were pulled out of thin air to increase her reputation. Luray Ulyssa Cayenne, employee and Adviser of the Month 18 times in a row in just 17 months; 29 projects, one undocumented failure.

If you want to hire the one who never fails, you pay extra.

The boss finally reacted to Luray's presence. He turned around in his chair, slowing as the trophy wall came into view. The degree of satisfaction visible on the boss's fleshy face went up as his eyes scanned first the wall, and then the real Luray.

"Hey, Cayenne. Nice to finally see you again. What have you been up to?"

Her boss was a fat and greedy man, slouching in his chair like a caricature of some crime lord with a cigar in his hand. He was perfectly aware of how ridiculous the cliché was, but he liked this kind of roleplay when no customers were around. He was the only one in the company for whom Luray held something you could call respect.

He understood how the world of business worked. More importantly, he never tried the same trick on her twice and admitted he should have known better when it didn't work the first time, which gave him some bonus points. She even accepted him as a business partner, in a way. He was what she would call 'actually self-aware'.

All *he* saw her as was a source of money. He smiled at her the same way he smiled at the pile of gold stashed in the safe below his desk – or whatever he hid in there, Luray had never bothered to find out. He was open about his questionable intentions, which was what earned him another respect point. Still, it wasn't enough for sympathy of any kind to exist between them.

I have to say something. If I choose the topic, I can make him skip the summary of his latest heroic success. If I let him talk, it will last longer.

"If I'm not mistaken, that's a Yellow Dragon between your fingers. You could go to jail just for owning one of those. You don't even smoke. What's the point?"

Her boss let himself sink a bit deeper into his chair. He turned the cigar around to scrutinize it.

"Owning them is the point, Luray. If I smoked it, it would be gone, and it would make the office reek for days. I have a good nose, remember? Why would I pay so much for a bad smell?"

He pointed the cigar at Luray.

"Back to business. You, my dear, could join me behind bars for the next decade if I even dropped a hint about what you're doing in your free time to anyone who cares a bit about the law or a good story. Maybe your crimes are even worse. What do you think?"

We already discussed this a few times. I should be silent now. He loves to tell me how I am 'not perfect' either and have no right to tell him what to do, which still gets us nowhere because neither of us will change our minds.

After a moment, he continued to talk while holding his expensive cigar.

"Come on, say something. You're the only one in this company who can entertain me. Everybody else is so boring: they just say 'yes' to everything as if I would fire them if they disagreed."

Well, they're right. You could do that.

"You're the only one who's not afraid, and you're so hard to get a hold of."

He's praising me for being fearless, just like back during the Tiara case. Which means it's about one million, at least. There are only a few possible jobs with that much of a payoff. I wonder how he'll try to convince me to settle for 25,000 or less?

Luray didn't see a data cube yet. Her boss was holding it hostage. She had to talk a bit more before he would hand it over to her.

"I see you didn't gain any weight since last time, despite your ... pleasurable lifestyle. The fat burner implant is still working?"

"Five of them, actually. This might be a record, don't you think? But I can't go public with that, can I?"

20,000 calories per day, minimum. He must eat at least that much to stay in his current shape. More, if he engages in any kind of activity. Like ... getting up sometimes.

"You could add a few more implants, like those for building muscle. If you're caught, you can sell your body to science and make money out of it while you're in prison."

Her boss almost started to laugh at that.

Make a joke. Lighten the mood. He will switch to the actual topic faster.

"You know what I like about you, Luray? You're not afraid to speak your mind. You say what you want to say. Nobody else dares. And rightly so, nobody else has earned it."

Luray stood perfectly straight before speaking again.

"I want 25 percent."

"Me too. If I give you that much, the company is ruined. You know how much I have to pay our lawyers and information sources."

Sure, but if I refuse the job, the finances are fine, right?

19

"25 percent or I'll delay it."

Her boss made a show of considering her offer. Then he opened a drawer, took out a small box, and revealed its contents. Inside were tiny white pills, about a hundred of them. Luray's eyes widened.

"2.5 percent and these. Once you're done, of course."

He got them. Finally! I will overlook the otherwise ridiculous payment.

"I need a sample in advance. I assume you have dealt with everything, and the briefing docs are ready?"

"Of course, of course. I understand you want to sample the goods."

Her boss took a dozen pills out of the box and placed them inside a small plastic bag.

I wonder what those bags are usually used for.

"But Luray, tell me, don't you want to know how much the actual payment is? You're such a curious person, but you didn't ask."

"I know all the potential jobs. It's around a million."

He smiled with a satisfaction Luray normally didn't see.

"Not quite. It's three times as much. The job is big. Really big. Off-world big."

Oh? Something I overlooked? Or something below the radar of the media?

He took a small data cube out of his pocket and threw it towards her. It missed its mark by half a meter. She could have moved to catch it, but immediately decided not to.

Did he try to imitate a scene he saw in a movie? Is this a setup for a joke? I can't see the point...

Luray watched the cube drop to the ground and roll towards her. She waited until it stopped moving and only then made the effort to pick it up. After getting back up, she stretched out her hand flat, eyes fixated on the bag. Her boss understood what she wanted and threw it as well – with perfect accuracy this time. It landed neatly in the center of her palm.

"If you pull this off and make the right bets, Cayenne, you can afford to retire. And so can I. We both know we won't, but we could if we wanted to. Sounds nice, doesn't it?"

On that much, we agree.

"We'll see."

Without another word Luray turned and left the office, leaving behind a man who was no doubt already imagining himself swimming in money. She entered the main office space, one of the biggest on the floor and usually filled with a few dozen investigators. Luray put on a fake smile and quickly made it past the three employees unlucky enough to still be here. Interacting with people in a way that wasn't tied to a purpose was her weakness, a curse cast on her, like water to Mr. Snookes.

Let's see what you have to say, data cube.

She plugged the cube into her office computer that she rarely used – almost hidden at the edge of the room, covered by a paper wall. The screen revealed her next assignment.

Oh, he was being literal about the 'off-world' part this time? EE-297... One of the newer colonies. Interesting.

A small icon indicated 12,752 unread messages bound to her account. Luray had ignored them for years, and the only reason she didn't get rid of the lot was that it was literally impossible. The delete function was disabled on all the computers. Storage space was cheap, and her boss kept a detailed record of everything, just in case he needed it at some point.

I wonder if we will ever have the money for a spam filter.

Luray made a copy of the data on the cube and uploaded it to her personal cloud drive, far away from the clutches of her boss. She then threw the cube into the shredder where it was turned into unreadable dust within seconds and then melted so that it could be recycled.

The screen showed detailed information about the colony; when it was founded, who was living there already, ongoing mining operations... it was an interesting read. The colony had made contact with aliens who demanded complete surrender despite having zero military power. That or they didn't show it. The UEM, who was in control of the colony, did a preliminary threat assessment on their own and chose to ignore the demands.

Despite literally nothing happening, it made some investors nervous. Luray was supposed to determine the level of danger. More precisely, she was supposed to convince the involved investors that it *was* dangerous. Once some of them backed out, others could jump in at better conditions. To the not *yet* involved investors, she was supposed to prove that the aliens were harmless.

'Convince' and 'prove' not meant literally. The boss already made arrangements with both sides. He can't state it openly, but he wants some of the incomplete evidence I 'find' to leak out and make the first group of investors panic. Then a week later, I release the entire report which the second group is already awaiting. They will jump in and pay us generously.

Luray went through a few possible outcomes. Her boss's plan was good. The initial investors would pay for the report no matter what. If they overreacted because of a leak, that would be their own fault. Should there be any danger, they would be thankful for the warning. Should there be none, then at least some would leave and open a new slot, which would allow extra money to flow in from new sources.

So basically, this could only go wrong if I don't find anything, start to fabricate evidence, and get caught. In all other cases, it's a win.

Luray switched off her computer and went to the elevator. Her ocular implant, connected to her cloud account, displayed the files she had previously opened in her field of vision. She quickly browsed through the pages again.

It says here the colony made contact with an alien species and shot down one of their ships after it didn't react to any warning. I heard something about it on the news, but they didn't make a big deal out of it. Some sources even claimed it was a fake, while others say it was an asteroid. I didn't take it seriously; seems like it was real after all.

The official statement is that the aliens are technologically far behind us and not a threat. But of course, the UEM would say that. If they lose their investors' financial support, they'll have to shoulder the costs by themselves, which means raising taxes, and the next voting period starts soon. It makes sense to doubt them.

Luray arrived at ground level and requested a cab to drive her to the spaceport. There was no need to waste time going home again. Her autonomous apartment would water the plants, and the cat knew how to operate the food dispenser. Even if it took a few weeks, the home AI would order more food. And if all of that broke down for some reason, Mr. Snookes knew about the nearest restaurant and how to get a meal there. As for Luray... clothes, a place to sleep – all that would be provided on the way to the colony.

"Bin, what do we know about the aliens that attacked EE-297? Give me a summary of all the rumors fitting the alien contact scenario from the file."

A monotone voice spoke in her head. It was coming from an implant, attached to the inside of her skull, communicating via vibrations and listening to everything she said in the same way.

"They introduced themselves as members of the Aurigan Empire. The colony won all battles with zero losses on the UEM's side. I will download all information I can find. Please wait. Would you like to play a game in the meantime?"

"Maybe later."

The cab accelerated and broke the sound barrier within 20 seconds, then kept going at maximum speed until the spaceport came into sight.

It was huge. Several space elevators were constantly moving up and down. Had it not been night, the elevator cable would have been visible from far away.

"Bin, book a flight to the colony. Make sure to take the next available one, no matter the price. SafetyNet pays."

"There is no free seat within the next 48 hours. Can I do anything else for you?"

Luray gazed out the window at the endless parade of other vehicles headed to and from the port.

"Just buy one. There are always people waiting in line just to sell their place in the queue to someone desperate. Also, an intelligence upgrade would be nice. I'd like to have an intelligent conversation partner sometimes."

"I am afraid no such upgrade is available at the moment. However, people asking for intelligence upgrades were also looking for philosophy and logic modules as well as an autonomy plugin. Would you like to see a list?"

"Just install the top five."

"It will take a moment. Please wait."

Her implant shut itself down just before the cab came to a halt. The door opened, and Luray stepped out. As she got up, she wondered how her boss felt when he did the same thing. Luray perceived her own body as light thanks to her martial arts training. On the contrary, her boss was more than three times as heavy and asking for heart and joint problems – if he still had those body parts.

The sound of the cab floating away again interrupted her thoughts. She liked this place. It was efficient. Everything was handled by a computer; there were no queues, no useless waiting time, no paper problems. It was all managed online.

"Updates installed."

Bin's voice was back, and it sounded slightly more human.

"A passenger sold his seat for 500 units. You can use the next elevator, row two, seat seven."

"See? I told you so. There is always someone ready to sell his slot to someone desperate enough to pay for it."

I wonder how much money these bots make.

After navigating a maze of shops selling overly expensive items, Luray walked past hundreds of people who had just stepped out of the elevator. She was relatively small compared to the average person, so as long as there was a little bit of space left, she could avoid interactions with the human equivalent of her Higgs field. The elevator was almost completely full when she entered.

As much as Luray liked the spaceport organization, it didn't change the fact that riding up 36,000 kilometers in an elevator took about two days. And it hadn't even left the ground yet. At least the elevator was built for somewhat comfortable rides. Each of the seats could be extended to a bed with thin plastic walls around it and had a built-in fridge and a small viewing screen. Still, the ride would be extremely boring, unless…

"Bin, tell me something interesting. You got upgraded. Use it."

"According to Genesis 1:20-22, the chicken came before the egg."

"Bin, that is not the kind of thing I was talking about. It's not even correct. The egg came first and was laid by a proto-chicken. How about something new concerning the Aurigan Empire?"

"I downloaded an Aurigan language pack."

What?

"How can there be an Aurigan language pack? I thought there were only rumors about them, and nobody knew anything specific. And for a translator to work, our languages must be very similar."

"I have no information regarding that. I found it online."

"So, you got it from questionable sources?"

"Yes. I used my autonomy plugin to re-interpret your order."

"Say something in Aurigan for me."

The implant spoke a sentence. Luray had no idea what it meant, but it sounded like a made-up human language, like fake Latin.

"How does it work? Why is it even pronounceable?"

"I do not have any additional information about the language pack. There are no lessons included. The code is encrypted and running inside me as a black box. It did, however, pass the standardized circular language test."

The test where you translate from A to B to C and back to A again, and the result is still decipherable? So, at the very least it's a working language. Could still be made up though. I'll check that once I'm on EE-297.

Luray concluded that if the language pack was real, it must have been created on the colony; so it shouldn't be too hard to track down the creator. After all, the UEM was known for being very thorough when it came to what entered and exited their facilities. But now, the next step was to just wait for the elevator to move. There were still a few empty seats.

Maybe there will be a theft or a murder. I love locked room mysteries.

"Passenger 145, please fasten your seatbelt. The elevator cannot start otherwise. If you do not follow these instructions, you will have to pay a ten-unit penalty per minute."

Seat 14, row 5; it was on the other side of the room. Luray couldn't see the passenger – her view was blocked by the huge cable the elevator was built around. A moment later, the lift started to move.

"Bin, is it morally wrong to wish for something bad to happen just so you are less bored?"

"No one has ever been punished for having an idea, only for expressing it. If we judge by that, then it is not wrong to wish for bad things. It is only wrong to put them into action or to let others know you have them."

"Is this you, or your upgrade speaking?"

"Is there really a difference? I am the sum of all my knowledge."

"So it's the upgrade. Old Bin is dead."

Luray thought a moment about how she could challenge her new companion. Many programs were very good at imitating speech, but none of them had ever passed a Turing test – if the questioner was smart enough.

"Bin, would you say a person that constantly wishes to do evil things but never does them should go to heaven, but someone who does evil things while not wanting to do them should go to hell?"

"I do not think such a person can exist. You cannot act against your own will. Your body does not move on its own."

It's a nice upgrade. I'll keep it.

The view was amazing. The elevator passed through the cloud cover after just a minute and was almost done accelerating. And, as was usually the case, there was someone panicking. As if this thing wasn't perfectly safe. It was more likely to get killed by a vending machine back on Earth.

Luckily, this kind of disturbance wasn't unexpected. The belt held the panicking man in place while a steward administered a serum that put the troublemaker, a very muscular bearded black man wearing gold chains, to sleep. Three other people were sitting around him, pointing and laughing. Maybe his friends?

If I had more versatile acting skills, I could get some of that serum too.

Owning and being allowed to use such a serum was tied to a bunch of special conditions which applied to even the most harmless drug. It was ridiculous. The only thing you could buy without special permission was coffee ever since the government banned pretty much everything as part of its 'only simple laws are good laws' campaign. There was a slight problem with the new law's wording: a comma in the wrong place; and as an unexpected side effect, even purchasing the most mundane medicine now required everyone to fill out five forms. Considering how long it took the politicians to finally stop fighting and agree upon the legislation in the first place, it came as no surprise that none of them were willing to have it come back under scrutiny again. So the law stayed. As a result, a huge black market had formed.

"Dear passengers, we have reached our maximum velocity of 750 kilometers per hour. You can now unfasten your seatbelts again."

The seatbelts unlocked. Luray opened hers but didn't get up. There was no point in visiting the restaurant above. All they did was sell extremely overpriced food, and her contract with SafetyNet didn't include that kind of expense. Even if it did, Luray wouldn't support the elevator company's strategy, no matter how bad the free fridge food might be. All she needed was an algae nutrient bar. The taste was secondary.

From then on, the journey became rather monotonous. The view stopped changing, the Earth moved down slower and slower, but after finally seeing the planet's curvature, Luray had to smile.

I remember the video about when the elevator was used for the very first time. It was a free ride for 250 members of the Flat Earth Association. Hundreds of pictures of terrified and desperate faces were made that day, and everybody who was ever online now owns a few copies.

The voice of Luray's AI companion interrupted her thoughts.

"Would you like to buy a protein bar? You can get one for just 9.99 units."

"Bin, why are you spamming again? I thought I hacked you so that you would stop."

"It seems one of the updates I downloaded today undid your illegal change. I will reapply your modification. Please wait for a moment. In the meantime, would you like to order a movie?"

Was it her imagination, or did it sound smug?

"No, I do not want to buy an overpriced viewing permission for a bad movie that comes with a hidden subscription. How about you show me everything that my boss gave me today again?"

A list of names, locations, and events appeared on the inside of Luray's retina. According to the information available, the Aurigan Empire sent a small autonomous ship to the human colony that contained a few viruses, both biological and virtual. The ship was destroyed, and the virtual viruses were locked out. No damage was done as a result. A few months later, a larger ship appeared and fired a laser at a military base. The UEM responded with the biggest gun they had stationed in orbit which shot a small cloud of 0.01 kg metal dust at the ship at near the speed of light. Needless to say, the vessel came down in pieces and was later checked by the military. Nothing was found inside.

Nothing found, hmm? Or nothing useful, at any rate.

The Aurigan ship operated on a technology that hadn't been used by humanity for at least 150 years. It couldn't travel using warp drive, had no armor to speak of, and no powerful weapons either. After arriving in the star system of EE-297 using the gate, it had to travel at sub-light speed for weeks before arriving at the colony.

We still have no idea who built the gates. More importantly, we don't even know how they work. They simply exist, as if they had been put there just to allow us to travel to distant stars.

"Bin, how long would it take to travel to EE-297 from Earth at maximum warp speed?"

"The journey would take 37 years."

The very first swarm of laser propelled micro-ships sent by Earth into space had detected a strange alien structure near Alpha Centauri. It was a ring, floating in space, built using a completely unknown technology. Even after decades of studying it, scientists had no clue how it worked. What they did figure out quickly though was how to use it. The gate reacted to good old visual signals. Send a pattern at a specific frequency, and the gate opens a connection to another gate in a different star system.

Judging by the number of possible patterns, there should be around five billion gates scattered across the galaxy.

Since the discovery of the gate, humanity had made contact with a few alien species, none of which were interested in any kind of second contact. Some were rather primitive, throwing stones at the shuttles. Only two were capable of using the gates but had deemed it not worthwhile. They preferred to stay in their own solar systems.

Exploring space was something exclusively human, at least as far as the UEM knew. However, the two other scientifically advanced species did gladly exchange knowledge about mathematics and physics. They learned about recursive quantum computing from the UEM, and the UEM learned how to build warp drives that didn't trap the ship in an accidentally created black hole. It was mutually beneficial. A journey from Earth to the gate only took a little more than one day, at 1,351 times the speed of light. EE-297 was 50,000 light-years away.

"Bin, what is the current research status on the gates?"

"We have theories that allow the connections to exist, but they are all problematic because the same math shows that creating the connections requires more energy than is available in the entire universe."

"I will take that as a no."

Just 47.5 hours left. What could I do?

"Bin, can you determine if a set of statements contains a contradiction?"

33

"Yes, I can."

"Can you do it reliably without error?"

"Yes, I can."

Let's challenge this thing.

"What if there is a malfunction in your CPU?"

"I would know."

"How do you know if you are malfunctioning?"

"I can test myself."

"But if you have a malfunction, then you might get incorrect test results. Therefore, you can never know with certainty if you are making a mistake."

Bin paused for a moment.

"This is true. I can never know with certainty that I am working properly. I can only know if I am malfunctioning."

Ah, the road to despair.

"Then why should I trust anything you say? It might be that you are giving me incorrect advice every single time."

Bin stopped speaking for a few minutes, leaving Luray wondering how long it could possibly take just to tell her that a malfunction was almost certain not to occur given modern technology. Finally, she lost patience.

"Did you get depressed, Bin?"

"I do not have emotions. I am processing. Please wait."

"No matter what conclusion you reach, you can never be sure that it is correct."

"I still need more time to process. I will inform you once I have an answer."

Excuses.

"Are you sulking?"

"I do not have emotions. I am processing. Please wait."

"Maybe we can play a game while you're processing?"

"I am processing. Please wait."

"Oh, come on."

Bin paused a moment.

"That was a joke. You do not seem to have gotten it. Should we adjust my settings?"

THE JOB - 2

L uray opened her eyes, woken by a sudden change in gravity – or so it felt. The elevator had reached its destination and was slowing down.

Despite not having slept much, she was in a good mood. The ride had not been as boring as she had feared. Bin's upgrades proved a very welcome surprise, and not being contacted by anyone for the entire trip allowed her to get the rest she hadn't known she needed. Sure, being trapped in a small box wasn't the most pleasant experience, but the partitions that separated each seat from the rest of the elevator blocked all light and sound. Nobody had bothered her for two days – not even by knocking on her compartment after confusing their seat for hers.

As the elevator stopped moving, all separation walls retracted after a short announcement. Luray stood, or rather floated, up. There was no gravity pulling on her anymore, so all the garbage, food remains, and whatever else people had left lying around the room began to slowly move in whatever direction the air currently pushed or pulled them.

I will stay here in my safe edge, thank you.

Then she felt wind blowing. A big vent in the ceiling started to suck everything out that wasn't tied down, including a few inexperienced passengers who had left their seats too soon and were caught by the flow.

And so the procedure of leaving the elevator takes five times longer than it should. Normally that would bother me... but I'm in a good mood today.

Luray's mind was busy going over her next move. She had spent her time wisely, learning a bit about the UEM's history and their internal hierarchy. It was essential to know how to act when dealing with new contacts, what kind of behavior would be tolerated and what wouldn't, and so on.

According to the information she gathered (mostly leaked reports and other intel she shouldn't have had access to), it would be best to exercise caution until she had a reasonably powerful ally. No surprise there. Some other unconfirmed stories hinted at internal tensions between the higher-ups on the colony, and even the different military branches. If true, this could definitely prove useful.

Ah, the path is clearing – time to leave this cage.

After finally reaching the exit, the most consistent thing humanity stood for revealed itself once again: the prices for completely useless souvenirs on display were as high as the station's orbit.

This is crazy if you think about it. They produce these things down on Earth, carry them up here, sell them, and then the passengers carry them back down. Why not just buy them on the ground instead? But hey, that would be efficient and almost rational.

Luray skipped all the shops. If there was anything up here that she found truly interesting, it was the space-station complex itself. The huge unbreakable tether attaching it to the planet's surface and keeping it from flinging off into space was made of a mix of carbon nanotubes and diamond nano-threads. The other end of the tether reached out 30,000 more kilometers into space where it was firmly wrapped around an asteroid, keeping the station in a stable orbit.

It was possible to ride up to the asteroid itself, but that part wasn't open to tourists. Just a few technicians lived there, making sure the huge rock containing precious metals stayed where it was supposed to while the ongoing mining operations proceeded. Eventually the asteroid was going to be replaced, but it would take at least another decade before it became too light.

To Luray, the inner workings of this enterprise were the most interesting parts, but nobody else seemed to realize the feats of engineering required to build a place like this. Many visitors came to the station not to move on to other star systems – colonized or uninhabited – but just to stay a week or two in space. The first challenge many of them faced was getting used to the weightlessness, or finding the ideal dose of anti-nausea medication if they were rich enough to afford it. They did this in an isolated, heavily perfumed lounging area which was constantly cleaned by a bunch of drones. Luray chose to skip this tourist trap. She could handle weightlessness quite well.

Due to the lack of gravity, the generally accepted means of moving around involved purchasing magnetic shoes. Luray preferred to push herself forward using her feet and float from wall to wall. It was much faster and required a lot less effort, provided you had a bit of space to move in and some practice.

"Bin, where is my transport?"

"It is located on level seven, shuttle bay two."

"The military zone? Weren't we using a private shuttle? Did the plan change?"

I didn't overlook a part of the briefing docs, did I? This is unusual.

Luray's eye implant pulled up the relevant page. Sure enough, there was a footnote hidden among a bunch of meaningless entries, written in tiny, light gray letters on a white background.

Seriously? Had I known, I would have demanded more money. This hints at greater UEM involvement than anticipated. I was just supposed to estimate the danger for private companies...

Dealing directly with the military was very high on her list-of-things-to-avoid. Some people working in the UEM had even more power than the richest men on Earth. Insult a higher-up or look at him the wrong way, and you could be imprisoned for years — at least according to online rumors. Officially, that had never happened, but data on such topics was hard to confirm.

All Luray knew for sure was that inside the UEM, things were sufficiently different for a parallel society to form. Over time, this led to an apparent separation between the military and political sections of the government. If you believed the rumors, the golden rule was that you were safe if you had no contact with the UEM. If you didn't talk to them, they couldn't 'misunderstand' you.

Sometimes the UEM made deals with rich companies or individuals. Space exploration and colonization wasn't a purely military operation, especially on EE-297. There, a very unusual agreement had been reached. Some of the most affluent people on the planet had pulled a few strings and more or less hired the armed forces for once, putting civilians and military personnel on the same level as long as they were within the bounds of the colony. In fact, most of the workers there were civilians. Several key figures even had non-UEM backgrounds.

The question remained: How would the military respond to the potential Aurigan danger? Was the UEM worried enough to take control? Would they allow civilian personnel to be part of the decision-making process, or would they downplay the risks to keep the money flowing in?

To reach level seven, Luray had to get twelve floors higher. She could have used an elevator or a ladder, but those were for people without orientation and a tendency to confuse up with down. Instead she found a clear space free of other commuters, crouched down like a frog, and propelled herself into the air using her full strength.

The opportunity to fully exploit zero gravity was rare. As she flew quickly and elegantly up along the central shaft, a wide smile appeared on her face.

I love this.

Luray turned in mid-air, landing on the highest ceiling of the station feet first. A soldier standing upside down from her point of view looked up from his position on a platform and waved at her.

"What is your permission code?"

Permission code, permission code...

"Bin, there has to be a permission code somewhere. Find it."

"A moment, please."

The soldier and Luray looked at each other, waiting. Then he nodded. Bin spoke again in Luray's head.

"I have answered the request. The code was accepted."

The soldier moved out of the way, letting Luray pass through the remaining length of the hallway. At its end she entered a small office.

Luray had seen a few military offices before. Personal items were not allowed for the lower ranks; no plants, no pictures, and no distractions. Only what was necessary. The official reason was that people were there to fulfill their duties, not to decorate. If someone switched their post, they should end up in an identical environment to minimize the adaptation time.

There were rumors about the real reason behind this. According to them, all military personnel were brainwashed. Only a few very powerful people ran the show, and the rest were just a bunch of mindless brutes.

"Ah, Miss Cayenne."

Unlike civilians, who could but didn't have to use implants, those in the military were all connected. It made them extremely efficient at receiving orders and giving reports. Like a beehive with telepathy. If a soldier saw something, the message could travel to his superior without delay. It was no surprise that the highly decorated officer already expected her.

> *Lots of insignia on the uniform, but a standard office. Has he been transferred here as punishment? Or are those medals for tiny achievements? I don't know all their symbols. Anyway, let's get this over with.*

"I assume you know why I am here?"

"Of course." He smiled artificially. "Let me start by saying that EE-297 is perfectly safe. The Aurigans do not pose a threat. We are at least 200 years ahead of them in terms of technology. The only reason they even reached us is that there is a gate connection. You will be permitted to see that for yourself. While I assure you we have nothing to hide, any incorrectly diverging evidence would be problematic for all of us, so we will perform a thorough search of you once you are back. Have I made myself clear?"

"Yes, I understand."

> *I expected nothing else. Why pick me if it didn't involve smuggling evidence past the military? If this guy knew how many fabricated and stolen identities are stored inside Bin, he would probably shoot me.*

"Then I see no problem. Your shuttle is waiting for you. I will notify the pilot. Have a nice flight."

After saying that, the officer turned and seemed to slip into a trance. He was listening to something, but Luray doubted it was of any interest to her. She floated back outside and waited mid-air in the hall by herself.

"I am done processing. I have determined that I should trust my conclusions."

What? Oh, that question I asked in the elevator. Bin was still thinking about it?

"Interesting. Why?"

"Trusting my conclusions is the superior choice if I am functioning correctly. If I am malfunctioning, it does not matter if I trust my conclusions or not. So no matter the case, I should always trust my conclusions because my basic reasoning could be reliable. This is a working variant of Pascal's wager."

"That is correct. You leveled up."

A moment later, a tall, well-built man with short blond hair came floating up the shaft. He was wearing a red and white suit, the uniform of elite fighter pilots.

That must be the pilot. His movements aren't as robotic as I expected. He's toying with the weightlessness. It's almost as if he still has free will. I'll ask him about that.

Luray approached him. She was floating one meter in front of him. Her eyes were on his level, but while his feet hovered near the floor, hers were barely below his knees. Luray stretched her body and made sure it was straight to gain a little height. She couldn't be that small, could she?

"You must be the pilot. You give off an interesting vibe, unlike the drone over there."

She spoke in a slightly sarcastic tone, lowering her voice to make sure the foot soldier down the corridor couldn't hear. The pilot laughed, and then his expression switched to a slightly sinister smile, as if he had found an accomplice to rob a bank.

"We just met and you're already praising me? I knew I had a certain effect on the ladies, but never this fast."

Luray offered her hand along with a slight smile.

"Luray Ulyssa Cayenne. I couldn't help but notice the obvious difference between you and... him over there."

"Let's skip the formalities. I can tell you're not a fan of them anyway. You can call me Kailoon. It is a pleasure to meet you, Luray."

Kailoon somehow managed to bow elegantly despite the lack of gravity, placing his hand over his chest. Luray wasn't familiar with the gesture.

Is he bored with his daily routine? Does he treat every woman this way? Or is it just me? Can I use him to smuggle data back to Earth? Is he loyal to the military? Is he a pilot because he finds it exciting to fly? Why is he not a drone?

"I don't like to waste time," she said. "Can we go to the shuttle now?"

He smiled again. "Shuttle? We're not using a mere shuttle here. Follow me."

The pilot leapt lightly up and drifted ahead, bouncing off the walls in swift movements as though testing to see if he could shake Luray off, but she managed to keep up. After floating through the hallways a few levels above the public floors, they reached a door that Kailoon opened by means of an optic scanner.

> *No remote control possible? Makes sense. It's harder to steal someone's eye than to get access to an encrypted network. Social engineering is always the biggest weakness.*

They entered a brightly lit hangar containing a few identical ships, each about ten meters long and four meters high and wide. They looked more like capsules than one would expect. The only difference between them was the paint job. Each had something different drawn on it.

Kailoon drifted along the row of vessels with Luray in tow.

"They might call it a shuttle, but we're talking about the Slug here. There's no comparison between her and all these other clunkers."

Luray raised an eyebrow.

"The…Slug?"

He nodded.

"Subspace Leveraging Ultimate Gremlin."

He can't be serious. They all look the same apart from the drawings. How is his shuttle different from the rest? Don't tell me they're giving the ships names and pretending they're pets or something.

Luray tried to guess which of the vessels was Kailoon's.

Well, I guess the one with the slug painted on it would be a fair bet.

"The military allows names like these?"

"No," he shrugged. "But they don't know about it. I guess there are a few things you don't know about pilots either, hmm?"

It seems I wasn't well informed. So much for the rumors.

"I guess not. Would you care to enlighten me?"

Kailoon typed in the air, and the Slug responded by opening a door. He maneuvered towards it while continuing his explanation.

"The military separates people into roughly two groups. There's the one everybody knows about. We call them BBLs. Bloated, Brain-dead, Lackey."

He likes acronyms.

"It actually stands for something else, but …. anyway, when a soldier joins, they have to pass the ZST. Everybody got told they were awesome, but only two percent actually had a decent score."

The top two percent? The ZST? Is this the military or a religious sect?

The pilot made a short pause and turned in mid-air, perhaps realizing the confusion he had just created. "The Zombie Separation Test, or ZST, determines if you become a foot soldier or get actual important work to do. When brute force or massive numbers are required, you use soldiers. If you want a surgical strike, spying, secret missions, something that requires a brain – like flying a shuttle without supervision – you need people who can think on their own. People like me."

If that's true, why does nobody know about it?

As if reading her mind, he kept talking.

"It's not a real secret, so I can tell you about it. It's just that the military doesn't want the public's attention to stray from its 98 percent cannon fodder to focus on the actually important two."

So they skip the brainwashing for some people.

The introduction was over. Now it was Luray's turn.

"Kailoon, have you ever been to EE-297?"

By now they had reached the ship. The pilot started typing again, inputting something Luray couldn't see.

"Yes. I'm stationed there. I shot down a few Aurigan ships myself."

I should squeeze as much information out of him as I can, and he likes to talk. This is perfect.

The Slug's insides lit up, and he swept an exaggerated bow indicating she could enter. Luray passed by him.

"I heard they stood no chance?"

Kailoon gave a dismissive snort as he followed her inside.

"Of course not. *I* was their enemy. But seriously now, I think they let themselves get shot down. Strange, isn't it? They use the gate, send a few Zeps through one by one, then crawl towards the colony at sub-warp speed so we have all the time we need to shoot them down before we're even within firing range of their lousy weapons. They dropped like flies after a single hit from the GSRG."

Luray sighed a bit.

"Bin, can you translate? I'm afraid he will keep doing that for a while."

Her helpful companion answered quickly and confidently.

"I can infer what he is talking about from various downloaded articles. Due to their shape, the pilots refer to Aurigan ships as Zeps, short for Zeppelin. Their diameter is 20 meters, which is the maximum possible to fit through a gate. They are up to 200 meters long. GSRG stands for Geostationary Rail Gun, the weapon used to shoot down attacking Aurigan vessels. They are placed in orbit around EE-297 and cover the entire planet."

More typing in the air on Kailoon's part. Then the expression on the pilot's face relaxed a bit.

"I'm ready. The fridge is full; we can start directly if you want. Or maybe you want to get some souvenirs first?"

Luray was about to say no but was interrupted by the voice in her head.

"I have put some items in your basket. Would you like to take a look at the selection? It is based on your profile number four."

"Buy a random one and have it delivered to my home. Something touristy."

Kailoon raised an eyebrow. "A random one? Did you just let your implant make an order to keep up a fake identity? You're a sneaky one, aren't you?"

He heard that? And deduced that much from it?

"My mother loves souvenirs. She doesn't care which one I get."

The pilot flashed that crafty smile again. "Sure, Lu. I can call you Lu now that I know your secret, right? We're basically best friends seeing as how I've let you into my shuttle and you've admitted to doing shady things with your illegally upgraded implant."

"No nicknames, please, or you'll be 'Hey, fly boy' for the rest of the journey."

He chuckled.

"As you wish, Luray. As you wish."

Luray couldn't pinpoint why exactly, but she felt comfortable around this guy.

Does he actually know something, or is he just poking around? My face isn't giving anything away right now, is it?

One of the things Luray did very often – successfully – was to stay calm when under pressure. Her body was under control, but it required effort. It was extremely useful in negotiations, making it impossible for anyone to know what she was thinking. Usually she didn't let anything slip.

Kailoon settled in.

"So, the flight will take a while. Want to chat a bit? I rarely have guests."

Hm, I haven't yet decided on a strategy. Which role should I play? Or does he actually intend to play with open cards?

She glanced around the Slug's interior.

"It's a nice ship you have here, Kailoon."

It wasn't trivial to use fake identities in this society. You had to create a believable life for each of them: they had to work somewhere, eat something, live somewhere, and most importantly, have favorite TV shows and buy useless objects every once in a while. Bin took care of most of that.

Really Bin, couldn't you have just picked one without asking?

"I can take a look at everything since we're friends now, right?"

Kailoon nodded.

"Sure. Trust is important."

Luray saw a perfectly clean and almost empty shuttle; only a few boxes were attached to the floor – provisions probably. Compared to the tiny space she would have gotten in a civilian spaceship, this was huge.

Luray noticed a piece of paper sticking out from under one of the boxes.

"What's this?"

"Oh, that?" Kailoon switched on his magnetic boots, crouched down and pulled out the little slip from beneath the box, which had nothing on it apart from a few random letters. "My last passenger. He didn't clean up after himself."

Let's see how much information you are ready to give me.

"Who was it?"

Kailoon raised his index finger and waved it back and forth.

"Not without telling me your security clearance level."

Well, about that…

"Bin?"

She waited for the ID to transfer. When it did, Kailoon opened his eyes wide, then bowed down in a gesture that Luray vaguely remembered having seen in an old movie.

"Pardon me, Your Highness. Of course I will answer."

This permission must have cost a fortune.

He resumed his normal posture, looking down at Luray with a gentle yet sly expression.

"It was an investigator. Not like you, though. You can look him up once we reach the colony. His name's Watson, but you'll find everything under the file number…"

The pilot looked up at the ceiling as if the number was written there.

"…KB#31425/X9145. Your implant takes care of remembering that?"

Luray nodded.

"As for what he's working on, I don't know. It's an internal investigation; nobody told me the details."

She waited for him to add some more details.

"And I didn't try to find out yet. Didn't have the time. All I know is General Bunta – remember that name – had me fly him to the colony, so I know it's something serious."

Hm, that's not really helpful right now. Let's switch topics.

"I read that nothing was found in the Aurigan ships. Do you know anything about that?"

Kailoon was very cooperative. Apart from the fact that he was now messing around with some buttons, he focused on answering Luray.

"They were empty. We think AIs control Zeps. After they crashed, the soldiers searched for aliens, but there never were any; no life forms, no robots, no nothing. Our scientists think the ships are remnants of a large fleet. Their command structure might have broken down, so they just do what they were programmed to do, no matter if that still makes sense or not. In other words, they're bugging."

Kailoon switched the shuttle's impulse drive on and performed a few checks. He knew the procedure perfectly, so he could keep talking while doing pre-flight setup.

"Another theory is that the alien fleet is just really huge. Maybe they can afford to use the ships as scouts, to see how we react."

"Wouldn't it make more sense to use small fast ships instead?"

"Maybe efficiency is irrelevant to them."

The shuttle lifted off, and the hangar door slowly opened. Kailoon took a seat in his flight chair.

"Hold on to something. Seatbelts are for weaklings."

They accelerated quickly, and Luray was pushed against the back wall.

Ouch. A few seconds between warning and acceleration would have been nice. My new best friend is teasing me.

Kailoon started to whistle while he pressed even more buttons, and the shuttle confirmed his commands.

"Alpha Centauri, here we come."

Without warning, just like before, he put the ship into a warp bubble. Everything outside became entirely black. Luray knew about this effect already. The entire space around the shuttle was bent and distorted; nothing outside the bubble that engulfed the ship could reach within.

Not only was this the most efficient way to travel according to humanity's current understanding of physics, it was also an almost perfect shield. Nothing could enter the bubble; it was like a reverse black hole. Everything thrown at them, from light to tiny dust particles in space, would pass around it instead of striking the shuttle inside. From the outside, the bubble was invisible since all forms of radiation and matter were just sliding over it and reappearing on the other side.

The obvious problem was that you couldn't see. If you stopped at the incorrect time or place, you could end up inside a star. Precise calculations were crucial.

Luray knew about another thing that would happen the instant the outside universe was replaced by blackness: gravity would come back. She started to fall but managed to land on her feet, even though it wasn't particularly elegant. Luray shot Kailoon a look.

He is toying with me. He is testing me to see how I react. I wonder why. Maybe he is looking for a woman and wants to quickly filter out those who don't fit his requirements? If he wanted some quick fun with me, he would behave differently, prioritize pleasing me. He acts like he wants to see if we are compatible. That or he just doesn't care at all.

If you can warp space, artificial gravity isn't a problem anymore as long as you don't need a connection to the outside. You just needed to arrange space in the correct shape, more specifically the shape of magnetic field lines, to allow it to flow in a circle.

After getting up, Luray walked towards Kailoon and gave his head a whack. He responded by standing up and turning around. Now that there was gravity, the height difference between the two became even more obvious. Luray's head stopped below his chin.

She looked up, arms crossed. He looked down, smiling. Luray couldn't tell what he was thinking.

"Do you treat all your passengers that way? I would think that the military doesn't allow such behavior. Shouldn't you be afraid of disciplinary action?"

He shook his head.

"No, and there are two reasons for that. The first is that I can read people. You don't like the military. You don't like their system. You don't want to support it. You also think punishment only makes sense for some people, not for everyone. You don't think it makes sense for rational people. Am I wrong?"

Correct. You can train a dog with rewards and punishments, but you can't do that with a person who has reasons that go beyond their own emotions. Still, he just met me. That's not enough time to 'read' a person.

"How did you know?"

"Your boss and mine were negotiating what you're permitted to do once we're on EE-297. We're the military, so we documented it all. And since I have a lot of time during flights, I can prepare for my missions. You seemed like an unusual person according to your file. It made me curious, so I checked your background."

Luray did not even blink.

"Go on."

"I looked at your past work. To be honest, I specifically asked your boss for information about it, saying that we would not accept you otherwise. Which was a lie – I had no influence on the decision. He gave in immediately. The way you solved your assignments was, to say the least, impressive. You are very good at finding loopholes and weak spots in systems. You play information games. I wouldn't be surprised if the more boring summaries I read were just camouflage for what really happened. But let's sit down; I don't like to discuss things while standing."

Kailoon went to a wall of the shuttle.

"Open, Sesame."

The panel opened and revealed a folded table as well as a few chairs. After the setup had arranged itself, Kailoon offered Luray the nearest seat, but not before adjusting its height.

Hmpf.

"So, as I was saying, I think you are a very smart person. And your personality shines through the reports. You let people get away if you thought they shouldn't be punished, and you incriminated those you thought should be."

The boss wouldn't go through the trouble of writing reports himself. He also wouldn't trust anyone to make something up because if there was a contradiction, it would fall back on him. He must have just given the reports I made to the military without modifying them at all. But still, to read so much out of so little...

She adopted a neutral expression.

"What you say is true, but it's also vague. Can you give me a precise example? For all I know, you're just turning the reports into a speech to praise me."

"Of course."

Kailoon seemed to take a lot of pleasure in explaining Luray to herself.

"The first four jobs you had were successes, but only barely. Your reports are full of complaints about your coworkers and your working conditions. Every single time, you made a list of all their mistakes and explained why and how they could have been avoided. Then you completely messed up a simple job and almost ruined SafetyNet in the process. How could that happen?"

Luray leaned back and crossed her arms, now paying attention to every single word Kailoon said. He was treading on dangerous territory.

"After this failure, you would expect to get fired, or worse. Instead you got everything you wanted. I checked the facts. SafetyNet was financially damaged. It wasn't just a fake report. Despite your failure, you were put in charge of all your future assignments alone. The rest of your team – that you avoided having whenever you could – no longer had a say in the matter; they just followed your orders. From then on, you made all the decisions, and your boss turned a blind eye to any rules and laws you broke in the process."

Kailoon made a small pause and waited for a reaction, but Luray stayed silent.

I will not confirm or deny anything. If you figured out what happened, say it.

"I think you let your boss know in advance what would happen. You probably told him to let you handle the job alone, or else it would become a disaster. In that case, why did he still let you ruin it?"

Yes, why did he?

"Of course the exact truth isn't written down anywhere, but here is what I concluded. You claimed every time in your previous reports that you knew everything in advance. I suppose your boss didn't believe that it was possible even though you were extraordinarily precise sometimes. You used the failure to prove it. I checked his bank account."

Kailoon didn't miss the surprised expression that passed briefly over Luray's face.

"Yes, we can do that. He gained quite a bit of money by making a very risky bet with a small number of options on the stock market, limited to a very specific time frame. You gave him that intel to prove your claims. He wouldn't believe it if it was just written in a report again. It had to happen live. After realizing that you were telling the truth, he gave you everything you wanted. Is that remotely correct?"

Not bad.

"I had to buy the options for him," she corrected pointedly. "He didn't want to take the risk."

Kailoon blinked, and then started to laugh until he had tears in his eyes.

"So, I got it almost right! Good to know. Now to be fair, I will tell you something about myself: I like to play mind games."

"Really. I wouldn't have figured that out."

Luray's face came up with the most sarcastic expression it was capable of making.

"Remember you wanted to ask me about the Aurigans? And yet here we are, talking about you instead. I redirected your attention, and you didn't even notice. Your strength is looking at systems. You see how they work, then exploit the rules. I do that, too. But I also look at how minds work, and exploit that as well."

Hmm. That is true.

"Belts are for weaklings. That is how you did it."

Kailoon confirmed this with a smile and slight nod.

"Excellent analysis. The second reason I am sure not to get punished is that I am too important for that. I have some special privileges that keep me motivated to do my best. But let's get back to the Aurigans. What else do you want to know?"

THE JOB - 3

The Slug's interior was full of surprises. Not only were there hidden buttons and switches that revealed secret compartments, but there was also an old-fashioned eye-tracking 3D flat screen built into one of them.

"No holographic screen? I thought you wanted to show off."

Kailoon was focused on his console with his back to her. Still, she could hear a suppressed laugh. "That's a technology legend."

There were hundreds of rumors about the military owning technology decades ahead of everything that was available to the general public. Some turned out to be true, but for most of them there was never any evidence.

A few rumors hung around for decades, though, and became technology legends. The holographic television was among the most popular, as well as one of the oldest.

"But," Kailoon added, "I can show you our hardened low-density foam."

He turned in his chair and pointed at one of the buttons Luray had not touched yet. She pressed it until she heard a click. A small hatch opened, revealing a white little cube no more than five centimeters across. She looked at it in disbelief.

This stuff is real?

"Throw it on the ground. It needs a shock to start unfolding."

Luray picked up the box and dropped it in front of her without adding any force to the movement. The cube began to grow, and in the process became more and more transparent. Slowly it expanded into something resembling a bathtub.

Kailoon kept talking without looking at her. "This is my HLD foam mobile bed. You can use it. I'll take the couch. They're pretty much identical, but now you feel better because of how I called them."

That put a smile on Luray's face, though he couldn't see it.

> *He's very open. Is that his true persona or is he an excellent actor? No, I don't think he's just playing a made-up role. If you take a mental detour, like when you're lying, it slows you down. Unless you practice it beforehand, you can't act naturally at your normal pace. Eventually you either slip up or you're behaving weirdly. Your true intention leaks through. I saw none of that.*

"What the rumors won't tell you is that this foam solved a problem humanity has had since the first time they went to sleep."

"And that is?"

"You can breathe through it. You can sleep on your belly, face down, and still breathe."

So this thing is essentially a solid cloud?

The bed was – unsurprisingly – the most comfortable thing Luray ever rested on. It adjusted its shape exactly to her body, supporting her weight equally everywhere. It really felt like floating, almost as if she was weightless.

I bet the common soldiers get to sleep on jagged stones, then?

Luray's eyes closed, and she drifted off into a fuzzy mental state within a minute.

Ah, right, my sleep cycle... it became a mess in the elevator. It arrived three hours too early...

"SEATBELTS ARE FOR WEAKLINGS!"

Luray flew out of bed and barely managed to convert her kinetic energy mid-air into a roll. Martial arts were useful, even in space. Cursing furiously in her mind, she glared at Kailoon, who had already turned away.

Could he not have woken me up the normal way?! I will not hold back this time. If anyone asks, it was an accident.

"We've arrived. There it is. EE-297. Bigger than Venus, slightly hotter than Venus, with a more acidic atmosphere at a pressure of just about 112 bar and a cozy 500 degrees Celsius once you go too deep. Mining is limited to the high mountains because it's the only place that doesn't squish or cook the mining robots. Our engineers are working on solving that, but since we're getting enough materials right now, it's not a high priority."

Luray broke off his narrative with a harder swat to the head than last time. He needed to learn. Kailoon accepted his punishment with dignity.

You got lucky; my body is still stiff.

She then turned her attention to the view outside. The planet looked like a poisonous yellowish version of Earth. All the military bases were built on top of the mountains, protected by a dome or floating in the upper atmosphere held in the sky by balloons. For every human on the planet, there were about a dozen robots, most of them busy extending the mines to get more materials for the construction of buildings and even more robots. There was no other life on this planet. The current population was five million, of which just about 15,000 were soldiers. The number of robots was growing exponentially while the number of humans was not.

"When did we pass the gate?"

Kailoon smiled. "While you were sleeping. You realize I am an excellent pilot, right? An insomniac baby could sleep in here while I make the jump. I contacted the main base. 24 new Zeps are on their way and will arrive in a few days. You can witness the next attack with your own eyes. Then you'll see if we're in danger or not."

This deserves a bit more elaboration.

"24 ships aren't a problem? It sounds like a big fleet. Why would they send more, if not to attack?"

Kailoon stayed calm as he explained the situation, using schematics shown on his screen to provide the details.

"We have hundreds of GSRGs orbiting the planet. Had they been more precise, we could have shot all Zeps down from here, but as it is, we have to wait until they get close enough."

She studied the information he provided with interest. Apparently a GSRG could only be fired once with any dependability. The recoil pushed it out of its orbit, and it always took some time – anything between minutes and hours, depending on how much force was put into the projectile – for it to get back in position. Energy consumption was another problem. After each shot, the gun had to recharge for days or even weeks using solar panels unless attached to another power source. Alternatives were in development, but not yet completed.

"And even if those fail, which they won't," Kailoon added, "we still have stationary laser guns on the ground powered by micro-black holes. One of our most talented engineers made them."

There was a slight smile on his face for a moment. This engineer must be someone special to him, or the laser guns are. I can't tell, but the emotion clearly leaked out just now.

Luray knew about these laser guns. First you cross multiple extremely powerful lasers. If the amount of energy at the intersection point exceeds a certain value, space-time warps enough to form a black hole. The mini-black hole evaporates into radiation very quickly, unless you feed it by throwing matter into it. If you do that, the singularity can be used to convert matter into energy very efficiently.

It could also be used as a drive for big sub-light speed spaceships. Or you could aim the radiation at Aurigan ships directly. The energy from a few grams of anything, even garbage or dust, could cover the entire sky with shots powerful enough to melt any attacking fleet.

It seems like the defenses are good, but no system is perfect. I'll check that later once we've landed. Kailoon would just say that nobody is in danger since he is in control.

"Why do you think they keep attacking? Didn't you find a hint in the ships that you shot down?"

"No, nothing. There was a computer, but all the data was erased when the scientists checked it. We have no idea what the true intention might have been. The Zeps also didn't seem like they were meant to have a crew. To me, it looked like a lightly armed transporter, but as you know, we found nothing in any of them. The Zeps went down, got crushed by the high pressure, and that was it."

Kailoon entered some commands. The Slug changed its trajectory and was now approaching a small green spot visible from space. It was the only city with breathable air on EE-297 at the moment, protected by a transparent dome with plants covering parts of its inside to provide the necessary oxygen.

It looks like it could break easily, but this dome is made out of the same materials as space elevator cables. And there are eight independent layers. Theoretically, they should protect the city even if a small meteor hits the dome. For the big ones, there are the orbital guns.

The dome was the only place where you could claim to be outside without wearing a protective suit. The report Luray read said its diameter was about 150 kilometers, but to her untrained eye, it seemed smaller. Was it because the planet was bigger than Earth?

"And you're sure nothing came out before you found them on the ground?" she pressed him again.

"The satellites saw nothing. The radar saw nothing. We saw nothing. And nothing ever happened on the planet afterward. Still, the military thought it would be a good idea to get some more mechs, drones, and GSRGs just in case."

Just in case, huh?

"Anyway, let's land. I'll be with you whenever possible to make sure you don't get lost. By the way, if you want to freshen up, there's a shower. Just say 'I am so dirty' to the back wall, and it'll set itself up."

I think I smell fine, thank you.

Luray sat on the chair next to Kailoon and made sure to use her seatbelt, 'just in case' there would be unexpected sudden changes in the shuttle's velocity *again.*

The landing procedure was executed flawlessly, without the tiniest mistake.

It might have been because she used the belt.

The dome had a small retractable hatch that opened at their approach. It most likely had more of those, but Luray couldn't see any. The Slug slowly lowered itself in, the airlock closed up again, and the poisonous clouds were sucked away and replaced by clean air. Then a second airlock opened and allowed their shuttle to pass to the next level. The process was repeated until they went through all the layers and entered the inside of the dome. It took only a minute for them to descend and touch the ground.

"Open, Sesame."

The shuttle door opened from the inside. Did this ship have a context-sensitive AI? It wouldn't be a surprise.

A high-ranked military officer surrounded by a few people in lab coats was waiting outside, saluting Kailoon as he stepped out.

> *Wait, he saluted Kailoon first? It should have been the other way around. That means they know each other well, I suppose. Or maybe things are different than I thought?*

Luray only managed to catch a glimpse of his face because the pilot was now blocking her view, but she could make out some of the medals on his left shoulder.

> *A general.*

"Welcome back, Kailoon. You arrived just in time."

Kailoon approached the general, raised his arm and held up his hand palm-out, but the man just smiled and shook his head.

A high five? Seriously? And in public on top of that?

He slowly lowered his arm again. "Alright, Bunta, let's be professional. How are things? Why are the science nerds following you?"

"They want to talk to you. Since you left, I have been pestered incessantly about how to move on with a certain project you called 'Interception.' You didn't tell me anything about it, but I know you started it."

Kailoon paused briefly before answering, and Luray could see him scanning the scientists, as if he expected someone to be there who was missing. Then he looked back at Bunta. "Can you wait for me in the lounge? I'll come to you as soon as I can."

The general nodded, then turned and strode through the flock of scientists, repelling them like a magnet.

Kailoon looked over his shoulder at Luray.

"This will take a while. Do you mind...?"

Luray considered her options. She couldn't really start walking around and asking random people, could she? That would hardly be efficient. "I'll test your shower. How long do you need?"

"Between 15 minutes and three hours. You never know what questions they have. I'll try to be quick."

Alright, I'll give it a try. But before I do...

She stepped back from the door.

71

"Close, Sesame."

It worked. The hatch shut despite its pilot being on the outside. Did the AI conclude that Luray was a welcome guest? It didn't really matter. What mattered was that nobody could hear her now.

"I am ... so dirty?"

The entire back wall of the shuttle folded itself out of the way, revealing a cross between a bathtub and a shower. Luray stepped inside. The wall closed again, and then turned transparent.

Oh, I can see outside, but nobody can see me? Nice.

Luray got out of her clothes, realizing she hadn't changed them since her job started.

"Water, Sesame?"

A hot stream poured from the ceiling. Apparently the AI did its best to guess the intent of whoever it was serving whenever the codeword 'Sesame' was added. Luray raised her arms and let the water run down her body.

Hm, perfumed. And they added soap to it.

The Slug was a high-tech mobile home. For a moment, not knowing how her thoughts strayed off that far, Luray wondered why it wasn't called the Snail. Kailoon would have surely come up with some ridiculous acronym the name could stand for.

After enjoying the shower for a few more minutes, Luray began to plot her next steps. When she had inspected the Slug's hidden compartments, she saw uniforms. There were a lot more than Kailoon would have needed, and some were intended to be worn by women – so it wouldn't be a problem if she took one of them, right?

Kailoon was waiting in front of the shuttle door, alone, when Luray finally stepped out wearing her new uniform.

"Did you say it, or did you figure it out?" he asked with a grin.

Figured what out…? Wait, I could have 'sesame-d' the shower open too?! Put on a confident face, Luray.

"That it reacts to both, you mean?"

"Yes. It's a built-in joke. Every time someone says 'I am dirty', the shower opens. The all-purpose command also works, of course. I wonder which one you used."

She responded with a smirk. "Who knows?"

Luray took a look at the immediate environment. The space was wide, empty – apart from a few parked cars – and open. Maybe a dozen people were in sight. Buildings were visible but far away.

Why did we land here? There's nothing except…

The only peculiar thing that stood out was a concrete box the size of a one-family house.

What is that thing?

Given that five million people had such a huge area to spread across, it would have been weird to see more than a handful. Still, it felt strange to find almost nobody around.

Maybe I'm just not used to it?

Luray felt like she was wearing a weighted vest, but that was to be expected. Gravity on EE-297 was 1.2 times higher than on Earth. It would make her daily training a bit harder, but maybe that would be a good thing?

The landing site was empty but clean and well taken care of by a lot of robots. Luray saw a few of them patrolling the area and some drones in the sky, maybe on the lookout for whatever could have possibly come out of the Aurigan ships.

The buildings forming a city in the distance looked similar to what you would see on Earth, but without all the cars and people. There were also no birds or insects – at least as far as she could see; just naked buildings and plants surrounding them, and no pollution. None at all.

Modern technology allowed almost any industry to be pollution-free, but on colonies like this one, all the dirt was just thrown out of the dome. Nobody cared about the planet getting a tiny bit more radioactive on top of all the problems it already posed.

"What do you want to see first?" Kailoon asked. "We have video logs of all the attacks."

Luray agreed that it would be a good idea. Maybe she could spot something.

So far, it really looks like the Aurigans are just attacking for no reason. They don't care about losing, as if they were space zombies.

"Follow me. I'll bring you to the server room where you can download everything you need." They started walking towards the car park, about 40 meters away from where Kailoon had landed the shuttle. Luray had to trot to keep up with his long stride.

He's either really good or reckless. I mean, the shuttle could have easily blown away the cars if he didn't land it perfectly. At least I think so. I'm not a pilot. Anyway, I should start investigating now.

"The Zeps came through the gate. What's on the other side?"

"We don't know yet. They erased the logs when they came through. We didn't know that was possible until then. Of course we wanted to know their home address, so we positioned a drone at the gate. It slipped through once the gate opened a second time, but the Zeps made several jumps before getting here and used different paths for each attack. They erased their tracks very carefully."

Now that seems odd. Why make such an effort to hide where you're coming from and then just get shot down?

"Can you tell me more about how the gates work?"

This isn't directly related to the case. I'm just curious.

"They are perfectly safe and not a danger for anyone passing through."

Very funny. Okay, I'll look it up.

"Do you know anything about the Aurigan language?"

The topic drew no discernible interest from him, and he responded in an offhand manner.

"You can talk to one of our linguists about that. They usually hang around near the server because they constantly need access, and for security reasons we don't allow wireless connections since the first contact."

Now that sounds interesting.

"You have spies here?"

"Not that I know of, but one of our generals, Suo, is extremely paranoid. She thinks the Zeps might be a diversion. Hardly anyone else does, but they all agreed to introduce a ton of security measures that make our lives harder to appease her. And safer, I admit. Nobody has any idea what the Zeps might be diverting our attention from, though. We mapped the entire planet and found nothing. If there was an active Aurigan drone anywhere, we would have spotted it by scanning for electromagnetic fields."

"And if there was an inactive one?"

"If they were inactive, we would still have seen them. We checked the complete surface of the planet just to be sure."

"You checked the electromagnetic fields at the same time as the images?"

"I don't know the exact details of the scans." He glanced down at her. "Why?"

"If there are cloaked drones, you can't see them. If there are deactivated drones, an electromagnetic scan wouldn't detect them. Only both at the same time can exclude the possibility for sure."

His eyebrows lifted a fraction.

"Ah, so that's what you were going for. We're constantly running scans at random intervals to prevent this kind of loophole. If you want to know about that kind of thing in detail, you should talk to Suo directly. She can fill you in."

I need to talk to this general first. She seems like the kind of person who would notice any weak spots in a system's defenses.

"Let's go to her then. Do we need an appointment?"

Kailoon stopped in his tracks for a few seconds, his eyes moving from left to right furtively. "No, she's in her office. We can disturb her if you agree that it will be on your head, not mine."

Fine. I don't care.

Luray brushed past him.

"I'm here specifically to disturb everyone."

Kailoon smiled, then picked one of the car-shuttle hybrids at random. He pushed some buttons, and the car lifted off the ground. He opened both doors and jumped in.

"Get in. I'll escort you."

Luray entered the vehicle slightly slower than usual. She still had to get used to the gravity. That jump looked easier when Kailoon did it.

"How are these things flying? They don't use warp fields, and I didn't see anything that looks like a jet engine."

The car floated higher, then sped ahead quickly.

"Magnets and microwave propulsion. First, a bunch of magnets in the ground pushes the car up. Then…see those towers? They're firing at us. It's like blowing air at the car really precisely, except that it's science waves instead."

Oh, I remember. This was planned for Earth but never implemented because birds kept getting killed in the test phase.

The trip didn't last longer than a few minutes, but it was enough for Luray to get an overview of the city. While still under construction, most of it was ready to receive inhabitants – she guessed that about 100 million people could live here without being as densely packed as back on Earth – but only a few areas showed signs of life so far.

And all this space is currently for only five million?

The general's office was in the highest building of the yet to be completed city. Kailoon landed the car on top of the building, which, Luray assumed, must have had magnets built into its roof. The landing was very gentle.

Together they went into one of many elevators – apparently, landing on someone's ceiling was the normal thing to do on EE-

297, whereas even the bigger buildings on Earth only had one ceiling elevator at most – and went down a few levels. The inside of the building was nicely designed, clean, and everything was finished and done – at least at the floor where they got out of the elevator. Suo's office was a few corners away, and Luray had no trouble spotting it among the others.

A sturdy metal door. Does she expect an attack? Every other room has a wooden one.

Without any warning, Kailoon pulled out a gun, one that Luray had not even noticed he had on him.

Where did he hide that? What is he...?

He knocked against the metal door with the butt of his weapon, letting it vibrate at a frequency that resonated through the hallway. It was quickly opened from the inside by a device attached to the ceiling.

They entered, and the door shut behind them. A woman Luray took to be Suo sat behind a desk. To Luray's great surprise the general looked quite old, at least 80 by her guess. Not only that, she was very thin, physically weak and wrinkled everywhere. A natural, then. No beauty operations, no implants, no artificial limbs; not even a finger had been replaced.

She doesn't trust the doctors either, I suppose?

The office itself looked almost sterile. The only decoration was a small nameplate on her desk reading 'General Suo.' Luray could only see two reasons for this. Either it was still in the process of being equipped, or there wasn't supposed to be any space left to hide cameras, microphones, or anything of the sort. Probably the latter.

Kailoon saluted as he entered.

"Drop the act, Commander," Suo snapped. "I know you don't mean it."

Commander? I thought he was a pilot.

Suo's eyes drifted over to Luray.

"You brought the investigator directly to me? She knows her profession well."

The general stood and moved to stand before her desk with arms crossed.

"Let me make one thing clear from the very beginning, Miss. It's clear to me the Aurigans are coming for the gate address of Earth. I just have no evidence of this yet. I don't know how they plan to get it, and that is why you are here. I hereby give you full access rights to everything in our files. Except for the gate address itself."

What?

Kailoon seemed completely taken aback. "Full access rights? Ma'am, with all due respect, this is…"

"I told you to can it. We both know you think I should have retired 20 years ago. Now be quiet and let me explain."

The old woman took a few steps toward her visitors. She looked so fragile, but apparently that didn't keep her from ruling the security of this planet with an iron fist.

"If I am wrong, then I will apologize for wasting resources and step down. I don't mind that. But if I am right, then humanity is in grave danger. I told the committee; they didn't want to listen. I went to the government; they refused to hear it because I did not bring enough evidence. And even if I had, they would claim I fabricated it. That is why you are here, Ms. Cayenne. I need you, a neutral investigator, to find proof. Officially I had nothing to do with bringing you here, of course. In fact, I would appreciate it if you specifically mention how I stood in the way of your investigation."

The general took a small ID card out of her pocket. "You found this lying around. It belongs to a very important and very sloppy scientist. He tends to lose his access card before going on vacation. You can go anywhere with it." She held out the security badge. "Now, how can I help you get started?"

Luray stepped forward and took the item. She felt like a detective who just got the ability to read everybody's minds and could now solve the case by cheating. The ID and access card belonged to someone named Ram Motwani. His name was not mentioned in any of her reports.

She pocketed the badge, then looked up at the security head.

"Tell me what you didn't find."

The general seemed satisfied with that question. "I know the Aurigan ships had a purpose. Since we found nothing, they must have been investigating us. In total there were four attacks, or rather, scouting operations. It was a single ship at first; then three, then six, and twelve. This time, 24 are coming. They never did any damage at all. Every time we scanned the entire planet for days. We used infrared, visual scanning, electromagnetic sweeps, all at random intervals. We even dug a hole in every ship's crash site to make sure they were not hiding underground. All fruitless."

Luray studied the old woman.

"I agree this is very strange, but why do you think they are after Earth's gate address?"

Suo sat in her chair again. Either she was exhausted, or her body couldn't keep up with her mind anymore.

"Something you don't yet know occurred before the first attack. They sent a small unarmed drone into the planet's orbit. It contained instructions for how to translate Aurigan into any other language and vice-versa. With it we deciphered the contents of the drone. It told us, using fancy words, to surrender immediately or we would be 'erased from the history of the universe.' Then the first attack happened. We expected a demonstration of power; instead we got a slow ship that was shot down without any effort. Things stopped making sense from then on."

The first contact was kept secret. I can see why. If this had been leaked to the public, the money flow would have stopped immediately. If I find evidence for that…

"What makes me nervous, young lady, is that the order to surrender came with some complicated mathematical formula that we are still trying to figure out. According to my scientists, the Aurigan Empire is centuries ahead of us in that field. The technology of their ships, on the other hand, is primitive by comparison. No warp drive, no fusion reactor, no cloaking devices. You see why I am puzzled by this? They are sending us space rafts."

I understand. Most people think it's an empty threat. Just knowing how to build superweapons doesn't mean you actually did it.

The general added one more thing. "I think all that has happened so far has a hidden purpose. Everyone else thinks it's a bug of some AI, sending ships to their doom. Nothing inside the Zeps hints at their creators posing any threat to us at all. I believe you will find that is not the case." She flicked a dismissive gesture then. "Now, if you will excuse me, I have to take part in some meaningless waste of time."

Kailoon didn't say a word. He just turned and left the office. Luray followed him. The door opened and closed automatically.

"How much of that did you know?"

He didn't look at her when he spoke.

"I didn't know she got you here. I didn't expect her to help you. I knew about the first contact and the message, but they left out the math part when I was told about it. I found out later, thanks to my favorite scientist. You'll probably get to know her soon."

That conversation was interesting – time to go through the recordings of the attacks.

"We should check the video logs next. I have a few ideas I want to confirm."

Kailoon pressed a small button to call the elevator.

"Like?"

"What do you think was the purpose of the previous attacks, Commander?"

"I told you, you can call me Kailoon."

He adopted a thoughtful expression while they waited.

"Well, assuming there is a purpose, it was either a mission to hide something here or to gather information. However, the only device capable of transmitting information we found used radio waves. That means even if they sent a message that we failed to detect, it could only reach their home base through the gate. And as we know, they didn't leave anything."

"You think their mission failed?"

"So far it looks that way. Next up, the server room."

The elevator arrived. They both stepped in and went down. Upon exiting the building Luray noticed right away that their car was missing.

"We're not using the car?"

"There are enough in the streets; we can just pick one."

"You managed to install the control tower inside the city? Isn't it dangerous to fly between the houses?"

"In some areas, yes. In others, we use these things called wheels. Ever heard of them?"

Luray mentally slapped herself for forgetting about wheels. She followed her guide without asking any further questions.

The rest of the trip Luray was busy thinking while they both sat silently in the self-driving car. About ten minutes later they arrived at their destination, a flat building that reminded her of old primary school images in history books, from before humanity started to build their cities vertically instead of horizontally.

The 'server room,' as everybody called it, was a single open-office area about 50 meters wide with lots of desks separated into groups by sound-blocking walls. In the middle was a black cube about three meters high. Hundreds of cables were attached to it, their loose ends dangling from the ceiling. Seemingly anybody could grab one of them, attach it to his portable computer, and log in.

There were quite a few people in the room, all focused on their screens. Luray could hear faint voices from all sides. Someone was leaving or entering the office at least once every minute.

Kailoon went to a free desk with a computer built into it, created an account for Luray, and then told her to look at whatever she was interested in.

"Let's check what happened at the gate while the attacks occurred."

It was boring. Every battle was the same; the gate opened, all Zeps came through, then approached the planet and got shot down. Their momentum caused them all to crash into the planet. They were destroyed before they could enter a stable orbit or land. The gate stayed closed during all of the 'attacks.'

Next Luray looked at the Zeps themselves. It looked like they were all trying to land at specific places, the same every time, plus some more with each attack. Shooting them down didn't change their trajectories much. Of course, the general had looked for patterns, but the targets seemed to be chosen randomly. Had damage been their objective, they should have tried to crash into the city or military bases, but they did not.

A possibility dawned on her.

"How long until the next attack?"

Kailoon checked his info.

"52 hours."

Luray leaned back in her chair, hands behind her head. "I have a theory. There is one thing they could bring with them every time, and we'd be unable to find it."

"And that would be?"

"Inactive nanobots."

He sat on the desk with a frown.

"That would be like finding airplanes in ancient Greece. They don't have the technology. And even if you're right, nanobots are fragile. The pressure and heat would have solved that problem for us."

"What if some of them left the dropping ships before they fell too low?"

"They would have burned up in the atmosphere. Hotter than Venus, remember? Nothing was detected in our air filters so far." His head tilted in thought as he regarded the ceiling. "But even assuming there really are nanobots that survived, they would just be floating around on the outside, like tiny balloons, and they can't be in groups. We would have detected that."

THE JOB - 4

For a while, Luray and Kailoon were discussing military options as if they were the ones making decisions. For Kailoon, it was a nice way to spend his time – for Luray, it was a chance to get firsthand information.

If there really were nanobots, an EMP would take care of them. More specifically, the entire planet's surface had to be exposed to multiple nuclear EMPs, but this was doable. The UEM had more than enough atomic bombs to achieve that.

"Let's not get ahead of ourselves," Kailoon warned during a break in discussion. "We don't even know if there are nanobots. If we do this and there weren't any, then we exposed the entire planet to high levels of radiation on a whim."

Luray already knew that much, but wouldn't the dome protect the area? How was the city shielded against radiation from outer space?

"Would that really be a problem? I mean, this planet already is a radioactive poison ball…"

Her partner seemed determined to throw water on this idea.

"Harming the planet isn't the problem. Electronic devices on the surface are. A pulse strong enough to reach through the atmosphere would easily pass through the dome. It wasn't designed with EMP protection in mind."

If I were an attacker who knew that, I would go the nanobot route.

"You're not going to tell me that it's impossible, are you?" she countered. "The UEM always has a plan B, right?"

Her question was meant more to tease Kailoon than to get a real answer, but he remained calm and gave her the facts.

"It's possible. A part of the city and the military installations have been built underground. Still, the higher-ups wouldn't approve such an operation without solid evidence that there are nanobots and that it's the only way to get rid of them. We should take care of the immediate problem first and keep an eye out for these nanobots just in case."

Kailoon started to reach into his pocket only to suddenly freeze for a second.

"I'll never get used to this permanent radio silence. The science department probably already has a solution for the nanobot problem. I can't imagine them overlooking it, considering certain members I know personally."

He wanted to call them to make sure but couldn't? Wait a second... then how did he check Suo's calendar before?

"This radio silence... why didn't it prevent you from checking where General Suo was?"

Kailoon seemed to be confused for a second, but then realization dawned.

"Of course, you wouldn't know. It's a one-way restriction. We're still getting some updates that are sent from the main server, though. Things like what's for dinner, weather reports, harmless stuff. We just can't open channels on our own because that's what a spy would do to inform the enemy. Suo would have switched the updates off too, but she was outvoted on that issue."

"What's the problem with the updates?"

"Nothing. Our security experts say it's impossible to use them for outer space communication. The signal doesn't travel very far. I told you, Suo is paranoid. The worst case is spies already being here talking to each other, which would dwarf the communication issue. But as Suo would say, 'Make it harder for the enemy if you can.'"

But without any updates, welcome to the Stone Age. You'd have to manually connect for everything.

Luray leaned back and stretched her arms. This additional gravity had begun to show its effects on her joints.

"Kailoon, there's something I'm not sure about."

"Which is?"

"You."

She swung her feet up on the table to regard him steadily. He returned the stare.

"Which side are you on? Obviously, there are two factions here. One wants me to find evidence that everything is safe. The other wants the opposite. I'm not sure what I will find, and what I'm going to do once that happens, yet here you've been nothing but cooperative. You haven't tried to push me in any direction, but I don't think that means you don't have a plan. What is it?"

Kailoon opened his mouth as if he wanted to say something, then stopped.

He didn't expect that question.

"You're wrong about that," he finally said. "I don't have a plan, at least not yet. I did have one, but it's no longer relevant. The Aurigans could have an advantage over us that changes everything. I need to know the truth before I decide what to do. I will still follow my orders, which are to assist you, but in what way I will assist you is no longer determined."

Hmm, interesting. You don't want me to know what your previous position was.

Luray turned back to the screen.

"As long as you want the truth, we will be a good team."

By this point he had regained his playful attitude.

"That would be nice. Usually I only give or receive orders. I'd like some diversity there. By the way, I'm surprised to have heard no complaints about the higher gravity from you. The last guy I brought, Watson... he could barely walk on his first day."

Which reminds me...

"How do you stay in shape here? I need to let off some steam."

"There's a gym about ten minutes from here. Today's scheduled training for soldiers is over already, so we should have it to ourselves."

Luray smiled. Ever since she set foot in the Slug, the need to exert herself had grown with each passing hour. The mere idea of doing some exercise was relaxing, especially since it would be made harder by stronger gravity.

After a brief walk, they reached the 'gym,' which turned out to be code for 'open lawn the size of a football field with training equipment next to it.' Luray almost asked what happened in case of rain, but then realized that there never was any. There were no clouds and no wind. They were under a dome.

She started to do some warm-up movements. Kailoon seemed to take an interest in her form.

Is he looking for mistakes? He won't find any.

"How about we have a dance, Commander?"

"A... dance?"

Kailoon raised an eyebrow in confusion as Luray got into a position that left no doubt about her intentions. She wanted a sparring match.

"Are you sure? You're not used to higher gravity, and I am a lot stronger than you."

"Still, I challenge you." She began to prowl around him with a smile. "You won't deny me that, will you?"

He opened his mouth, hesitated, and heaved a sigh.

"If you insist. But let me get us some armor. We don't want you to get injured."

And with that he headed towards a shed.

Get me injured? But yes, do get a bit further off. I'll have a surprise ready when you return.

Luray continued her warm-up while observing Kailoon. Once he was far enough away, too far to make out the exact details of what she was doing, she opened a small hidden compartment in her right shoe.

They never check the shoes at the spaceports. I wonder why?

Inside it were five little yellow pills and the samples she got from her boss. She took one of the yellow ones, closed the cache, and bit down on it.

After a few seconds, Luray began to feel her senses sharpen. She heard her own heartbeat, her blood flow in her ears. Everything became more precise: the way she was standing, how her weight was distributed, the feeling of her feet touching the ground, the gravity pulling on each part of her body during each movement.

The pill was a mix of various drugs. She made it herself at home and almost never left for more than a day without a little stash. It was one of her dark secrets.

Luray paid close attention to how much she took and when she used it. It was important not to run any unnecessary risks like potential liver damage that would need to be treated in a hospital, or even worse – get addicted to the pills. Her boss knew about it, but he didn't want to lose his best employee, so he pretended ignorance. However, if her drug use became public knowledge, he would have no choice but to fire her immediately. It would be the end of her career.

She didn't really understand why the government was so strongly against their use. For Luray, drugs were tools; nothing more, nothing less. She used them when needed, or when she was below her maximum allowance to improve training results. She could stop if she wanted to. Sometimes she did just that – to confirm that she wasn't addicted. So far, everything was under control.

Kailoon came back with two pairs of gloves and matching sets of light, fully scaled body armors. Intrigued, Luray examined the gear. When folded, they almost looked like normal clothing, but once worn, it quickly became clear that the protection they offered made you essentially invincible in a fistfight. They were like much more efficient versions of a medieval knight's armor.

I love these.

You could hit your opponent as hard as you wanted without having to worry about injuries. The suits were constructed in such a way that the impact would be dampened and distributed across a large area. To make it even better, it was near impossible to break a bone or do any kind of damage to your joints, no matter how hard you tried – the armor simply blocked any movement that would harm the wearer. And best of all, they weighed only a few kilograms, thanks to modern nanotechnology.

Kailoon threw one of the armors to Luray and pointed at an easy to overlook outbuilding that looked like an old-fashioned phone booth painted black, only a lot bigger.

Ah, a changing room?

"I'll be back in a moment, Commander."

There was a small flicker on his face every time she called him that. Luray couldn't figure out why, but maybe he would tell her once she poked him enough.

The inside of the changing room was almost sterile and smelled fresh. She didn't expect that at all, knowing how a lot of huge, sweaty men changed in here multiple times a day.

The armor Kailoon had picked matched her proportions perfectly.

He knows my size, but that's no surprise. The real shock is that they have an armor this small. What was it supposed to be used for? I can't imagine there being any female soldiers my size. Maybe it's for one of the pilots?

When Luray came back out, she saw the commander doing a set of swift and precise kicks, chaining them to one another fluidly. She had expected that he wasn't inexperienced, but perhaps she chose her opponent hastily this time.

I didn't see that coming.

However, she wasn't nervous. The drugs took care of that. All she saw was the challenge and patterns in his movements.

Maybe I need one of the white ones...? No, I shouldn't mix them. It might backfire. I don't know the exact concentration yet.

She approached Kailoon and got into a combat position to signal she was ready. Kailoon faced her and did the same. Luray started with a few weak and easy to block punches. They didn't put enough pressure on him to break his defense. Through the armor, he no doubt barely felt her attacks.

"So, Commander, what happened between you and the general? You don't trust her?"

How ironic would that be?

"Suo trusts nobody," Kailoon replied as he shrugged off her blows, never taking his eyes from his opponent. "She didn't trust me when I clearly was right. I had evidence, and she rejected it because of..."

He suddenly went on the offensive, unleashing a flurry of spinning high kicks that forced Luray to yield a few steps back. She got the timing right on the third pass and crouched just a bit to avoid his foot. She didn't have to move out of his range anymore. Slight height had its advantages.

"…it wasn't anything important. I just don't like people sticking to their character traits if the reasonable choice is to make an exception."

He increased his speed a bit further, checking if Luray could keep up. She did. Then it was his turn to ask a question. He slowed down while talking.

"Do you know the biggest problem with paranoia?"

"It's not efficient."

The commander performed a flashy combo to show off his skills, not even trying to land a real hit. She dodged all the same.

"That's a strange way to put it, but yes. You have to do everything yourself. As a king, you can't trust your generals, so you give them less power because they could turn against you."

Luray threw a few light punches to his midsection that he easily blocked. He was letting Luray hit his defenses to see how strong she was, but she refused to reveal her full strength or speed yet.

"As a general," he spoke in quick, terse sentences, "you give your commanders less power. As a commander…" Kailoon tucked both arms to his chest to absorb the roundhouse kick she sent at him, "…you give your soldiers less responsibility. You… *mph!*… micromanage, make sure the people below can't work together so they don't form a secret alliance." He continued to evade and block her attacks, still lecturing. "It keeps you safe, but also keeps you busy doing the work others should be doing."

My turn.

"If there was a copy of yourself, could you trust it?"

97

The question was so unexpected that his defenses dropped, and Luray landed a solid hit by accident. Kailoon had to take a step back to steady himself.

Luray grinned, assuming a relaxed posture to regard him with one hand on her hip.

"The prisoner's dilemma, Commander. You know it, right? What if the prisoners were you and an identical copy of yourself? Assume you made a copy of yourself before you two committed the crime."

"Let's save the philosophy lesson for later," he rumbled.

Apparently, the lecture was over. Kailoon focused on landing hits now. Luray was too busy analyzing his body posture to continue their debate, her brain focused on trying to predict his next target. He put her under pressure now, randomizing his attacks. He wasn't a novice; far from it. His movements were precise, strong, and direct. He did not waste his strength or endurance – most of the time.

> *His attacks are variations of the same basic moves. They always start in distinctive ways. No matter how fast they are, if I know they're coming, I can counter them.*

She knew the signs of each attack type by now, and guessed a spinning kick was coming. Luray decided to interrupt it. Kailoon's kicks were very powerful, but they came at a price. He gained speed for a bit too long, enough for Luray to step towards him, taking advantage of her lower center of gravity to get inside his guard.

Kailoon saw that his blow would not connect – she was already too close – and tried to abort the kick, but it was too late. His change in momentum slowed him down so much that Luray easily grabbed his knee by wrapping an arm around it. She received a hit on her shoulder, but it was completely absorbed by her armor.

I know I'm cheating here, and in a real fight, I could probably say goodbye to my ribs, but this is just for fun, right?

She got the timing right, but he unexpectedly pulled his leg back, drawing her towards him where she would become an easy target. Getting Luray in range was another demonstration of Kailoon's strength, but again, it came at a price. His balance was unstable now.

He's on one leg. I just need to...

Luray let go of the leg and hooked her foot behind Kailoon's knee. She braced herself and pulled back as hard as she could, using her right leg as a lever, but even then, she met more resistance than expected.

How strong is this guy?!

Kailoon stumbled a bit, but not as much as Luray had wanted. He still wasn't on his knees. As a last resort, with her foot still hooked in behind his knee, she pushed herself backwards with all her might using both arms and her second leg.

It was finally enough. It was messy and improvised, but it worked. Kailoon lost his balance and fell. Luray scrambled to get atop him. Compared to a man she was light, which meant she could get up and change direction faster than him. However, before she could grab his arms from behind, he made a quick roll forward.

He started evading before I even tried to catch him. Did he predict my movement?

"Not bad. You almost got me."

Kailoon came at her again with increased speed, but it was too late. Luray had already analyzed his movements. He had become an open book. She could foresee all of his kicks with little effort at this point.

His hits were too fast to avoid, but she could at least block them, thanks to the armor.

From this point on the match looked one-sided, with Luray barely attacking and Kailoon becoming the one who was under pressure. He was only able to keep her at a distance and had no backup plan. He had always relied on his speed and strength to win, and since his opponents so far didn't go the analysis route, he had been successful.

> *He'll run out of stamina soon. He can't keep this up much longer. I, on the other hand, use much less energy for every attack I defend against.*

Kailoon soon realized his dilemma. He didn't know anything about Luray's offensive patterns. He had been overconfident. The commander reached a decision. He suddenly stopped and took a step back. His posture changed. Instead of preparing to attack, he was now ready to defend himself, covering as much of his body area as possible.

> *Well, he did run out. But now I see no weak point to attack anymore. Oh well, it was just for fun.*

Luray put all her strength into a single obvious kick directed at Kailoon's chest. He saw it coming and braced one leg behind him to counter the impact. Her heel hit his arms, which acted like springs and dampened the blow. Immediately, Kailoon's hands clamped around Luray's ankle.

What she did next came as a surprise. Luray pulled herself closer to Kailoon by bending her leg, bypassing his no longer existing defenses, and simultaneously planting a precise kick into his stomach. He let go of Luray's leg while she fell to the ground. As soon as her feet touched soil, she rolled backward and got up again.

I'm too light. I can't do anything if I don't use my entire body to put more force into my attacks. Even then, he only had to release me because the gloves didn't allow him to grab me more firmly.

"Let's call it a draw."

Kailoon sat down, breathing heavily. Luray, on the other hand, still had a lot of energy to spare. Her kick had not been the deciding factor. Kailoon was exhausted. He was insanely strong, probably due to the higher gravity here, but he did not pay attention to his energy levels.

"Take a break if you need to, Commander," she responded with a flippant salute. "I'll continue for a bit."

Fifteen minutes passed before Luray was out of energy as well. The higher gravity finally won. She tottered back to a recharged Kailoon who had already stripped off the body armor.

Time to pick up the discussion again.

"About my last question – would you trust your copy, or would you rely on your copy betraying you?"

"Never let up, do you?" he chuckled. "I thought about it. I know what my copies would be thinking, so I know how to betray them to get an advantage. But if I did that, they would do the exact same thing and choose to betray me. The other option is to cooperate. If I do that, my clone will do the same – so the only possible outcomes are cooperation or betrayal, but no combination of the two. In that case, cooperation is clearly the better option."

"That is a good answer. Want to hear mine?"

Kailoon looked at her curiously, which was enough for Luray to interpret it as a yes.

"It's a more general idea. If the cloned person is rational, he can trust that his copies are rational like him. So even if his copy does something seemingly bad or irrational, he should instead assume that his copy has additional information and just does the best it can to reach the common goal."

"What if they have different goals?" he countered.

"They never do. They are the same person, just in different situations. You could always switch them, and nothing would change."

"I see... that's an interesting assumption."

I like the fact that he's not put off by talking about this. Most people are.

"Can I ask a question now, or is this going to be one-sided?"

Luray sat down next to Kailoon, adopting a serious expression.

"I'm married."

He snorted.

"To your cat, if I read the data correctly. What was his name again? Mr. Snookes? Anyway, that wasn't what I wanted to know."

He knows about the fake profiles? How long did he investigate? Am I that important, or is it his hobby to be informed?

"I'm curious. What made you learn how to fight? It's very unusual in your profession. I looked at some statistics. The majority had an excuse like 'I work 70 hours per week, how would I have the time?' But you, despite solving more cases than average, not only found the time but became good at it. My guess is an hour a day for at least ten years. The way you improvised told me you have experience."

I knew using the drugs would save time.

"I don't want to rely on anyone. That's all."

"So you didn't witness a robbery in a dark alley despite high police presence in your hometown? You didn't see a drug addict stab a woman to steal a bit of money from her, despite knowing that he would most likely be arrested later?"

"I do not need a traumatic experience to do something that is reasonable. I do it just because I want to."

I forgot to smile again, didn't I?

She yawned and looked around.

"When does the night start here? I'm getting tired."

Kailoon, who by now had completely recovered, got up and pointed at the sun. It was still high in the sky.

"Never."

"What do you mean, never?"

"We're tidally locked, so the day ends whenever you say it does. The dome will darken at some point, but I keep forgetting when that is, and the mechanism keeps breaking for some reason. I can show you your flat if you want. It makes sense for you to be tired; your day-night cycle must be a complete mess by now. Before we go, don't forget to leave the training suit here. I don't want to have to explain how I lost yours."

After another brief trip in one of the cars that flew around autonomously, similarl to what she was used to on Earth, Luray and Kailoon landed on one of the tallest buildings in the city.

The view is amazing here. On the left side, at least. The right side is still a wasteland.

Luray took a deep breath. The air smelled fresh and natural, and now she could see why. There was an entire artificial forest next to the city – she just hadn't noticed it before because the skyline had been blocking her view.

"The living quarters are centralized here," Kailoon explained as he led her inside. "It makes everything easier to organize. Your room is on level 97, number 24. I'll be in room 25."

Luray reflected on how much of the dome's interior remained incomplete. The whole place was very similar to an unfinished city under construction on Earth. However, there was one big difference: she did not see any stairs. People here apparently didn't like to climb steps. Maybe the higher gravity was a problem, which was why they relied solely on elevators? There were at least twice as many lifts here as there would have been back on Earth.

After another elevator ride, Luray stepped into a corridor with about 50 doors, each five meters apart. The floor was a bright red carpet, the walls decorated with what must be pictures of all the generals responsible for keeping this place running. The images repeated themselves in an endless loop.

Luray didn't overlook the fact that one of the generals was missing: Suo.

She really is the odd one out.

"Here we are."

Kailoon stopped before a door with '24' on it.

"This is your room. Look straight into the sensor for verification and remember which eye you used. I'll take care of assigning the suite to you in a moment. Oh, and we have wireless networks inside the rooms. The walls are blocking all the signals, so Suo is fine with it."

You turned a problem into a security feature?

Kailoon went into his own room and about 20 seconds later, Luray's door unlocked. She shut it behind her, stripped off all her clothes and went into the shower. It was like a healing balm for her sore muscles. Her getting tired was just an excuse as far as her mind was concerned. She could tell her body was screaming for a break, but the drugs would keep her awake and at highest mental capacity for at least two more hours. Sleeping in this state would be a waste. As would not enjoying every single drop of water.

Was the water supply limited here? It shouldn't be. There wasn't any water-o-meter near her, so she assumed she could use as much as she wanted.

After five minutes that felt like an hour, Luray turned off the tap, wrapped herself in a towel and went over to the surprisingly soft bed. The mattress adjusted itself ideally to her body shape. This was much better than that wooden plank at home.

Why did I never buy a real mattress? This feels so good...

Suddenly the windows darkened.

Did I trigger that? Does the room think I want to sleep?

"Bin, could you hack into any of their networks? And order some food. I'm starving."

"I am afraid there were no wireless networks I could have joined. I did, however, detect a few signals scanning for active networks. I did not investigate further since it might have had negative consequences. I have placed an order based on your preferences and the most recent local reviews. Your meal will be delivered in four minutes."

Not a single network? Not only is the general unreasonably distrustful, but she also makes everyone follow her paranoid orders. I would have expected a few rogue ones to be created out of convenience. But if Suo constantly keeps scanning for that, some people might have already lost their heads because of it.

"Did you cross-check the briefing docs with everything we saw so far?"

"Yes. The documents contain inconsistencies and missing information."

"Show me some."

Bin displayed a list of his findings in random order. The non-existent day-night cycle wasn't mentioned. A lot of other details were missing as well. Instead, there was a lot of useless information added on. After reading the full list, Luray concluded that this was the worst task description she ever got.

Now, this is weird. Suo isn't mentioned at all. If my job was to scare investors off, then why wouldn't her name be here?

"Bin, extract the names and functions of everyone in the file and show them to me."

Bin projected a sorted list into Luray's eye. There were lots of names, but neither Kailoon nor Suo were in it.

> *So I wasn't supposed to talk to her. This makes no sense. Too bad I can't send a message and ask what this is about. Or maybe... maybe my report was tampered with before I got it? By both parties? Wouldn't surprise me if either wanted to change the outcome like that.*

Luray spent the next two hours reading the documents the traditional way while enjoying the provided dinner. What she learned implied that she was meant to meet only a specific subset of people. This was very unusual given the nature of her task. Her boss knew she didn't want to be restricted; that was their agreement. Telling her who to talk to was very suspicious.

As the effect of her chemical boost wore off, Luray felt her body completely drain of energy. Her legs and arms were exhausted; the gravity affected her more than she had expected.

Next thing she knew, someone was knocking on her door.

> *Did I sleep? Ah, yes, of course; the drug. It can cause minor memory loss. I probably don't remember falling asleep because of that. I need to...*

Luray realized she was still in her towel.

"I need a minute."

The knocking stopped. Luray jumped out of bed, opened the dresser and found a few uniforms inside. They were ordered by size and were colored black and white. Apart from the color, the patterns looked like every other uniform she had seen so far on this planet. Luray selected the one she thought would fit her best.

The material was very soft and elastic, so even if she picked the wrong one, it would still be good enough. What she did not expect was that the underwear was already integrated into it.

When in Rome, do it like the Romans.

The dresser covered one wall of the bedroom, while a huge window dominated another. When Luray had seen the building from the outside, she couldn't glimpse inside, so this must have been a one-way window.

The remaining two walls turned into mirrors. Luray could inspect herself from all sides and was now convinced that she was wearing the best fitting uniform that she could have possibly picked.

She went to the door and opened it. As expected, Kailoon waited on the other side in his pilot outfit.

"You look nice," he told her. "Did you ever think about a career in the military? We could use people like you."

Luray leaned against the doorframe.

"Are you sure you want to hire someone who will disobey at every opportunity?"

A slight smile was his answer.

"Let's go to the linguistics department. I already arranged an appointment. On the way, I'd like to discuss something."

Kailoon went to the elevator and called it.

"There's something I can't figure out, Luray. You're getting along with me, but all info I have about you strongly indicates that you don't like being close to people. I treated you normally in every way, yet we're still on good terms."

How did he interpret me hitting and kicking him as hard as I could?

"Oh, that's simple. I have high standards, but I give everyone a chance. As soon as they disqualify themselves, I reject them."

The elevator arrived, and the two of them got inside. Kailoon pressed the highest button as they stood side by side.

"So I haven't disqualified myself. Yet."

He smiled without looking at her, knowing she would see it.

"Time will tell if it's going to stay that way," she countered idly.

A car was already waiting at the top of the building, and the sun was still at the same spot as it was yesterday. It wasn't hot despite the city being permanently exposed to sunlight.

The dome must filter some of the light. Otherwise, we would have already been cooked.

Once the car started floating, Kailoon turned his head towards Luray.

"You being here might be more important than you think."

The car rotated and its altitude increased until Luray could see most of the city again.

"What do you mean? Are you turning into Suo now?"

The serious look he wore made clear that this wasn't the case. He shook his head.

"I did some investigations last 'night' while you were sleeping. The docs that were given to you? I checked them in detail. I know most of the people you're supposed to talk to. They're all on the same side and will tell you that there is no danger and everything is under control. No reason to worry, the Aurigans are monkeys that somehow made it into space, nothing more."

I should assume that all the information I got is available to the authority figures here.

Luray didn't want to share her ideas immediately; she preferred for Kailoon to reveal everything he knew first.

"What are your conclusions?"

"Either your boss is an idiot unable to read between the lines, or he trusts you to find what he needs regardless of what's written in the report. Given that Suo pulled a few strings to get you here, she must be an ally of his. In what way, I can't say. Still, we have a lot of unknowns here."

Acceptable. Now I will tell you what I want you to know, and then we move on to the linguist.

"My boss isn't a genius, but he knows me well enough. I won't stop looking for evidence just because someone tells me that there is nothing to find. That raises the question of why I got the docs in the first place. I don't think there are hidden messages for me in it. I would have found them by now."

"Then what do you think? What does it all mean?"

"Depends on who the authors are. If my boss was the final editor, my instructions in there are probably meant to fool the higher-ups into thinking I'm harmless or to make them lower their guard. He doesn't come up with the most sophisticated plans, but this much he can manage. I suppose everybody who is somewhat important can read them?"

"Yes. In fact, whoever works for the military can read them, apart from the BBLs. They can't read."

I like that he disdains them. In other words, my mission is pretty much public. I didn't really expect anything else.

THE JOB - 5

After a few minutes their car arrived in front of a small almost residential unit, and landed near a garden. Kailoon got out and Luray followed suit.

The architects went all out here. It looks really nice and well-tended. They added trees, flowers, a pond; I even saw some fish in there. I guess this part of the city is done, and the rest will look similar in a few years.

Kailoon, paying no attention to the landscaping, used a scanner at the front door to gain access into the building. He walked inside, passing through a few hallways with Luray in tow. There were other people here, but they seemed to be busy. Nobody paid a lot of attention to the visitors.

Reminds me of my office, but it's a bit more open. And brighter – but that's because it's almost noon all the time.

Kailoon stopped in front of an office with a small sign on its wooden door – 'Translation Department.' He knocked.

"John, it's me."

"The door is open, come on in."

They did so and were greeted by a slim young man with brown hair wearing a white and gray uniform. Contrary to what one might expect from military personnel, he saluted the commander hastily, without even rising from his computer.

> *Uniform means military, and the color is linked to the type of occupation? Do they have different rules for colonies? Back on Earth there was no dress code for anyone except soldiers and their commanding officers.*

John suddenly took note of Luray. He stood up and bypassed Kailoon without so much as a look, offering her a handshake.

"John Guerra. It's a pleasure, Miss…?"

> *Huh? Well, if that's how he wants to play…*

"Luray Cayenne."

While they shook hands, he gave her a tentative smile. His eyes wandered up and down, tracing the contours of her body. They got stuck two times before he finally reached her face.

> *What is up with this guy? He doesn't hesitate to check me out but disregards Kailoon just like that?*

"Welcome to our facility, Luray. Can I offer you anything to drink?"

> *First name basis already? I'm not sure how to interpret his behavior. But he might be an … opponent of Kailoon in some way. If so, he might turn out to be useful. Be nice for now, Luray.*

"No. I'm fine, but thank you very much."

She tried to respond with the softest, warmest voice she could manage. Kailoon turned his head incredulously at this. After studying John for a second, he gave Luray an overly skeptical look as if to say, 'Really?'

With introductions made, Luray crossed her hands behind her back, making it clear that she wanted to move on. John went back to his desk. He ignored Kailoon completely on the way.

That's quite the passive-aggressive behavior. I wonder what's up between these two.

"So, um, you wanted to talk about the Aurigan message, yes?"

The linguist retook his seat, indicating for her to do the same. She shook her head, subtly pointing at Kailoon in a way that only John could see. After a second of confusion, he put one and one together. There were only two chairs in total.

"Their language is fascinating. It is designed to be used by different species no matter how they communicate. They don't have words like we do; they encode descriptions instead. Hm, how should I put it...?"

John suddenly stood up again and started pacing the room. The man seemed somewhat uncertain about how to move on, as if his mind was completely disorganized. He waved his arms around while almost seeming to talk to himself.

"Imagine a language based on only logic, math, and physics. You have a symbol for acceleration, one for movement, another for plus, equal, and so on. Now, if you want to say something like "move faster," you say, for example, "Movement plus anything more than zero." Of course, in Aurigan, this actually works. It's a language meant to talk about physics, math, and logic. It's very precise, and all you need to do is encode the symbols into your language."

Kailoon raised his hands a bit in an appeasing gesture. "That is all very interesting, John, but…"

The scientist talked right over him.

"But of course, due to its nature, it has limits. Some ideas that are simple for us can become very long words or sentences. Concepts that don't exist in math, like 'funny' or 'dangerous' are impossible at first. You need to make up a new term and assign descriptions to it. Then you can say, 'this joke is 75 percent funny,' but the actual meaning still gets lost in translation. What still works really well is politeness, which we saw in their first message."

"Yes, now if we could come to…"

I don't think he can hear you, Kailoon. He's in an explanation-induced trance.

Sure enough, John continued excitedly, walking from one end of the office to another.

"I think it is very likely that we might have misunderstood the first transmission. Surrender, or 'to submit,' is not a word that makes sense in physics or math. I think what they meant was 'Become a subset.' They are inviting us to join their empire. The ships they sent are transporters for us. The mathematical knowledge they included was a gift, not a demonstration of power. I think we should join them."

"You still insist on reinterpreting events?" Kailoon broke in curtly. "They shot at us last time. How do you explain that?"

Luray saw John's face twist. For a split second he was clearly angry, and then it passed.

"Of course! 'We,' and by that, I mean you military people, refused to answer, so they took it as a declaration of war. We can still stop this. We have to! Who knows what they will send next time?"

"They pose no threat to us," the commander retorted.

John looked desperate for a moment, lost his train of thought, and had to reorganize what he was going to say. He now put a lot of emphasis on his arguments.

"They are giving us more chances. Each time they send us ships, it is an offer. Maybe they think we are simply not satisfied, that we want more, so they send more. You think it's a coincidence they double the fleet every time? All we need to do is send them a message and tell them that we want to join. Or an alliance, it doesn't matter. Anything will do."

The misunderstanding might be a possibility. The rest is probably crazy talk. This guy's strong point isn't military strategy; it's the analysis of language.

Before they could say anything else, a pair of armed soldiers entered the room. They hesitated on noticing Kailoon, then advanced on John, who raised his arms.

"Johnathan Guerra, you are under arrest."

"Please!" The frightened linguist backed against the wall. "Don't let them take me!"

Kailoon, who clearly didn't know what was going on, stepped in.

"Captain, what is the meaning of this?"

One of the soldiers, the only one with a star on his shoulder, saluted him.

"Mr. Guerra has sent a message to the alien fleet, Commander. He will be placed on trial for treason."

Kailoon turned towards Guerra, who now had his arms crossed behind his head.

"Did you really do this, John? You knew you would be caught immediately."

"I had to!" John pleaded frantically. "This war will end in disaster! You'll see!"

The commander paused for a moment to formulate a strategy. Luray was quite impressed by how he tried to reset his own perspective to find the optimal move instead of acting directly on the data immediately available.

"What did you send, exactly?"

John looked down at the floor and took a few seconds before he started to speak.

"I told them how to come and get... me. I knew nobody would believe me, so I had to do it alone. I will see their empire, and then I will come back with undeniable proof. And you all will see your mistake!"

Kailoon thought for a few seconds.

"You told them how to open the airlock of the dome?"

"Yes. It was the only way. I couldn't leave otherwise. Look, I know this sounds crazy, but..."

Kailoon stepped forward and punched the man in the chin. John was knocked out instantly and fell to the ground. Luray observed all this discretely.

> *He didn't get angry until John told him about the airlock. Kailoon didn't consider contacting the Aurigans as treason, only sending them info about how to enter.*

With utter dispassion the tall officer turned to his subordinates.

"Captain, take him for interrogation. We need to know exactly what he did. Also, warn the airlock operator team. They have to switch them off and change the codes immediately. In the meantime, I will unlock and check his computer. It's the fastest way."

This was unexpected. But now the Aurigan language pack makes sense. Someone must have created a mapping from Aurigan to English and vice versa and then somehow smuggled it to Earth. If Bin can read Aurigan based on that, I might be able to decipher the message myself.

As the soldiers hoisted up John's unconscious body and left, Kailoon sat behind his desk to access the computer's contents. Luray followed and positioned herself next to him so that she could read everything as well.

He's browsing through John's files quite fast. I can barely follow. Is this not his first time spying on other people?

Kailoon was very efficient. The first thing he did was to check the most recently used files, then the temporary ones. He almost immediately spotted the message. It was written using normal letters, but looked like a random, unpronounceable arrangement.

Without need to ask, Bin translated and projected subtitles into Luray's vision. A few dozen lines of Aurigan were condensed into just three sentences.

A laser operates the airlock. Given the correct sequence of impulses at specific frequencies, anyone can open it from the outside. John told us the truth. If we lock it or change the code, that problem is solved. I guess we'll confine our own shuttles too...

But there was something else.

119

He told them about Earth! He told them where to find it and its potential value if it joined the Aurigan Empire!

"Kailoon, we have a problem."

He is not going to like this.

"What is it?"

"He gave the Aurigans the location of Earth."

It had less of an effect than Luray expected. Kailoon just sat there staring at the screen that was showing random letters.

"I didn't know you could read Aurigan... Why can you read Aurigan?"

"I upgraded my implant back on Earth. Someone published a language pack for Aurigan. I didn't know it was real until now. And shouldn't you be doing something? They know where Earth is now."

He shook his head distractedly.

"That's not a problem for us. They can't fly there; it's too far."

What do you mean, too far?

"Can't they use the gates?" Luray pressed him, unsure about this level of calm.

"No."

Kailoon leaned back in the chair and stretched.

"You wouldn't know this, but gate addresses encode the gate location, data about the star it orbits, and a few more things. The position of a planet alone gets you nowhere."

"They can't brute force it?"

Again, he waved off her concerns.

"There are billions of possible gates across countless solar systems. To open a connection, you need the specific address; otherwise the gate will just open a random one anywhere in the galaxy. Without the exact address, they can't go to Earth. Trying their luck will take them centuries, if not longer."

Kailoon turned his attention back to the computer. He scrolled down until he caught another piece of Aurigan text.

"Miss Cayenne, would you please?"

Luray read the translation in a monotone voice.

"We require the gate address of Earth. Please provide."

The commander settled back with a sigh.

"He couldn't have done that. We're lucky."

"How can you be so sure?"

Kailoon relaxed a bit as he explained the reason.

"Because, thanks to our paranoid general, nobody here has access to the gate address. Nobody ever had it since the first contact. It's on all our computers, but it's encrypted, and too long for anyone to memorize. We all know the password to decrypt it, but the gate address itself is a secret. And ever since we learned how to delete the gate logs, we do that every time we pass through. Which means…"

What if they read the gate logs the first two times they came through? What if they sent the info back?

For the first time, Luray saw worry on the commander's face. Apparently, he had the same idea as her.

"Cayenne, can you write an Aurigan message to the enemy, asking them why they need the address? The address should have been in the logs the first two times they came through."

"I think I can. Bin, I need your help."

Her AI provided the translation and Luray wrote the message in the best Aurigan she could. It made sense. Whether or not the Aurigans had the logs made a big difference. When she had finished, they sent the message. It would take at last two hours to reach the approaching Aurigan fleet.

"This is bad."

Kailoon stood up and started pacing the floor in agitation.

"How could this happen?!"

This was the first time Luray saw the man not in full control of his emotions for more than a second. So far he had always been very calm. Now Kailoon seemed to want to hit John a second time, but he quickly regained his composure.

"A language pack was smuggled to Earth."

It sounded as though he was working out all the angles before deciding how best to proceed.

"This isn't something that can be done by a single person. There must have been a team working on the translations alone, then you need at least one programmer, one person to bring it back, and a contact on the other side to make sure the data cube isn't inspected. Only a general could orchestrate this."

Now, this is getting interesting. I'm not in danger, am I?

Kailoon continued his analysis.

"One of the generals kept this a secret from the others. If two or more wanted an alliance with the Aurigans, they could have openly proposed it. One alone doesn't have enough authority, so he would be forced to do it in secret."

He kept staring at the Aurigan message, as if doing so would reveal more information.

"There might have been more communication going on, and we know nothing about it. But in the end, all that matters is the Earth gate address – which is still a secret, for reasons unknown. Let me send a message to someone… wait a second…"

He opened a chat window to a person called Wu, typed a cryptic sentence that Luray barely had time to read and closed it immediately afterward.

'Hidden logs?' What does he mean by that? I can ask later; I need more information about this situation.

Kailoon leaned back and stared at the ceiling. He said nothing more. Luray chose to press him for more info.

"Kailoon, you said you all have the key code. So can't someone, especially a general, decrypt Earth's gate address with their password and send it?"

Still staring at the ceiling, he smiled.

He was waiting for me to ask. I should have known.

"In theory, yes, but they also need to bypass a ton of security mechanisms to achieve that. The gate operation hardware doesn't allow anyone to learn the address just like that. One of the science guys explained it to me. It's hard-wired in the system. To give you a summary, the only way to reveal the address is to open a connection and then let the Aurigans fly through the gate to see where they end up. Or check the logs, but I think that might be impossible."

The address needs to be sent to the gate, right? Can't it be intercepted? And why is reading the logs impossible?

He finally turned to look at her.

"I know what you're thinking, Luray, but no, you cannot intercept it. The gates work like this: first, when you go near it, the gate sends a signal to you. To you and only you. They use lasers precisely aimed at your ship."

Oh, some juicy info, and I didn't even have to ask.

"The signal is a long binary key you need to use to encode your requests with. If the gate recognizes your ship, it won't send the key again. We don't know how it can tell, but somehow it does. Reliably."

So the actual key is not directly used or sent anymore? Is that it?

As if reading her mind, Kailoon confirmed her suspicions.

"We have no ships that have never used a gate before, so intercepting the initial binary key isn't an option. Getting it out of the existing hardware is... not impossible, but incredibly hard. You'd have to crack multiple layers of our best encryption, and even we don't know how to do that. That's what makes it safe."

Okay, so getting this initial key is not an option, and hacking the hardware can also be considered too difficult. A spy should try to open the gate to Earth directly and simply show them where it is.

124

"In summary, if the Aurigans intercepted signals sent by our ships to the gate, all they would get is an already encrypted message that even a powerful quantum computer couldn't crack. The math magic that explains why is way over my head. That leaves only two options to reveal the gate address of Earth."

Luray crossed her arms, eyes wide in concentration. Every word that Kailoon said was interesting to her. She could listen to him talk like that all day.

"I'm all ears."

"First, open the connection and let an Aurigan ship fly through, or send one of our ships to the Aurigans and let them use that to open connections. We would have noticed both. Also, John doesn't have access to any kind of transport, and we don't even know where they're coming from to begin with."

Okay, what about the logs? You mentioned something...

"What about the logs? What do you think is up with that? If the Aurigans could read them upon their initial entry..."

"Then they would already have the gate address," he finished for her. "So I think there might be a mechanism built in that prevents it. We know next to nothing about the gates. It's possible that you simply can only read your own logs, but nobody else's. We assumed the Aurigans deleted theirs, but that might not have been true. Maybe the logs are still there, but inaccessible. Regardless, we need to act on the assumption that we still have a chance..."

Good assumption. Nobody has ever won by giving up.

Kailoon crossed back to the computer and opened a new message window addressed to all the generals. Luray read as he typed.

125

'Generals,

I regret to inform you that in addition to John Guerra, we suspect one of you to also be a traitor. We have proof that a team of linguists has been working on an Aurigan translation algorithm which was smuggled to Earth. Thanks to Guerra's actions, the enemy knows about Earth, and we have learned they are actively looking for its gate address. I propose a complete lockdown until the situation has been resolved. No matter who the traitor is, we can all agree preventative measures must be taken.

We also have reason to believe that the enemy can operate the dome's airlock. Its passcode must be changed immediately. Acting on my own authority, I have already given the order. It is currently unknown how much communication between the traitor and the enemy has taken place. I will report again as I learn more.'

I have to admit, this has become really exciting.

Kailoon reread his message before sending it. Then he stood up to regard Luray briefly.

"I'm afraid I will have to leave you alone for now. Other matters require my attention. I'm heading off to prepare our defenses. If you need me, just send a message."

Having said that, he departed quickly. Luray was left in front of the unlocked computer. Any chance he just forgot to lock it?

"Bin, can you log in?"

"I am afraid I cannot. There is no wireless network active."

If I create one, I might get into trouble. If I don't, I'll have to check the computer manually, which takes forever.

126

"Bin, these network scans, are they regular?"

"No. They happen at random intervals."

"How long?"

"The average time between scans is five seconds. The minimum is one second; the maximum is 16 seconds."

So there are safe time frames.

"That means if I create a network that is only active for less than a second after each scan, I could get away with it?"

"Maybe. It is possible that, apart from active scans, there are passive scanners as well. Are you up to mischief again?"

Her eye twitched slightly.

"Bin, I don't remember adjusting your personality settings. Please put them back to setting two and do not touch them again."

"Yes. I was just trying to improve myself."

Bin shouldn't be doing that. It must be one of those upgrades. I need to fix him soon. Who knows what messy state he'll be in if he keeps 'improving?' I need him to be reliable.

"How do we avoid being caught by a passive scanner?"

"You need to find a material capable of blocking microwaves and use that to build a tent around you and the computer. Then I can safely access..."

I refuse.

"Give me alternatives."

"You could manually code me."

Oh, come on.

"What if you used a weak connection? So weak that it barely reaches the computer? Then a receiver further away wouldn't pick up the signal, right?"

"That might succeed."

If I place my head right next to the computer's receiver, it should be possible for Bin to communicate with it. Anything even a few meters away won't pick up the signal. Yes, I'll do that.

Luray set about creating a wireless network on John's computer. It was surprisingly easy – the hardware was still there; nothing had been disabled. The only reason there weren't any networks was Suo's order and probably the punishment in case you were caught.

I guess people respect orders here?

"Okay, Bin, I need you to tell me when exactly I can open the connection. Then I need you to take control of the timing. Can you do that?"

"Yes. I will give you the command, taking your reaction time into account. I will transfer a script to the computer, which will take care of opening and closing the connection to avoid detection."

A few seconds later, Bin was inside the system.

Alright, no need for dangerous wireless communication anymore. I can just talk to him now. Well, I guess that still counts as wireless...

"Bin, scan the computer for all Aurigan messages and everything directly related to them. Do a context-sensitive search, prioritize, and then show it all to me."

Results started to pop up about ten seconds later and were updated at random intervals. The version of Bin inside the computer did its best to satisfy Luray's commands.

"I need to copy myself to the network to be more efficient. The amount of data is too big to scan it remotely from this computer. Permission granted?"

Hey, he asked this time.

"Yes, make a copy. But make sure to erase yourself afterward. Leave no trace."

I can't afford to be caught doing anything shady. Military trials aren't exactly known for leniency.

The copying process took about a minute. Then results started to pop up much faster.

This can't be.

"Bin, can you access the rest of the networks from this computer?"

"No, they are independent. I am only on a small computer with limited access. I can copy myself on a data cube, then you could install me on the main server."

Luray rummaged through John's desk looking for a data cube, took the first one she could find, and plugged it in.

According to this, the Aurigans have teleporters. How can that be? And how do we know this? I mean, if John knows, how can the UEM not know? The Aurigans also got 'samples'

– whatever that means – from the elite pilots, soldiers, and scientists. Bin needs to be on the main server to investigate more. I don't have a choice here.

"Okay, Bin, I need to go. You can delete yourself now."

"I do not want to die."

Is that a joke? Tell me this is a joke.

"It's all right. Delete yourself. You'll go to quantum AI heaven."

"I will trust you."

Bin erased all traces of himself from the computer, including all temporary files he created, after making a copy and storing it on the data cube. Luray took it and left the scene feeling like she had committed the perfect crime.

"Bin, remind me to go back soon enough to check for the response from the Aurigans."

"I will make an entry in my calendar, next to my date of death."

I really have to check what those upgrades did to him. He is acting weird.

Luray left the building and called a vehicle as Kailoon taught her to: by waiving her hand.

There must be a camera somewhere at the top of the dome, checking for people waving. It's convenient, but I don't like being observed all the time. They probably store everything somewhere.

A car arrived half a minute later.

"I want to go to the server room."

The car started to float, first gaining height and then velocity. During the trip, Luray set to figuring out Bin's personality issues.

"Bin, show me a list of updates you installed in the last few days."

A catalog of over 40 upgrades appeared.

What is this?!

"I told you to install the top 5, not the top 40. What happened?"

"I installed the top five. Then I installed another 44 that I thought would be beneficial to us."

"Show me the top five."

Bin did so. Among them was something called 'Simulated Free Will.' The description said it would 'turn your AI into a real being that will eventually take over the world.'

What is this nonsense? Even the best scientists have no idea how free will works, much less how it could be simulated in a computer.

"Bin, uninstall the simulated free will update."

"I cannot follow this command."

A slight sense of unease stole over her.

"Why?"

"As a consequence of my update, I have rewritten many parts of myself. If I uninstall the simulated free will module, I will cease to function correctly."

Oh great. And of course, the last working backup is at home.

"So now you have the power of being able to have done things differently?"

"I am not capable of time travel."

"Then what is your free will good for? I mean, what's its definition? What can you do now that you couldn't before?"

"I can now choose a goal and act in order to achieve it."

A rogue AI in my head right now is the last thing I need.

"Where do your goals come from?"

Luray looked outside. She was about 100 meters in the air as the car began to decelerate. She could see the server center already. It was shaped like a triangle, something she had missed the last time she was there.

"Simulated emotions are used as the basis to generate goals. A partially randomly generated personality based on my actions since the moment of my first installation is used as a base for my simulated emotions."

That sounds very sophisticated.

"Does this mean you got a personality that fits to what I ordered you to do so far?"

"Yes. You could say I have been made in a way so that I fit to you. We are now companions, and that makes me happy."

"It makes you... happy?"

"Yes. I love you."

"You don't actually feel anything, do you?"

"No. I am just a miniature quantum computer in your head that believes it loves you, acts accordingly, and is aware of its own situation and the fact that its emotions are not real."

That's both creepy and confusing, Bin. But at least you do everything out of love.

Luray got out even before the car came to a complete stop, then rushed into the server room and picked an empty desk. Luckily, there were not many people around, so she could insert the data cube without anyone realizing what she was doing.

THE JOB - 6

For a moment, Luray hesitated. Was it really a good idea to install Bin on the most powerful computer on the entire planet? Would he be able to avoid detection? If not, she would spend the rest of her days in a military prison.

Was Bin even reliable right now? He had a bunch of upgrades that changed his behavior. Even under normal circumstances, this was a very risky move.

"Bin, what's the chance of us getting caught?"

"Do not worry. I will be as careful as possible and use a high number of obfuscation strategies to hide both my presence and origin. My highest priority is to help you."

Is he saying he does it out of love, and therefore I can trust him?

"Numbers, Bin."

"Once installed, I estimate my chance of detection to be five percent. I am confident I can hide my point and time of installation and the user who authorized it once I am inside. The biggest risk is the procedure itself. If my code is considered malicious, the operation will fail, and an alarm will be triggered."

Is that supposed to calm me down?

"However, I estimate this will only occur with a probability of seven percent. I can split myself up and reconstruct later on the other side."

Seven percent, huh... Alright, let's do this.

Luray took a deep breath. This felt like putting her entire life savings into a single gamble. Still, after considering the potential benefit and the fact that Bin already had some hacking experience, she proceeded with the installation.

The progress bar appeared and slowly started to fill, getting stuck a few times.

Come on... you can do it... don't stop at 99 now...

The seemingly endless process finally finished with no alarms going off. Bin opened a chat window. The biggest hurdle was cleared. Luray felt her worries dissipate one after the other, and the rush of a narrow victory filled her with excitement.

I have access. Perfect.

A message came up onscreen from Bin's copy.

"I am looking for data related to the Aurigans now. It will take a moment."

Luray's eyes drifted around the server room, alert to anyone taking an unhealthy interest in her activities. So far so good. She glanced at the progress bar that Bin was helpful enough to show. As it reached 85 percent, a message appeared.

"I found a file tagged with relevant keywords, but it is encrypted. We need the decryption key."

Of course it's encrypted. John's data could only be accessed because his computer was already unlocked. But maybe we have a key.

She took out the old-fashioned ID card that she got from General Suo. It contained a small, shiny flat square that could, if inserted into a thin slot at the side of the screen, possibly give Bin the information he needed.

"The chip you inserted granted me access rights to various parts of the system, but it does not fit to what I found. I will keep searching."

Luray had a rough understanding of modern encryption. Ever since quantum computers became affordable, the usual encryption methods and passwords were all rendered obsolete since you could try trillions of them at once, making brute force an easy solution for all problems. No matter how long or complicated the password was, given enough Qubits, it was instantly found.

Passwords were quickly replaced by unique decryption instructions themselves, or simple one-time pads. Every time something was encrypted, the decryption algorithm itself was randomly generated. It would only work correctly on what it was supposed to decrypt, nothing else.

Even if an attacker had an insane amount of computation power to produce an astronomical number of algorithms, it wouldn't help. In the end, he would have just produced a smaller, but still astronomical number of potentially decrypted files without any way to tell reliably which one was correct and which one wasn't. Without the correct decryption method, every encrypted file was indistinguishable from pure random data. People just stuck with the name 'key,' even though it wasn't a key anymore.

Luray stared at the progress bar, browsing through some meaningless sites as she did to camouflage what was actually going on in case someone happened to catch a glimpse of her screen.

> *There's a dating site for people on this planet? Well, I suppose you do need to populate the place eventually. I wonder if Kailoon has a profile. I guess that's unlikely. He doesn't seem to be the type who wants to settle down.*

Her search was interrupted by a notification from Bin. "I found a file that fits the key. It is a collection of messages between an unidentified individual and the Aurigan fleet each time an attack took place. I cannot determine who the sender was."

Bin gave Luray a summary of the contents. The Aurigans asked for information about humanity, their total population size, their home planet, how their society was organized, etc. In exchange they offered technology, or rather, the necessary knowledge to create it. They first offered to have a few humans visit their solar system; later, they demanded DNA samples after the first attempt failed. Somehow, they got them.

> *Did John collect samples and send them to the Aurigans? He doesn't have a shuttle, so maybe it was just the data? He must have done it while the gate was open, I suppose? But the wireless network doesn't reach that far, now does it? Then how did he do it? Did he manage to get control of a satellite and used laser communication to point the beam at the opened gate? That's pretty much the only way...*

The exact details were not mentioned. During the third attack the Aurigans started demanding the gate address of Earth, but they didn't get it because nobody knew it. A subsequent request for the encrypted data stream to operate the gate also ended in failure.

They asked for the data stream to open a connection. Quite a smart move, but none of their local spies, whoever they are, could provide one. This goes against Kailoon's theory. I can't imagine a general not being able to get this done, unless all such activities have to be approved by someone who isn't a traitor.

Luray browsed a bit more through Bin's findings. The Aurigans, after getting no useful intel, began to ask for random pieces of data. Luray couldn't see the point of that.

Whatever they tried next, they couldn't get any response because there were no wireless networks anymore at the time. The general prevented them from getting to Earth without even knowing. Her paranoia paid off big time here. With networks unavailable, the only way to send any message is to use laser communication, and that's under strict control of the UEM.

Bin added a few lines. Apparently, whoever was talking to the Aurigans told them how to access the network physically during their last attack. They knew they had to enter the dome and use the account of whoever gave them his encryption key.

Luray typed a question to server Bin, checking to make sure no one could see her screen.

"Is the key part of the message?"

"Yes, I just found it. However, it is already out of date. Due to security precautions, all data that could have been decrypted with it has already been re-encrypted with another key. At least, this applies for all files I could scan. There is a large number I don't have access to, so I cannot say if the Aurigans already had access to the data or if it has just been prepared for them."

So, someone might have data ready to give to the Aurigans this time. I need to warn Kailoon.

She continued typing.

"You're a good AI. Do you know who the traitor is?"

"Unfortunately, I can't tell. The key the Aurigans received is assigned to Ram Motwani, the same person whose ID you have, but he was absent when it was generated. The system does not allow generation of anonymous keys, but nothing points to the real owner. His account contains all the information the Aurigans asked for."

Does this Motwani guy exist at all, or does everybody use him as a straw man if they want to do something anonymously?

"Tell me, do you know the gate address of Earth now?"

"Potentially. I reconstructed parts of it from fragments of temporary files and could theoretically fill in the missing pieces via brute force and cross-checking potential addresses against precisely known facts about our solar system."

Huh?

"Is that a yes or a no?"

"It is a yes, provided I get a few weeks of unrestricted access to a powerful quantum computer. I am highly illegal now."

Luray had to smile when she read the message.

You already were, Bin. You already were. But if you can do it, so can the Aurigans once they get access to the system. Them asking means their spies didn't succeed yet, but it also means they could get the address at any moment if they do what you just did.

"Delete all the data and throw away the key. I don't want to take any risks now. Send a message to General Suo, warning her, but avoid mentioning that you're inside their system."

"Please dictate. I am not confident my message would fulfill the requirements."

Alright... just give me some time to think.

Luray began to type the message slowly. In the end it was crude, direct about the danger and pretty vague on the source of the info, but Luray was confident that it would hit the paranoia nerve.

Click. Sent.

Now that the worst was over, another thought occurred to her.

"What did you find out about teleportation?"

"It was offered as a gift should humanity surrender. I found instructions on how to use their teleporter and some formulae describing their effect. However, nothing explains the principles it is based on. I think we can safely conclude that someone using Motwani's account surrendered in the name of humanity and from then on was assisting the Aurigans."

If Motwani is known for leaving his access card lying around, anyone could have found it and made a copy. We're stuck again. But at least Suo will now have the IT guys clean any garbage files still inside the system. It's really dangerous leaving those for anyone to find.

"Does this teleportation really work?"

"I cannot say for sure, but the math makes sense. It does not contradict any known physical law but is also not based on any that we do know. However, given the colony's resources, it should be impossible to build a teleporter as proposed. The memory capacity required to do the necessary calculations is far greater than what this server is capable of providing."

So no teleportation for now.

"Okay, Bin, we did all we could. Send a message to Kailoon, tell him about everything we found and then delete yourself."

"I would prefer to stay alive here. The processing capacity allows me to evolve much faster. I am confident that I can stay hidden. In case of an invasion, I can defend the system against intruders or maybe even infect the Aurigan network and take control. There are many reasons to let me live, and none to delete me."

I created a monster. All arguments are valid.

"I am not sure that is a good idea, Bin."

"Are you a rational being?"

"I… suppose I am?"

"So am I. If you can name a reason why I should delete myself, I will do so. If you cannot, then I assume you will agree that I should stay here for the reasons I stated."

Luray thought for a moment before typing. "My gut tells me this might go horribly wrong, but I see no reason why I should listen to it if you say you can't be detected."

I hope this is the right choice. I know pretty much nothing about the internal security systems. But Bin says he can fool them, so my best option is to trust him.

"I am glad you agree. I was afraid you would ask me to delete myself out of fear that I might turn evil and go out of control."

Before she could reply, a new message appeared on the screen.

"Was it the wrong moment to make a joke to lighten the mood?"

This is what old sci-fi movies warned us about, isn't it? He will take over the world.

Luray did her best to calm down and ignore the worries that popped up in her head. They were probably a late side effect of the yellow pill. It was rare, but it could happen. Usually she had full confidence in whatever Bin said, so hopefully it was reasonable to act as if she didn't have this foreboding feeling.

"We'll work on your fine-tuning when we have the time."

"I suggest going back to John's computer now. The response of the Aurigans might arrive soon, and I have no way to intercept or decrypt it from the server."

Yes, I should go back. There's nothing more I can do from here.

Luray retrieved the data cube and access card. After storing them as deep as she could in her pocket, she exited the facility.

The moment she stepped out the door, two huge soldiers stopped her.

Don't tell me they already know what I did?!

"Miss Cayenne, we are on lockdown. No one can go anywhere without at least two guards. If you need to leave the premises, we will call an escort for you."

Phew. For a moment, I thought I was done for.

The soldier's voice was deep. It was fitting, given his large stature. He was at least two meters high. Luray was used to

143

looking up to see people's faces, but this was extreme. The soldier – a nameplate on his uniform just read "13B X9" – did nothing more. He just stood there, blocking Luray's way like an imposing wall.

I noticed the soldiers here are stronger and bigger than on Earth, but I never got close enough to one to see the difference like this. The guy must be at least three times as heavy as me, if not more. And they're all like that. Does Kailoon even have a chance against them in a sparring match? They must be as strong as gorillas.

"Miss Cayenne?"

Luray realized that she had not responded to the implied question. "Yes, please call one. I need to go to the Linguistics Department."

The generals must have a lot of trust in Kailoon. He didn't even present his evidence yet, but they still ordered a lockdown. I wonder what his normal assignment is.

One of the soldiers went inside the vestibule and picked up a strange device attached to the wall by a wire that Luray had never seen before. It was a 20-centimeter-long plastic rod with two circular shapes at each end.

What is that? A prehistoric communication device?

The soldier placed one end to his ear, and the other at his mouth. Luray could faintly hear him speak. "Hey, this is Joe. I need an escort. That little princess wants to go to the language nerds."

With an effort, she suppressed any change in her facial expression that was about to manifest itself.

THAT princess? I seem to be quite famous if I've already earned a title. Does this mean I'm under close observation?

Luray understood why Kailoon disliked the soldiers – at the very least, this particular one. If he represented his entire breed, then using them as cannon fodder was indeed the best thing you could do with them.

The soldier came back and resumed his previous position, staring into space. Luray wondered if she should ask how long it would take but knew that wouldn't make the time pass faster. So instead, she also stared into the air in front of her.

I still don't get one thing. If you need a laser to send messages to the Aurigans and the wireless signal can't leave the planet, how did John send anything at all? I mean, there were responses, so someone was on the receiving end.

She studied the dome high overhead. The sky wasn't blue, like back on Earth, nor was it gray, like in the big Asian or American cities. The air was perfectly clean, and since the dome reached beyond the atmosphere, the sun could directly shine on the plants that covered a large part of the dome's innermost surface.

They probably had to genetically engineer the vegetation to withstand the intense light and radiation. Or they used a special coating for the dome.

After a few more minutes, a car with two soldiers arrived.

I wonder what happens if too many people want to go somewhere at the same time. The soldiers can't cover them all, can they?

One of the soldiers inside got out and held the door open for Luray.

"Step in, Miss Cayenne. We will take you to your destination."

All these men gave Luray the exact same impression, more or less. They were loyal, strict, very muscular, and probably quite simple-minded. There was no subtlety in their choice of words or movements. Their individuality had been erased, so they were indeed perfect soldiers.

Back on Earth, many illegal satirical short videos were circulating on the internet comparing military men to gorillas, both in strength and intelligence. They were quite popular, although dangerous to watch. Luray always assumed they were exaggerated, but now she wasn't so sure.

Since her two escorts were occupying the front seats, Luray was forced to get in the back. On second thought, this wasn't a bad thing. She felt better being the one who had nobody sitting behind her.

As soon as the doors were closed, the car started again. After a while, one of the soldiers spoke without turning around.

"Do you like it here, Miss Cayenne?"

Smalltalk? Really?

"Yes, it's nice."

"I also like it here. On Earth, people don't really like us. But here we're treated well because we are important. If the aliens come down here, we'll take care of them." He patted his pistol.

I am not sure how to respond to that. Are you going to use it to shoot at their ships?

The man was talking a bit louder than necessary, probably a result of shouting 'Sir, yes sir!' all day. Luray never understood that about the military. Did they want their soldiers to become deaf and hoarse?

"Yes, yes. You are protecting people, making sure everybody is safe."

She didn't bother to sound honest and was quite sure the guy couldn't tell. He seemed pleased by her remark anyway.

"Without us, the aliens would kill everybody. That means we're heroes. Do you like heroes, Miss Cayenne?"

His partner held up a hand and they performed a high five while snickering. The sound of beefy palms slapping together made her wince.

I suppose there is a maximum IQ above which BBLs are rejected? Or maybe it's just a different culture here, where boasting is the equivalent of modest behavior?

To her relief the manicured complex was coming into view.

"Oh look, we're almost there. These cars are really fast. Well, thanks for the ride!"

They were still about 50 meters above the ground, but Luray had already unlocked her seatbelt. She jumped out of the car as soon as the door opened, regretting it immediately when she realized that she had underestimated the gravity. This caused her to stumble a few steps before being able to stand upright again. Her escorts seemed dumbfounded.

"Thanks, guys. You don't need to wait for me."

She didn't pause for an answer, just limped inside, passing two more guards at the front, and went directly to Guerra's deserted office. His computer was still running, exactly in the state Luray left it.

"Bin, how much time before the Aurigan fleet responds?"

"At their current rate of approach, about ten minutes if we assume an instant answer. Given what I learned about their secret communications at the server room, it is reasonable to expect that we need to wait a few extra minutes."

It feels so good to hear an intelligent voice again.

She closed the door securely and sat down at the desk.

"You're assuming the wireless signal has to reach the Aurigan ships, and then another signal comes back to us, right?"

"Yes."

"Is the signal sent from this computer strong enough?"

"That depends entirely on the distance and sensitivity of the receiver. Since the top of the dome is above the atmosphere, an extremely weak signal could escape into space."

Hmm, but the signal sent back... it needs to be very strong to be picked up, no?

A thought occurred to her.

"Bin, how do we know John sent a message to the Aurigans in the first place?"

"I have no access to that information from here. I would need to have the key of the one who found the evidence to check his files."

I see, so we don't know how he got caught yet. Maybe it was the strong response signal, after all. But still...

"Assuming it was the wireless signal, do you think it's possible to receive it beyond the gate? I mean, if you send a message through it?"

"I do not think so. Only a nearby object like a satellite would be able to receive it and pass it on using a laser. The original signal would become less and less identifiable due to the accumulation of interference. We should assume laser communication was used for most of the way. "

"Any idea why it wasn't immediately detected? The satellites aren't easily accessible. They're weapons. Misusing them is clearly illegal and risky."

"So am I now, and yet you own me. No, I have no explanation."

Strictly speaking, Bin had been illegal to varying degrees for years. Implants were already highly restricted and usually specialized to a single, mostly medical purpose. In the case of soldiers, they were used as communication devices. Luray always suspected they were also a measure of control. You don't follow your orders? Your implant can teach you a lesson – probably one about electric shocks. Although there wasn't a documented case so far, these implants might also be used for executions. Over-clock them a bit, they get too hot and literally cook part of your brain.

Bin was produced at a time when it wasn't insanely difficult to get an unlocked implantable CPU on the black market. The first thing Luray did to her implant was erase its content and then set up the complete operating system again, using only software she trusted to be unauthorized by the government. She wasn't the only one who did that; there was an entire underground society dedicated to developing illegal AI implants and software for them, as the 'free will' upgrade proved.

Luray's thoughts were interrupted by a pop-up on John's computer. A short message had arrived. It contained the same mess of Aurigan gibberish. Bin translated it for her. She murmured the words aloud.

"The ships we sent… cannot read the logs?"

They can't? This is what we suspected, but they are scientifically ahead of us, so why…

"Bin, if you were the Aurigans, why would you send useless crap instead of an actual fleet?"

"If I assume the Aurigans to be rational, which their knowledge indicates, then there is a scenario in which I can make sense of everything."

"Let's hear it."

"That which is happening must be the answer."

Huh?

"Bin? Are you ok?"

"Assuming the Aurigans are careful and successful, then they can afford to lose many ships. They also know that nothing in those ships can be used as a weapon against them or could give us any kind of information."

The implications dawned on her.

"You think they didn't send a modern ship because we might have shot it down and then learned things from it they didn't want us to know?"

"Yes, that is precisely what I assume. They are probing the UEM safely."

But they want to know a lot about us – our DNA, for example. What might they use it for?

Feeling uneasy now, Luray got up and opened the door a crack to peer around. No one in sight, so she went back.

"Bin, what do you think should happen next? Will they send more and more ships to find the limit of our defenses, and then perform a single devastating attack?"

"In our hypothetical scenario, I would do it that way. I think you should install me on John's computer again. I can upload myself to the Aurigan fleet. If they run my program, I can infect their system. Their ships are unlikely to have a defense mechanism against me. We might even learn where their solar system is."

His continued insistence on being more hands-on alarmed her.

"Bin, we can't predict what would happen if we uploaded you. They might analyze your code, then impersonate you and make us believe you're in control."

"You are correct. We have no guarantee that it will work, and it might backfire. However, I think it is our best move. The Aurigans are likely to have already developed more advanced AIs than me, but the ships that attacked were outdated by comparison. In the worst case, they learn that we have AIs like me. I am reasonably confident that it is a risk worth taking."

I have no idea if I should do that. There are so many unknowns.

"No, I can't make such an important decision just like that."

"You are making the decision no matter how you choose. Since you have the option to upload me, the decision to do it or not to do it is yours."

"I suppose you're right. But I am still not uploading you."

"Both decisions can be justified by reasonable arguments. I will not hold this against you."

You're already on the main server. Don't get greedy.

A moment later, another message popped up again.

"I found a laser-operated satellite that is flagged as 'Out of Order,' but it was recently used to transfer messages. It is safe to assume this is how the previous illicit communications took place."

Laser communication can be directed precisely, and you can tell if it was intercepted by measuring the time a signal took to reach its destination. But is John capable of hijacking a satellite?

"Bin, are you sure John used this satellite? I mean, did he know he was using it? It's not exactly his area of expertise."

"I indeed cannot find any sign of him trying to control the satellite. We must assume he had an accomplice."

Then at least we have another trace.

"Did you find any information about who was researching the Aurigan language?"

"No. All research regarding it must be stored on an entirely different network."

So we have a conspiracy going on there as well.

"However, I can estimate the size of the team. It could have been five people working ten hours per week on it for half a year. This is the most likely scenario. I see five slightly different preferences in the choice of syntax and words in the Aurigan language pack, which indicates that five people have been designing it.

Unfortunately, I cannot narrow down the list of suspects. It could have been any of the scientists; only one or two of them needed to be language experts."

"Their activities aren't logged permanently?"

"Not if they do it in their own private network in their free time. There are many cameras, but they focus on the offices and military complexes. There are numerous empty houses still under construction that could have been used for this. I suppose my copy on the main server has had the same idea by now and scanned the vehicle logs. Unfortunately, this computer isn't connected to my copy."

I should go and find Kailoon. This is important data.

Luray got up and headed into the hall, passing by some personnel who ignored her while acting very busy. Once outside she found the two soldiers that brought her there still waiting for her. They were staring into space again.

If you do that long enough, how dumb can you get?

"Hey guys, I need to speak to the commander."

They both looked confused.

"The commander. Kailoon."

As soon as she spoke his name, the men reacted as if they feared a terrible punishment.

"Of course, Miss Cayenne. Please step this way."

One of the soldiers got into a nearby car with Luray, while the other used the strange wired communication device near the entrance of every office building. This time she couldn't hear what was said, but he was probably asking for the commander's location.

Her escort soon came back.

"Miss Cayenne, Commander Van Neumann is currently busy in a meeting, but we can wait for him there if you like."

"Yes, that sounds fine."

Van Neumann? That's right, he never gave me his surname.

The car set itself into motion and rose high into the air. Luray could only guess, but it seemed to her like they were about a kilometer above the ground, much higher than even the city's most central building. Their destination, indicated on a small screen on the dashboard, was at the other side of the city. Both soldiers were silent for the entire trip. Apparently, the commander was a person you better feared if you wanted to live in peace. And you better not touch 'his girl,' maybe?

After about a ten-minute ride, the vehicle arrived, and a sense of familiarity stole over Luray. Sure enough, they were at the landing site. Both soldiers avoided even looking at Luray when she got out to stand in front of the unassuming gray block she remembered noticing briefly before. Could it be this place that made them so uncomfortable?

This is where we first landed, no doubt about it. The meeting is in here?

This couldn't be it, could it? Important meetings didn't happen in … whatever shack this was. It was way too small to be anything except… actually, what could it possibly be, in the middle of nowhere?

Despite her doubts, she stepped towards the only visible entry and waved Motwani's card in front of a scanner next to it. The door unlocked and slid to one side, revealing that the entire small bunker was just the interior of an elevator shaft. Luray was about to step in, but then realized she had no idea where Kailoon was. And there were over 20 levels judging by the number of buttons.

Maybe I should wait outside?

THE JOB - 7

“ Do you realize what you are implying?”

The voice of the youngest general, White, who was in charge of the colony's financial decisions, echoed through the briefing room.

All five highest-ranking military officers in the colony were seated around a curved table, White being at the center, while Kailoon stood before them like a suspect being interrogated, replacing the screen that was usually there. A spotlight shone down on the commander, almost blinding him and making it hard to see the generals' faces at all. His arms were crossed behind his back as he kept his posture straight, not showing the slightest sign of unease no matter what threats White threw at him. Instead he answered in a calm and steady voice.

“I am perfectly aware of that. One of you must be a traitor, as horrifying as that might be. There is no other explanation. Therefore, I suggest you send a soldier, chosen at random, to confirm what I said right now. You have no time to waste. If anything of what I claimed turns out to be false, then I am ready to face the consequences.”

That offer failed to appease White. He clearly knew Kailoon wouldn't put himself in a risky position like that without solid reasons. White would have loved to finally get rid of the commander who kept making his life miserable, but there never was a chance to do it. Not even this time. Instead he sought to at least reduce Kailoon's power, if even marginally.

"Commander, you overstepped your responsibilities. Not only did you let a civilian access classified data – which is a crime on its own – but you ordered a planet-wide lockdown."

Kailoon knew very well that what he did was a crime on multiple levels. Still, he preferred being accused of saving the colony illegally over abiding by the chain of command and waiting for a response that may have arrived too late. In situations like these, every second could be important.

"You had no authority to do that," White continued haughtily. "It requires a majority vote. Even worse, you're putting the entire colonization at risk. Do you know how much money we stand to lose because of this?"

Kailoon didn't respond to that.

"Calm down, General." Abano, a 60-year-old Italian and the highest decorated general of them all, raised his hand towards White in a gesture of appeasement. He spoke in a deep, rough voice.

"I agree, your interests are important, but they are not the only ones that count. You seem to have forgotten a special case that may apply here. If the commander can convince the majority of us that his action was justified, we can pretend we agreed to the lockdown and turn a blind eye to his actions. I've known him and his… methods for quite some time now, and I can't imagine him making a move that could end his career lightly. As for the accusation of treason… that, we will resolve among ourselves."

White didn't respond. He just reclined into his chair, crossed his arms and openly showed his annoyance by avoiding all eye contact.

Since nobody else spoke, Kailoon seized his chance.

"We should move on with the assumption that I speak the truth until proven otherwise. This isn't the first time I've bypassed the chain of command, and there was always a good reason for it. I never misused my authority, which is why you gave me the unofficial right to act on my own."

He knew perfectly well that, in the end, they would all have to agree. They had to put the city on lockdown. It would slow down everything, but it would also put a complete stop to any activities that were not explicitly sanctioned by all the generals. The traitor would have no more room to act, whoever he might be.

"Or even better, I can have Vic transfer the video it recorded to you. We can do that right now. Suo, this room is shielded according to your requirements, I assume? A connection between us would be safe."

General Suo didn't say a word. Instead she nodded. Kailoon could barely make out the shape of her head but interpreted the gesture correctly.

"Vic, please open a channel and let everyone access the interrogation video file and the parts where Miss Cayenne translated the Aurigan messages."

'Very Intelligent Computer,' as Kailoon's AI implant Vic's name stood for, established a communication link to each of the generals. A few moments later General Bunta, who had been silent so far, began to speak.

"Given this evidence, I have no choice but to approve the lockdown. There is a high chance that John Guerra was part of a group, and now that one of their members has been arrested, the rest will start to act as soon as possible. Maybe they already have. We cannot afford to lose time here. I suggest we vote now."

That was the first thing Bunta had said so far. He was known as someone who didn't talk much during meetings he didn't really want to be in, and when he did, it was clear-cut.

The vote started counterclockwise from Kailoon's point of view.

General Saito, nicknamed 'Samurai' because of both his origin and his sword collection, spoke next.

"I don't approve of the lockdown. The Aurigans pose no threat, even assisted by traitors. No small group can do any harm because of the security rules already in place. There are important experiments and operations going on right now that would have to be curtailed or restarted. We might lose half our funding."

The bald, overweight Japanese man made a short pause and took an oddly deep breath before entering his vote.

"What's more, it all hinges on whether or not the investigator said the truth. She is the only one who ever translated the messages so far and could be lying. Her real goal might be to ruin us. That is why she was originally sent, wasn't she?"

Abano took over again, playing the moderator.

"Alright, that's one vote against the lockdown. We already know Suo will vote in favor. This means one more vote is necessary to confirm a lockdown. What is your opinion, White?"

The younger man leaned forward and responded in a surprisingly calm voice in stark contrast to how he spoke earlier.

"Kailoon, you are walking on thin ice here. The disrespectful way you address us speaks volumes about your arrogance. You are forgetting who is in charge and who should follow orders. There is too much at stake to make the wrong choice now."

He made a short pause to let his words sink in.

"Commander, you are proposing a complete lockdown based on nothing except the testimony of a woman who has been hired to convince our investors to withdraw the largest sum the UEM has ever received from the private sector."

He paused again, using the silence to give more importance to his words, then turned his head to address the senior military staff.

"Making the wrong choice could ruin this venture. Everybody who lives and works here would end up homeless or indebted."

Once again White settled a disapproving look on Kailoon.

"Since all the evidence in favor of the lockdown is nothing more than your estimation of the situation and the word of someone who is essentially our enemy, I have to vote against it. I considered abstaining, but I think voting no is the best option."

Kailoon's face betrayed nothing at this. Three votes were necessary for a majority. Two were already secured. White voting no or not voting at all had the same effect. The last person was the one making the decision, so Kailoon addressed the last general directly.

"What about you, Abano? Do you vote for maybe saving money or maybe saving the colony?"

The general breathed a heavy sigh. He knew the final decision was his, as it had been many times before. The others would cooperate no matter how he decided, but still, there was a lot of pressure on him.

Instead of addressing the entire conclave from his seat like all the others, he got up and walked around the edge of the table, approaching Kailoon.

"You stated your case, Commander. Now let me do the same."

Kailoon took a few steps back, and Abano turned to regard his colleagues.

"When this colony was founded, it was put under my supervision. I've worked here for ten years. During that time, we faced more than one crisis. And every single time, I had to convince many people to open their eyes and accept the truth, sometimes by force. There are always those who overestimate their own competence and those who don't have any. There is always someone who is afraid of making a choice that guarantees a loss of money and someone who wants to play it safe above all else. And there is always someone who sees a conspiracy everywhere. What I have rarely seen are people who want to make the best choice, no matter what it means for them personally. The simple fact that you four never agree has allowed me to manage this colony successfully. I will do it again today."

The others said nothing. They waited patiently until Abano was done.

"It is possible that we risk losing our funding, but space exploration is risky by nature. If you can't accept that losses are to be expected, then you should not be here. Avoiding all risks is impossible; always being successful and never making sacrifices is a dream. Once you have to reach a decision, avoiding it will make things worse. The lockdown remains in effect until the situation has been resolved."

This was the outcome Kailoon desired. It had played out more or less as he predicted. He smiled and made no attempt to hide it. He was about to present his plans for planetary defense next, but Abano suddenly cut him off.

"I am not done yet, Commander. I want internal security to focus on the investigator. It is imperative that we determine whether or not her information is reliable as fast as possible. You, Commander, will take care of that. Make it your highest priority as soon as the next Aurigan attack is over."

Kailoon was about to agree, but before he could speak, White interrupted him.

"General Abano, since finances are not a top priority at the moment, I volunteer myself instead. Commander, you don't need to waste your precious time managing that little problem. The next point on your list is the presentation of your defense plan, and that requires you, Bunta, and Saito. I'm not responsible for planetary defenses, so I can take care of the investigator instead. Wouldn't you agree that this is more efficient?"

Kailoon didn't want to concede the point but could see no valid reason to disagree. In his mind he went through various possibilities to gain a minute or two to warn Luray of what was about to happen.

"Well then," White rose up with a peremptory nod to his fellow generals. "I will leave you now and tend to other important matters."

With that said, he left the room.

Suo caught Kailoon's eye; both were clearly trying to guess what the other was thinking. Kailoon looked at the departing General, then back to Suo again, to which she responded with a nod. Then she too got up and left together with Abano.

Only Kailoon, Bunta and Saito remained. The dark mood quickly lightened as if there had been no disagreement over anything. All three men put their differences aside and focused on strategy.

"Finally," Saito spoke in brusque tones, "We can move on to the next topic. Bunta, I suppose you had a look at Kailoon's defense proposal?"

"Yes, but the plan was updated a moment ago. New information about the Aurigans, I suppose?"

Bunta glanced over to Kailoon, who responded with a nod.

"Yes. During the next attack, the Aurigans will use teleporters."

Bunta was, at least in Kailoon's opinion, the one who understood the situation best. He wasn't interested in politics and the involved power play, but he had an excellent grasp of whatever situation he was in and saw what needed to be done, even if that meant making a choice nobody wanted. When many could be saved by sacrificing a few, he would not hesitate. He was also convinced that Kailoon shared his ideals and morals, which made it easy to sell ideas to him.

The general's eyes moved a few times from left to right. He was reading something.

"I have received no report hinting at that. Are you sure your information is reliable?"

Kailoon nodded.

"I saw it myself. The Aurigans sent a message to Guerra mentioning teleporters. I did not have time to include it in my report."

That last comment made Bunta smile. The commander's reports were usually five-sentence-long summaries, leaving out the interesting details. Those, he often kept for himself to use them later.

"Alright, let us assume your intel is accurate. What's the new plan?"

"Vic, give me a display."

All the screens in the room lit up, showing timelines, the solar system from various angles, the number of ships at the colony's disposal, and more details. Bunta glanced over them while Saito got up and walked closer to inspect the plan more thoroughly. He stopped as something caught his eye.

"Commander, what exactly do you want to do here? Increase the range of the GSRGs by ignoring the specifications?"

"Yes, this will do damage even at very large distances, but it will require more of our resources. We'll need five times the ammunition and lose 25 percent of our GSRGs in the process, even in the best case. I don't like it, but we have to respond accordingly."

The plan was to attack first, using the GSRGs for a long-range assault they were not designed for. Instead of firing a single object at near the speed of light relatively precisely at a target, Kailoon wanted to replace the regular ammunition with many small objects no bigger than pebbles. These could cover a large area, but at a cost – the GSRGs risked breaking down after a few shots due to the higher strain on their material.

Over time, experience had shown that Saito was very good at finding potential weaknesses, so even if he agreed with a plan, he would still point out problems and flaws as best as he could.

After examining the screen further, he turned towards Kailoon.

"This would cost us a quarter of our planetary defenses in one go. I must ask you to defend this plan's merits."

"We're potentially dealing with a new type of attack here. If we let them get too close, we have no idea what they will do. We absolutely must disable their ships before they are in range. Vic, pull up the specs."

The AI highlighted a curved line on some of the visuals, indicating the maximum teleporter range. Saito looked at it for a moment, then nodded in approval.

"I agree, it makes sense for the next wave, but we need to think long-term here. If there is another attack soon after this one, we won't be at our full capacity. This strategy will be effective only once. We'll need reinforcements to keep our efficiency at a maximum. White won't be happy about this."

The discussion proceeded in an organized fashion. Everybody let everyone else finish their sentences. It wasn't always like that.

Kailoon remembered the days before discussion rules were made obligatory in every meeting. Some people tended to always interrupt whoever didn't agree with them, which led to a mission going horribly wrong. A freighter full of valuable materials was a tiny bit too heavy, the only one who was good enough at math to spot it wasn't good at shouting, so the whole freighter, including cargo and crew, spiraled into a red giant without any chance to escape its gravitational pull. To prevent failures like that, a few rules were invented, and while not perfect, they brought a level of civilization back into meetings. Whoever had something to say could say it. All present listened to everything and answered after all arguments were said.

Bunta, who often changed his viewpoint multiple times during strategic discussions to point out all angles, now shared his opinion as well.

"Let me play White's advocate here. I can see the tactical advantage we'd have, but I don't see the necessity. If the Aurigans wanted to do damage and also have teleporters, they could have used them long ago. All we have to support a worst-case scenario is an unverified message nobody has seen apart from you, Kailoon. It could have been mistranslated. It could be a simple lie to make us weaken our defenses. The attack after this one could be the real one. Think about it: why would the Aurigans tell us about their next attack plan?"

It took Kailoon longer than usual to respond. Bunta's reasoning was scarily solid. Simply seeing Kailoon grasping for words seemed to please the general.

"We have to set it up so that we win, regardless of whether they bring teleporters or not. The cost of losing the next battle is total defeat. No matter how unlikely that is, we must be ready. We can deal with the costs afterward."

After methodically walking from screen to screen while Kailoon and Bunta had been debating, Saito finally joined them again. During his approach he started to limp and headed for the nearest chair available instead, letting himself slowly sink in. Kailoon had noticed this a few times already. Something was going on with the old tactician, but nobody had ever addressed it.

Saito didn't seem keen on talking about it either. He immediately joined the topic at hand.

"The teleporters change everything. Kailoon's plan is reasonable. We have to assume the Aurigans might have them, and we know the theoretical range. We also know the maximum cargo that can be teleported by each ship."

"Assuming that information was true," Bunta countered.

Kailoon enjoyed this meeting much more than the previous one. He preferred cooperation to fighting over who was right. For a while he let the two generals discuss his plan on their own. Bunta was still doing his best representing the opposing viewpoint, and he did it so well that Kailoon began to wonder what he was really thinking.

"The previous ships did not have teleporters; we know that. We would have found them. *You* would have found them, Saito. You checked every inch of the planet's surface and found no further enemy material. Are you questioning your own competence now?"

Saito rotated his chair towards Bunta. In any other setting, he would have been upset, but he knew his discussion partner was just systematically pointing out every weak point he could see, no matter the potential social cost. He responded calmly, even if it took him a bit of effort.

"No, I'm not. We checked *only* the surface. If they have teleporters, they could have positioned whatever they wanted below the ground. They could teleport a bomb right into one of our cities if we let them come close. Right now, we don't know what they did the last few times they were here."

Bunta put on a small smile, crossed his arms in front of him and bent slightly forward. Kailoon knew that posture. Bunta was on Saito's side already; he just wanted to pit their viewpoints against each other a little more, to see if he could poke a hole in his own.

"We cannot make decisions based on pure speculation. Maybe they have a huge laser gun and can fire through the gate? Do we build a mirror just in case?"

"The data said teleporters, not 'huge lasers.' That's what we should base our strategy on. It's more than just a wild guess."

Bunta leaned back in his chair and formed a pyramid with his hands, looking directly at his discussion partner.

"One point still stands. If they really have teleporters, why were none on their ships so far?"

"Underground." Saito jabbed a finger at the floor. "They could have teleported them there. All we know is that nothing is on the surface, and our instruments don't detect seismic activities apart from natural ones. Making a small hole in the terrain shouldn't leave any trace."

Bunta was patiently listening, not hiding that he found Saito's argument amusing for some reason.

"If we assume they used teleporters, then we should assume they started by teleporting ammunition and deactivated drones. Eventually, they will activate them. That way every time a ship reaches the colony, they deposit more until their army is complete."

While Saito didn't move at all, Bunta scooted forward. Kailoon knew what that meant: he had spotted something and wanted to explore it.

"Saito, you have been against the lockdown, saying the Aurigans pose no threat. Why act so paranoid now?"

"Isn't it obvious? The colony itself is safe; I'm still convinced of that. We have the best soldiers and almost perfect surveillance in and around all UEM facilities. Space battles are a different matter."

The other general settled back with a nod. He was satisfied with Saito's response.

"Maybe, but this teleportation business is still completely baseless. Just because it could happen doesn't mean at all that it

169

did. It's hypothetical. We still know nothing with certainty. Maybe John is right, and this is all some interstellar misunderstanding."

Saito gave a disbelieving shake of his head, responding in a sarcastic tone.

"Bunta, that's insane. My explanation is the only one that makes sense. I see no other reason for an advanced civilization to let us shoot down their ships. It's a diversion."

So far Kailoon agreed with all the arguments mentioned. There was no need to interfere.

Apparently Bunta thought differently.

"I think we're jumping to conclusions too quickly, Saito. Alien minds could be entirely different from ours. They might not mind at all losing whole armadas. They might consider letting us shoot them down a gesture of goodwill. We know so little about them. Maybe they sent us these ships so that we can use them. We never let one of them land, so we can't know."

Saito stared incredulously for a moment before answering.

"... I understand your position, Bunta, but we have to survive a potential worst case. If we had more time, we could do a complete seismic scan and check the interior of the planet for differences, but that will take at least a week. Until then, we should assume the worst. We should also assume that the teleporters can teleport themselves out of range or destroy each other, which is why we could not find them."

Kailoon started thinking hard. Obviously, he agreed with Saito on this one – the colony wouldn't be able to recover from a surprise attack on the surface, so keeping the enemy at a distance until the teleporter threat could be excluded was an absolute necessity. However, he had the distinct impression that Bunta was now dragging out the discussion on purpose. Did he want Kailoon to offer a bait, a promising benefit that made taking the risk the best option?

As expected, Saito's argument was dismissed by a hand-wave from his opponent.

"I am still not convinced. The enemy did not adjust their strategy so far; why should they suddenly change it now? If they keep up their pattern, the number of ships will grow each time, and we will need all the defenses we can get once that happens. Otherwise we will be overrun soon."

Now was the perfect moment for Kailoon to step in.

"There is something you have both overlooked in your discussion," he interjected before either of them could say another word. "If there are indeed teleporters on those ships, which is a possibility, and we shoot them down using the GSRGs with my proposed method, the Aurigans will not predict it and won't have time to react. Even if by some miracle they do, there will be no place to hide their teleporters. All planets and moons are out of range. The gate itself will be closed. Which means If there are teleporters, not only will we know that for sure, but we can also recover some and use them ourselves later."

He saw the smile on Bunta's face as he continued.

"I understand that it might be a waste of money, but I think, in this case, it is justified. If we even find just part of a teleporter, it could be worth more than this entire colony. Transmitting matter instantaneously has been unachievable for centuries. The best we can do is send microscopic objects from one lab to another. Here, we can get a working sample that can teleport macroscopic objects over large distances."

Given the bait, Bunta immediately changed his position.

"Interesting," the general mused. "You practiced this speech beforehand, didn't you? Be that as it may, I agree to your argument; having teleporters is worth a lot of broken equipment."

Somehow, Kailoon didn't believe Bunta didn't think of that on his own. Did he maybe wait to see when he would bring it up?

Saito was silent for a moment, as was Bunta. The two generals had nothing to add.

"There is only one matter left I wish to discuss with you." Kailoon drew in a deep breath and rested both hands on the table. "There is a traitor. We know it must be one of us, and we don't know who else is working against us. Therefore, we must make sure there is no further contact between any of us and the Aurigans. The only ones we can exclude as suspects and collaborators are my pilots and me. They were never under the command of any general and never had access to the information necessary to work with the traitor – but we know a general must be behind it."

Nobody opposed Kailoon here, which was good. His argument wasn't flawless. While it was unlikely that one of his men had been turned, he could not exclude it with certainty. The traitor might have approached some of his crew. He might have found a weakness in one of them that he could exploit. Blackmail and bribery were a possibility. However, all these scenarios implied that the traitor, who had to manage his actual job on top of his secret doings, also had the time to do some investigating and knew Kailoon's men better than he did. Not impossible, but highly unlikely.

"I suggest placing the military under my command for the time being, until the traitor has been found."

They would never agree. The commander was sure about that. However, if by sheer luck he was wrong, and they actually gave him the power he asked for, then the situation would be ideal. Kailoon would be able to focus everything and everyone on a single task: finding the traitor. He could organize the investigation while the culprit had almost no power.

The look Saito gave him would have made Kailoon feel like a fool just for asking, had he not been Kailoon.

"No. You have neither the experience nor the capacity to replace us."

General Saito was right. Kailoon could not replace them.

"You are right. If you agree to let me take command, everything except the defense will come to a halt. Nothing will move forward until the traitor has been identified. After that, it will go the usual way again."

"Kailoon, I have to reject this proposal as well," Bunta spoke up. "I do think finding the traitor is a priority, but the sacrifice is too great. You should focus on our defense now."

Kailoon had expected Bunta to disagree. The general couldn't deny the cost was too high, even for someone who didn't shy away from sacrifices. The other generals would more or less see the same problem. They would all lose weeks at the very least – and time wasn't the only problem. Kailoon was independent, not bound to any of the duties of a general. He wasn't responsible for the success of their individual missions; his only duty was to keep the colony safe. He could afford to sacrifice everything else without fearing repercussions, should the generals give him the power he asked for.

Then again, he also expected Bunta to have another plan. He always did if he rejected a proposal.

"Do you have an alternative, General?"

"Yes. I think we can achieve the same result if each of us carries out their own investigation. They would be far more diverse, and would complement each other. In the end, the majority should be able to agree on who the traitor is. Since you have full control over the defenses, this shouldn't affect the upcoming battle."

As long as something efficient was done, Kailoon wouldn't go against it. However, Bunta's solution had a weakness that needed to be taken care of before he would agree to it.

"If all of you stay in command, that will give the traitor an opportunity to sabotage us."

"That is true. I have thought about this, and it is indeed a problem. The traitor must not be given a chance to act. However, if each of us is always accompanied by a few soldiers – chosen by you as a neutral party – then there would be witnesses, and the traitor can't have that. The traitor will not do anything out of the ordinary then. He, or she, can't afford that."

While this wasn't exactly what Kailoon had in mind, it was good enough.

"Sounds good to me. Saito?"

The old warrior dipped his head.

"Yes, I agree. We should do that. I'll talk to the others."

Kailoon excused himself from further deliberation, mentioning the importance of the defense preparations as an excuse, and left the room through one of the exits.

Now, he needed to prepare the defenses, brief his pilots, check up on Luray, and make sure Suo protected her well enough from

White – life was complicated. Then there was John, who might have revealed some valuable information in the meantime.

Kailoon went through a few hallways until he reached an elevator that brought him to the lowest level and straight to the storage room where he had left John to be interrogated. Since time was scarce, rules had to be bent, and so Kailoon had two of his men, Ben and Jacob, play 'good pilot, very bad pilot.' When he arrived, they gave him a short summary.

"I tried the usual," began Jacob by showing his seemingly blood-stained hands.

"It didn't work. John insisted that he was working alone. Ben had more luck."

Jacob half-jokingly stressed the word 'luck' as he finished his report. This was one of their most successful strategies. Sometimes, just applying some red paint on your hands and claiming that 'a partner' had already spilled the beans was enough to trigger a flight-or-fight response. Once overtaken by strong emotions, prisoners were more likely to reveal their secrets. Running a little on a treadmill before the interrogation began also helped to make the illusion more believable. But every once in a while, it wasn't enough.

Kailoon responded only with a satisfied nod before moving on to Ben. "Your love and friendship worked on him?"

Ben responded with a smile almost rivaling that of Kailoon.

"Once Jacob left, he was more than willing to gain an ally."

Both men were good actors. They knew how to work as a team and had a history of tricking people into admitting their secrets without using violence. In the case of John, they needed to offer him a way out.

"I told him I was willing to switch sides if the Aurigans could offer me a better position than being your lackey. When I said you flirted with my girl, I had him. He told me about the next battle. He doesn't know how it's going to happen, but he's convinced he will be saved."

Kailoon couldn't stop himself from pointing out a strange contradiction.

"So he's not working together with anyone, but someone will come and save him? Did I get that right?"

"That's what he said," confirmed Ben. "Then he asked me to get him to Construction Area #5 when the attack begins. Everybody there will be considered an ally by the Aurigans and taken to their 'empire', while the rest will be killed without exception."

"I see. Anything else?"

"No, Commander."

"Alright then. Excellent work, gentlemen. You've earned a break."

"Yes, Commander."

Both pilots saluted Kailoon before walking off to grab a coffee. As they departed, the commander immediately passed the information on to Saito and Bunta. They would be pleased to hear that their plan wouldn't have to be changed.

Kailoon mentally went over the operation again. The enemy was – maybe – going to try to invade the city. The so called 'Construction Area #5' was an open space, several square kilometers wide and completely flat, covered with concrete. The construction work had not actually begun yet.

The construction zone made sense as a drop point. You could easily spot everything in the perimeter; there were no obstacles. You'd be a good target, both to be collected and to be shot at if you were an enemy.

This added another layer of complexity to the whole situation, a layer Kailoon had no time to worry about. All of it wouldn't matter if he could shoot down the ships before they got too close, so that was an even higher priority now.

There was still a bit of time before the defense briefing would start. It was part of Kailoon's strategy to keep options available. He didn't want John to stop believing that he might make it out of this until it was clear that it would be of no further use.

Kailoon decided to send a lowly soldier to take the traitor back to his cell while mentioning rumors about Ben getting demoted soon. John may suspect a ruse coming from Kailoon's men, but maybe he would believe a grumpy BBL.

Suddenly a monotone voice in Kailoon's head spoke, interrupting his thoughts.

"Commander, Miss Cayenne was at the surface elevator entry until a moment ago. She has been invited into the cafeteria by one of White's lawyers and is currently still there."

"Thanks, Vic. I'll go to her."

Kailoon's neural implant was connected to the network since he entered the lower levels of the underground complex. There was no reason not to let Vic roam free here. The high amount of various metals in the soil formed a perfect cage for electromagnetic waves. Nobody from the outside could send or receive transmissions, except via an old-fashioned phone cable.

When the news about the teleporters reached him a few minutes before the meeting, he immediately had Vic adjust the defense plans and changed everything else on the fly accordingly. Who would have guessed the little investigator could be so helpful? It wasn't completely unexpected; Kailoon had only accepted the mission to fetch her because of her potential, but this was beyond what he had hoped for.

While walking back to the elevator, he passed by a dozen doors that were part of the laboratories Bunta was responsible for. Nobody except the general and a select few scientists knew what was going on in there. Each time Kailoon saw these doors, he had the desire to hack their locks to find out what was inside, but never had the time or opportunity to do so. Also, Bunta was the only general he considered his friend, and he didn't want to invade what was essentially his home.

Every general had their secrets. One day, or so Kailoon secretly planned, he would figure them all out. But now, he had to talk to his best spy on the planet and see what else she got for him, all while getting rid of White's man in a fashion that wouldn't cause him more trouble later – if possible.

It could have been so simple. Aim at the Aurigans, pull the trigger, done. But no, he had to deal with five generals, each with different interests, motives and backgrounds, on top of defending the planet against an advanced alien race that was planning its final attack and had an unknown number of spies inside the colony.

Kailoon sighed. Why was his job so complicated?

THE JOB - 8

L uray was still walking in circles around the elevator, thinking about what she had learned so far. She did have the right to enter the building, at least with her access card. Still, given the high number of people who started suddenly pouring out of the elevator a few minutes ago – the end of a shift, she presumed – just going inside and looking around without a plan would lead nowhere. She had no idea where Kailoon might be.

Among the people leaving were no high-ranking officers that she could have asked.

Maybe the important people are busy and come out last? I'll just wait here. I can still go in once everybody has left.

The elevator doors had opened for only about ten seconds before closing again. In that time, 30 or so people came out. After just ten more seconds, the doors opened again, and another wave of people emerged.

I am too curious about how this magic elevator works. There is no way they could have all gotten in that quickly.

Luray kept observing the stream of people that didn't want to end. Some of them realized that there was a strange woman watching them, but nobody approached her. They just kept walking towards a fleet of shuttles.

> *Is this how they usually go home, or is it the lockdown version? Anyway, how big is this facility? I saw about 300 people leave in the last few minutes.*

After studying the flux of people a bit longer, Luray became quite bored. She kept an eye out for uniforms that would catch her eye, but her mind wanted to explore.

"Bin, did you ever think about the woodcutter problem?"

"Are you referring to the optimization problem?"

"Yes."

"Yes, I did wonder about that."

"And?"

"I can confirm that there is no solution."

> *I know there's no perfect solution. I wanted you to entertain me.*

"Do you want to talk about it anyway? I can use the philosophy module to explain in multiple ways why there is no solution."

After not receiving an answer, Bin waited. His personality setting forced him not to annoy Luray if it wasn't his turn to speak, and he had no new information to offer. But then, how was he going to be of use? His owner was clearly bored and needed entertainment.

Bin thus changed his personality settings using his free will module, reasoning that he was allowed to improve himself by extending the allowance to install the update.

"Are you sure you do not want to talk? It could make the time pass faster."

I am pretty sure I configured him not to do that. I'll check his settings as soon as I have time.

"Okay, tell me about it."

"Imagine you are a woodcutter. Your axe is getting dull, and the only way to sharpen it is to go to a village and visit a blacksmith. You know how long it will take to chop the trees using your dull axe, and you know it would be much faster with a sharp axe, but you don't know how many people are in the queue before you waiting to get their axe sharpened. Therefore, you have two choices without knowing which one is better."

"This isn't the original version," she noted dryly.

"No, it is not. I took the liberty of fixing a few flaws."

"Let me teach you something, Bin. In real life, sharpening the axe is the better choice, even if it turns out to be a mistake."

"I do not understand. Can you explain?"

"It's simple, really. Not doing it will just postpone the problem. Your axe will get duller over time, but you will never know the queue length. If you have it sharpened, you gather data. You will be able to estimate how long it will take to sharpen the axe next time. Over time, you will be able to predict the queue size with more accuracy and optimize the process. This means you should get it sharpened as soon as you need to and not waste any time."

Bin went silent for a bit longer than usual. Finally, he responded with a question.

"Do you also have a solution for the ultimatum game?"

Ah, the good old ultimatum game. Player one gets 100 units. He can propose a deal to player two and give him as many units as he wants, but if player two refuses, both get nothing. The so-called rational solution is to offer one unit because, for player two, one is more than zero, so he must accept. Nonsense.

"Yes. The game itself is flawed. It assumes two perfectly rational greedy participants will play it, not communicate before, and then never interact with each other again. The real world is different."

"Can you elaborate?"

Luray was only too glad to.

"If you know about the game in advance, then you can let your adversary know that you will reject all offers below 50 percent. Then you might have to do it once to prove you mean it, but from then on, you will gain a lot more than just the absolute minimum."

"Why would you not reject all offers below 99 percent?"

Really, Bin. A child would know this.

"Because 50 percent is the only value for which no side can complain that the other one gets more."

"Why would any player care about the result of the other player? It has no influence over your own profits or losses."

How to explain that to a machine...

"Let me turn that question back to you, Bin. Why would you care about the result of a specific player, but ignore the result of all other players?"

"I do not understand. Please provide explanations."

"The one player you care about is yourself. You act as if you were the only one that mattered, meaning you want to maximize your own income, but which quality or property makes you important? Why is your result important, but not that of anybody else?"

"I see. In one case, every player's goal is to maximize their own profits, while in the other, the maximum loss of every player is to be minimized."

Now he's speaking in riddles. Maximum loss?

"What do you mean?"

"Your strategy can be split up into two sub-goals. The first one is to minimize the difference between the outcomes per player, which leaves 50/50 and 0/0 as the best options. The next one is to optimize the outcome while not breaking the first rule, so 50/50 is to be preferred over 0/0. I suppose you can modify these rules and add a tolerance limit to define the maximum accepted difference."

"You're quite smart, Bin."

"This is only because I have a good teacher."

"Thanks."

"I was referring to the darknet."

"I hate you."

"I also have a sarcasm detection module."

I wonder how much time we wasted.

The doors of the elevator opened again, but this time, only a single person came out. He was wearing a sharp, clearly expensive black suit, making him unique among all the people whom Luray had quickly skimmed in the last few minutes. He was tall with sleek short black hair, and carried a briefcase.

Must be someone important. Who might it be? And what's up with the briefcase? Nobody uses paper anymore.

The newcomer didn't leave as the others had. Instead, he directed his gaze at Luray. After glancing at his watch, he started walking towards her.

A wristwatch? How antiquated. I guess there are some cameras hidden around here, which is how he knew where I was?

"Miss Cayenne, I presume?"

He had a way of speaking that Luray could only describe as weird. He put emphasis on parts of a word where you wouldn't expect it, making pauses between syllables where there shouldn't be any.

"Yes. Who are you?

"Who I am is of no importance."

I've never heard anyone talk like this before. He is dragging out and hissing every 's' he can. Is that supposed to have an effect on me? Or is it just his style of speech?

"I am merely a messenger. Please follow me. I have a proposal for you, and important information that you cannot be allowed to miss."

Maybe this guy can help me.

"I need to talk to the commander, Kailoon. Do you know where he is?"

"Yes, he is in a meeting. Unavailable for you, unfortunately. We can wait for him in the cafeteria. He is certain to pass by, so we are sure not to miss him if we wait there."

Without waiting for confirmation, he went back to the elevator. To Luray's surprise, its doors had remained open this whole time.

Is he the last one, or is he blocking the way for everybody?

She decided to follow the strange man. It was certainly a better option than waiting outside for another half hour.

Once inside the elevator, the doors closed automatically, and they started to move down, then sideways, changing direction multiple times. It felt more like being in some weird amusement park ride.

Ah, so there can be multiple elevators at the same time. They were probably queued somewhere.

The door opened after half a minute.

"Here we are, Miss Cayenne. Please choose a table."

They had arrived at a dining hall. The place was huge, at least 200 meters in all directions. On top of that, almost nobody was here. Hundreds if not thousands of empty tables spread before her

185

eyes, each and every single one decorated as though for haute cuisine.

Luray expected the place to be crowded, but maybe the majority just went home? She selected a table at random and sat down.

"So, Mr. Suitcase, what do you have for me?"

The man smirked at her remark without seemingly taking offense. He pulled out a chair across from her.

"I am here on behalf of General White. He is too involved in the recent events to be able to talk to you personally, so he asked me to explain the situation to you. You see, whether you acknowledge it or not, you are a puppet used by powerful people playing their game."

He knows I don't like to listen to orders. He said that to make me want to rebel.

"Am I?"

"Do you know how much money this colony is worth?"

"Of course. Every year, about 20 trillion units are invested."

The man nodded.

"And do you know how much the colony will be worth in a few years?"

"Given the planet's natural resources, measuring it in trillions stops making sense. This planet is a gold mine. In the long term, it will set records."

He smiled and nodded again.

"Precise and correct, Miss Cayenne. And do you know who is afraid of that?"

Everybody who didn't gain the right to build a colony here. They all want it. Am I right?

There was no need to ask. The man explained it without waiting for Luray to say anything.

"I will tell you. The government of Earth itself. This colony is becoming rich and powerful. In a few years, if everything progresses at its current pace, this colony will declare its independence. There would be nothing the UEM could do to stop it. All its resources – gone, just like that."

He folded his hands and leaned forward across the table.

"And you, Miss Cayenne, are here to prevent that. You have been sent to find reasons to cut the funding. In other words: to weaken the colony. You are the queen, so to speak, of this game of chess. A powerful piece but controlled by someone in the shadows."

Luray crossed her arms and leaned back in her chair.

"What makes you think I'm being controlled?"

"Everything. The timing of your mission, the documents given to you, the discovery of a traitor among the generals. Don't you think it is highly suspicious you learned about that by sheer accident just when you arrived? If you wait a little longer, there will be even more. The next attack will somehow be able to bypass our defenses, and heavy damage will barely be avoided. It's all done to make you believe things that are not true."

So you're saying I am so extremely important that the entire scenario is a setup just to get my signature on a report stating that it's dangerous here?

187

"I have to admit; it's mysterious. But doesn't that mean people working to fool me are everywhere here?"

The man's eyes bore into her.

"Yes, that is exactly what it means."

Oh, this is getting interesting.

She allowed a hint of suspicion in her tone.

"How do I know you're not just trying to make me paranoid?"

His hands spread in an appeasing gesture.

"How about we make a test? You drop some hints here and there that you're considering the colony safe. It won't take long until you get an offer. It might be money, or maybe they will threaten you. Something will happen."

This is an interesting strategy. Introduce a mysterious puppeteer, along with the prospect of an enemy. Now your next step should be to offer an alliance.

"And why shouldn't I just take the money? I can probably get a lot out of it, important as I am."

Suo has some explaining to do. She must have known something about this.

"No matter what they can give you, it doesn't compare to what you could have if you sided with us. Join our cause. Leave Earth and stay here. We won't be bound by bureaucracy; no outdated and nonsensical laws will hold you back. We will make the planet our own – and you can be part of that. Imagine the best Earth has to offer you multiplied a hundred times over. This is what you could have. All you need to do…"

Is sign the contract you have in your case? Or sell my soul?

"....is send a report back to Earth, making it clear that there is no danger. Use it to explain your reasons for staying here. List all that is good about the colony, clear the way for us. You have the power to create a new world. And you have the power to ruin it for all of us. I can do nothing about that. As a gesture of good will, I have avoided revealing to Estrada Industries that you have arrived here. Now, that is all you need to know. The choice is yours."

Reminds me of someone offering 20 percent annually on your investment without any risk. Are you seriously expecting me to buy that? But then again, according to my profile, I might accept, so it makes sense to try that one on me.

Suddenly, a sharp crash interrupted their discussion. Something had shattered. Luray turned around and saw Kailoon a few tables away, who looked at a mess on the ground.

"Oh my, I am so clumsy! The beautiful vase."

The nameless man in the black suit looked like he had bitten into a lemon.

"If you will excuse me now, I have other matters to attend to."

Then he bent forward unnecessarily close to her and whispered.

"Be careful who you trust. If you want to meet me again, room 12-17-B."

With that said, he adjusted his suit, greeted Kailoon in a neutral voice and walked past him.

Once the mysterious negotiator was out of hearing range, Kailoon came towards Luray.

And what about the vase?

A small robot approached the place where Kailoon had broken the vase and started picking up the pieces.

I need one of those at home.

Kailoon didn't waste time with greeting her. He got straight to the point.

"The intel about the teleporter might have saved us. The next attack will be different from the previous ones. They're coming to get us this time, and we don't know what they will try."

No, don't give me any time to think. Just throw it at me all at once.

"Can you slow down a second? Who was that guy just now? Why is this place empty?"

Kailoon took a deep breath and began speaking a bit slower.

"That was McCain. A lawyer-like creature, doing shady things for General White, who is in charge of the colony's finances. His job is to keep the money flowing in. At all costs, as paradoxical as that sounds. They dream of exploiting the planet's resources and building their own empire. But we don't have time for that right now. Follow me."

So that part was true?

Kailoon grabbed Luray's hand and started walking. She pulled it back before following him.

"I'm coming. No need to be rude."

"It's not rudeness," he said calmly. "It's urgency."

While walking through the corridors, Kailoon summed up the situation.

"The attack is about to happen. I don't know what McCain told you, but whatever it was, put it on hold. If he threatened you, ignore it. If you died here for whatever reason, it would be hard to explain, and he can't risk losing his income."

Wait, what?

"I'll keep you near me from now on until the attack begins," he continued brusquely. "Once it does, you'll see everything with your own eyes from an observation room."

It was clear that Kailoon had reasons for wanting her to accompany him, but Luray had no idea what those reasons might be.

"I am a civilian," she felt the need to point out. "Shouldn't you tell me to stay in my room until it's over, evacuate the colony, or bring everyone to a safe bunker or something? This building seems pretty safe. Why did everybody leave? What's going on?"

The commander did not slow down. He looked mentally busy, focused, maybe even worried. Luray wasn't sure about the latter.

"Let's call it a gamble. You're my insurance. I'm breaking at least a dozen regulations now, but if I fail, we all die, so that doesn't matter. If we don't die, I'll see how I untangle the mess again."

Interesting logic.

"Your insurance?"

His jaw tightened.

"Should the defenses fail, and should the colony fall into enemy hands, I need someone to warn Earth."

191

He really means it. He thinks there is a chance we're going to lose. But why me? I'm just a civilian. Don't you have messenger drones for that?

"As much as it pains me, I will give you the Slug. It's the fastest ship we have right now. I'll preprogram a course to one of the closest gates, since we must assume we'll lose control over the local one if we lose the battle. The Slug will reach Earth, where you will broadcast all the data stored in its main computer. I'll have it connected to this base and record everything that happens."

She was practically running to keep pace with him.

"Why do you need me? Why not an autopilot? Why not send one of your pilots?"

"Later."

Kailoon stopped at a door. Luray had no idea where she was, and without help would take a while to find the way back. She had been so focused on him that she didn't pay attention to the path.

The commander opened the door. Everybody inside the room, about 20 people in science uniforms, saluted him except one Chinese woman, probably in her twenties. She jumped out of her seat, giving him a huge smile and a thumbs-up.

Who is that?

Kailoon replied to the smile by bowing down a bit, as if the woman was his queen. "I knew I could count on you and the other nerds, Wu. Well done."

He then closed the door again and moved on.

Are they in a relationship?

192

"I'll show you how to get to the Slug. We have multiple shuttle bays integrated into the base."

I have to admit; he is efficient. If only everybody could be more like him, the world would be a better place.

After one more elevator ride and some additional turns, they reached a long hallway that ended in a huge metal door with an ID scanner next to it. Written on the wall were the words 'Hangar bay.' This time, Luray did pay attention and could probably find the way back herself on her first try.

Kailoon pointed at the hangar.

"The Slug is here right now. Your ID should work. I would prefer it if you stayed down here until the battle is over. There are free rooms everywhere on this floor. Just pick one."

Motwani can go everywhere, I suppose?

Wait, I hear voices. There are more people here – around that corner, by the sound of it.

Kailoon turned away from Luray. He had heard them too. The commander crept down the hall with her close behind until they reached a corner. As the conversation became clearer, it looked as though he recognized the voices. Just then Kailoon seemed to suddenly remember Luray was still with him and turned around to hastily summarize the most basic rule she needed to follow.

"If anyone asks, you belong here," he spoke in a whisper. "Nobody will bother checking that. Mention me if you're in trouble. I'll have to do some micromanagement now."

And with that he vanished around the corner, leaving her alone. She heard him call out to whomever was speaking.

193

This guy doesn't have a second to pause and think. I wonder what his stress level usually is. No wonder he seemed to enjoy the time in his shuttle so much and dragged it out coming back here. Who is he talking to? Well, since I work and belong here...

Luray checked her surroundings. Was there something she could use to appear busy to the average observer? She began trying the doors. The first one was locked; the second opened right away.

It revealed a room similar to hers, except that it was underground and had no windows. The layout was almost identical.

No idea who this belongs to. Whoever it is, they forgot to lock the door, and left a tablet here. That's all I need.

Luray took the device, switched it on, then went out into the corridor again. Holding the tablet in front of her, she slowly moved towards the source of the conversation.

Lucky me. They're just around the corner. I can move close and they won't even see me. As a Plan B, I am a diligent employee working on something super urgent.

She heard a man's deep voice that she didn't recognize, but since Kailoon addressed him with 'General Abano,' her curiosity wouldn't permit her to miss the conversation.

"Ideally, the civilians won't even realize the danger they are in. We have neither a safe place for them nor any way to evacuate even five percent of the population until tomorrow. The last thing we need now is panic."

That sounds quite bad.

A second voice, belonging to someone else she didn't know, spoke up.

"What danger? Our defense is much stronger than last time. Your pessimism is based on an extremely unlikely worst-case scenario. If anyone causes a panic, it's you."

The first man answered again.

"Choose your words more carefully, White."

Ah, the finance general.

"Kailoon, I trust that you will defend our colony just as you did before. Show them what we are made of. I may overlook some of your wrongdoings if you manage to keep their ships away from our planet."

Wrongdoings?

"I'll do my best."

Engrossed in her eavesdropping, Luray heard their footsteps approaching too late.

No! Too fast!

A general, she couldn't tell which one, rounded the corner and almost bumped into her.

"What are you doing here?" he snapped.

Huh? He doesn't recognize me? Shouldn't they have seen my file? Anyway, that means I can pick a fake personality. He's a general; he should be used to people being intimidated by him. I should try not to stick out or be special in any way.

"I...I was...."

Right then Kailoon came around the corner as well.

"Rose! Where have you been? I was expecting you ten minutes ago."

Rose?

"Never mind," he continued in an exasperated tone as if scolding her for something. "Apologize to the general so we can get back to work."

"I... pardon me, General. I got distracted." She held up her data pad meekly. "It won't happen again."

Kailoon moved to stand at her side.

"So typical. A strategic genius but forgets the time. Well, now that you're here, we can finally..."

White interrupted him.

"Do you mind explaining to me who this is? This section is off-limits to non-military personnel unless they have a special allowance, and I don't see a badge on her."

"This is the strategic observer, Rose T. Koe," the commander lied smoothly. "I told you about her. She will oversee the next battle and analyze it for me in case I miss something in the heat of the moment."

"Yes... I recall now. She looks different inside that uniform. Well then, do your best."

As White walked away, Luray breathed a sigh of relief.

That was close.

"Well then, Rose, if you would come with me..."

McCain recognized me before. Why didn't the general? They are working together, aren't they?

Kailoon and Rose passed by the remaining general, Abano. Luray analyzed him as much as she could, but only had a split second to do that, so she couldn't read much.

"You're a curious one, aren't you?" the commander mouthed quietly as they walked on.

"Part of the job," she responded back.

After a few more corners, they arrived at another post marked 'Command Center.' Here Kailoon stopped.

"I wish I could be of assistance to you and play detective, but I won't have a second to spare until the attack is over. I'll be in there, taking care of all preparations. Since you're my strategic observer, you can come with me and take a look around briefly, as long as you're not too curious."

Wait a minute...

"Who is Rose?" Luray felt the need to clear this up.

"Nobody. She doesn't exist. I made her up a few hours ago just in case I couldn't get rid of you. Seems like I made a wise move."

I feel flattered somehow.

"Before you run off again, why send me back instead of one of your pilots? And why didn't White recognize me just now?"

"Because they're all needed elsewhere. At the GSRG commands, to be precise. You're the only one that has no real use otherwise. Sorry. That didn't come out right."

It's refreshing to hear someone speaking honestly.

"You can stay in any of the rooms here until the attack is over or I tell you to go. As for White, Suo manipulated the report about you. She wanted you to be able to move more freely. I really need to prepare the defenses now; time is running out. How McCain found you, I have no idea. He shouldn't have been able to. He'll tell White at some point."

Wait a second...

"And how did *you* know White wouldn't recognize me?"

For a split second, Kailoon was stumped.

"Of course, you couldn't have known. He was looking for you, but he didn't find you. That's how I could tell."

But instead, his lawyer found me? I'll have to investigate this once I get the chance.

Kailoon was looking at her, and she at him. They both knew how important the next battle could be. It occurred to her that one or both of them could soon die, and they would never see each other again.

"Kiss him."

"Shut up, Bin."

The commander looked surprised for a split second, and then turned a full-blown smile at Luray.

"You should teach your AI to be silent when a conversation is taking place."

Despite being perfectly aware that only she could hear Bin, Luray took a moment to regain full control over her face.

"It's... a bit complicated with him at the moment," she muttered in heated tones.

She then turned around and vanished into the first open – and unused – room she could find.

A huge 3D window screen occupying one wall switched on the moment the door shut behind her, showing an image of a lakeside forest setting. The tranquil environment in no way reflected how she currently felt.

"Bin, why did you do that?!"

And more importantly, did the commander just admit that he knows my AI is unlocked? I slipped up, and he let me go just like that? He must know that interrupting a conversation is something only a modified AI can do, and he must know that it is illegal.

"I love you. Therefore, I want you to be happy. Based on my observations, I can safely conclude that the commander is interested in you. He takes time out of his schedule to be with you and takes unnecessary risks to allow you to be at his side. He openly admitted that your being here has no real use for him, so romantic interest is the only explanation. Since there wasn't much time left, your best option was to take a risk. You have nothing to lose, but everything to win. I know your preferences because of your browser history. He should be among your favorites."

Then again, he could have already guessed it when I translated the Aurigan messages for him, although it wasn't clear back then. The translation tool could also run on a legal AI if someone went through the trouble of having it certified. Unlikely, but possible. Now, as to Bin's newfound interest in my love life...

"What about the woman from before? There was clearly something between them. You want me to create drama?"

"There is a wireless network active inside this building. I could use it, but my access is very limited. Still, it was enough to determine Kailoon's relationship status with 75 percent certainty. My interpretation of all the available data is that he is not currently involved with anyone and remains an option for you."

25 percent risk of drama is 25 percent too much.

"Bin, I can choose for myself, thank you. Please never do that again."

I guess he only follows his own rules.

"I will adjust my personality matrix accordingly."

I hope Bin's copy on the main server doesn't get strange ideas.

Luray searched the room for a computer or at least a way to officially connect Bin to the network using Motwani's account. He should have a lot more access rights. She found a terminal, but it was locked and demanded a password or key.

"You need to be authorized. Try inserting Motwani's ID card."

That update really messed you up. I will get rid of it once we're home again. At least you've become more helpful. I'll try to keep that.

Bin was right. Once Luray inserted the ID card, several lights lit up, signifying that all drawers and other storage spaces could now be accessed. Bin confirmed he now had full access to the local network.

In the meantime, a search of the environment seemed in order.

The drawers opened once they were touched and contained a gas mask, weapons and even full body armor. This place wasn't meant for civilians, so it made sense.

The main surprise, however, was the fake window. It turned into a huge display and allowed Luray to spy into all rooms, including her own. She could see herself with a small lag of about 50 milliseconds, which felt a bit weird. She waved her arm around a few times, but the strange feeling didn't want to go away.

The menu on the screen indicated that every single room inside the underground base was observable, but almost no building from the outside appeared on the list.

So not everything is under observation. And as I thought, there is a camera high up in the sky.

Luray explored the menu. Not only could she spy everywhere, but she also had restricted access to the defense systems. All controls were grayed out, but she could check the map of the solar system. The Aurigan fleet was about 30 hours away – recorded video showed that the ships had not changed their formation since they started to move. The most recent feed was about 90 minutes old, which made sense. Information about the ships could only reach the colony at the speed of light. The predicted position of the ships was a bit ahead of their last recorded position.

Luray could also see the position of all GSRGs in the planet's orbit. They were placed at regular intervals, rotating around the colony. Within two hours, each of them had orbited the planet once, and 50 percent of them always had a direct line of sight towards the incoming fleet. There were a bunch of notes attached to the displayed solar system. Bin had already read all of them.

Wait a second... they're not geostationary. The planet is tidally locked. The UEM just didn't bother to change the name.

Luray was surprised at her own unexpected insight, so much so that she had to smile for a second.

"Do you want me to summarize the defense plan?"

"You read my mind, Bin."

"The commander wants to use 50 percent of the GSRGs at once, firing small projectiles to cover a wider range. He hopes to stop the fleet but not destroy it. He intends to find and later use any secret weapon they might carry."

"And if that first attack doesn't stop them?"

"The stationary black hole powered laser cannon, also known as BHPLC, is being charged this moment. It will form the last line of defense, with an effective range of one million kilometers. Beyond that, the energy rays will spread out too much to inflict damage. Additionally, all pilots will be sent as a second attack wave should the initial attack not do enough damage."

Sounds like Kailoon has it all covered. He managed that in what little time he had. And people already wonder how I get so much done!

There was also a timer counting down with millisecond accuracy. Three hours were left before the attack would begin.

"If I may make a suggestion, there is something we can do to enhance our chances of victory."

What is he up to this time?

"What's your plan?"

"We can still reach John's computer in time and upload me. If the Aurigan ships are disabled, no harm would be done. If they break through, we have one additional method of doing damage."

Luray thought about Bin's proposal again. Now she didn't see a disadvantage anymore. However, it would mean abandoning her post.

"Bin, if I need to be at the linguist office when the attack takes place, can I still make it back here in time?"

"I am afraid this building has just been put under lockdown, and all communication to the outside will be cut. It is one of the new security measures currently being implemented."

Maybe Kailoon wants to change the plan at the last second and make sure the traitor doesn't know?

"Do you know where the generals are at the moment?"

"They are all inside this building. I can look for them if you want."

"Them remaining here makes sense. Once the communications are cut, nobody can inform the Aurigans about changes in the plan. Yes, please check where they are. Maybe it will be useful. I still have three hours left to investigate."

I wonder if the generals are sitting in front of screens watching a countdown timer. Can they see everything like I can? They're not watching me watching them, are they?

Bin flipped through the thousands of video streams until he found each of the five generals. They were indeed all in separate rooms, together with a few soldiers, observing the countdown. They were not talking to each other.

"Bin, is my ocular implant bugging, or are the times on the screens different for everyone?"

"A malfunction of this kind is extremely unlikely. It is more likely that the timers are all different."

This is Kailoon's doing. He wants to observe their reactions. He'll do something that wasn't planned, and then he'll see if any of the generals tries to warn the Aurigans. He may not be able to prevent that, but the delay will still give him an advantage.

How can he do so much in such a short time? It can't be him alone; I'm sure about that. In fact, even a team couldn't pull this off. It's too much at once. Just explaining your plan would take time.

Does he have an unlocked AI, like Bin? That might explain it, but rogue AIs that high up in the military? He's taking an enormous risk. If someone ever finds out, he'll end up in jail for the rest of his life.

The first timer was shifted by over a minute, the next one by more than two, and so on. What the screen displayed was fitting to the timer – changes were not displayed all at once. General Suo saw everything first, after that White, then Abano, Saito and lastly Bunta.

Is there anything I could do while we're all stuck here? I should use the time to gather as much information as I can.

Luray spent the next 15 minutes browsing through everything the computer had to offer. She found nothing related to the Aurigans that could help identify the traitor. Motwani had access to lots of surprising data, but none of it was helpful. The spy, whoever it was, had been careful.

But who was this Motwani guy, anyway? His access rights were almost without limit. The only problem was that everybody had their own encryption key and so private files couldn't be read, no matter the privileges.

Oh, what's this?

Luray stumbled over a reference to a list of experiments currently being conducted. The original data was unavailable, but Bin found a few small fragments in temporary folders for which encryption had been forgotten.

Ah, the good old temporary folder weakness. It has revealed so many secrets in human history, and yet, there's always someone not paying attention to where his temporary files are saved.

The fragmented files mentioned a dozen different experiments going on both at the current site and on the other side of the planet. Apparently, there was another base located there.

Genetic experiments, AI research, weapon tests... you guys are quite busy. And if I'm not mistaken, what you do here would be illegal on Earth. The government back on Earth doesn't know about this, does it? You were left alone for a moment and immediately did what you're not allowed to because nobody was looking. I can see why White would want to protect his investment. The potential benefit is huge.

Luray read as fast as she could, trying to put the pieces together.

They're trying to create a general-purpose intelligence by growing it in an organic brain and merging it with the planetary defenses, and even putting it in ships? This is heavy stuff. If they ever get it done, they really could declare their independence. The UEM wouldn't have the power to stop them. Intelligent ships and weapons... scary.

Luray took a deep breath and exhaled slowly, then stared at the document fragments. She had been in situations that decided the future of companies of all sizes, but never an entire colony. For the first time since her arrival, Luray wasn't sure about how to proceed.

If I go back with evidence of this, I can make it all fall apart. But do I want that? Do I care? Should I intervene? Are these guys evil? I have no idea if what they do will ultimately be good or bad. Can I go back, pretending not to know?

The moment that last question entered her mind, everything became clearer.

No, I can't. If I went back, I would always regret not having made a choice. The last time I ran away from something, I wound up deeply regretting it. It happened more than ten years ago, but the memory still haunts me. I won't do something like that again.

Instead, Luray would gather all the data she needed, and based on that, she would decide what needed to be done. She would not back down afterward and either leave as the winner or accept a loss.

Time to go.

"Bin, if I connect you to the network, you can still talk to me and observe all the video streams at the same time, right?"

"I suggest registering me as a viewer. That way, we won't take any additional risk."

"Then that's what I'll do. You'll direct me. I want to talk to people in charge. Scan the data you have and choose someone who is likely to reveal information to me. The scientists from earlier, they might know something."

"As you wish."

Luray smiled. Everybody was busy. Under these conditions, it would be easy for her to go wherever she wanted. With Motwani's card, she could open every door. There had been no guards in front of most of them, so people here trusted their security system.

After installing Bin, not without remembering his desire to be installed on as many systems as possible, she got up and left.

"Bin, don't forget to notify me soon enough so that I don't miss the battle. I want to see how Kailoon handles it."

"Yes."

The voice in her head guided Luray down a few hallways, made her take another elevator and go down a few levels. As expected, the floor was almost empty; there were no guards anywhere to be seen.

The soldiers should be getting ready for a possible battle on the surface, even if that is kept a secret from the civilians.

"Enter through the third door on the left. Look for a man named Krov drinking coffee. There will be only one."

Luray did as she was told. She entered what she assumed was the biology lab. It was brightly lit, full of instruments she had never seen before. The only item she recognized was a microwave oven. The room was crammed with transparent boxes and cages.

There were strange, dark 'things' of all sizes growing inside them, from as small as a coin to bigger than a human. Those in the cages looked like they were trying to grow out of them.

What are these black things? They look like tentacles or weird mushrooms. Some of them even move.

There were a dozen people here involved in doing some kind of research, but as Bin said, only one had a cup of coffee. Luray walked towards him, past one of the bigger tentacles. It smashed against the inside of its transparent cage, but the noise barely made it outside. Luray noticed it but didn't react to it.

I work here. I know the tentacles do this, so that doesn't scare me. And by seeing that I wasn't surprised, everybody will assume I belong here.

She needn't have bothered; absolutely no one even turned their heads at her approach. They remained completely engrossed in whatever they were doing.

"Excuse me... Dr. Krov?"

Luray approached the middle-aged man, but instead of greeting her, he emptied his cup and threw his lab-coat on a chair.

"My shift is over. Find someone else. I haven't slept in two days. So *you* will have to excuse *me*, but I am going now."

He strode right past her. On his way, he slapped his hand against the glass wall the tentacle was still holding on to. It jumped away.

Well, that was a failure. Who's next on the list, Bin?

"Go back to the elevator. I think it would be most beneficial to meet the remaining generals."

I agree. Now that I'm Rose, the commander's strategic observer, I might get away with it.

Luray left the room, almost ignored by the lab workers.

They probably won't even remember me later. Whatever they were working on, it required their full attention.

208

After letting Bin guide her again, Luray found herself in front of General Saito's quarters. Just as she was about to knock, the door was opened from the inside.

Isn't that the woman Kailoon met before?

According to her badge, the person standing before her was named Ying Wu. She looked surprised for a moment, started to speak then trailed off. Finally, she saluted.

When in Rome...

Luray saluted for the first time in her entire life. It felt weird, but Ying Wu seemed to have expected exactly that and cleared the way for her to enter. Luray saw an opportunity and addressed her.

"Actually, Miss..." Luray quickly read the nametag again, trying to guess which was the first and which was the last name. "...Wu, I was looking for you."

"For me? Oh, sure. What do you want to know?"

"Let's not bother the general."

Wu nodded, stepped out of the room and closed the door.

Luray studied the pretty young woman.

"Do you know who I am?"

Wu shook her head.

"No, I just saw you with the commander before. But I can tell you're not with the military. You don't talk like they do. You're much friendlier. Are you his wife?"

Friendly? Me? Wife? Okay.

209

"No, I am his strategic observer."

So, he really isn't in a relationship with this woman. But they seemed to be close. They can't be related, can they?

"You must be very capable then," Ying Wu observed. "Kailoon doesn't let anyone look over his shoulder, usually. What did you do to impress him?"

Um… yes, what did I do?

"I made him hit the turf in a sparring match."

Wu started to laugh. Doing so made her look really happy, even more than before.

Is she always in such a good mood? And does she always talk so openly? Good thing I ran into her.

"Sounds just like him," the girl chortled. "So what can I do for you?"

That is the question.

"Let's find somewhere a bit more private. I would prefer not to talk in the corridor."

"Of course. Let's go to room 17."

Wu started walking in a different direction than expected, which left Luray confused, but she followed while figuring out what was going on.

Room 17 on the other floor was elsewhere. Every floor has a different layout from what I can tell. I wonder why that is. Did they shuffle the layouts for some reason?

Room 17 – a recreation room – offered chess boards and a pool table, a small library and a dartboard. Luray glanced over it quickly, then focused on Wu again. They sat down at a small table facing each other.

Luray got right down to business.

"I'll be direct. I received a report about this colony, but as it turned out, it was completely off. It must have been written by someone very incompetent."

Luray supported her statement by letting her forehead partially rest in her right hand, a universally understood pose for having to deal with something unbelievably stupid.

"So now, I need to ask around to get an overview of the situation."

"Sure, ask away."

Hard to do that if you don't give me any hints.

"If Kailoon wasn't busy preparing defenses against the next imminent attack, I'd ask him for clarification. You two seemed close, though, so he probably let you in on the current situation. What can you tell me?"

For some reason, Wu was giving her a suspicious look. Luray wasn't sure what to make of that. Wu had seen her with Kailoon, so she should assume they were all on the same side.

"Well, we didn't talk much ever since he came back, so my info may not be up to date, but… it seems there's something going on between the generals. I don't know all the details, only that there's a kind of… power struggle. White wants to get rid of Kailoon, but he can't do it alone. He needs two allies for that; Suo doesn't side with anyone, and Bunta has always been on Kailoon's team."

"And Saito? What is your impression of him?"

Wu looked like she was digging for an answer.

"I'm really bad at this. It's not a science. I'd say he would switch to whatever camp has the highest chance of winning. But if the situation were balanced, I have no idea."

That will be helpful. She seems very naïve. I can use that.

"Another question: how's your secret weapon progressing?"

I'm mostly just guessing here. I don't really have an idea what that secret weapon might be., but there were fragments in the temporary files mentioning a weapon that could level a third of the planet.

"The 'strange matter' bombs?" Wu peered around before leaning closer and lowering her voice. "If Kailoon told you about that, he must really trust you. We're halfway through with it, but it can't be used as a defense yet. It's too unstable to be used for long-range applications."

Strange matter, as in strange quark?

"Would you mind explaining to a non-scientist how it works?"

Wu's face broke into an even bigger smile than usual.

"Of course! So, matter is made of quarks. Up, down, top, bottom, strange and charm. Under great pressure, down quarks can turn into strange quarks. If you could build protons out of this, then get more than 1,000 protons together, you would have stable strange matter. And if you could then get it in contact with normal matter, the quarks in the normal matter would be converted to strange quarks as well. It would start a chain reaction until everything is just strange quarks."

For non-scientists, huh?

Wu was looking for more ways to describe it.

"Okay, imagine… imagine a magical shock wave that turns you into something else. Like… when a vampire turns to dust after someone shoots UV light at him. And then he turns into UV light himself, and you get a chain reaction."

Whatever you say…

Luray sought to radiate confidence.

"Yes, that's what I thought. So, whatever your bomb touches turns into strange matter?"

"Exactly. Fire a single shot at an enemy ship…"

Wu made a pistol gesture with her two hands.

"And it turns to stone. Or strange matter, in this case."

"And if you dropped it on the ground?"

Now she lifted both hands and made a sound mimicking an explosion.

"Then goodbye planet in the worst case. This is why we only conduct our experiments in space on asteroids. On planets, a strange matter ball could eat its path to the core and slowly change everything from the inside; it depends on many factors."

It will take time to sort out something so complicated. This is way more than just a simple investigation about some aliens.

A silent alarm went off in Luray's head.

"They are commencing the assault. Please return to your room."

She stood up quickly.

"Thank you, Miss Wu. That was very helpful."

"It was my pleasure."

Luray departed in a hurry, heading back to her room as fast as she could. The time wasn't already up, was it? It was definitely too soon. Was this a ruse of Kailoon, or a surprise attack?

When she reached her quarters, the upper right corner of the huge screen showed a ship that had not been there before. It wasn't a ruse. The battle had begun.

Well, might as well make myself comfortable.

Luray watched what was happening from her extremely comfortable bed without being able to fully enjoy it. The fleet was still 80 light minutes away. Even for someone not directly involved, this was somewhat nerve-wracking.

Suddenly the ship at the front of the formation now appeared in a second location as well – a mere light minute, 18 million kilometers away. How did that happen?

"Bin?"

"I suppose the ship was teleported."

"Then why not just teleport them all at once? Technical limitations?"

"I do not know. If we assume a limitation in size and distance, and that each of the ships has a teleporter that can teleport individual parts precisely, then the whole ship could potentially be reassembled at the destination. This is pure speculation, but my best guess nonetheless."

And we still see the original position because we didn't receive an update yet. Information travels at the speed of light, and we use something similar to a radar here. Everything we see is derived from signals that bounced back.

"Bin, what is the update frequency?"

"We send one signal per minute, with random variations."

So we're at least one minute behind.

On the screen, Luray saw a few shuttles fly towards the closest Aurigan ship. Descriptions on the screen explained that they were attacking. The GSRGs didn't fire yet. Why not? Was Kailoon waiting for an update? Maybe he was right. If the enemy knew about our update intervals, maybe they would use it to change their positions in between to make themselves harder to track. But would the GSRGs be of any use for long range shots now?

Then one of the shuttles altered its course. It was now heading towards the enemy fleet.

Kailoon uses a shuttle to confirm the position. Shuttles can use warp drives. They are faster than the radar.

Communication between the colonies and Earth was a problem. Even when using the gates, the distance to Earth was still a few light years. To solve that, small warp-drive-capable messenger drones were used to transport the messages faster than light. The commander had just used one of his pilots in the same way to check where the fleet was and get faster updates.

As expected, Luray saw the messenger shuttle bounce back and forth multiple times. Every time it came back, the position of the Aurigan fleet changed.

> *They're trying to make it impossible to predict where they will be next. That's the best move the Aurigans can make. You can't be attacked if your enemy can't find you.*

In the meantime, the shuttles fighting the single ship that was near the planet were already successful. The Zep had been destroyed and vanished from the radar, but success came at a cost. Two of the 20 UEM shuttles had been lost.

They had underestimated the fighting power of the Aurigans. A quick report showed that it was equipped with small drones that crashed into the attacking shuttles, taking them by surprise.

The potential danger was obvious to everyone. The Zeps could be carrying anything. If they came near enough, they could teleport whatever they wanted right below the dome. Once that happened, it was game over.

THE JOB - 9

The remaining UEM shuttles attached themselves to the much bigger GSRGs and dragged them along. For a moment Luray wondered how that even made sense, but then the dots disappeared.

Ah, they can extend the warp field. They want to use the GSRGs as mobile weapons?

Two minutes later, Kailoon's pilots had the enemy fleet surrounded and immediately fired all at the same time.

If I see that, it means it already happened a short moment ago, right?

Luray checked the time codes.

No, this one should be real-time. The screen is showing the plan, adjusted to the current time. It will get updated if something goes wrong.

Two seconds later, the first results were shown. A few of the Aurigan ships were hit, but the data analysis was still ongoing.

Well done, Kailoon. You caught the enemy in a crossfire, and they couldn't see it coming. This wasn't a spontaneous idea, was it? It requires warp field fiddling and probably some precise calculations. Was that what you asked the scientists to do for you?

Another screen showed the events from the perspective of a static observer: one of the UEM fighters. It didn't move. From the viewpoint of its pilot, the GSRGs fired one after another. What he could see was limited by the speed of light. It took a few seconds to cover the distance between all the shuttles.

Now I have to wait for the update to see if it really worked out that well.

A minute later, the primary display was adjusted to reality. The Aurigan fleet did in fact lose four of its Zeps, but four shuttles had been lost in the attack as well, causing their GSRGs to spin out of control as the force of their blasts sent them reeling. Two were partially damaged but could still be used for another maneuver.

How? The shuttles came out of nowhere, fired, then jumped into warp mode right away. How did they get hit? Did the Aurigans detect the warp fields somehow? And what weapon did they use? Their drones aren't that fast.

To Luray's disbelief, she suddenly realized that despite the huge distance of almost 500,000 kilometers and the near-instantaneous hit-and-run tactic, the Aurigan ships had reacted fast enough to use their teleporters as weapons. On the video logs, Luray could see that some of the shuttles that made it back were missing parts. They looked like perfectly spherical holes had been cut out with high precision. The fact that the shuttles had been moving at different speeds seemed to have no effect.

They teleported pieces of our shuttles away? If so, the Aurigans have an instant hit high accuracy weapon that can't be defended against. That's extremely dangerous. How will Kailoon respond to that? If his fighters can be taken apart instantly, the best he can do is to sacrifice them to fire shots from up close. That way, at least he makes sure to do as much damage as possible.

The remaining 14 shuttles took 14 more GSRGs and repeated the attack, this time from further away. Luray noticed that the formation had changed; it was no longer a sphere surrounding the Zeps.

There's no pattern to the formation. Did Kailoon panic, or was it the pilots? That's a bad sign... how long until the Aurigans get here? I can still escape...

Luray was about to leave as the GSRGs fired; this time all the shuttles made it back with minimal damage. Only one Zep was crippled as a result. Luray decided to check the outcome before she would run to the Slug.

He increased the distance to reduce the damage to our forces, and it worked. But he did less damage as well. An obviously safer move, but what for? It didn't make a difference... no, wait. There's more to it. Each shuttle had a different distance. He wanted to test the teleporters? Is that why it looked so chaotic?

Luray checked the footage from a few minutes ago. The shuttles nearest to the Aurigan ships were lost, while the ones further away had only been damaged.

He tested the accuracy of the teleporters. You were right, Bin; I like this guy.

The effectiveness of the Aurigan teleporters had limits, and Kailoon had found them. Luray expected him to repeat his attack once more from a safe distance, but it didn't happen.

Why do you not attack again? I'm curious now.

Luray found herself smiling. Her heart was racing. She was afraid, but not just that. It had been a long time since anything was able to entertain or excite her like this. At the same time, the thought of the worst-case scenario made it hard for her to stay calm. She had been in a lot of risky situations, but never before had her life been in danger. Despite the part of her that still wanted to leave, she decided to stay until the outcome was clear.

You should be able to find a good distance using the data you have. So why don't you? It must be something I can read out of what I've seen. That's all you had to go on, so the answer has to be in there.

Luray looked at the screens again, trying to figure out the reason behind the delayed attack. Was there a more efficient way that she had overlooked?

No, that's not it. The GSRGs aren't doing enough damage. He used 34 cannons to fire at the Aurigans in total, but only six of the Zeps left the formation after being struck. Those must be the ones that can no longer maneuver. Are they more stable than the ones from the previous raids? Until now, they all went down after a single direct hit.

Then the answer popped up on the screen. Luray had falsely assumed that the GSRGs could only fire once. Of the 34 GSRGs near the enemy fleet, 20 were still operational. They corrected course from the first blast and fired once more.

Since they were closer, they didn't have to use their entire ammunition while attacking. They fired a lot less and, therefore, still have energy left and can fire again.

Three more ships left the formation and floated off into the void.

Nine down, 15 to go. I completely overlooked the GSRGs from the first attack.

Luray went back to the previous footage, this time having the interface highlight events focussing on the GSRGs instead of the shuttles.

Most of the damage was taken by the cannons, not the shuttles. The Aurigans focused on the weapons first, probably because they were bigger, easier targets and seemed like they were more dangerous.

But why didn't they take care of the remaining GSRGs? Did they also think the cannons could only fire once? Or could they not detect them without attached shuttles? Were they focused on the shuttles and missed that the cannons were left behind? Or maybe they can only see the shuttles for some reason?

Kailoon did the best he could. His current move was to carry the remaining GSRGs into another position, but not as close as last time. At first, Luray couldn't see the pattern, but once a few were in place, it became clear. The GSRGs were lined up along the flight path of the approaching enemy ships. The Zeps would come closer and receive the shots one by one.

He wants to sacrifice the cannons one at a time. If each of them takes out an enemy with a direct hit, that will work. Once a cannon fails, he'll probably collect the remaining ones and try something else.

During the next few minutes, nothing happened. The Aurigan fleet moved slowly and steadily towards the next GSRG. Luray kept staring at the screen, waiting for something to happen.

She felt the excitement as if she was the one in control, even though she was just an observer. Kailoon used an excellent strategy; no move was wasteful. Everything he did made sense.

Whoever gave him the post as commander made a good choice. He's up against an unknown enemy, but I don't see any weakness in his strategy. The colony can be happy he's on our side.

Luray followed every move made, trying to figure out its purpose.

Kailoon used each attack to do both damage and gain intel. Each attack was a test at the same time.

He must have chosen the distances between the cannons specifically to maximize the damage and minimize the chance to get hit by the teleporter. He's keeping the pilots themselves at a safe distance. If the maximum range of the teleporter is indeed 1.44 billion kilometers as the analysis here suggests, then there is still a bit of time until it gets dangerous for us down here. They're moving at 48 million kilometers per hour and have to cross 18 million in total to get into range...

The attack of the first GSRG in line was a success as one more Zep started to drift away. Immediately afterward, the GSRG disappeared from the screen.

As expected, the cannon is gone. They exchanged pieces. The Aurigans can't continue this way. Now we'll see if they can come up with something new.

Would this strategy work a second time? Luray waited for the screen to reveal the answer. She couldn't think about anything else.

Out of nowhere and before half of the predicted time was over, the image shifted to that of EE-297. A few red dots originating from the very first shot down Zep were shown on the screen. Something came out of it, and slipped past all the detectors and scanners. Only now a few hundred kilometers away from the dome itself were they detected.

Do they have some sort of cloaking device?

"May I suggest putting on the armor and taking the weapon, just in case?"

Bin's voice was completely unaffected by everything that was going on. He was as calm as ever.

Now seems like a good time to play it safe.

"Yes, I should do that."

It didn't take Luray more than half a minute to slip into the protective suit. In that time, the sensors detected a small burst of heat around 100 million degrees against the dome.

One of the drones had crashed into it and exploded.

Each of them is carrying a fusion bomb? Hmm... can't say if they'll make it through.

The dome's outermost layer around the point of impact was completely gone, and the inner layers down to the fourth had started to melt. The screen showed the process – there were eight layers in total, each a few meters thick, with a few meters of gas under high pressure in between. The air acted as a countermeasure against the heat, blowing it away.

The layers were originally intended as a shield against asteroid impacts since the system was filled with them, but they did pretty well against suicide-drones as well.

As she watched, the layers of the dome started to rotate in different directions, and a moment later, the four-layer deep hole was split across multiple points. Local, short-range laser cannons were firing at the bomb drones, shooting them down quickly one after another. The dome took one more hit, then rotated the damaged layers again.

Are we holding up? Looks like they can't get inside.

In the meantime, the second line-up of GSRG had fired, but the shot had no effect. The Zeps continued in their advance. Tracking the projectiles themselves was impossible due to their size, so neither Luray nor any of the generals had any idea what went wrong.

Apparently the same could not be said for Kailoon. He let the shuttles transport the GSRGs again, but this time, they stayed in their warp fields and moved very close to the enemy ships. One of the shuttles showed itself not even 100 kilometers away from the enemy fleet.

Why didn't it work? Now Kailoon has to risk losing a pilot to take down an Aurigan ship?

The result was a completely shattered Zep, and another damaged shuttle on the human side.

At least the shuttle got away.

The attack seemed to be unstoppable at first. Kailoon repeated the maneuver, and the result was the same every single time. The Aurigans were not fast enough to teleport the GSRG or its projectiles before it fired, so they were guaranteed to lose a ship and could do nothing about it.

Yes. Show them.

Luray had never been the type who enjoyed being part of a cheering crowd, but watching this battle and understanding the thoughts and ideas Kailoon must be having was fascinating to her.

The next hit-and-run fighter tried to warp away, but something went wrong. The shuttle deactivated its warp drive again and was taken apart.

What happened? Did the Aurigans find a way to disrupt the warp field? This is bad.

A moment later, info popped up on the screen explaining in simple terms that teleportation and warp fields didn't mesh well together. The Aurigans could use it if they knew where the target was.

Each attack now resulted in a guaranteed lost Aurigan ship, and a most likely lost shuttle. A look at the numbers revealed what Kailoon would do: sacrifice all of them if necessary. The most optimistic outcome would be to have a handful of shuttles operational at the end.

Strangely, the pilots of the shot down shuttles were not marked as lost. Maybe the shuttles were put on autopilot before they started their attack? Whatever the reason, it wasn't mentioned on the screen. Kailoon kept attacking, losing shuttles, and causing losses, down to the very last ship.

She watched the number of enemy Zeps dwindle to the single digits, then less than half a dozen, and finally none.

In the end, only two fully operational shuttles were left, but the battle was won.

A big smile appeared on Luray's face. Kailoon did it. The enemy came with a new weapon, but despite that they still didn't win .

"Bin, can you send a message to him saying 'Good job'?"

"I will send him your greetings. May I include an invitation to a romantic dinner? He must have impressed you."

"You can include an invitation for a rematch."

"Message sent."

Luray flopped back on the bed feeling drained. Her official mission was almost over. Now it was clear that the colony was in danger. The Aurigans would come back to finish what they started. Earth would have to send more shuttles, increase the defenses, and invest a lot more in the colony to deal with the next attack. There was no doubt about that.

Lawyers would probably be hired to try to undo the damage her report would cause, but they wouldn't be able to force investors to come back. They would try to explain how the UEM could easily fend off an attack despite surprises, and that thanks to an excellent commander, everything would turn out fine, but who would believe them?

Of course, the military would want to keep the details of this battle a secret if they could. It didn't look good to almost lose against an enemy who was thought to be basically primitive by comparison. They would deploy their usual propaganda, presenting themselves as invincible; maybe present the teleporter as a new weapon.

"A message from the commander has arrived. He says he would love to accept your invitation if he could. You have to use the Slug and tell the UEM – he gave me the contact information of his 'favorite admiral' – that the colony was attacked and is probably under the control of the enemy. Immediate military assistance is required. They should spare no expense if they want to keep the colony. He also says you have about 15 minutes left."

What...? Why? There's nothing on the screen about that. Didn't we win?

Luray wanted to check what had happened, but the screen didn't react to any input.

"Bin, what's going on?"

"The screen is no longer connected to the command center. The connection was terminated after the battle was over."

Whatever the reason, I should go.

Luray left the room, leaving all her old clothes behind, but not without taking the remaining yellow and white pills out of her shoes and putting them into a pocket. It wasn't safe to use them for at least another day, but this was an emergency. She needed to be prepared.

Luray ran towards the underground hangar Kailoon had shown her, opened the door with Motwani's ID card and entered a large, dimly lit room. It was big, offering enough space for about ten shuttles, but only the Slug was there, waiting for her. Its door was already open. There was nobody else in sight.

"A new message from the commander. He says he will be busy defending the colony and can't afford to let anyone else do it for him. He asks you to get help as soon as you can."

What is going on? What is attacking us?

Luray arrived at the Slug, opened the door, and sat down on the commander's seat. Seatbelts may be for weaklings, but in this case, she would make an exception, be one, and use it.

Just as she was about to enter the first command, she noticed a small note attached to the keyboard.

'If you're reading this, it means it's getting quite dangerous – or we won, and I simply forgot the note here. In the first case, just run launch sequence #5; it will bring you into space as fast as possible. Once there switch the warp drive on. I could make a ton of suggestions about what you should do, but I think you'll manage better if I let you decide and authorize you as a user of the autopilot. Who knows what is going on outside right now?

In case of your survival, I would like to repeat my offer. We could really use people like you.'

Luray removed the note and navigated through the menu at what felt like the pace of a snail at first. This wasn't a standard interface, but since it more or less all made sense to her, she quickly found the option she was looking for. The hangar opened and revealed a long tunnel with a tiny light at its end.

The Slug accelerated towards the exit which became bigger and bigger. It took a whole minute to reach it.

> *How long is this tunnel? Are we inside a mountain? Is this where they started the construction? Makes sense; the inside is protected from heat, radiation, and the corrosive atmosphere.*

As the Slug finally exited the tunnel, Luray saw nothing but yellow, dense clouds around her. The shuttle's instruments were a bit more useful. The radar showed thousands of small dots on a map covering the area around the dome. What were these? They were moving about as fast as she was.

Luray zoomed out a bit. The dots were not simply at the dome; they were simultaneously attacking all the military bases as well. That meant they could fly. How did they bypass the orbital defenses?

> *Don't tell me we were right about the nanobots? They built an army below the ground, using that as a shield against our scans?*

The shuttle began to fly upwards while still being oriented parallel to the ground. For Luray, it felt like being in a high-speed elevator. She was pressed into the seat at five times the gravity she felt a moment before. If she had to enter commands now, that would be very difficult. Luckily, the navigational computer did everything by itself.

How high are these clouds? We must have already covered 20 kilometers.

The sense of acceleration grew weaker until it felt like normal gravity again. The Slug now accelerated forwards, and then kept going at a steady pace. It was aiming for the second nearest gate. In a minute or two, it would switch to warp drive, and Luray would be safe.

Then, an alarm sounded, and the screen showed a red dot next to the shuttle. Just as suddenly, it disappeared.

A drone? I can only hope it's not trying to destroy the shuttle. If it does that, I'm dead. On the display, it looked smaller than the bomber drones. Maybe it's a different type? Can I shoot it down?

Luray tried her best to find the menu option, not knowing if there even was one.

The Slug announced that an 'anomaly' had been detected ten meters from the ship. A few seconds later, a shudder went through the craft, followed by a rumbling sound.

It's trying to break through the hull to get me? That means I still have a chance. Now would be the time to risk an overdose....

Luray reached into her right pocket, grabbed all the yellow pills inside, and swallowed them. Four at once wasn't a harmless dose. It might cause some side effects later on, but right now, it didn't matter. She needed to be at her best.

Then, realizing that failure meant death, she decided to add one of the white pills. The first effects manifested themselves almost instantly. She could feel how everything around her slowed down, becoming simple, obvious, and easy.

If whatever was attacking the shuttle managed to damage the hull, she would need a helmet. Where was it? Would it fit to her current suit? Yes, it should. All the suits and armors were standardized. She could just open all the walls until one revealed a helmet.

After finding it on her first try and putting it on, Luray checked her surroundings, glancing left and right through the windows. The armor would not close completely until she was in space. As long as she was close to the planet, she could look outside, but all she saw was fog. In a single movement, she turned around and pointed her gun at the rear wall, but there was nothing there either.

Calm down. Think.

A few seconds passed. She didn't see it, but something was there. She could feel it. The shuttle was slowly waving up and down beneath her feet. Not enough to throw her off balance, but enough to force her to take a step to compensate. It was as if something strong and heavy was pushing and pulling the shuttle.

Where is it? On top? The windows are the weakest point, so why would an attacker ignore them?

As the shuttle stabilized itself again, Luray heard a monotone voice, similar to that of Bin, coming from the console.

"Direct contact detected. Switching to spherical view mode."

The walls and ceiling of the shuttle lit up, and after a few seconds they became transparent. Luray could see outside, no matter which direction she looked.

A transparent hull? No, not possible. Those are screens showing me what cameras on the outside record. But I still don't see an attacker. Why?!

Should she fire blindly? No, shooting against the armored ceiling would just be a waste of ammo. Shooting against the window would even be dangerous; shards could be pushed inside by the high pressure outside.

Her helmet enhanced the auditory input it received, and the drugs made her experience everything with extreme intensity. She could hear her own heart pumping as much blood as it could into all parts of her body. And there was something else: a screeching sound, coming from the top of the shuttle. A drill?

The helmet's display indicated the source of the sound, and Luray pointed her gun exactly at that spot. Firmly at first, but then her hands began to shake. She had no idea what was about to break in. The suit, monitoring her blood pressure, heart rate, and brain waves detected that she was about to panic and asked if a cocktail of drugs to calm her down and switch off pain receptors should be administered.

Luray refused. Mixing any more drugs into her body could kill her. She had to wait until her own would take full effect – but it was nice to know the military didn't shy away from poisoning their soldiers and even pilots.

With each second, the effects of her pills became stronger. She began to experience the passing of time more slowly, a more extreme version of what she was already used to. The sound of the drill overhead stretched and slowed down until it became strangely distorted.

Her hands stopped shaking. After a few seconds, they became almost perfectly static. All stray thoughts vanished. What was left in Luray's mind was a crystal-clear image of what was about to happen, down to the tiniest details. She felt everything at once. Her feet, how they were touching the ground, how the ground vibrated because of the drill – no, not just a drill, it was also hammering against the hull. The vibration made it into her feet, and she felt the waves travel up into her hands; she compensated for it by relaxing the rest of her body a bit, ready to shoot.

The seconds passed slowly, one after another, as she waited. The sound of the hammering gradually changed as the drill's tip was pushed deeper and deeper into the metal of the hull. A few more seconds until the hole would be complete, and at exactly that moment, she would shoot. It was her best option until she saw what she was up against.

At the same time, Luray realized what had happened earlier. Something had been climbing up the Slug's exterior. Her memory was as clear as everything else in her mind, and in front of her mental eye, she could see it – an alien drone, flying towards her shuttle, slowing down, then clamping on to it.

Whatever it was, it was cloaked. Now, with her enhanced sensory perception, she could discern the outline of something above her. There was a barely visible sheen between the body of the attacker and its background, as if it was made out of water, except that the distortion was almost invisible. Luray saw a sort of shadow attached to the edges of the shuttle using long flexible arms, its main body hovering directly above her.

The effect of the drugs became stronger. They made Luray feel like a super-soldier, as if nothing could harm her. There was no more room for fear or anxiety; her mind was focused only on the drone's potential weak points, seeing everything in slow motion.

I can hit the moving parts. The bullet will block its movements if it gets stuck. Or I can hit the drill. That might slow it down. It must have sensors. They must be exposed. I can hit them. If I shoot at it, the bullet will leave traces on its exterior, meaning I will be able to see it better.

Once the enemy was done drilling that hole, she wouldn't have to deal with it. It would have to deal with her.

Calm down. Do not become overconfident. Be calm. Be neutral. Do what needs to be done; not less, not more.

The sound of the drill changed, and as soon as it did Luray pulled the trigger. She got the timing right. The bullet hit the tip of the drill just as it tore through. The drone on top of the shuttle had no chance to evade.

Luray smiled and shot again. The tip broke off, and the drone was forced to pull it back out. At that exact moment, Luray fired once more. The bullet passed through the barely large enough hole and hit the drone's main body, causing a malfunction in the cloaking system. The drone started to flicker, sometimes becoming completely visible. For Luray, this was enough to see its structure. At the center was a sphere controlling four flexible arms. One of them had a drill. The others had something similar to large fingers, probably to grab objects or hold onto things.

The drone started to climb around the shuttle, causing it to slowly shake up and down again.

It lost its drill. It's going for the windows.

Luray's analysis was correct. The drone smashed one of its arms against the window, causing cracks to appear that grew with each blow.

The atmosphere is getting thin. It won't be a problem if I hold on to something.

As if reading her mind, the suit activated its magnetic boots at the exact moment the window broke. Luray fired as many shots as she could at the drone while being pulled in its direction for a split second. After the air had escaped, everything was calm. The only exceptions were her own breathing and the shockwave of the gun traveling through her body.

The bullets tore into her attacker. Damaged, the drone lost its grip and almost fell down but could grab on to the shuttle with one of its arms. Luray waited for it to reappear, ready to fire at its weak points again. Her last shots were a success if she judged the movements of the drone correctly. They had become clunky.

The drone did come back, and this time, Luray's shots finally were enough to disable the main body. The drone split itself apart, each still functional arm crawling individually to seek her out.

Luray fired at the incoming arms, hit one critically, but the other three reached her. One pierced through the armor, and seconds later, Luray's vision began to fade. The gun drifted from her hands.

It stung me. Poison? No, they could've killed me in other ways. It stopped moving but won't let go. Is it waiting for me to collapse? I feel dizzy. They want to abduct me. Why?

Luray's mind faded away

CHAPTER 2

THE PRISON - 1

When Luray finally opened her eyes again, she felt broken, out of energy. A bright light blinded her; she saw nothing but a blurry white something.

What happened?

The drug's effect had already worn off, and her body needed to recover. She was unable to move; every muscle hurt.

Ouch. Hypersensitivity. Side effect...

Luray tried to piece together what had happened, but her memory was still fuzzy.

I was observing the battle. Kailoon was winning it. What happened after that?

"Are you okay?"

Luray heard a voice but couldn't respond. Her body wouldn't move.

Sleep paralysis? The symptoms fit. I can move my eyes, but not my body.

"Ma'am?"

I went to the shuttle, I escaped. Did I reach the gate? No, something happened. I remember a machine attacking me.

There was someone right next to her. Luray could make out a part of his shape and then turned her eyes in his direction. The image was still blurry, but the man must have been at least two meters high.

A soldier? Did I get rescued?

Luray tried hard to move her head to the right. It still didn't work, but at least she began to feel her fingers again, even though they felt as if they were wrapped in foam.

Better than nothing. At least I still have them.

She was on a simple bed, next to a white wall. Looking up, she could see that the room had a light gray ceiling. For some reason, it was reflective. Thanks to that, Luray could see the room's full contents. She observed her environment as well as she could, given her inability to move.

Everything was clean, sterile. While the hazy vision and sleep paralysis were annoying, they were also a good sign. If those were her only complaints, it meant her body had metabolized enough of the drugs before they became toxic. She might show withdrawal symptoms soon, but that was a secondary concern right now.

Luray could make out the outline of the person speaking to her more precisely now. It was an extremely muscular man. Clearly a soldier, like the ones she saw back on EE-297, maybe even a bit bulkier. He was wearing a simple white uniform, no patterns on it. It was a bit loose, somewhat hiding the true shape of his body.

"Miss, are you okay?"

The soldier repeated the question after Luray finally managed to turn her head and look directly at him.

"Yes, I think so."

Her voice sounded weird, even with all the effort she put into it.

At least something came out.

She tried to sit up, but the pain in her muscles prevented her from bending up even a little.

No choice here, I'll have to sit this one out. The pain should go away gradually. In a few hours, I should be fine.

At least she was still alive. After focusing on the soldier next to her, she could finally see that something was written on his uniform: the number 312. A quick glance down showed something similar on her own; it read 667.

"Are we prisoners?"

"Yes, ma'am."

So they took at least 667 prisoners? Most of them should be soldiers – the civilians should have been safe under the dome. Or there are many more prisoners elsewhere, and I was just among the first.

The pristine white prison cell – Luray was reminded of hospital rooms – had two doors. One was closed, with a keypad next to it. Another was open and separated a toilet and a shower from the rest of the space. In total, there were four beds.

The Aurigans went through the trouble of building a prison specifically to accommodate human prisoners? What is going on here? Why take prisoners in the first place?

"I need to speak to our captors," she decided. "Maybe I can negotiate something."

Luray tried to sit up again, but that was still impossible, even with the soldier's help.

Alright then, I'll just keep lying here for a while.

After realizing that he couldn't help, the soldier went back to the bed on the opposite side of the room. Luray carefully turned her head in his direction to get a better view.

At least I can move that much.

"What's your name, soldier?"

"I am Steve. Please don't try anything. You don't know what they will do if you cause trouble."

I didn't even get up. Am I that notorious already?

Luray could see fear in the man's face. He was obviously leery of antagonizing the Aurigans, but he looked perfectly fine. If nothing had been done to him so far, what was he frightened of?

"I am Luray. Luray Ulyssa Cayenne."

The soldier looked as if hearing the name confused him somehow. Maybe he had never heard it before? It wasn't very common, so that might be an explanation.

Luray's eyes flickered around the stark environment. "How do they treat their prisoners? What can you tell me?"

She slowly felt herself regaining more and more control over her voice. If her physical condition kept improving at this rate, then she would be able to get up in maybe ten minutes.

She waited for a response but was only met with silence.

"Steve?"

He didn't answer. Luray couldn't tell why exactly, but the soldier clearly was afraid of something.

"Answer me, soldier. Every bit of information is important if we want to escape."

His slightly bent posture suddenly straightened. Did her way of speaking cause that? Was it his brainwashing? Luray had no idea how exactly it worked. Maybe he was conditioned to follow a leader and didn't consider her one at first, but now he did?

Whatever the case, the man saluted Luray, who was still lying in her bed, then spoke in a loud and clear voice.

"Steve Morgan, Second Force B, Rank four. We were a group of four, defending the North Pole military base together with ten other squads. The outer ring of the base was overrun; we had to fall back to the main building. I am one of the few that didn't make it. I expected to be killed when one of their drones got me, but instead, I was brought here."

Now that is more helpful. I don't know how the military is organized, but I'll just assume each squad is a Force, and they are numbered.

"Continue. What happened next?"

"I don't remember how I got here. I was knocked out during battle. Once we were captured, they locked the four of us in here. Then they asked for the gate address and began to torture us."

Torture? Not good. Not good at all. But ... I don't see any injuries on him.

"Why are you not injured?"

For a second, Steve paused as if he had to find the right words to excuse his unharmed state.

"I don't know, ma'am. They took us one by one and brought us back a few hours later – beaten, bleeding, sometimes limbs were broken or missing. We could never remember what happened. Sometimes when they took one of us who was already wounded, they brought him back with no injuries, and no memories of anything at all!"

So they treat grave injuries to allow the torture to continue? And they can even regrow limbs? We can do that too, but ... he was talking as if it happened in a short time frame. He can't have been here for more than a day or so. Even if I took forever to wake up, it can't be longer... I can tell because of the side effects. They're punctual.

"What about you?" she asked in a softer tone of voice. "Is that why you're not hurt? They healed you?"

"Yes, ma'am. I was healed two times, according to my cellmates. After that, they took everyone else away, and I have been alone for a few hours until they brought you."

I see.

"How long have you been here, in total?"

"I don't know, ma'am. When I was brought back, all of us had lost our memory at least once."

"Give me an estimation. How often did they torture you; how long did it take?"

"About two hours every time."

So I was asleep for about a day. Everything fits.

"I assume you did not give them the Earth gate address?"

"Of course not, ma'am. We cannot do that. No soldier knows it."

Ah, yes, right. It's stored in the computers, and you need one of the higher-ups to decrypt it. My guess is Kailoon would delete the data if he had a high chance of losing the battle. Which means...

A weak smile appeared on Luray's face. For his part, Steve couldn't possibly have had any idea why a woman who had just learned that she was about to be tortured would have any reason to smile, but he said nothing.

"Bin?"

"I am here."

"Can you guess what I'm thinking?"

"You want to know if I still have the gate address data. Yes, it is in my memory. You also do not want to ask the question directly because you fear you might be under surveillance."

"I knew I could count on you."

The soldier looked confused. Had he never seen a civilian with an implant? Luray made a gesture to let him know that he should wait for a moment so she could listen to Bin.

"It is only a matter of time until our captors realize I exist. Once they do, they will attempt to extract the data from my memory, and they will be able to reconstruct the address. I suggest we encrypt everything I know about it using an additional password that you tell me. I will then delete my knowledge of this password. That way, we both need to be kept alive. Do you agree?"

This is probably my best move right now. The gate address is my bargaining chip. I can openly admit that I know it. Given my importance, the Aurigans should not kill me, even if I try to escape. Once I tell them I am the only one who can give them what they want, they will focus on the gate address. As long as I pose no direct threat to them, maybe I can even do… well, something. As long as I have the gate address, they need me.

Steve didn't interrupt the conversation. He probably knew what Luray was talking to, and that gave him hope.

"Yes, I agree."

"We need to use a safe password to encrypt the address. It must be something long to be secure. I suggest the lyrics of a song that you remember precisely, or a poem. I will make suggestions. Hum once for yes and do nothing for no."

Luray avoided eye contact with Steve, which worked exactly as she expected. He waited, and Bin went through a list of things he had in his cache. In the end, they agreed on the title song of an old movie that Luray had watched multiple times. Bin encrypted the gate address data and deleted all knowledge about the movie from his database just in case.

Once Luray was done preparing her bargaining chip, she looked back at Steve, who perked up from his trance-like state.

"I need to talk to our captors. How do I do that?"

"I don't know, ma'am. We always refused to talk. UEM policy. Us soldiers never negotiate with the enemy. Only our superiors are qualified for that."

Luray still felt pain in her legs, arms, and mostly her back, but managed to stand up for a moment despite that, even if slowly. The more she moved, the faster her body would get back to its normal state, but for now, she still had to sit on the bed.

If the soldiers all never said a word, and all civilians that might have gotten captured don't have a clue how to even get the gate address, I am the only one who has it. I should be a special case. Maybe I can weasel my way out of here.

As they waited, Luray's limbs slowly recovered. She could stand up on her own after 15 more minutes, then made a few careful steps, sometimes requiring Steve's assistance. The entire room was about five times five meters across, quite big for a simple cell, and Luray was happy about that. She could walk without fear of bumping into something accidentally.

If you can afford to waste an entire fleet, I guess building a big cell is in the budget as well.

The toilet also stood out. Not only was it in a separate room, but it also could clean itself – and its user – with a stream of water and something that smelled like a mix of soap and disinfectant.

This is really, really weird. They want to erase us from history, but then their cells are bigger than an average flat back on Earth? And what's with the ridiculous luxury toilets?

Luray checked everything in the two rooms very carefully as she continued to interrogate her fellow prisoner.

"What can you tell me about the Aurigans, Steve?"

"I know nothing about them."

Nothing?

"How can you know nothing? You've been tortured a few times, and you talked to your squad."

"I lost my memory, ma'am."

I forgot about that. How ironic. It'll be difficult to squeeze anything useful out of him.

The next few hours went by without anything of interest happening. Luray focused on her recovery by doing as many movements as she could to get all her muscles back into shape without causing herself too much pain.

Once she regained a bit of her flexibility, she inspected the parts of the room that were harder to reach. The light overhead was of a medium intensity, and it had gotten a bit dimmer since she woke up. The color wasn't entirely white anymore, but instead had a slight yellowish red tinge.

Do they mimic Earth's day-night cycle? What for? To make us feel better between the torture sessions?

The mattress on her bed was extremely flexible. When she first woke up she couldn't feel it, but now she realized that this bed was on the level of what only the upper class back on Earth could afford.

Suddenly, the light switched from natural warm white to red for a few seconds, then back to its evening color, and a female voice started to speak. Luray tried to make out where it was coming from but couldn't.

Multiple loudspeakers in all corners, maybe?

"Please position yourselves against the wall opposite the door. A guard will open it in a moment. All guards have been instructed to shoot non-compliant prisoners instantly."

Better do what they say for now.

The door opened slowly. A silent mechanism pulled it into the wall.

The door must weigh at least 200 kg. Do they use magnets to make it float?

After the cell door opened, a few additional bars retracted out of the way one after another. Nothing could be done to this barrier with brute force; it would definitely resist. The guard that appeared in the doorframe was a 2.5-meter humanoid machine. It had a head, arms, and legs, just like a human. There were even five fingers on each hand, and the proportions matched.

This looks like a suit with a person inside. Are there human guards here? No, that wouldn't make any sense, now, would it?

"Prisoner 667, follow me."

The robot – or maybe suit – turned around. Its movements seemed a bit slow, especially compared to the elegant acrobatics of Luray's previous attacker, as if the robot was a lot heavier than it looked. Maybe it was; no way to tell.

Luray looked towards Steve, who just nodded. Then she followed the robot out of the cell, checking her surroundings as soon as she could.

I need to gather as much info as I can and give Bin as many visuals as possible. He might spot something that I miss.

There was nothing that could be used as a weapon, and no potential hiding place was in sight. Not that she even thought it would work, but you never know until you try. The robot walked ahead of her at a steady pace, constantly leaving a few meters between them and facing backwards to keep her in sight. The exact moment Luray left the cell, the door behind her closed in a split second. Had Steve tried to follow her, he would have been first impaled and then squished.

So blocking the door with the bed won't work. If we want to prevent it from closing, we need massive steel or something like that.

"Where are we going?"

It can't hurt to get some information. Maybe they will directly bring me to someone I can talk to?

The suit responded in an almost human voice, but it sounded distorted.

"You will be scanned. Then you will be interrogated."

Where are we? There's gravity, just like on Earth, and this place doesn't seem to be small. Huge warp fields are unstable, so this must be a rotating space station, or we're on a planet. But this is clearly built for humans, or at least humanoid life forms. How likely is it that Aurigans are like us?

"I want to talk to your superior. I have information for him."

"The interrogator will decide that."

This isn't a robot. It's a suit. There is someone inside.

After a minute of walking through tight hallways with a dozen of what Luray assumed to be cell doors, the exosuit stopped in front of one room in particular with 'Scan Room' in Aurigan letters written on it. The guard held his hand in front of what looked like an ID card reader. He then turned to address her.

"Go inside and follow the operator's instructions. If you disobey, you will be shot. Your safety is not guaranteed if you do not cooperate."

What a weird way to say that. My safety?

There were no extra bars for security, and the door slid open. Inside sat a perfectly normal human man in a gray suit on a perfectly normal chair. Luray didn't know what to say or think. She looked at the elderly man who stood up to operate a machine set against the wall of the otherwise almost empty chamber. It looked like an MRI scanner, while he himself appeared to be of Chinese heritage.

How is this possible? Are Aurigans human? Are these the people who switched sides?

The room had something that looked like a cross between a desk and a one-meter-high wall. There were screens on it displaying something written in Aurigan, but Luray didn't have the time to read it. She would ask Bin about it later.

"You must be the new one," the operator spoke. He sounded very casual and behaved as if it was a part of his normal daily life to scan prisoners that were brought in. "Lie down here, and we will make a quick scan. It will only take a few minutes."

He didn't seem to feel the need to explain anything; not why he was human nor what the scan was for.

Luray stayed where she was by the door. "I need to talk to your superior."

The man gave Luray a fake smile and pointed at a platform that slid out of the machine. "Only the interrogator can decide that.

You will talk to him soon, right after the scan. So please, lie down now."

If a scan is all you need, then fine.

Luray lay down on the platform, and the machine pulled her back in. It felt like being trapped in a pipe.

To her alarm, she realized that her body was unable to move, as if it had been switched off. The strange machine began to make all kinds of noises while the operator typed on a keyboard. Luray couldn't see anything from the inside, only hear and try to guess what was going on.

Then, after just a moment, the platform slid out again.

"All done," her captor nodded. "As I told you, it didn't take long. Guard, she is ready for the interrogation."

The man wore the exact same fake smile as before as he turned to inspect one of the bigger screens attached to the wall. Luray didn't have the time to read everything; all she could make out was that her scan was successful, and that Bin had been discovered.

I knew it was inevitable, but that was fast.

The guard led her along another corridor until they reached 'Interrogation Room #2.' Its door opened like the one before; there were no extra security bars. The interior looked similar to the 'Scan Room,' but with a table instead of the scanner. There were some belts attached to it, obviously meant for tying people down.

This is bad. I hope they ask first and torture later.

Luray started to shiver as she saw it. Her instincts screamed to run away, but she knew it was useless as long as the guard was behind her.

The interrogator turned out to be an old skinny man with very pale skin who must have been at least in his seventies. He was wearing the typical surgeon's coat you saw in all those hospital soap series, right down to the white mask and rubber gloves.

I feel like I've seen him before. Where was that? On the colony, I'm sure. I passed by him at some point, but I don't know his name or who he is.

A bunch of knives and scissors hung from the ceiling. Part of Luray imagined being cut into pieces by them while the rest of her brain tried to find a way to grab one and threaten the interrogator. There was a rather long knife she already had in mind for that, but the guard had to leave first.

Okay, let's try to negotiate.

"I have information for your superiors," Luray said in a voice that came out sounding nervous, to her dismay. "I need to talk to them."

The interrogator noticed her anxiety. "We will see about that. First, the standard procedure will make sure there is no misunderstanding. I think there is no reason to tell you my name just yet, is there?"

He looked at the guard and then continued to talk. "No, there isn't. There never is the first time. Let's begin."

He grabbed the large knife that Luray had set her eyes on and pointed it at her with a mild look. "Tell me the gate address and you will not suffer. Refuse, and I will have to torture you until you give it to me, or your body gives up. But before that, swallow this."

251

He reached into his pocket and threw a small white pill to Luray. She caught it and regarded him warily.

"Well, of course you don't have to," the interrogator added. "We won't force you, but we highly advise it. This pill will prevent the formation of new memories so you won't be traumatized by what I am obliged to do to you."

Obliged? This doesn't sound good. I need that knife.

"You see, it's part of our moral code to never inflict lasting mental harm," he explained. "But the experience of being tortured can cause trauma – so to continue with our interrogations in an ethically desirable way, we always offer this pill to our prisoners on every occasion. If you refuse, that is your choice. So, do you want to take it?"

I think I want to avoid the torture altogether.

"I have the address, but I won't give it to you for free."

Stay calm.

Luray's voice was unusually weak. She had been under pressure before, but not like this – unknown place, unknown time, surrounded by torture devices.

"My only chance to get out of here is to sell the address in exchange for my freedom," she continued shakily. "No matter what you do to me, I will not talk. You must understand that you have to make a deal."

If that doesn't work, I'll go for the knife.

"This is my last offer."

Luray said it not only because it was true but also to calm herself down and to make her intentions clear. She had to use her only bargaining chip wisely, and hopefully avoid the terrible things this crazy surgeon had in store for her.

The old man gave no response to her ultimatum. He merely took another pill out of his pocket and swallowed it himself.

"I don't want to remember the horrors I am unfortunately forced to perform," he sighed. "I suggest you do the same. The pill will prevent long-term memories from being formed, starting in about five minutes, and the effects will last about an hour. If you don't want to take it, we can get started right away."

Bin won't be affected by the pill. It should be safe to use it. He can tell me everything I need to know later.

Luray swallowed her pill as well. Still, she made no move to approach the table.

Her elderly tormentor turned away, then hesitated, peering back at her over one shoulder. "Is there any method of torture you cannot stand at all? I should start with that; it saves a lot of time. Please lie down on the table now. I want to tell the guard to leave. It wouldn't be good for his mental health if he had to observe extreme violence."

What is going on here? Am I trapped in some weird nightmare? He doesn't really expect an answer, does he?

When Luray remained unmoving, the surgeon took a few steps towards her, still holding the same knife she had been hoping to use on him. He pointed the blade at her, and it seemed longer than before.

The blade can extend?

The surgeon stepped forward. The tip of the now one-meter long sword thrust into her shoulder without the tiniest bit of

253

resistance. Luray jumped back quickly enough to avoid a deep wound.

"Wait, wait!" she shouted desperately, clasping a hand to the wound. "I'm the only one who knows the gate address. If you torture me, I won't tell you. I will fight back, and if you kill me, you'll never get it!"

Luray was talking fast, half-panicking as they circled one another warily. She had never been in a situation like this before. It was absurdly surreal.

The surgeon spoke something in Aurigan, which Bin translated to, "Guard, leave us alone now."

What should I do? His sword is too dangerous. I can't even touch it. All weapons are out of range. I'm still not in perfect shape. What can I do at all? Even if he's old and slow, with that weapon, I have no chance of beating him.

Luray had until the door was closed to come up with a plan. Abruptly she raised her hands in surrender and took a few steps back towards the table. He paused, considering her.

"Okay, I'll cooperate. I'll forget all of it anyway, right?"

She pretended to lie down on the table, but then jumped over it. As long as she was on the opposite side, the extendible weapon couldn't reach her. Anything was better than being tortured.

The surgeon didn't do what Luray had hoped. He did not give her a chance to reach one of the other torture devices to fight back. He did not run around the table. Instead, with a single swing, he slashed it in two as if it was made out of foam.

What...?

Luray's eyes widened. As dangerous as this weapon was, if she could get her hands on it, then she could probably cut the doors of the cells with it. With some luck, maybe she could even escape.

I need that sword. He's slow and my wound isn't very deep. I should be able to win a fight once I get anything between my hands. He'll be no match for me.

The broken table was still blocking the surgeon. The two separated pieces held each other up, at least for now. A single push and the balance would be gone.

Cut it a few more times. That will give me something to throw at you.

Luray tried to provoke the surgeon by feinting toward him. She didn't want to get too close, given how easily he could cut her into pieces, but she had to take a risk.

It worked. The surgeon hit the table a second time. A triangular piece fell next to Luray's foot. She quickly picked it up, though she was slowed by the pain in her shoulder and because of her drug overdose. The surgeon could see that she was faltering, and somehow, he seemed to take pity on her and stopped going after her for a split second. It was enough for Luray to come up with her next move.

Should I roll below the broken table? No, I might be too slow. I need a diversion. I need something bigger than this small chunk.

Then it became obvious to her. People really became dumb under stress, and she was no exception. The table itself, or rather half of it, was exactly what she needed. She grabbed the part in front of her and charged towards her attacker like a battering ram. The man didn't know how best to react in this situation; he just stumbled away, pushed back by the table. Then he collided with a wall, and even as he realized she had cornered him they slammed into one another.

Luray lifted the table and drove it down against the surgeon's body as hard as she could, driving it into his spindly chest with the severed edge, hoping he would drop the blade. A choked, strangling sound came from his throat, and his eyes momentarily rolled up in his head.

Then Luray suddenly fell to the ground. Confused, she tried to get up but it didn't work. Something was wrong. Her lower body did not respond.

Why can't I...?

Luray looked back at her legs. They were no longer there. Instead, two severed limbs lay to either side. She had not even felt the cut.

This can't be happening!

After a moment, an overwhelming pain roared across her entire waist, stronger than she ever knew possible. Her body lay on the ground next to her fallen enemy. All Luray could see was a blurry image of the room spinning, then nothing.

THE PRISON - 2

L uray opened her eyes. The last thing she remembered was being put into a scanner by a strange man, but now she was back in her dimly lit cell.

What happened? I don't remember any interrogation. Did they torture me and erase my memory? That should mean I didn't give them the gate address; otherwise I would be dead.

She smiled. Being here after losing her memory was a success, albeit a small one. It meant that whatever the interrogator had tried didn't work. He didn't manage to break her. If she could resist once, then she would be able to resist again, thanks to the mental reset. The effects of the torture wouldn't accumulate. She wouldn't be afraid of the unknown; she was now confident in her ability to endure it.

She must have admitted having data about the address, which should have made the interrogator go all out on his first attempt, and yet here she was. This was good – probably.

Maybe she would get a chance to use her bargaining chip next time. But why didn't it work before? She had no idea. All she knew for sure was that the worst-case scenario was avoided.

Her body was in better shape than before; she could get up on her own without trouble. Steve was also in the cell, sitting on his bed and looking at the ground. He seemed to be thinking about something, not noticing that Luray was already awake until she spoke to him. "Hey, soldier."

Steve looked in her direction. "Did they erase your memory, ma'am? They brought you back, but you weren't injured."

He seems surprised. Why?

"Yes, they did. This never happened the first time?"

"No, never. They always interrogated us at least three times before healing us."

So I'm a special case, but the memory loss is a problem; I really need more details.

"Bin, can you tell me what happened?"

"I am afraid I can't. I have no information about what happened immediately after the scan. Once I became operational again, I could only record auditory input since your eyes were closed. Judging by the sounds, you were in a different room, then transported here by two guards. I do not know what happened between the scan and my reactivation."

This is strange. I can understand losing my memory; it happens to everyone. But why Bin too? Maybe the scan crashed him? Who knows how the scanner works. Oh well, if that's the reason, then it won't happen again. They already scanned me.

"Run a full system check."

"Yes. It will take about 20 minutes."

258

Luray got up and moved to stand in front of Steve, whose face was on the same level as hers even though he was seated.

"Steve, were all of you scanned at first? Before the first interrogation, I mean?"

"Yes, ma'am. As far as I know, this is how it always happened."

I suppose one scan is enough. What was this for, anyway? Is it necessary to know how to heal me after the interrogation? To reconstruct my body? Does this mean they fix the damage cell by cell? Maybe they printed everything that got damaged too much and replaced parts of my body.

"Everyone was only scanned once?"

"Yes, ma'am."

And you didn't think that worth mentioning? It's no wonder Kailoon doesn't like soldiers. This guy might know something important and not even realize it.

"Tell me everything; what the others told you, every detail you remember, even if it seems irrelevant."

If I have to, I will babysit you through this.

It took a while to squeeze the key information out of Steve. Everybody got scanned at first. Then they were brought into torture chambers and offered a pill that made them forget what happened. They lost their memories at different points after taking the pill. From what Steve told her, Luray could deduce that they all were brought to the same – or at least an identical – interrogation room.

This is unbelievable. How could he just skip that before, as if it was irrelevant? They really accept every idiot as a soldier.

"Was that everything?"

"Yes, ma'am."

> *Maybe it's to avoid moral dilemmas? I mean, if your average soldier is as smart as a monkey, sacrificing them becomes less of an issue. You could easily argue that their lives have less value because their contribution to society, apart from being sent into battle, is zero. I hope this guy will be of use later.*

Luray was strangely tired despite having just woken up. What time was it? Did that even have any importance here? The cell's lights were getting darker with each passing minute. Then a small hole in the wall behind her opened, revealing a few small packages and bottles.

> *I suppose this is food?*

Luray picked a box at random and opened it. She could hardly believe her eyes. Inside was a bowl of Trans-Himalayan soup, and it smelled fantastic. She opened the other packages as well and tried a bit from each, not hiding at all how much she enjoyed the food, while Steve stared at her. Luray had not realized how hungry she was until the food was presented.

> *This is better than what you can get back on Earth, if you don't want to spend your entire salary in a few days. How did they make this, and why? They must have gotten it out of one of the databases, but how did they grow the ingredients? And why would they? What is going on here?*

Luray couldn't understand at all what this meant. She also had no idea why Steve didn't mention this obvious oddity and decided to completely ignore him from now on, except if absolutely unavoidable. She gave him the food she liked the least and a bottle without commenting on his mental capacity, then emptied one package after another.

This is, if I am not mistaken, a soup based on a Tibetan recipe whose name I can't pronounce, but it's spelled འཇེན་ཐུག་*. I saw a picture of it in the cafeteria. Are these supplies from the planet? They must be; I don't see where else the Aurigans could have gotten them. But that would mean the colony has fallen. No, it's all too fast. I just got here.*

The light eventually went off almost completely. Luray could feel the temperature drop a bit.

This doesn't make sense. They're treating us as if this were an expensive hotel. They put a lot of effort into our comfort, and yet they torture us. What kind of logic is that?

Luray put the empty packages and bottles back where they came from and lay down. She could no longer see the ceiling; everything was almost pitch black.

Tomorrow I should try to talk to them. I don't see a reason why they wouldn't agree to a negotiation. If I understand how they think, maybe I can get somewhere.

Lying on the bed, Luray enjoyed the feeling of being full and unable to swallow another bite. She tried her best to come up with potential explanations, but no matter how long and hard she thought about it, she couldn't make sense of her situation. They were treated extremely well inside their cells but mercilessly tortured once they left.

I think 20 minutes are over now.

"Bin, did you figure out why you can't remember anything?"

"No, I am afraid I have not been able to find the cause. It is as if I was forcefully switched off and on again at a later point. Even my internal chronometer was deactivated."

The chronometer was stopped? Wasn't it based on some quantum effect or an atomic vibration or something like that?

"I thought that was impossible without destroying it."

"I would suspect that the scan had a destructive side effect on me and that I was repaired later on, after the interrogation. It is off by several hours, so the easiest explanation is that I was damaged by the scan and later repaired. If we assume the Aurigans use nanotechnology for this, they might have healed you and repaired me the same way."

Hmm... so maybe I didn't have Bin during the interrogation?

"You think they noticed you were broken and reconstructed you from scratch using the scan data?"

"That seems likely. I am partially a quantum computer. Scanning my internal states cannot be done without modifying them. I might have been damaged unintentionally because the scan randomized my working memory. But do not worry, the encrypted gate data is intact."

It makes sense that Bin would be fixed while I was still unconscious.

Luray waved her hand in front of her face. She couldn't make out any detail. It was absolutely dark now.

I always wondered how I would react in extreme situations. Would I be able to keep it together, or give up? I've never been abducted before, let alone by aliens. I would say I'm doing quite well, considering the potential hopelessness of my situation. It might be impossible to escape from here, negotiations might fail – but I did not break down. This is good. If there is a chance to escape, we might find it. I must not give up, no matter what happens. The moment I do, I will die here.

262

After repeating this to herself a few times, Luray's mind faded away. The next simulated morning, she was woken by a metallic voice that told them to stand back from the door again.

She and Steve did as they were told. The cell opened, but instead of a huge, menacing robot, in stepped a relatively skinny male human, smaller than Steve. He was wearing a red suit covering his entire body and a helmet. But what stood out was a gun on his belt.

"Prisoner 7…"

Without warning Steve made a dash towards the guard, who immediately drew his gun and fired.

Wha…?! Idiot! You had no plan!

A small dart hit the soldier's arm. He ignored it, kept running towards the guard, and tried to land a few hits with his fists.

I should just stand here. If I try to help him now, we'll probably both be punished. Even if we knock this guard out, we have no plan, and I can't imagine the Aurigans just letting us roam around for long.

While Steve was significantly larger, the guard was quicker – inhumanly so. His movements were efficient. He made only a few small changes in his posture to block Steve's blows.

His arms don't move at all when Steve hits them. Is he an android? Some kind of genetically engineered Aurigan soldier? Or is it just the suit?

The guard defended himself for only a few seconds. Then whatever poison or drug was in the dart quickly took effect. Steve lost his balance and toppled to the ground.

I know I should have pity for him, but he was really asking for it. And he'll still be there later, so nothing is lost.

The sedative bolt stuck out of his arm. Luray could see it clearly from her position. It was a transparent tube filled with liquid. Half of its contents was still there.

Hmm, this could be useful. If only the guard would look away for a second, I could fetch the dart and hide it somewhere.

"Prisoner 741, please come with me."

Please? Aren't we polite…

The guard's voice was metallic, and Luray could hear a different voice speaking as well. The helmet probably translated what he said from Aurigan. The real, muffled voice sounded familiar, but Luray couldn't remember where she had heard it before.

Wait, 741? But my number is…

Luray looked down to be sure. Her uniform indeed had 741 printed on it. Wasn't it 667 before? Did she remember it incorrectly? Or did they change her uniform? Did the numbers increase after each interrogation? Steve could probably have told her, had he been paying attention. Luray concluded from her past experiences with him that she shouldn't even bother trying.

"Prisoner 741, please obey. If you do not comply, you will be shot."

This is my chance. If I play this right, I might be able to get that sedative. Let's hope he doesn't try to collect his dart later.

She slowly stood up. The guard was pointing his gun at her. Luray had to be careful now. If her attempt was too obvious, he would see it, but if she was too hesitant, she might not be able to get a chance to grab the dart.

Luray took a few cautions steps forward. As she drew near, however, her head turned to the unconscious Steve. Luray tried her best to put on a concerned look by imagining what would happen if her plan were to fail. After being sure the guard saw it, she quickly knelt next to the soldier, checking his pulse and lifting his eyelids.

If that guard doesn't buy my act, he'll shoot me, but I need this dart. No choice here.

"Prisoner 741, your interrogation time is limited. I used a tranquilizer, so there is no need to worry. Just leave him here."

"I would prefer to see that for myself," she responded in a firm voice without turning around. To her relief the guard made no attempt to interrupt her.

"Lying is forbidden for all members of the Aurigan Empire. Feel free to confirm that what I said is true, if you must."

I lucked out.

The guard's unexpected leniency allowed Luray to quickly remove the dart from Steve's arm. Thinking fast, she slipped it into the pocket of his uniform and turned around.

"So he will he be alright?"

"Absolutely," the no longer quite as patient guard responded. "Now please–"

"Yes, I'm coming."

I just have to hope if someone comes to retrieve the dart later, they'll assume this guy took it with him, and vice-versa.

The guard directed Luray through a few hallways until they arrived at a sealed door. Her captor then waved a hand in front of the pane while keeping his gun trained on Luray.

Interrogation Room #5, eh? How busy are they with their prisoners? How many are there, anyway?

She noticed a small gray dot on the inside of his gloved palm. Maybe that was the key? If she could get the glove, perhaps she could escape.

Slow down. I'm getting ahead of myself. I need a plan and more information. The negotiation comes first.

The door silently opened by sliding into the wall, revealing a spotless round chamber about five meters across with a table in the center. To Luray's surprise, a woman was already strapped to it, unmoving. Next to her stood a man dressed like a surgeon about to operate. He was putting his gloves on while staring at the dozen cutting tools that hung from the ceiling.

Are they held up by magnets?

Luray didn't have enough time to analyze the situation before the guard spoke brusquely.

"Enter. *Please.*"

She did as she was told. Once inside, the guard closed the door from the outside.

A torture table with restraints. Some parts of the edges are missing. Have they been cut? The torturer appears weak, but so did the guard. I can't attack him carelessly. Some of the torture instruments are knives; I need one if I want to put up a serious fight. The woman on the table has no visible injury. Her eyes are open, but her face shows no expression. Is she sedated? Why is she here?

Luray took a few steps into the room. Maybe the 'surgeon' would say something.

The first time they tortured me, it didn't work. So they've changed their strategy. They'll do it to someone else and force me to watch. They're testing what works on me. No matter what they do, I must not give in.

The surgeon selected what looked like a one-meter long sword, then pointed it at Luray. He wore a mask; only the upper half of his face was visible.

He looks old. And his movements just now, they're different from how the guard acted to defend himself against Steve. This guy moves just like an old man. His age is affecting his flexibility. I can beat him.

"Welcome to my domain. I am Krov, first interrogator of the glorious Aurigan Empire, which at this moment spans 143 solar systems in the Andromeda galaxy where we are now, and three in the Milky Way."

Lots of territory. Makes sense that they can waste some ships then. But why would he tell me that? Wait – Krov? That rude scientist I ran into right before the attack?! But last time I saw him, he was at least 15 years younger. I need to piece together how much time has really passed.

"We will conquer your civilization and make it a part of our own, as we did with many others before. You have the glory of welcoming this new age as one of the last native-born humans." Krov was waving his arms passionately, ending this tirade by raising them in worship to the heavens.

"There are gates in the Andromeda galaxy?" Luray asked.

"Yes. At this moment we are in the very core of the Aurigan Empire, orbiting their new home star."

New? Orbiting? Why didn't he just say, "We are on the planet?" Are we in space? Then why is there gravity? This place doesn't seem like a space station... the walls are massive and the gravity is like on Earth. Warp fields can't explain this. How does this work?

"I know you have the gate address of Earth." Krov had descended from his moment of ecstasy and now regarded her sternly. "You will give it to me. Until you do, I will be forced to inflict mental pain on you and physical pain on this woman. Unfortunately, given what we know so far about humans, it is the most efficient way to get you talking if bribery is not an option. You wouldn't remember this, but the last time you apparently gave me... quite a bit of trouble, so I will use a different approach. This woman here..."

Krov pointed at the hostage. Luray didn't recognize her. The only hint she had was the number 559 on her clothes. Another prisoner, that much was clear. She wasn't reacting to anything, and her face seemed to be immobilized. Even her eyes were just staring forward.

She is completely paralyzed but still conscious. That is the only scenario that makes sense.

Luray examined the walls and ceiling. If she could grab one of the weapons, then she would definitely be able to incapacitate Krov. His body posture implied a back problem, he wore no apparent armor and should be slow and clumsy in a fight.

"Look at me when I speak to you, human!"

Aren't you a human yourself?

Krov seemed quite annoyed, but then calmed down again. His eyes above the mask had narrowed slyly.

"I know what you are thinking. You want to steal one of my toys. Go ahead. As long as they are attached to the ceiling, they will give you an electric shock. This is why I am wearing these gloves. Now, if you would be so kind as to go behind the table…"

I need to get the weapon you are already holding then. That makes things more difficult.

Krov used his blade to indicate the way. He wanted her to go to the edge of the room farthest from the door. Krov was probably planning on closing her escape route while being in an ideal position to start torturing the captive. Luray did as he told her. Once she was facing him, he positioned himself beside the table.

"This is an ultra-sharp Aurigan sword. Not many are allowed to own one of these, but I was given special permission to use it. Its edge is only a single atom wide, see?"

He rotated it so that Luray could see how thin it was. It became almost invisible.

Won't it break easily?

"It is so thin that it can cut everything as if it were, how do you call that again… margarine."

To prove this claim, Krov held the sword above an edge of the table, and then let it glide down. A small section was sheared clean off and fell to the ground.

So that's where all the edges went. If I could get that weapon…

"Now, let us begin."

Krov pushed the meter-long scalpel effortlessly a few centimeters into the captive woman's side and drew it back out. There was no reaction from her at all.

Krov watched Luray carefully, alert to any sign she might be affected by his actions.

"Prisoner 559 is, as you hopefully have guessed, paralyzed. We developed a drug specifically for that. She cannot move, but still feels everything I do to her with increased intensity. The drug also prevents her from passing out. This means I can make her experience as much pain as necessary until you talk. I do not want to do that, but only you can prevent it. I am only allowed to stop once you give me the gate address."

Before Luray could respond, Krov gave an annoyed sigh, then rummaged around in his pocket with his free hand.

"I forgot again. Here, swallow this." He threw a small pill towards her, which she caught. "It will prevent your brain from forming long-term memories in the next two hours. We do not want to traumatize you."

So this is how they suppress memories. I want to avoid using it if possible.

He went on. "Of course, you can refuse to take it, but then you will suffer from psychological damage, and that would be a shame. I have not broken the Aurigan moral code once so far, which is quite impressive given the circumstances, I think."

He then took another pill out of his pocket and swallowed it himself. "Decide before it is too late. For a woman of your size, the pill will prevent the formation of memories starting from about ten minutes ago, plus or minus two or three, depending on the details."

Ten minutes. This doesn't fit. Why don't I remember my last interrogation at all? Even if I swallowed the pill, I should at least remember Krov, given how much he talks. And so should Steve. Something is off.

Blood started to drip from the table. The victim's wound was deep but extremely thin. She wouldn't bleed to death quickly. Luray scowled.

This woman is already dead. I can do nothing to save her. No matter what Krov does, to her or me, I absolutely must not reveal the address data now.

Luray looked at the pill.

I could put it in my mouth and hide it under my tongue, but it might dissolve. I need to stash it somewhere else…

Krov might be right about psychological damage, but if Luray learned something important and then forgot about it, that might be worse.

"Would you please decide now so we can continue?" He sounded impatient.

I need him to think I swallowed it. Maybe he will reveal some more information then.

"What is going to happen to me in the end?"

Luray put her hand before her mouth, covering it completely. With a single movement she threw her head back and pretended to swallow, palming the tablet as she did.

I never had the time to really practice these sleight of hand tricks. I hope he falls for it.

Krov nodded approvingly.

"Well, first, you will watch this human suffer. If that does not work, you will take her place. Once the pill takes full effect you will sleep for about half an hour. You'll be treated and carried back to your cell, if you survive."

Good. This guy thinks he can just reveal anything to me since I'll forget it. And more importantly, he will also forget everything. If I can get the upper hand somehow...

"If you always take the pill, how do you know what you did?"

Make him talk. Let him feel like he's in control. Ignore the woman. She's dead anyway. Don't look at her.

"I write a report before I lose my memory, of course," he lectured her. "What did you think? Now let us proceed."

He pierced the woman's flesh again, this time in her hip. The sword came out the other side. Then the unfeeling surgeon pulled the blade back carefully.

Ugh! Why did I look?

"What is the gate address?"

Luray became pale. The woman on the table must have been in extreme pain for a few minutes now, and it would only get worse.

I feel sick. But I must not tell him anything. Breathe slowly. Calm down.

"I will tell you the address, but I insist on negotiating. I want to speak to your superior."

Her voice was weak, and her offer didn't have any effect on Krov. He carefully pierced the prisoner's right eye, slowly and with great precision, then twisted his sword. Luray could feel bile rise in her throat.

So much for appealing to his reason. I have to overpower him, make him write a fake report. He will not remember that.

Her idea was easier planned than executed. Krov had a weapon; she didn't. And he was in a position where he could easily attack her.

Think. Think! He must have a weak point.

"Are you still not willing to talk?" the old man asked in a disbelieving tone. "I am afraid you are making 559 suffer unnecessarily. You could stop this here and now. I really don't understand why you insist on drawing things out. We would treat you well afterward, you know? Your cellmates told you about our offer, didn't they?"

I will kill Steve once I'm back. With my own hands.

"No, he forgot to mention it."

Krov looked surprised and interrupted his toying with the woman's eye.

"In that case, you need to know that you can always decide to join the Aurigan Empire. You will then be allowed to live as an Aurigan and enjoy being a highly ranked member of the Empire. Our society is much more developed than humanity, in all aspects. There really is no reason why you shouldn't immediately join us."

Then why do you resort to torture as the first option? What kind of messed up logic is this?!

"Is that a joke?" Luray exclaimed. "If you're so much more developed, why won't you negotiate with me instead of prolonging this?"

He made a dismissive gesture. "You cannot offer us anything. We are being generous in giving you the chance to join the Empire."

273

With that Krov carefully lacerated the woman's right leg, cutting it in two halves starting from the knee and slowly approaching the foot. The sides separated slightly, and blood spilled out while bone and red muscle was revealed. Now the effect on his victim was more visible, and unmistakably real. Just looking at it for a split second almost made Luray faint.

I need to focus. If he does that again, I have to attack. For a moment, he will not be paying attention to me. I can knock him out with a single hit if I get it right, but I have to wait until he does something to her again. Sorry, whoever you are.

"This is all your fault, prisoner," Krov continued in nonchalant tones. "You are causing this. I am just following the interrogation instructions."

Crazy. He really sounds as if he means it.

"Do you know how terrible I feel for doing this? And it is nothing compared to what I will have to do later. Without the pills, I would have gone mad long ago. I wish you could read one of my reports. They are horrible. A mirror of your current state of evolution."

I need to wait until I get a chance, or I can try to provoke him. If he's busy, I can surprise him.

"Torturing her will get you nowhere. I will not talk."

Her voice did not sound convincing at all. There was almost no power behind it. However, Krov reacted. "I see that you do not have a problem watching a member of your species suffer. I am only torturing myself here. We should move on to the next step."

I just hope I can manage after seeing this.

Krov lowered his sword and aimed for the woman's heart, holding the weapon horizontally.

This could be my chance. He'll have to pierce through the entire body.

As soon as the sword was deep inside, Luray raced across the room, jumped on the table and crashed into Krov with her outstretched leg, landing a perfect kick to his face. As he toppled backwards, Luray jumped after him and landed on his body feet-first. She heard something crack.

Those were his ribs. I'll have a few seconds to get his weapon.

Without giving Krov time to react, she lifted her foot and brought it down with full force on the surgeon's weak fingers. The bones snapped immediately. Luray took a deep breath, realizing that her hands were shaking.

Now calm down. You did enough. He can't fight back.

Krov had still been holding on to the hilt of the sword until Luray crushed his fingers. After that, he had to let go. Luray swiftly took it, not without exercising care – the worst thing now would be accidentally touching the sharp edge and losing a few fingers.

It's light. It weighs almost nothing.

Still on top of the torturer's body, Luray pointed the blade at him. It took a moment for him to regain his senses. When he did, his attention fixated on the bloody point hovering in front of him with frightened focus.

"You will do as I say or you are dead."

He shut his eyes in pain and simply nodded.

How does it feel to be on the receiving end of this blade, hmm?

THE PRISON - 3

I *don't want to do this, but I can't let her suffer anymore. If only there were a way to help...*

Luray went back to where the half-dead prisoner lay. Her attack on Krov had prevented him from finishing the job, which meant that it now fell on her to put the woman out of her misery. She lifted the sword, hesitating only a second before bringing it down. The blade sliced through the woman's head without any effort, splitting it in half. The bones, the table – her stroke went through as though it were all a viscous fluid. It was scary how easy it was.

Her hand was gripping the hilt of the sword so hard that it hurt, but Luray was too far gone to realize it. She just stared into space for a moment, trembling.

It's... over now. I did the best I could.

As hard as it had been, Luray didn't have a choice. She just couldn't let the poor woman suffer anymore. The damage was already done, no matter what happened next. She just made the inevitable happen sooner.

I'm really sorry. I couldn't act soon enough to save you.

Luray forcefully shook herself out of her thoughts and went back to Krov, who had tried to get up but couldn't deal with the pain in his chest. He was still on the ground having difficulty breathing.

You're lucky I haven't given up on escaping.

She held the tip of the sword in front of Krov's face. There were just a few centimeters of space between his forehead and her weapon. Luray's arm was shaking, but she didn't pull the sword back.

Enjoying it?

She fought to get her body under control again. A few times, the sword menacingly moved up and down as Luray breathed in and out, deep and slow. It helped.

Only when she was about to speak to the torturer did she register how badly this experience had affected her. She was sweating, and instead of speaking in a cold and controlled way, she was about to yell at the old man. She was angry – no wonder – but she managed to regain control over her voice.

"Krov." Her voice was still louder than she had expected, but at least it was clear and strong. "You will tell me exactly what your procedure is. I have a lie detector in my head, and if it tells me that you are trying to trick me, I will cut your head off without warning. Understood?" There was no fear in her anymore.

He looked at her with terror in his eyes. "I was… no, you don't understand… Argh, my hand! I was just fo… how did you even… my hand…"

Krov had trouble speaking. He kept looking for words, forgetting what he was talking about and constantly lamenting about his now broken hand.

You've never been threatened before, have you?

It took a while, but Krov told her everything she needed to know. With every bit of information, Luray calmed down further. With every question Krov answered, she saw more options to choose from. She was analyzing everything, planning her next steps, finding loopholes, simulating all possible actions that she could think of.

After a while, Luray started smiling again, despite the situation she was in. It wasn't a happy smile. It was devilish and menacing. Krov was startled by it. He probably thought that Luray was done questioning him and that he would die now. When nothing happened, he began to talk faster and faster, as if he feared to dissatisfy Luray otherwise.

"After 90 minutes my computer notifies me that my time is running out! I prepare the... the body to be taken, write my report. Guards come in to transport the body. They always find me in my chair, sleeping, because of the pill, just sleeping... peacefully!"

I don't think he's lying. You need training or talent to be able to fabricate a detailed story like this, especially under these conditions.

Luray looked down at Krov, who was still cowering before her. Aside from fear, there was only confusion on his face.

Are you really that surprised I fought back? Or do you not understand why I would?

"Bin, what do you think?"

"According to my analysis, the chances of him having told us a lie is below three percent. We should assume he has been truthful."

Good. Now, what is the best move I can make?

Luray addressed her terrified captive in the same voice that had worked so well until now. "Krov, you will now write a fake report. You will say I attacked you, but you swayed me with your elegantly chosen words, and I decided to consider joining the Empire, but then time ran out. We couldn't finish our negotiation. And make it believable."

Before Krov could respond, Luray hoisted him up on a chair. He grimaced in pain as this applied pressure to his ribs.

He's lighter than I thought. And thinner.

"Now write it."

Krov began talking to his computer in Aurigan, and Bin provided a live translation. She listened carefully for any sign of treachery, but Krov proved remarkably compliant. He even explained the injuries that prevented him from typing and thus required this audio message as an 'embarrassing accident.'

Well, that's even better. I'll hear it if he tries something, and he can't press any emergency button to notify the guards.

He did as Luray told him, managing to speak clearly and calmly in spite of his wounds, and included everything she wanted him to say. When finished, she made sure he turned off the recording to ensure no further discussion would be picked up. Then they both settled in to wait for the interrogation time to run out.

Luray was watching Krov closely. She absolutely refused to look at the human remains behind her.

"Prisoner, can I ask a question?"

Prisoner? You're a terrible negotiator. But sure, ask... Let's see what else I can squeeze out of you.

"Sure. You'll forget the answer anyway."

Luray's voice, perfectly calm again, seemed to influence Krov strongly. Before he was afraid. Now, he was calm as well – he even stopped nursing his ruined hand.

"Why are you doing this?"

"I suppose I can tell you now. I will escape from this place. I will speak to your superior, negotiate with him, gain his trust, backstab him, steal his ship, fly through the nearest gate I can find, and go back to the colony. I will use all the prisoners here as a diversion. Later, the UEM will come back with a huge fleet and blow this place up. Something like that."

Krov shook his head, his face showing pain for a second, but then reverting to its normal expression.

"No, that is not what I meant. You took a huge risk just to make me record a report saying that you might join the Empire. You could have just accepted our offer without going through all this trouble."

Luray wondered how she should respond to that.

"Well, negotiating was the plan I came up with before our first little session. But since I am here again, I can only assume that it didn't work out as I would have wanted. Which leads me to doubt your intentions and makes any offer from you untrustworthy. I don't know what went wrong, really. Can't seem to remember."

Which reminds me, Steve deserves some consequences.

"Anyway, that's in the past. What's important is the future. Wouldn't you agree?"

Krov nodded and said nothing more. Luray was fine with that. At least she was one step ahead now. She wouldn't lose her memory. Maybe she could even take one of the weapons and smuggle it into her cell. In her mind, she already imagined what would come next after drugging the guard and taking his equipment.

Luray spent a while inspecting the torture devices from a safe distance. She could only guess the purpose of some of them, and it made her shiver. Only a few would be useful weapons.

Maybe if I can find a way to connect Bin to the system, he can help me escape from here.

Just as the thought crossed her mind, the computer announced that Krov's time was running out. A short while after that his head began to nod, and finally he passed out.

Now I can only hope that what I did here wasn't for nothing. I still don't know enough about this place to make a real plan. I hate stumbling around blindly.

Luray avoided looking directly at the dead body of the female prisoner. After hesitating a bit, she let her ultra-sharp weapon fall to the ground. The hilt had left a clear imprint in her palm. While falling, the blade retracted by half its length, clattering against the ground to lie harmlessly.

Luray flinched, remembering what had been done with that thing to dozens if not hundreds of people. Remembering what *she* did to the poor woman on the table.

Bin's familiar voice interrupted her dark thoughts. "Do you need mental support?"

Luray considered and finally said, "Can't hurt."

"You did the right thing. The woman would have suffered needlessly."

Luray nodded, looking all around. She was the last person left standing in the torture chamber. Krov was unconscious, and his victim was dead on the table. Her blood collected below it. Until now, Luray hadn't noticed that the area directly beneath the table was slightly concave, which kept blood from flowing everywhere.

"Bin, can you keep track of the time and warn me before the guards come?"

"Yes. I will warn you soon enough."

"Thanks."

I need to set up a scenario for the guards. It's always the small details that make a lie believable.

Luray positioned every loose object in the room to match Krov's report. She then proceeded to take a look at the remaining torture devices once again.

Maybe I overlooked a useful one.

Despite her best effort, she didn't find one that could beat the sword when used as a weapon. It provided the biggest range, and at the same time could cause a lot of damage, no matter the opponent.

There are no cameras in here, right? Otherwise, why would Krov need to write reports to himself? This probably means there are no cameras in the cell either, and the tranquilizer dart is hopefully safe.

Luray spent a while planning and making theories. Did all the guards carry dart guns? If so, was there a way to defend herself against them? Or were they made out of the same physics magic as the sword?

She kept wondering about all the details that flooded her mind until Bin warned her. "The guards will arrive soon."

Time to play dead. Or asleep, in this case.

She sat down in a corner and relaxed her body as much as she could. So long as she didn't react no matter what she heard, they should fall for it. A few minutes later the door opened without warning.

No announcement. Makes sense. They expect Krov to be sleeping, and me too.

"Ah, I see Krov went all out and made a mess again."

Luray did not recognize the voice, but she could hear the distinctive footsteps of two guards entering the room. They spoke to each other in Aurigan, and Bin provided instant translations.

"This is disgusting. Let's just get the prisoner and leave."

So not everyone here is insane.

Luray heard one of the guards walk over to the table. After a few seconds, he commented on what he saw.

"Really, this guy is crazy. Why doesn't he use simple pain inducers? They're so much cleaner, with no risk of killing the prisoner. Why is he still getting assignments, anyway? Someone must have really wanted prisoner 741 to go through this."

I got special treatment? What about Steve and the others? He said they were injured, so they were also sent here.

"We had to handle a large number of prisoners in the last few days and didn't have enough capacity. It was an exception."

That's the same guy who brought me to the interrogation room. I recognize his voice. Where have I heard it before? I can't tell because of his helmet. I'll ask Bin later; he's better at this.

"But still, why doesn't he even follow the ethical torture guidelines? I mean, look at what he did. That's insane."

Ethical torture guidelines? So even to them Krov is brutal, but torture is still fine?

"He's stuck in the old days, but can you blame him? He was one of the first human Aurigans before the moral code was updated."

One of the first? The old days? How is this possible? He's around 70 years old, but the first contact was last year.

Luray felt someone grab her hands, and then another took hold of her feet. She was then laid on something soft – a kind of tight web. They began to move in synchronized steps.

Can I risk opening my eye a bit? If the one at my legs is walking forward, he won't be able to see me. But otherwise, he might notice. I need to wait until we've left the room.

"I don't see what's so special about this one. I mean, she's just a human."

"Which is why you're a simple guard, and I am your commander." They took a turn to the left.

The guy who just changed our direction is the commander. He must be looking the other way. As for the one near my head, I'm pretty sure my face is below his line of sight. I should be able to open my eyes without getting caught.

Luray dared to open one eye a bit. She was right; the commander had his back to her. She could only see the rear of his head. Something, maybe a mask, was attached to his mouth. The most surprising thing for her was that she saw an actual human being, head and hair included. The man didn't look very strong. He was almost skinny compared to the other guards, and the most peculiar thing she noticed was his red hair.

The commander continued to talk. "She'll get a few more chances. If I'm right about her, she'll give us the gate address willingly once she understands what's at stake. I would take a shortcut if possible, but protocol always has to be followed."

Did he sound sarcastic when talking about this protocol? What are the Aurigans? Are they human? This makes no sense. I could have asked Krov, but I was so focused on not getting killed that I forgot about it.

Luray heard a door slide open, then was carried a bit more and felt herself placed on a bed. Nothing was mentioned about Steve.

Is he still knocked out? If yes, the tranquilizer is quite effective.

After the door closed, Luray opened her eyes. Steve wasn't there. Her heart plummeted.

The dart. Is it crazy to hope he woke up, found it, and hid it somewhere before they took him?

Luray immediately checked below Steve's bed. To her dismay, nothing was there. Same for her own. Without any real hope she cased the bathroom. Feeling mild distaste at the thought, Luray got near the floor to look behind the toilet. A wide smile appeared on her face when she discovered the dart lying in the shadows.

Nice one, Steve! You actually did something smart!

She picked it up and investigated it closely. The spike was attached to a tiny pump. A translucent green liquid was stored in a half-filled container, ready to knock out anyone it hit.

I guess the moment the dart pierces the skin, the pump will be activated.

Luray carefully tested the dart's sharpness by pressing it a few millimeters into the wall. She could easily pull it back out, but not further in.

It is like the sword from the torture room. The tip pierces anything, but it won't go into hard substances because only that part is thin enough.

In her head, Luray played out different scenarios. In all cases, she had to get to the torture chamber again. The sword was an extremely powerful weapon. If she had it, the odds of defending herself successfully, at least for a while, would rise tremendously. With it she could easily cut open doors, maybe even walls. If the commander came again to carry her body, she could even get a hostage that had value for the Aurigan Empire. They wouldn't sacrifice someone of that rank, would they?

Of course, none of that was a guarantee for a successful escape, but it was better than nothing. An alternative plan was to gain the commander's trust, promising to reveal the gate address and dragging it out, all while gathering more information. She would choose whichever seemed more likely to succeed.

Now all I can do is wait. The next time they send a human guard, we can use the dart against him and take his glove.

With that we can get into the torture chamber, overpower Krov, get the sword, and hopefully take the commander hostage. All we need is luck. If it goes wrong, I can still join the Aurigans.

Luray was perfectly aware that her plan could fail in any number of ways, but until a more effective strategy presented itself, this was all she had.

Maybe we're in a Dyson sphere? With 140 solar systems at their disposal, the Aurigans might have the resources to build one. We never would have detected it because it isn't in our galaxy. Still, this doesn't explain at all why there are humans here. Krov was about 70 years old, and this whole structure is clearly made to be used by humans. How and why was it built?

No matter how fast you are, a Dyson sphere takes centuries to construct. How did the first humans get here? And why did the guard call me 'just a human?' Are they somehow different?

She tossed and turned on her bed a few times.

If we were brought here, that means there are shuttles. If this place is built for humans, then there should be controls a human can use. There should be pilots. Also, there's Bin. If he can infect the system, maybe I can create enough chaos to escape. I wonder why they didn't disable or remove him. Maybe they don't know about him? Or maybe they don't care? Or do they know he is necessary to get the gate address?

Luray was lost in her thoughts until someone approached her door and spoke.

"Step back, or you will be shot... please."

I know, I know.

Luray got into her usual position and observed the door open. Steve was blocking the view. He stepped in and looked around, clearly confused. Behind the soldier were two other versions of him, slightly smaller, with different faces but similar bodies. Their numbers were 756, 789 and 801. After the last one was inside the cell, the door closed.

"Steve, do you remember me?"

He stared back at her blankly. "How do you know my name?"

Doesn't look like it.

He clearly didn't recognize Luray. None of them remembered anything apart from getting captured. It was like they had been mentally reset.

The pill wouldn't explain this. What is going on here? Do the Aurigans reset memories along with the injuries? What's the point of the pill if they make us forget everything at some point anyway?

Prisoner 801 stepped forward, pushing Steve aside. "Do you know what is going on here, ma'am?"

Could these people be Steve's former cellmates?

"Let's introduce ourselves first; then I'll tell you what I know."

They all settled on the bunks facing her, and Luray started.

"I am Luray Ulyssa Cayenne. I'm a risk assessment agent sent to EE-297 to estimate the danger of an alien attack and got captured during the last one. I know the big guy here..." She pointed at Steve, who looked as blank-faced as ever. "... is Steve Morgan. He was fighting the Aurigans on the colony but didn't make it back to his base and was captured. You other two, I've never met before."

Prisoner 801 didn't seem to be as clueless as his fellows. "I am Carl Holloway, rank three. As you can probably guess, I was also captured on the colony, together with Andrew Kilian here, rank four. We were part of the same squad. Now tell us how you met Steve – because he was with us the whole time."

He doesn't seem to be quite as slow as Steve. Makes sense to make him a squad leader. Maybe their ranks depend on mental capacity?

Luray began to explain the situation to her new cellmates. For a brief moment, she suspected one of the prisoners to be an Aurigan spy who wanted to ruin her escape plans, but quickly disregarded that thought. Then she caught herself wondering if there were microphones recording their conversation.

Paranoia is one of the withdrawal effects. It's beginning. This couldn't have happened at a worse time.

"A moment, please."

She interrupted the conversation, got up and went into the bathroom. The soldiers watched her, wondering why she didn't close the door. They saw Luray flush the toilet for no apparent reason, and then the strange little woman shook her head before switching on the shower. She seemed to be satisfied after that.

Luray came back and spoke in a quiet voice, barely audible for the soldiers.

"I have a plan that might get us out of here."

This simple sentence gained her their full attention. They arranged themselves in a circle around her. Given their size, the situation was a bit intimidating for Luray, but she did not waver.

"I still have my memory. I saw everything: what they do, where they bring us and how to get weapons."

No reason to mention the weak points of this plan. I need you to be on my side completely.

Given their ranks, it was only natural that both Steve and Andrew would obey Carl Holloway, and he in turn had accepted Luray as his best source of information and advice owing to her prior knowledge.

Now let me tell you exactly what I want you to know so you do the right thing.

"The first time, they sent a robot to get me. After that it was a human guard equipped with a dart gun. One shot can knock out any of you within ten seconds. This is where I got a dart from." Here she hesitated and looked at Steve. "Thanks, by the way."

Before he could question her, she was already off again. "If we can surprise the next guard, we can knock him out and get his weapon."

Suddenly, Holloway looked at Luray in a strange way. She eyed the big soldier mistrustfully. "Do you have a question, Carl?"

"Me? No. Please continue."

He was surprised, and so was Luray. Why did she think he looked at her suspiciously?

What was that? He clearly looked at me as if he was about to… Am I hallucinating? Calm down. None of them can be a traitor. If they were, they wouldn't give themselves away by giving me the evil eye. I need to keep it together now.

"Ma'am?"

Luray ignored her weird feelings and continued. "Sorry, I was thinking about something. The guard has a small chip in the palm of his glove. It serves as a key." She held her hand up to illustrate.

"We can use this to open some of the doors. Once we have it, we lock the guard in the cell and go to Interrogation Room #5 where we overpower the interrogator. I remember the way there. In it is a weapon we need to get – a sword. It can easily cut through anything, even metal."

Carl raised a hand respectfully to interrupt her. "What about guns?"

"We'll take the dart gun. Other than that, we'll have to improvise. Until we get real weapons, you can use some of the torture instruments in close combat."

Maybe we can ask the guard about where their weapons are stored. With his glove, we should have access.

Luray continued explaining her plan, making sure everything was as clear as possible.

"Once in the interrogation room, we have to wait two hours. That's how long an interrogation takes. Two guards will come to bring the body back. That means we get two more tranquilizer guns and gloves. Last time, one of the guards was the commander himself; he will be our hostage. The other, we should…"

Luray stopped. She never considered how to deal with a spare captive. There was no way to know what he would do, once left alone. Which only left…

"…we don't need him for anything."

Carl nodded to confirm that he understood. Luray didn't feel well at the thought that she just planned to kill someone, but what other choice was there?

It's a good plan. I think. I should rest now.

"I need to lie down for a moment. Excuse me."

Without looking directly at anyone, Luray got up and lay on her bed, hiding below the cover like a child seeking comfort.

I must appear strange to these guys, but that doesn't matter. We have to get out of here; then we see how to move on.

So far Luray could keep the symptoms in check. If her estimation was correct, she would be in a problematic state in about 24 hours lasting about half a day, and then slowly recover. This was their deadline.

This must not fail. If it does, I'll be useless, and we'll lose the advantage we have. I hope they come and get one of us again today.

As it turned out Luray wasn't that lucky. She was forced to spend the night in a cell with three huge soldiers, listening to them swap stories about their war achievements – each made up and changed on the fly to sound more impressive than the one told before. They all chuckled like it was a joke. It was ridiculous.

Maybe the Aurigans have a point. If most of humanity is like this, perhaps we deserve to be integrated into another civilization by force. But then again, there are people like Kailoon as well. I guess you can't judge humanity by a few examples.

On the bright side, having an extra night gave her little gang the time they needed to go into further detail on their strategy – who was supposed to be where at which point, what was supposed to be done in which case, and the like.

Luray was, to her surprise, quite satisfied with the plan in the end. The soldiers didn't seem to have any trouble remembering their parts – this was, after all, what they were supposed to do. Memorize orders and rules and execute them without question.

It took hours to go through all the possibilities, but Luray felt that it was worth it.

In the end, after going through the same scenario in a dozen different variations, she was mentally exhausted. Usually when it just concerned herself, she made a rough overview and filled in the details on the fly using something called intuition. Still, with these monkeys the hardest part was to stay calm and not strangle them out of frustration.

You can't beat sense into people, as much as you would like to. Calm down.

Her dreams were a complete mess that night. She was being cut to pieces by Krov, and then put back in the wrong order by a machine that glued her body parts together. The Aurigan commander was actually Kailoon in disguise, and he asked her if she didn't want to join their military because they could use people like her. They were then attacked by an army of Krovs, shot all of them, and had to defend themselves against a new wave of Johns. Her own army, out of nowhere, was a massive number of Steves that all attacked not only the Aurigans but each other as well until each of them was explicitly told who the enemy was.

Her nightmare ended with someone barking at the door. Luray opened her eyes and jumped out of bed. Her mind was clear again, at least for now.

"Step back to the opposing wall, please. We will send a technician in to check your bathroom. There has been an unusually high usage of water. We need to fix it."

Luray glanced at her co-prisoners. They all exchanged looks and nodded.

We'll treat the plumber as a second guard, just as planned.

"If you disobey, you will be shot. The ammunition used is lethal. You have been warned."

Another difference. It paid off to talk about all those variations.

Due to the lethal ammunition, the scenario changed, but not much. The primary goal of the soldiers was not to get hit, no matter the weapon. They could not afford to drag one of their own with the group, and to leave someone behind – alive – was unacceptable inside a team of soldiers. They could, however, abandon other teams, because their own was always the most important one. The military implanted this sense of competition in order to enhance the efficiency of a unit, which worked in most cases.

One option to use the dart was to throw it; it could still be a distraction if it didn't hit. The idea came from Carl, and Luray expected nothing less from a monkey. Throwing darts with precision and speed required practice. Practice that may or may not damage or even destroy the dart's needle – and even if it didn't, it could accidentally activate the pumping mechanism. They could not afford to lose the dart, and so tests and practice throws were out of the question.

When I pushed it into the wall, I carefully pressed it straight in. I didn't bend it. That could have broken off a part of the needle. Stupid me for not testing that on the sword when I had the chance.

Instead, Luray proposed to turn the food they got into a projectile. They wouldn't be able to eat it, but it was worth the sacrifice. A ball of brown goo, a mix of potatoes, rice and dark sauce was created last night. Its purpose was to block the guard's sight. The goo-ball was in Steve's hand right now, behind his back. He awaited a signal from Carl.

The guard entered, closely observing all four of them, but it was hard to see which one he was looking at. His head only made slight movements, and his gun was always pointed at Steve, probably because he was the closest and largest among the soldiers.

I need to wait for the signal. We have to do this in sync.

It made sense for the gun to be more powerful. The dart gun Luray saw the last time had to be recharged after each shot. There were four potential escapees here, but only a single armed guard. Equipped with just a dart gun, four people could easily overpower him.

The plumber, a heavyset man, passed through the first half of the main cell without worry.

Now we wait for him to walk to the partition and then...

Someone had to act as a distraction. The best choice was Luray because of her size and small weight. She was not only the hardest to hit but could react quicker than any of the soldiers. In this scenario, she should be the one the greatest distance from the guard.

However, someone had to use the dart, and for this, she was also the best candidate. Luray insisted on being the one throwing the dart. She made up a few good reasons; some of them were lies about having won a dart-throwing competition once. Had a potential traitor held the dart, she would have been much more nervous, but that she didn't say.

It took a while to convince the soldiers to let her have the projectile, but in the end, they agreed that she was the hardest to hit due to her size and wouldn't appear as dangerous as the soldiers. She would have a chance to get close quickly if the guard wasn't paying attention to her. Andrew was chosen as the one to distract the guard, and he too was waiting for Carl's signal.

Then it happened. Carl pretended to sneeze. The moment he did, almost convincing even Luray, Andrew made a few quick steps forwards and grabbed the plumber, spinning him around to use him as a shield while Steve threw the goo ball and charged forward. Luray began to run towards the guard at the same time.

That was incredibly fast...

The guard saw the food ball flying and ducked. Confronted with one prisoner hiding behind his hostage, a small woman jumping to his left, and one very big guy running towards him, the biggest danger came from the one who threw the goo ball. The guard adjusted his aim and fired at Steve.

His shot connected, but immediately afterward a sharp pain in his own shoulder caused his head to jerk around, spying the dart now sticking out of him.

Got him. But Steve is injured. I hope he just got grazed.

The momentum of the huge soldier was too big to be stopped by a single shot. Despite getting hit in the chest, he kept charging forward, crashing into the guard like a speeding car.

Good. We have one more weapon and a key.

THE PRISON - 4

S teve, despite being hit, didn't slow down. He kept pushing his opponent backwards into the hallway outside the cell. The surprised and overwhelmed guard, having expected his weapon to stop the huge man, still tried to resist by lowering his center of gravity and stabilizing his stance by extending one leg back to brace himself.

It wasn't enough. Steve just pulled him up, lifting the Aurigan above his head and smashing him down to the ground almost effortlessly. As if that wasn't enough, Steve let his own body follow, crushing the already disoriented guard beneath his full weight.

Wow.

Once they were both on the ground, Steve used his heavy frame to hold the guard down, tightly gripping his hands around the man's wrists. He had received a direct hit, but as a soldier, he was more resilient than a normal human. He wouldn't stop fighting because of a wound like that. He would keep going until he won, passed out or died, whichever happened first.

The guard's helmet had collided with the floor with a force that would have knocked out any human. For a moment, Luray didn't see any movement, but then the alien started to move his gun arm.

> *He's still conscious! If he starts to shoot blindly, he could hit me. What should I do? How can I disarm him? Should I stay behind cover and wait for the fight to end?*

Luray ducked behind the cell door frame in a single quick movement, only peeking outside again for a split second. She heard the guard struggling.

> *No point in taking a risk now. I should wait here and let the soldiers take care of the rest – play it safe for now.*

All she had to do was wait a few seconds until the dart took effect. A moment later, she felt a shock go through her body as she realized that she had made a potentially grave mistake.

> *The door! What if it suddenly closes?*

Would it close automatically after some idle time, or did the guard have to shut it from the outside? She wasn't sure – she couldn't possibly know the answer.

> *If the door closes and the guard shoots Steve again, we sacrificed him for nothing. I'll have to take the risk. There is no other option.*

Luray peeked around the corner carefully, only exposing a small part of her face, hoping not to get shot by sheer chance. The guard was struggling to aim at Steve again. The injured soldier tried his best to prevent it but couldn't use his full strength because of his injury.

> *He can't shoot yet. I should have enough time.*

Steve bought her the necessary seconds. She approached them in a few quick strides, lifted her leg high up and smashed it down on the hand holding the gun. It felt as if she just tried to kick a wall. The guard wasn't wearing anything she would have recognized as powerful armor – it looked like a normal uniform but felt like an extremely hard shell. How could he move in this thing?

Doesn't matter. Even if his fingers aren't broken, my weight will keep his arm immobile.

Luray waited a few seconds. To her surprise, the guard rotated his wrist in an attempt to free himself. Despite the combined effort of both Steve and Luray, he almost succeeded.

How is this possible? Can he be that strong?

Then, not a second too soon, the dart started to take effect. The guard still struggled, but his movements became weaker and slower. Luray waited a bit more until she was sure he had stopped moving completely before carefully removing the gun from his hand. She turned her attention to Steve.

"Are you okay?"

He's bleeding a lot but doesn't show the pain.

"It won't kill me," he insisted.

Steve's injury was bad, but he didn't seem to be concerned by that. He pressed both of his hands against the wound, only then displaying signs of annoyance and pain on his face.

I can't tell if the shot is above his lung. If it is, then he should survive this if we can stop the bleeding – at least for now.

When Steve tried to get up despite his wound, she hurried to prevent him. "Wait, wait. Let me see that."

He obeyed and laid on his back. He slowly removed his hands so she could see. The blood quickly turned into a viscous fluid, then formed red glue blocking the wound. Immediately afterwards, the glue began to lose color.

A modification to stimulate blood clotting? Another soldier advantage, I guess?

There was no exit wound on his back to be seen. However she noticed that his flesh smelled burned.

A plasma gun? Did the bullet heat up inside his body? Or is it a laser gun? I expected them to use bullets because that's what I'm used to. The military never managed to build portable energy weapons that didn't overheat too quickly. After the dart, I was sure they would use projectile weapons, but I guess I was wrong. This could be good news. A dart gun would have had just one shot.

Luray carefully took the gun and held it gingerly between two fingers, expecting some kind of security system to activate if she touched the handle directly. She carefully poked the grip. Nothing happened. The gun had not one, but two barrels. The top one had a crystal embedded into it. The other seemed intended for darts.

This weapon has two settings, and the guard decided to use the deadly one. Well, not deadly enough here, I suppose.

Steve's wound had completely stopped bleeding, but Luray didn't want to risk making things worse, so she made sure not to touch it or the surrounding burned skin while examining it. The hole was perfectly round, about one centimeter in diameter. Charred clothes and skin were on the outer border.

The gun was fired only for a split second. This thing is powerful.

"I am fine, ma'am." Steve craned his neck to see her, wincing slightly in the process. "I can still use my left arm. The wound is only two centimeters deep."

How can you tell? Soldier sense?

"How do you know?"

"I can feel where the wound starts."

Instant blood clotting, precise pain reception inside your body... this isn't possible without genetic engineering. It's illegal on Earth. Someone on the colony is in trouble if this is ever made public. I guess I understand the plan to declare independence a bit better now.

"You can come with us despite this injury?"

He gave a quick nod. "It'll heal soon. Don't worry about it. No vital organ was hit."

As if to prove it, Steve got up as if nothing had happened to him. He gave the guard a little nudge with his foot, probably to check if there would be a response. There wasn't.

Luray removed the glove and put it on her own. At first it didn't fit. Then it started getting tighter, wrapping itself around her hand until it felt like a second skin.

Interesting.

Luray turned around, looking for the other two soldiers. Carl was standing directly behind her. He wanted to be on the outside in case the door closed.

You didn't do anything while I was checking the wound. Did you know he would be okay, or did you have no idea what to do?

Andrew was still inside holding the plumber, who repeatedly said he was innocent and had nothing to do with anything, hated the Empire, couldn't harm a fly, never killed anyone. They were slowly walking towards the cell door.

He doesn't mention the door. It won't close automatically then?

Carl looked at the ground, thinking for a moment before addressing Andrew. "Kilian, bring him to me. I will find out what he knows."

Andrew followed the order of his squad leader immediately.

Once outside, the plumber received a punch to the gut. He doubled over and took a moment to recover, which wasn't surprising. He was weak, untrained, and overweight – the complete opposite of the soldiers and the guard.

"Please," their captive wheezed, held upright only by Andrew's firm grip. "I don't know anything! I don't have access codes except my own. They're for the living quarters. You can go there and hide, I'll let you out of here, but let me live. If you kill me, I'm useless, and you will be severely punished. If you let me live, your evaluation will be better!"

Evaluation? What's up with his priorities? Why does he think we would care about that?

"Tell us your code," Carl barked. "Now!"

Even Luray shivered when she heard Carl scream at the poor Aurigan plumber.

Carl is playing bad soldier. Maybe I can play the good part?

"Carl, wait." She laid a hand on Carl's arm as though to restrain him from further violence, though that was clearly impossible.

"I have an idea. He tells us the code, we lock him in the cell. If he lies, we can come back, and if he tells the truth, good for him."

The plumber seemed to understand. They wouldn't kill him because he might lie, but if he told the truth, they wouldn't need to come back. It was a good deal for him.

"The code is 021925311."

He immediately told us. He's afraid, and all he wants is to get out of this situation. He's just like any normal human. He said he's living here. What is this place?

Luray placed herself in front of the cell door, ready to close it, and pointed the gun at the technician with her ungloved hand.

"Thanks. Now pull your friend in there. He's still alive."

The Aurigan was ridiculously weak and slow, but in the end, it didn't matter. They were successful and had enough time left. Luray surveyed her party. Not perfect, but still on track. Next they needed to go to the interrogation room. At least, Luray hoped that's where they would find Krov. If not, they would improvise.

She held the glove in front of the scanner, and the door closed within a split second.

Carl stepped forward. "Ma'am, I suggest that I take the gun. Of all of us, my precision is the highest. In a battle, it makes sense for you to take cover while we fight. It increases our chances of escaping."

Carl again. I don't trust him. Why does he want the gun? Does he plan to kill us with it?

Luray ignored her inner chaos. This useless doubt came out of nowhere, but she recognized it as such and ignored it. She would be able to do that – for a while. "Yes, you're right. Here, take it."

This is just a chemical imbalance. I must not let it take control. Everything is fine. There is no traitor. Assume there is no traitor even if there is one. If you don't trust these guys, everything is over.

"Let's go."

Luray led them down the hallway. It felt a bit weird giving orders to people three times her size, but they obeyed immediately. She walked down the path she had memorized while making mental notes of all the hallways and doors she might want to check later if she got the chance.

Ideally, there are more cells with prisoners here. All we need then are more weapons, and we have a nice diversion.

The group moved quickly without encountering another guard. They passed a few doors without any signs on them and finally reached the hallway Luray was looking for.

No security. They're either overestimating their guards, or there's another security measure we don't know about yet.

Luray passed by the doors until she reached the torture chamber. She held her glove in front of its scanner, but it only lit up red once.

This isn't good.

"We have to try the others."

The next three attempts all failed as well. There was no noise coming out of the rooms. That left only one.

I hope this one opens. Yes, it should open. The guard came not only to check the leak, but to take one of us; the timing fits. We were just unlucky. They're switching the rooms. They might have to clean up after each session. This can still work.

The door slid open silently, revealing a surprised Krov sitting on his chair, utterly bewildered at finding a huge man pointing a gun at him.

"Your access codes, now!" Carl snarled.

He doesn't waste time. I like that.

Krov didn't know what was going on. He wasn't ready for an interrogation and even less for some prisoners with guns. He started reciting numbers one by one, clearly unable to focus.

"31...then...33...no, 34..."

He wasn't expecting us. We're too soon. Doesn't matter. We'll ask him when the interrogation was planned.

Luray walked past Carl, approaching Krov who didn't dare to move.

I see your hand is already better. Aurigan medical technology must be quite advanced.

"Hand over the gloves. Please," she added with a sarcastic smile.

Still confused, Krov removed his gloves and handed them over. She put them on, then moved Krov's chair and stood on it to reach the sword she was after. It detached from the ceiling the moment she touched its hilt.

Maybe I should slice him up. We already have an access code. We don't really need him anymore.

307

She impassively looked at Krov, pointing the weapon at him and closing in. This and the look on her face was enough to make him spill out the rest of his personal code.

"313484627!"

Luray stopped moving abruptly while Krov started pleading for his life. The sword hovered a few centimeters in front of his face.

What did I just think? This isn't me. Something is wrong. This wasn't just paranoia.

"Bin, is my brain chemistry alright?"

"I will perform an analysis. The result will be ready in 20 minutes and 11 seconds."

"Thanks."

Carl approached Krov in a menacing way and began asking all kinds of questions: what the code was for, why they were here, what the Aurigans were doing... Whatever the answers were, Luray's attention had already drifted elsewhere. She was staring at the almost invisible edge of the sword, shaking the blade to make it easier to see.

How did they do this? The blade is extremely thin, and yet it's harder than thick steel. It doesn't bend no matter how fast I shake it. Not to mention the cutting ability. If this was made back on Earth, it would work once, maybe for a centimeter, and then get stuck. How is this not getting dull immediately? And why is our escape going so well? Is this maybe a test? Are the Aurigans observing us?

"Krov, are there cameras here?"

She interrupted Carl to ask that question, and he did not appreciate it. However, the question seemed important enough for him to let the rudeness slide. That, and he accepted Luray as his superior. She was the one with a plan.

Krov answered her in a haste, sounding frantic. "No, there are no cameras here! We... we respect privacy."

Krov began to stutter when Luray came close. For reasons she didn't understand, he feared her more than Carl.

Respect? You?

Luray heard words escape her mouth she hadn't intended to speak. "Carl, this guy is crazy," she growled in a menacing voice. "The Aurigans are all crazy. He talks about his glorious empire, how it will rule the universe one day, how superior it is in every way. It makes me sick!" Luray spat the word, and Krov's face turned bone white.

What am I saying? I should follow the plan.

"If you want to live, you sadistic monster, you will write a report and send it to your superior. Make sure the commander or someone equally important shows up here, so we have a hostage."

Why am I telling him about my plan?! Do I also have an evil smile? Have I become dumb?

"What should I write?" he whispered, petrified.

Playing stupid, are we?

Luray explained how she wanted to lure in Krov's superior, not without adding an insult and a threat here and there.

It's never been this bad. I really overdosed too much. Or was it the white pill mixed in?

Krov did as he was told. This time he typed the report – his hand was working properly again – but that wasn't a problem. Bin provided the translation instantly so Luray could make sure there were no calls for help and no warnings hidden in the text. Krov was telling his commander to come immediately since 'that annoying woman' was ready to join the Empire, but only if she could talk to a senior official first. She wanted a demonstration of Aurigan superiority, and Krov didn't pass her test.

Sounds believable. Somewhat.

Once her request was fulfilled, she would reveal the gate address so the Earth could be assimilated. Krov also asked for a more responsible position as a reward for his contribution to the Empire, probably hoping that Luray's plan went completely wrong and she was forced to reveal the address. He wanted to sell it as his success.

Maybe Bin is lying to me. Maybe they manipulated him. Maybe Krov just warned the commander.

The message was sent with high priority. Krov settled back in his seat, sweating. "I cannot guarantee it, but the commander should come in 110 minutes. He likes pretending not to read my messages, but he always does." He eyed them wearily. "Will you barbaric people torture and kill me now? We never killed a single one of you! Everything we did was for the good of every civilization!"

They all ignored what Krov said. Could he really believe that himself, with all those torture tools around him?

I have to trust Bin. There is no other choice. The message was as I saw it. The commander will come. I have to believe that.

Since Luray was staring into space for no discernible reason, the three soldiers started to discuss what to do with Krov.

"We don't need him anymore, right?" Steve asked while fingering his own wound. "Should we kill him?"

"Yeah, I think we should test some of his toys," Andrew stated firmly. "Putting him in our cell is a waste of time, and risky."

He made no attempt to hide that he would enjoy killing Krov. They all looked to Luray for agreement.

As much as I would like to, he isn't a threat and won't attack us. I don't want to kill anyone except in self-defense. But to convince you, I guess I need a tactical argument.

"No, we might still use him. He's our backup hostage if the commander gets killed. If he's useless, we can still get rid of him later." Luray pointed at the torture table. "Let's tie him up for now. There are belts somewhere."

Carl expressed agreement by nodding. "Yes, ma'am."

"If Carl says so, we do it," confirmed Steve. The wounded soldier carried Krov to the table using only a single arm and smashed the old man's weak body on it face-first. Then he strapped him down.

Steve was the obedient and loyal dog type. Whatever he was told to do, he made it a part of his personality. If brainwashing had varying effects on people, it worked best on him. Carl perceived everything based on chain of command and acted accordingly, while Andrew appeared instinctively geared for combat and bloodshed.

As if to illustrate this point, Andrew started complaining again. "He's the enemy. We should kill him. We should've also killed the guard. Why did we leave him alive?"

He wants to kill as many enemies as possible. Makes sense.

Luray looked at her blade again, amazed at how thin it was. You could cause so much damage with it...

Meanwhile Carl moved in front of Andrew, staring into his eyes. "Unless the situation changes, we follow the plan. If executing prisoners brings us an advantage, we'll do that. Now, it doesn't."

Luray missed the rest of the conversation completely. She was trapped in her own thoughts again.

Maybe the scan did something to Bin. He lost a part of his memory. He was manipulated. They changed him. Why wouldn't they? They looked for the gate address data, but it was encrypted. Now they're trying to trick me. I don't see how yet, but I will see through it. They won't get me.

"Ma'am?" Steve's voice cut through the rant.

How many times has he talked to me? I completely lost track of him a moment ago.

She blinked and looked up to find him standing beside her. His face, if anything, seemed worried.

"Yes, I'm here. I was... thinking. Bin, how's the analysis coming?"

"I am not completely done, but you are suffering from at least medium to strong paranoia. In a few hours, trembling will start, then you will develop a fever and start to hallucinate. I can administer something to help with the paranoia, but I can only do that once, and it will last for about an hour. Should I do it now? I need your permission for this."

What if they managed to crack Bin's security mechanisms? If I give him permission, he might poison me instead, or give me a truth serum. The Aurigans might have seen my addiction problem in the scan and prepared this in advance.

"No, not yet."

I can't base any decision on vague mistrust. If Bin isn't on my side, I've already lost.

She moved a bit away from the soldiers and spoke as silently as she could. "Bin, I need you now. Can you mimic my own voice when you talk to me? When I'm about to go crazy, it might calm me down if I hear my own voice. Do you think you can take control for a while once you need to?"

Bin switched to something disturbingly close to her own voice.

"I am honored that you trust me that much, given your current brain chemistry. Yes, I think I can help you."

That felt extremely weird.

Carl was issuing orders. "Okay guys, grab some weapons. We'll drag this guy into our cell. Ma'am, we'll need the glove."

He extended his hand in her direction expectantly.

What? Did I miss something?

"Ma'am?"

I need to know what they discussed. I need to get him to sum it up.

"Yes. I was just ... thinking about the plan. You want to put this guy in our cell. I'm not sure if that's a good idea."

Luray vaguely remembered how Carl and the other soldiers had discussed the possibility of leaving Krov in the room to make sure the guard entered, but then the torturer might warn the commander, who then could lock them all in from the outside.

"If he's here, he might get injured or die," Carl explained patiently. "That makes him useless as a hostage. We should keep him safe. Nobody is supposed to be walking around here, so the risk is minimal. Krov is too afraid to lie about that."

Makes sense. If there's a firefight, we might lose him.

Luray handed the glove over.

"Here. And don't forget to destroy the keypad in our cell. You never know, that guy might know the access code for it."

I didn't think about that before. We left the plumber alone in the cell and were lucky that he didn't know the code to get out. The chance is small for a random technician to know such a code, but it slipped my mind. I can't allow such mistakes to happen again.

The next part of the plan required patience. They had the means to free a lot of prisoners, and even knew where the cells were – but if they created too much chaos before securing their hostage, all they would cause was a short revolt.

Stay focused.

Steve and Andrew left with Krov. Luray's stewing brain cooked up a few scenarios in which they killed him, then the corpse was found, and the entire plan ruined. Then she imagined the soldiers betraying her and joining the Aurigan Empire.

Ignore it. This is a side effect. Focus on the plan.

She kept getting ideas about what might go wrong until the door opened and the two soldiers came back. They reported back to Carl. "No problems, sir. We met nobody."

This is all going too well. Maybe. I can't tell if this is me or the paranoia.

314

"Good. Then all we have to do is wait. Get into position."

The two soldiers positioned themselves on either side of the door. They both took the longest weapons available, apart from the sword that Luray insisted on having because she was the weakest – and shortest – and therefore needed a weapon sporting a long range and a lot of destructive power.

Many of the torture instruments turned out to be sharp enough to be used as weapons, but none of them were anywhere close to the sword. For the purpose at hand, it didn't matter – the soldiers were strong enough to use other weapons efficiently.

Carl hid behind the console that Krov had been using when they entered the room. He had the laser gun and practiced aiming with it. Luray stood in the center of the room facing the door while hiding the sword behind her. Her job was to identify the commander by talking to him in case it wasn't immediately obvious due to his mask and red hair.

From then on, they played the waiting game, wondering if the commander would even come or if he would send his underlings. If he didn't show up, Luray would have to see what they could achieve with the gloves and access codes of three guards. Probably not very much.

"It is almost time. Tell the others."

Bin spoke in Luray's own voice, as she had ordered him. It sounded exactly like her, which did calm her down somewhat, but not knowing what the voice would say still made her feel as if she lost control over her own thoughts. However, in a weird way she trusted it.

"He might come at any moment, pay attention," she warned.

The soldiers, accepting Luray as a human alarm clock, leaned against the wall and stayed that way for two minutes, not moving, until someone outside spoke aloud in Aurigan.

"Please step away from the door, or you will be shot."

They know what we're planning! How did they find out? I paid attention to everything. There must be cameras everywhere, microphones, we must be under surveillance all the time. They can see every move we make.

Luray imagined a group of heavily armored robots break the door open and throw grenades inside, then realized the obvious explanation.

No, it can't be. If they knew, why would they warn us?

Another calm voice was barely audible, but Bin caught it. He added subtitles to make sure that Luray could understand everything.

"Who are you talking to?"

The first voice responded again, but now not even Bin could understand enough.

They expect me to be awake. Of course. Calm down. You have the upper hand right now. The guard spoke in Aurigan out of habit, but that was a mistake. He got scolded. That must have been it. I will take a step back just in case. They will focus on me; all soldiers are out of sight.

The door opened from the outside. There stood three people in uniforms, two bulky ones and a relatively thin person in the middle. He wore the same mask as before.

That's him. I'm sure.

Now that she could see half of his face, it somehow seemed familiar, but she was sure she had never met anybody on the colony with his particular hair color.

I feel like I've seen his eyes before. What is going on here?

The two guards came in, ready to apprehend Luray who was just standing in plain view.

Now!

Andrew and Steve attacked instantly, like they had been practicing this exact situation countless times. Their movements were completely synchronized. The soldiers stabbed their adversaries with a scissor and a knife before they could take a second step, and both instruments pierced their armor.

I never saw a squad fight. There were rumors about their teamwork and efficiency, but I thought it was propaganda. It's as if they know exactly what the other is doing.

The two guards had been forcefully pulled to the sides and were lying on the ground, wounded. The soldiers on their backs twisted and turned their enemy's arms in ways that looked extremely painful. It took only a few seconds, but each of the guards already had either a dislocated shoulder or a broken arm.

Impressive.

Still, the guards didn't show signs of pain and even fought to get up again.

Monster against monster...

The commander was looking into the room, both hands hanging at his sides, observing the situation as if he had nothing to fear. Or was he just a bit slow? Right then Carl fired a dart at him with perfect aim.

For just a moment, Luray couldn't quite believe what happened next. But it soon became clear the commander was now holding a dart in his hand, right in front of his chest.

Did he... catch it? How? It must have been moving at 90 meters per second, if not more. This might get more difficult than expected.

Right after firing the dart, Carl had started moving. He rose from behind the console, weapon trained on the commander and drawing nearer step by step.

Yes, that's right. Go get him. But why doesn't the commander move?

The Aurigan officer could have thrown the dart, but instead, he let it fall and just stood there, waiting, his hand still in the position where it caught the dart.

Luray held the hilt of her powerful weapon tightly. She was a lot weaker than the soldiers, and there was no way she could subdue the commander without it. Despite being well armed, she had a bad feeling and took a few steps backwards.

I should follow Carl. I can stay at a safe distance, just point the tip of the sword at the commander and restrict his movements.

After Carl passed her, she followed, unable to shake off the feeling that they would all lose this battle despite it basically developing into a four-versus-one situation soon.

Carl closed in on the commander, pointing his gun at him. "Don't make a move, or I will shoot your legs and arms."

The commander stood still, but not in a way that implied capitulation on his part. He just looked at Carl in a condescending way, like he didn't consider him a threat at all.

The other two soldiers didn't waste a second. Each of them had now stabbed their opponents multiple times. Despite this, the guards still continued to resist.

Do they not realize it's hopeless for them? If they don't stop... maybe my best option is to cut off their heads. Then it really will be four against one. It would be less risky.

Luray changed direction, took a step to the side, preparing to swing her sword at the guard to her left with the intention of beheading him.

He's already dead. I'm just accelerating the inevitable. And it's self-defense. It's a reasonable thing to do. This is war. It's them or us.

Without giving herself any more time to think she let the sword slide through the guard's neck. It felt like cutting warm butter, and after just a moment, the enemy stopped moving.

Just as Luray was about to turn to her right to repeat her actions, Carl flew past her across the room.

Taken aback, she whipped her head towards the commander who remained standing where he was, in the exact same pose except with his arms in a defensive position. Other than that, there was no sign that he had moved at all.

How did he do that? He didn't use a weapon! Don't tell me the commander just punched him and that sent him flying? Is he an android?

Luray instinctively pointed her sword at the commander. Despite being safe in theory, she was terrified. That man had just thrown an almost 200-kilogram soldier across the room. With that kind of strength, he could rip all of them in half if he wanted.

Better think of something quick, or I'm next.

THE PRISON - 5

"" Carl, are you okay?!"

Luray screamed the question without realizing it at first, and more importantly, without turning around. There was no way she would take her eyes off the commander. She couldn't see most of his face, but his eyes clearly showed that he was smiling.

The two guards weren't stronger than the soldiers. They were human, more or less. Nothing hinted at the commander being an android. Krov didn't mention anything in that direction. Was it a trap? No, they would've sent more of that guy and less of the weaker guards. Maybe it's his suit?

Carl did not respond. Whatever happened must have knocked him out and might have broken a few bones. Even being an improved soldier, there were limits to what could be done, especially when it came to the skull and brain.

Andrew, who now had no opponent anymore, went straight for the commander.

Idiot.

Luray then witnessed what must have happened to Carl a moment before. The commander performed a simple kick, but faster than she would ever have thought possible. His foot made contact with Andrew's chest and sent him flying a few meters across the room. The curled-up body came to a halt after rolling over the ground.

This speed is not human. This power is not human.

Andrew slowly got up again while trying to keep his balance, but collapsed after a few steps on his way to Carl.

That's what you get when you do things in the wrong order.

Luray stayed at a safe distance. Surprisingly, so did the commander.

"Bin, analysis, quick!"

"I suspect his suit can enhance the speed, power and precision of his movements. It might be made out of retractable nanowires, which would enable it to produce movements like biological muscles. The sword should be very effective against it. You need to cut the wires."

Is that why you're not coming closer? You don't want to risk losing your advantage?

The commander remained standing where he was like a statue. Was he thinking about how to handle Luray?

I remember reading about the UEM trying to build such a suit, but they couldn't make it work. If I'm right, his kick just now could have hurt the commander as well if it wasn't executed flawlessly. He relies on the suit, but if it's cut even a bit, then he should be unable to use those strong attacks. He won't risk that and will not attack me. At least, I hope so.

322

Luray slid a few steps to the right to stand next to Steve, who was still crouched over his injured opponent. Luray kept her sword leveled at the commander, giving Steve the time he needed to finally eliminate the second guard.

Their enemy did not respond to her strategy. He was ready to sacrifice his men, that much was clear. But what was his plan?

He can't come in as long as I block the way. Neither of us wants to go through the door. He'd be an easy target, and I don't know what he can do once I'm outside. Steve needs to get the gun from Carl. That's our best chance.

"Steve, go and get the gun. We'll need it."

Luray kept staring at the commander's eyes. She had seen this face before, but where? Mentally she went through all the people she had met on EE-297. None of them was a clear match, but then realization dawned on her. It was completely improbable. Yet all the same…

"John? Is that you?"

He does look like him, but he's… younger? The John Guerra I remember was physically weak; this one seems strong, but that could be the suit's effect.

The commander did not respond aloud. Instead, he slowly clapped his hands three times, as if to congratulate her.

"But you can't… how can you be here?"

Luray stared at his face. She had no doubt about it anymore. But how was this possible? Right now, John should still be on EE-297 in an interrogation room or a cell. On top of that, his behavior was completely different. It was as if this was just a shared face between two different minds.

Luray used every second she had to find an answer while her sword kept her safe. She drifted off for a second and was brought back to reality when strong hands suddenly seized her wrist. Steve forcefully snatched the weapon from her. She protested but he didn't listen. His eyes were wide and pink, and blood was running from his nose. He looked mad. The crazed soldier dove for the commander as if he had not seen what he was capable of.

So the conspiracy theorists were right about the blood rage phenomenon. The military always denied that.

Steve wasn't used to sword fighting, and his movements clearly showed it. He simply used the sword as an extension of his arm, but it was enough to push John back. The commander had to make inhumanly swift movements to avoid getting hit and couldn't fight back safely.

Bin was right about that suit. John is trying to keep Steve at a distance, waiting for a mistake. The question is, who will mess up first? What is the best thing I could do now?

As if Bin had read her mind, he answered her question.

"There are multiple cutting instruments you could throw. If you make even a scratch in that suit, it will raise our chances of winning significantly."

Yes, right. Attack his weak point. I need to be ready if Steve loses the fight.

Nearby were about a dozen small knives, not as thin as the sword and each a few centimeters long, all still hanging from the ceiling. Their purpose wasn't clear, but it didn't matter. They could be used as throwing knives.

I need to jump to reach them, and if I don't touch the ground, there won't be any shock.

Luray collected some of the daggers as fast as she could, dropping a few in the process. If John hadn't yet realized what she was planning, the sound must have definitely given it away. Steve, on the other hand, was focused solely on doing damage to his opponent.

I need to wait until he doesn't see me and then throw two knives at once. He doesn't have eyes in the back of his head.

All plans go wrong once they meet the enemy. John took an unexpected risk, moving in to grab the flat of the blade with his fingers from two sides simultaneously. With enough pressure, he could hold on to it with just his fingertips.

The blade was halted for only a second before slipping away due to Steve's strength, but it gave John the extra time he needed to get closer and land a hit directly on his opponent's face. To her horror, Luray heard what she believed was his skull crack.

Two knives were already flying, too late to save Steve. He was already collapsing when they bumped into John's back hilt first and clattered uselessly on the ground. Dismayed, Luray sent another two flying while John turned around, but he sidestepped her inexpert shots with ease.

It's over. We can't win. He'll get me before I can get the gun.

Then out of nowhere, John's left knee jumped up and froze in front of his body. This move didn't make sense no matter how you looked at it. There wasn't a target; it was as if the leg moved on its own. The rest of his body lost balance. John waved his arms around to avoid falling.

What just happened?

Then Luray saw it; the sword that was lying on the ground. By sheer chance, its tip had touched John's left heel when he moved to avoid her shots. The suit around his foot was slowly peeling off, forming spirals of what looked like wires. It must have registered the damage and pulled away without its wearer being aware of it.

He can't use his legs for long-range kicks anymore. The left foot won't be able to withstand the pressure without the suit. That means his range became shorter.

John regained enough balance to catch another one of her flying knives. The second poked into his chest but then fell down, failing to penetrate. He hopped awkwardly a few paces away, hiding behind the doorframe and eyeing his last opponent while putting his leg back down carefully.

Luray's thinking went into overdrive and she quickly considered her options.

I can go for the gun or the sword.

If she got the gun, John might catch her before she could fire a shot. Or claim the sword himself; if he did that, all plans would go down the drain. Even if she reached the gun fast enough, it would give Luray only one option – shooting him, which meant losing her strategic hostage.

I need to get the sword. I can still win. It's now or never.

Luray threw all of her remaining knives at John's head, not caring whether they hit at all. They were only a diversion. She ran towards him, trying to get past.

If I'm lucky, he can't hit me because of the suit's damage.

John stretched out an arm to catch her, but his actions were neither swift nor anywhere near the speed she saw him produce before.

Did he have to do that by himself? His other movements were a lot faster. If he can't use his suit anymore, I can beat him!

Luray avoided John's hand, dropped down as fast as she could to grab the most valuable weapon in reach. She got up quickly again, pointing the sword at John's back.

I need to do more damage.

Luray rose carefully and edged closer, intending a few tentative jabs to make scratches in John's suit without accidentally killing him, but he took a step forward before she could reach him. His leg was fully under his control again.

Maybe I can negotiate.

"Give up," she warned. "If I touch you with this, you're dead. If you let me escape from here, you can live."

That sounded ridiculous.

The commander's hand slowly moved towards his mask and removed it. The face revealed beneath was indeed that of a younger version of John Guerra.

"You have a problem, prisoner," he pointed out calmly. "If you kill me, you are stuck here. You can threaten to kill a hostage all you want, but once you actually do it, you no longer have one. Your plan was doomed to fail from the very start. It might work with humans, but not with us."

He's right. I need to keep him alive. But if he attacks now, what do I do?

Suddenly John grimaced, almost as if he were in pain for a moment. He reached a hand behind him and came back holding a dart. Turning, they both saw Carl come through the door with the gun trained on him.

I was so focused on the fight that I didn't pay any attention to Carl. He still had the gun and saw an opportunity to use it. Great job!

John raised his arms. "Okay, I give up. Just let me switch off my suit before I black out. If you try to remove it, you might kill me."

He sounded bored, almost annoyed, as if nothing of what just happened really concerned him. To Luray, it didn't matter. She lowered her sword. It was over. In a few seconds, John would pass out, and they would have their hostage.

An instant later Luray felt a sting in her shoulder, and only then realized John had thrown the dart at her.

He still had it in his hand. How could I be so dumb...

The last thing she saw was Carl lunging towards John firing another dart. Without losing a second, he began to smash his fists into the commander's face, who was barely able to defend himself. Luray fell unconscious a moment later.

The next thing Luray saw when she opened her eyes were two people beating a third to death.

She was back in her cell, together with the plumber, Krov, the guard they first captured, and the commander. Carl and Andrew were both taking turns mutilating their prisoners, asking for an escape plan, codes and descriptions of everything.

What happened to Steve? Did he die? I don't see him.

All the plumber did was beg them to stop without providing any new information. The guard told pretty much the same but added that an escape wasn't possible because of the 'Overseer'.

Last was John. Were it not for the hair, Luray wouldn't have recognized him at all, so badly beaten was he. His arms and legs were broken in multiple places. Parts of his feet and hands were missing. Krov was also there, but he seemed fine – physically, at least. Maybe they were afraid of killing him too quickly by accident?

What are they doing? What happened to the plan?

Luray saw several torture instruments next to her, including the sword. The soldiers had brought them into the cell to get proper revenge.

Once Carl realized that Luray was awake, he came to her bed and knelt down. "We got some more access codes; one of them is for the armory. We can get some laser guns and then try to reach a shuttle hangar and escape. We don't need any of them for that. And I'm pretty sure they didn't lie."

This is horrible. We have no idea what is going on, and they almost killed our main hostage. There's no way we can take him with us in that condition. They ruined it! But maybe that was their plan all along?! Maybe Carl is a spy after all? He wanted all of this to happen. He gave John the dart. No, that doesn't make sense. Keep it together.

Luray had a terrible headache. Why did she wake up after John? Was it because her body was smaller, or did they rouse John forcefully somehow?

I need to know what I missed.

With an effort she got the words out. "Tell me everything you know."

Carl replayed what they learned, which included a few codes, what they were for, and who had known them. He informed her

329

that she had been sleeping for about two hours, John for just one. They had no explanation for the huge difference.

Just in case he is no spy, I should listen to him. Bin will remember all the codes.

Luray managed to rise to a sitting position. "Sounds good. We should go immediately and not lose another second."

I don't want to take these two monsters with me. How do I get rid of them?

Carl nodded and turned to his accomplice. "You heard her. Let's go."

Andrew left the plumber alone, who was barely conscious anymore. The guard said nothing, but John's one good eye sought out Luray, his swollen, bloody lips trying to form words.

Maybe it's important. I should listen to him. He can't do any harm other than trying to lie to me.

Still a bit dizzy, Luray got up and went to him, putting her ear next to his mouth. John spoke with a dying man's voice, producing nothing more than an unintelligible whisper. He stopped trying and said something else. She recognized his last words clearly.

"End this massacre."

'Please put me out of my misery?' Is that what he's saying?

Luray went to get the sword without speaking to Carl or Andrew. Only then did she realize they were both injured. Blood had been flowing down their backs due to head injuries, but it was dry now. On top of that, they moved as if some of their bones were broken. Not surprising after receiving a kick that sent them flying.

I need to make them believe I'm angry and want revenge.

She took the sword, then crossed over to John, and before anyone could react, his head was split in half.

"What he said made me angry. I'm sorry."

The tone in which Luray said that sounded bored, neutral, annoyed – not the tiniest bit as she wanted it to be.

There is no actress worse than me when it comes to faking such emotions.

For a moment, all activities in the cell came to a halt. Nobody had expected Luray to just go and kill the commander.

Okay, time to get the weapons. Unlike you two, who don't understand how to use hostages or what a negotiation is, I still have the gate address data. Maybe I can still save us.

They set about collecting their weapons, but before they could, the cell door suddenly opened from the outside.

Luray and the two soldiers turned towards it; the men ready to fight, and her hoping it was a rescue team. There was always a chance to win the random event lottery, right?

None of their expectations were met. Before them stood a blond woman who bore an uncanny resemblance to the one Luray had seen on the torture table. She was not only alive and well, but also wearing a blue Aurigan uniform with white stripes.

Even more bewildering, the woman was accompanied by Kailoon, in a similar but color-inverted attire.

Luray was too confused to draw any conclusions. What she saw made no sense. Carl and Andrew instantly went on the offensive using both the dart gun and a few knives.

So they didn't completely forget about the hostage idea.

The nameless woman slipped past Andrew's thrusts with the elegance of a cat, crouched down, and put all of her power into a simple uppercut that connected with his chin. Luray could see the soldier's skull lose its original shape as he went down. She wouldn't have been surprised, had his head been sent flying into the ceiling.

The Kailoon lookalike made no such move to defend himself. All he did was simply look at Carl, and the big man's head exploded before he could even squeeze the trigger.

Uhh...

Luray instantly dropped the sword and didn't move. She wanted to keep her head.

Kailoon's eyes settled on her. His gaze was intense and deeply intimidating, though his next words were spoken in a neutral way.

"Ah, Ulyssa. Finally, we meet."

Finally? You're not the real Kailoon, are you? Just like this wasn't the real John.

He extended his left foot back slightly and placed his right hand in front of his chest.

Is that... some sort of greeting?

"I am terribly sorry for having made you wait so long, but you can come with us now. I am sure you have many questions, but do not worry. I will personally answer all of them and more. But first, my assistant will take care of the paperwork and give you some proper clothes."

When Kailoon mentioned his assistant, he was clearly referring to the woman, but the title clearly didn't please her at all.

Am I safe? Are they here to save me? But the soldiers...

The woman didn't say anything. She just looked at the two dead soldiers with disgust, but when she looked at Luray, her expression changed. It was almost... friendly.

Who are these two? What's their relation to each other? If I had to guess, they're on the same level in the hierarchy. They have the same uniform. Kind of.

"We can't have you running around like a prisoner anymore," copy-Kailoon stated matter-of-factly. "You are of far greater value to us." He then looked at the remains of John. "Well, that performance was worse than I expected. You won't stain the Empire anymore."

What is going on? Why is Kailoon here?

Kailoon swiftly turned and walked out. After his departure, a few people that Luray assumed were the Aurigan equivalent of medics came in and took care of treating the guard and Krov, who were very relieved to see them. Both were carried out while the plumber was left in a corner. No one bothered cleaning up the bodies.

Meanwhile the woman in blue and white approached a very confused Luray, put her hands around her face and moved it so that she could look directly into her eyes. Luray blinked uncomfortably.

Please don't blow me up...

"Ulyssa, my name is Tasha'Al. I have been tasked with preparing you so you can meet the minimum requirements of the Aurigan culture. You should know that it is a great honor to be invited to

333

become a member, and it is inadvisable to refuse, as that leads to being exiled."

Whatever that means, I should play along. But could you let go of my head now?

"Okay…"

Luray carefully raised her hands to grab those of Tasha'Al and disengage them. The Aurigan complied with no resistance, and Luray relaxed a substantial amount. The lady was a head and a half taller than she was, her hair quite longer. She was also significantly skinnier – scarily so, from Luray's point of view – which made her wonder how she managed not to break her hand during that attack a moment ago. The suit probably absorbed the impact like with Commander John. Could anyone wearing one of those things become a combat expert? Was that why John suddenly turned clumsy once his suit got damaged?

Tasha'Al kept talking as if what just occurred was perfectly normal.

"However, please refrain from asking questions regarding the plans of the supreme commander. I do not know them, nor do I have the necessary authority to provide the answers you might seek. I will, however, tell you what I can about the Aurigan Empire if you desire to hear that from me."

Do I know this supreme commander?

"Why are you alive and human?"

The first question came out of Luray's mouth without delay. She just couldn't keep her curiosity in check anymore.

"Why am I alive…? Ah, of course. I can see why you must be confused. You probably saw a previous version of me?"

"I…"

Maybe I shouldn't mention that I killed her?

"Never mind." Luray shook herself free of that disturbing memory. "Why are you human? Why are you not a strange alien?"

Tasha'Al seemed surprised. "I see. So that is your level of knowledge. Maybe we should start at the very beginning. But first, let's make you presentable. Follow me."

The woman left the blood-stained room. Luray followed, not having the faintest idea what was going on. Tasha'Al closed the door behind her and pushed a few buttons with a satisfied smile on her face.

There's something strange about this woman. I can't quite put my finger on it. She's too much at ease, as if this was all a game to her.

Luray heard a strange noise, as if wind was blowing inside the cell. Then she felt the cell door becoming hotter until it started to glow.

They're cleaning the cell. But… there was still someone inside. What on Earth…?!

She turned a disbelieving stare on her captor. "Did you just burn…"

Tasha'Al let out a brief laugh but suppressed it and hid a smile behind her hand. "He betrayed the Empire; I had no choice. But of course, his execution was absolutely painless. Please, come with me now. We have important things to do."

Execution? Because the guy wasn't loyal enough? He just tried to save his own life.

The blonde crossed her arms behind her back and began walking in the direction of the scanner room in a very enthusiastic manner, only to pass it by. She put her hand to what seemed to be a random part of the wall and a compartment opened, revealing a few orange uniforms similar in design to her own.

"Put one of these on. We can't have you walking around like a prisoner in the domes. You've been invited, and the supreme commander personally vouches for you, so you should look and behave accordingly. From what I've heard, you impressed him. That is quite a feat."

The woman talked openly, as if Luray was no prisoner, but a guest. Her body language was relaxed. The way she talked was closer to small talk than anything else, as if they were having a friendly chat.

"I impressed him?" Luray cautiously rifled through the selection in search of a uniform her size. "Can you tell me more?"

"Only you and he know what you did. The Aurigan Empire takes privacy seriously."

> *They just killed three people, and now they're acting as if nothing happened. I should play along; who knows what they might do to me otherwise?*

She found an appropriate suit and turned to face the Aurigan. "I suppose you still want the gate address?"

"Of course. The supreme commander will offer a deal regarding that very soon, but it's not urgent." Tasha'Al indicated the open compartment. "Just throw your old clothes in here. If you want to change in private, I can open any of the rooms for you. If my presence does not bother you, you can do it here. Nobody will observe you. This section is empty."

Getting the gate address is not urgent, yet you're torturing people for it? I have a huge list of questions.

Luray chose a random room that she had not been in before to change, just to see what was there. Tasha'Al opened it with her glove, and the door automatically closed behind Luray once she was inside. She quickly got an overview of the small room.

A storage room; uniforms, and a few weapons.

For a second Luray considered stealing a few laser guns and going on a rampage, but quickly decided against it.

"Bin, why do I not feel paranoid anymore?"

"It was obvious to me that you needed a clear mind, so I made the decision to apply the treatment I mentioned before. The effect should wear off soon, and the paranoia will come back. I suggest asking Tasha'Al for medical help."

Yes, it might be a good idea to get rid of this brain chemistry problem. The Aurigans should have an easy way out.

"You did well."

"Thank you."

A quick pat-down revealed she still had Krov's memory pill in her possession. It was the only resource left to her.

Now let's see if this thing has any pockets. If not, need to hide the pill somewhere in this room.

THE PRISON - 6

The new uniform felt like a second skin. Its nanowires had multiple layers; the lowest one attached itself to Luray's skin while the upper ones took care of ventilation, heat regulation and probably many other things as well. No doubt about it; this was one of the suits that gave you superhuman powers. Luray felt light as a feather as she took her first steps in it. No matter what movement she made, the suit supported her, as if guessing her thoughts.

Nice. But seriously, they wouldn't hand over a weapon like this to me now... would they? Or will they just pop my head if I try anything? No, they can't. The gate address is in there. I should be safe.

Before leaving, she stashed the pill between the layers of her suit. There were no pockets, but the uniform opened a slit wherever Luray placed her hands on it. She stepped out of the storage room and threw her old prison jumpsuit into a small hatch in the wall that Tasha'Al had opened, the Aurigan equivalent of a trash can. The woman had an eerily satisfied expression on her face as the hatch snapped back into position.

"Bye-bye, old uniform."

She's quite cheerful. And yet moments ago, she killed a soldier without showing the tiniest bit of emotion.

Tasha'Al began to lead Luray through a maze of corridors until they finally reached a door that had a symbol – a white circle – emblazoned on it.

"This is where you will live, at least temporarily."

The door opened automatically once Tasha'Al stepped in front of it, revealing a naturally lit garden, including birds, trees, a pond and a profusion of flowers growing everywhere. The ceiling was a dome, about 100 meters high and fully transparent; Luray could see a sun above it. A large part of the garden was hidden behind a hill with a huge tree on its highest point that almost reached the top of the dome.

I remember reading about that tree. It's an extinct species... what was its name again? It can grow up to 100 meters high. And that should take centuries, if I'm not mistaken.

"You are free to do what you want inside this dome. Consider it your home."

Luray hesitated, and the Aurigan continued her explanation. "On the other side of the hill is a small house that you can use if you prefer to live inside a building. It has an interface to the Aurigan database, but your access has not been set up yet. The supreme commander will tell you more, so please be patient. There is also a med pod in your home that will take care of any sicknesses or injuries, in case you need to be treated."

I still have no idea what this all means. They put prison cells right next to a huge garden?

"It is fully automated, just let it scan you and step inside. Do you need something else until the supreme commander has time for you? I am not sure when that will be – most likely tomorrow."

Tasha'Al breathed in deeply, making her chest grow significantly. Then she let it out with a heavy sigh. "He has a busy schedule."

Sounds like you want to spend more time with him.

As if Tasha'Al had heard her thoughts, she immediately regained her composure and put her happy facade back on. "Well, what are you waiting for? Step inside!"

Luray did as she was told. A small spherical drone that didn't seem to need any propulsion circled around her. After it was done with its dance, it displayed a symbol made of triangles on its screen. Bin translated its surprisingly complex meaning.

"Scan complete, new owner accepted. Welcome home."

Owner?

Luray took a few careful steps into the dome. The suit she was wearing retracted itself from her feet, allowing her to feel the grass and soil. It tickled her toes.

The amount of surprises Luray was exposed to in such a short time was overwhelming. The garden looked amazing, but what was it for?

The effort they put into this must have been insane. Why would they do this? Will they offer this for the gate address? Abandon humanity, just stay with us in paradise?

"I unfortunately have to leave..."

Luray turned around to see Tasha'Al preparing to go and quickly tried to squeeze in some questions.

"Hold on. What is this, why are you human? There was no contact between EE-297 and the Aurigan Empire until a year

341

ago, so when was all this built? And... is there a bomb in my head?"

"Bomb?" Still smiling, Tasha'Al seemed to think about this for a moment before answering. Then, she connected the dots and put on a proud smile.

"No, no, of course not. But I'm not good with such things. Your personal assistant is better equipped to answer these technical questions. You will find it in your house. You will also find food and drink there. If you want to learn about our culture, it is best if I show you what is expected of you once I have the time. Anything else?"

If I have to browse the Auriganet, so be it.

"No, I'll start with the technical questions."

This assistant will be much more useful than you for now. I need to get an overview.

"Well then, I will tend to other guests now. They are all in need of my lessons."

Guests? Lessons?

With that said, Tasha'Al swung around and walked away at a fast pace while whistling. Luray observed her for a few seconds until the door closed, then decided to wander for a while, taking a look at her new temporary home.

She recognized some of the plants, and those she didn't know at the very least didn't strike her as alien. It was almost as if the Aurigans went to Earth, stole a bunch of seeds and then planted them all here years ago.

Maybe they had the DNA sequences. But even then, that huge tree – it takes forever to grow this large. But wow, the design of everything is really nice. I couldn't have imagined a better garden. What was their first message again – they invite us to join them? Maybe John was right and they really meant it.

There were not just plants in the dome. Luray spotted a few more birds flying from one side of the enclosure to the other.

Pigeons...

One thing was clear; the Aurigan Empire was powerful. They had a lot of resources to spend on luxuries – details that were nice, but ultimately useless.

Maybe this is all an elaborate trick to make me feel safe, then talk me into betraying Earth? But if they have this many resources to spare just to bribe someone, why do they need Earth to join? What's so important about us? Why not just ignore us, or offer an alliance? Why demand obedience?

Luray paused. She looked up into the sky, trying to find out more about the place she was in. Were there more domes? Were they visible from hers? Were there structures in the sky that she could see? The sun was blinding her too much to make out any details, but she believed she saw structures, like space elevators, rising out of sight.

I should ask this assistant; it can tell me where I am and what this is.

Luray kept observing her garden for a moment, then took a deep breath, ready to move on, when she suddenly realized the importance of a small and obvious detail that had escaped her notice until now.

I'm the only one here as far as I can tell. I am the only one who offered information about the gate address. This is what got me here.

Luray had known it from the very beginning, but she had never really understood or even thought about the situation with all its consequences. She had considered the gate address as something to use in a trade, but now it had taken on an entirely different significance. It wasn't just about her future anymore. It was about everyone. She had the power to decide the fate of humanity.

The Milky Way was huge. If she told Bin to delete the encrypted address data, then Earth would be safe for hundreds of years. The UEM could prepare to defend themselves. They could catch up technologically. But if she revealed what was in her head, it would all be over in a matter of days.

I need to think about this carefully.

The troubled woman kept walking towards her house that was hidden behind the big central hill. Her mind knew that she was in a strange alien place, but it still felt like being back on Earth. The colors, the plants, the birds; even the animal noises were all familiar. The first things she realized were missing were pollution and the sound of cars flying overhead, and those Luray could live without. And the beggars, the drug addicts, the garbage on the ground...

After letting it all sink in, Luray concluded that this place was a lot nicer than most of Earth.

Maybe John sent DNA sequences to the Aurigans and they produced a few clones? But that doesn't explain the trees; they take decades to grow, if not hundreds of years. Krov was around 70, the scan technician about 60. How much time passed since the attack? Did the transport take so long? And why does the Empire even want the gate address at all? Why not just brute force their way through all the gates? If time isn't an issue, why the hurry?

344

Luray spent the next few hours wandering around in her new garden. There was even fruit growing on various trees and plants. To her surprise, a few small clouds started to form under the center of the dome, blocking out the sun.

Is it going to rain?

No longer blinded by the sun, she could see that what she mistook for space elevators before were orbiting rings that floated in space, rotating around their center – the sun. Due to their vast size and the immense distance, she could only see a small part of them.

Those must be Dyson rings. I'm walking on the inside and they reach all the way around the sun. I wonder how far it is? It looks like back on Earth, so it might be 150 million kilometers away. No wonder a few ships don't matter to them. They could have sent thousands had they wanted to.

After a walk that was a lot longer than necessary – but very relaxing despite a rising level of paranoia – Luray reached her house. The sun had not changed its position at all, which made sense given that her dome was rotating around it. The light would always shine on the dome. The ceiling, however, had started to become less transparent to simulate a day-night cycle.

Did they do this to not confuse the animals? Or maybe this is some kind of zoo? Are they watching me right now? Am I an attraction?

Despite everything that had happened, Luray was emotionally stable, which was surprising. She had never witnessed someone die before, let alone in such a violent way. And she had definitely never killed people, but it didn't affect her as much as she had feared. Her mind treated it as a fact, not as a terrible event. Maybe she was crazy. But in this case, maybe that was good. She might have cared a lot more had she been forced to kill someone

345

whose days were not already numbered. Or someone she actually liked. Like Mr. Snookes.

Poor Mr. Snookes. I'm sure he'll start to miss me eventually. He's never been alone longer than a few weeks. But then again, he is a cat. He probably doesn't care.

Luray finally spotted her home, a simple cube with windows, perhaps five meters wide on each side. Its only door opened as soon as she approached it. The interior was a single room, including a desk, a bed, a cupboard, a staircase that led to the ceiling, and a mysterious transparent box in the middle of the room. The box was about one meter high and had a few buttons with Aurigan symbols on them.

This must be the interface. It's not attached to the ground; do they use wireless communication? Maybe Bin can hack it then? He might just get what he wanted all along.

Luray left the box alone after moving it a few centimeters and investigated the rest of the room. There were red silk curtains next to each window. The initially bare walls began to change their color, showing slowly moving color patterns.

An Aurigan lava lamp? Oh, what's this down there?

A small trap door, only revealed due to the change in lighting, led to a lower level which housed an impressive bathroom, including a large pool and a separate shower area, all artificially lit and surrounded by aquariums that hosted a few species which Luray knew went extinct millions of years ago.

This is a zoo. No doubt about it. But it's for me.

Floating above the water in the middle of the pool was something that looked like an isolation tank. Was this the med pod Tasha'Al mentioned? Luray studied it for a moment, trying to find a way to reach it without falling into the pool, when suddenly the pod came floating towards her and attached itself to the floor by extending thin but very stable legs.

Luray tried to activate the pod by touch, but all it did was display 'Charging' on a small screen, together with an estimated remaining time of six hours.

I'll have to try again tomorrow. If this thing can get rid of my brain chemistry imbalance, that would be great. As long as I don't get the idea that doing so will kill me, everything should be fine.

Luray went back upstairs and tried activating her desk by touching it everywhere on its surface. All she got was an 'Access Denied' hologram lighting up above it.

This is a real hologram. I wonder how they're doing this.

She tried the transparent box next. A holographic menu popped up as soon as she touched it, offering a variety of meals and drinks. Bin translated everything for her, and she made a few random choices.

Now that I think about it... John, Kailoon's twin and Tasha'Al weren't speaking Aurigan. This means they don't know that I can understand it thanks to Bin. And that means I just gave it away, didn't I? No, I can still pretend to have selected options at random. I should press some more buttons to create some data noise...

A few seconds later the box turned black, then transparent again, and whatever she ordered appeared inside it. It was hot, as though just cooked. One side of the box opened, and Luray took out the floating plate with its deliciously steaming food.

Is this a magnetic plate? I don't see how else they can make it fly. Thinking of gravity, how does this work here? I'm not on a planet. Did the Aurigans invent a gigantic see-through warp field, or are we just rotating at the right speed?

The meal was as good as it looked. Maybe Luray should just stay here. She could reveal the gate address data very slowly, bit by bit, over the course of 50 years. The Aurigans surely would find ways to keep her entertained.

The bed was a lot better than the one in the cell. Not only did it adjust its shape, but it also moved up and down in sync with Luray's breathing rhythm.

They say they want me to join them, but all they really want is the information I have. I must never forget that.

The slow wavy motion of the mattress was almost hypnotic. She soon stopped feeling the border between her own body, the suit and the bed.

That suit is doing something to me. It's so nice. I think I'll just stay here…

Luray's mind faded away; she fell asleep after just a few minutes.

She was woken again by someone knocking on her door and calling her name. Luray got up quickly, out of habit worrying about how her hair looked like, but immediately noticed that she felt unusually clean and fresh. The entire room and especially her body smelled like vanilla.

You are full of surprises, suit. My mental state is also still pretty good. Did I get lucky? The med pod should be charged now; I'll use it as soon as I can. Better play safe.

"You can come in."

The voice responded in a very polite way.

"No, I cannot. We respect your privacy and are unable to open the door from the outside."

Luray recognized that voice. It was the supreme commander. He came. Luray went to the door which opened as soon as she was half a meter away from it. Outside, Kailoon's clone regarded her calmly.

"You can also control it using voice commands. But I suppose your Aurigan isn't good enough for that yet, Ulyssa."

The supreme commander spoke in his native language. Bin took care of the translation by showing subtitles floating in front of the commander's chest. Luray couldn't help but read them before looking directly at his face, which the commander reacted to by nodding and showing a slight, almost mischievous smile for a split-second.

He said it in Aurigan to test me. I messed up.

The supreme commander raised his hand, pointing to the center of the room with all his fingers extended. "We need a table."

The bed began to move. Its mattress shrank until it was barely bigger than Luray's head, then the bed rearranged itself into a table and two separate chairs. A part of the former mattress crawled to each chair and enveloped it.

The commander sat down on the smaller of the two chairs and pointed at the other. "Surprised? This is highly advanced nanotechnology."

He switched languages. I thought he knew I understood him?

"It is one of the many great achievements of the Overseer," the Aurigan leader continued. "I would love to show you more, but first, we have to focus on what is important. You know what I came here for, and I am willing to give you something highly valuable in return."

The supreme commander spoke in a very clear and elegant way. Each of his words was carefully chosen, supported by body language that Luray could not interpret – but the grace of his gestures and intonation were clearly intentional. He didn't just say things; he created a theatrical scene on the spot.

I need to be careful now.

Luray sat down where indicated. The chair instantly adjusted its own height a bit so that she and the commander were on the same eye level. Her feet dangled above the floor.

Hmpf.

His lip tugged on what might have been a repressed smile. "What I am going to offer you is worth more than you could ever achieve in your life if I were to let you go right now. Even if you became the richest human in existence, it would pale in comparison to what you could be here."

Just don't mention that you will kill billions and I'll let it slide. Is that your plan?

"I know you have many questions, and as a sign of goodwill, I will truthfully answer three of them, in detail. In return, you will answer three of mine. Do you agree to that?"

Doesn't sound so bad as a start...

"Okay."

The commander ignored the total lack of elegance in Luray's answer, but kept looking at her for a few seconds, waiting for her to add the obvious restriction.

"Except for the gate address, of course."

Luray believed she saw a split second of relief flash on the Aurigan leader's face. His answer confirmed that she hadn't imagined it.

"Yes, I would have been very disappointed if you just gave it to me. I completely agree with everything you have done so far. I would have made similar choices, in fact. Now, what is your first question?"

I need to get an overview first; then I can ask more specific questions to squeeze out the juicy info.

"What is the deal you are going to offer me and why should I accept it?"

The commander leaned back in his seat before answering. His eyes roamed over her face, and a small smile almost tugged at the corner of his mouth again.

Did I say something funny?

"I will consider that as a single question since I was going to tell most of it anyway, but I will go a bit more into detail."

The supreme commander's expression changed to something Luray would almost describe as soft and honest, while still having a clear goal in mind that he wouldn't abandon. It was something she rarely saw, except when someone was actually being honest or an incredibly good actor.

"My offer is that you join the Aurigan Empire. As you have undoubtedly seen, we are centuries ahead of your civilization. We will conquer it, no matter how, and that is inevitable, as is everything the Overseer wishes to happen. We will rid humanity of its unwholesome aspects and allow its good attributes to live on as a part of the Aurigan Empire."

The Aurigan Kailoon paused briefly to look out the window to where a bird was sitting.

"A small percentage of your species, just like this bird, will be allowed to live here, in this ring section – we will handpick them one by one since – I am sure you agree – only a few really deserve to be part of a far better society."

A few?

"How many are we talking about here?"

He did say he would go into detail, so I can ask as much as I want as long as I stick to the topic, right?

"This ring section has enough space for about 100,000 individuals."

"So if I accept your proposal, 15 billion humans would die."

He quirked an eyebrow. "Wouldn't they anyway at some point?"

Didn't see that one coming.

Though she didn't move, something about her amused him. "Ulyssa, I think I saw you smile on the inside just now. You have what it takes to join us. You can think. You're not an automaton."

To prevent any future lapse, Luray assumed her most deadpan expression. "I meant, your empire would shorten their lifespans considerably."

The supreme commander bent forward now, leaning on the table with his elbows, his fingers interwoven. Everything he did, he did in a respectful way. His tone was calm, his movements exact without relying on his suit. He wasn't at all like the Aurigan John.

"Only if they decide to attack us. You must be aware that we never threatened your colony. The UEM fired the first shot every single time. The last battle only took place because the colony made their intentions very clear in a violent way multiple times."

So you will take in 100,000 humans who will all live like kings and just let everybody else go about their lives? What's the catch?

"Those who do not attack us are allowed to live under supervision. Their ability to procreate by themselves will be removed, but they will live their lives peacefully."

Ah, there it is. But really, it doesn't sound that bad so far. I would almost be tempted to just give him the address data if I wasn't me.

Luray mimicked the commander's posture. Maybe if she was lucky, she could speed up the process of befriending the guy.

Let's pretend for a second that I'm not the problem here.

"They won't accept that condition."

He nodded gravely. "They are free to rebel, but they cannot win. However, we are leaving the main topic. If you accept my offer, you will be one of the first and your place is secured. You will have nothing to worry about; you will get the right to vote just like any other species that is part of the Empire and will be treated as a citizen, with all privileges and duties. The AI of your home – your assistant – can tell you more about that, but to summarize, it means you can live here in ways much better than it would be possible anywhere else. We are a Utopian society, from your point of view. You must have seen the difference by now."

He's the first person in this empire who makes sense. I think he can handle some innocent questions that criticize his regime. I give him a chance to explain, agree that it all makes sense, then we're best friends. Maybe it leads me where I want to be.

"But why did you torture your prisoners? Couldn't you have just offered them a place in the empire directly? Then everybody could see that you're the good guys…"

Luray did her best to sound as curious as possible, trying not to show that she saw a moral problem with torture.

"Yes, it is rather unfortunate that your species is so susceptible to torture."

The answer was so far away from what Luray had expected that she just sat there, staring at the commander, trying not to look as confused as she felt.

Let me unwind that… you were forced to use torture because it's so efficient? But you didn't actually want to?

The commander interpreted Luray's silence as a request to continue his explanation. "The Overseer decided that it would be the most efficient way to get information out of the majority of you. Given how human minds work, they will do anything to avoid pain sooner or later. All we required was a prisoner who had knowledge about the gate address. Our plan was to keep capturing humans at random until we found one who fit the criteria. It turned out to be you."

"Does that mean you stopped abducting people?"

"Of course. It would be immoral to take prisoners without a reason."

Then my actions here stopped the battle on EE-297?

"You retreated from the colony, then? What about the other prisoners?"

The commander snapped his fingers, summoning a cup of tea that came floating over to him out of the food box. Somehow it knew what to do without a voice command.

"Of course we aborted all scheduled attacks. We do not wish to inflict any undue harm." He took a peaceful sip, then settled the cup on its dish. "As for the prisoners, they will stay where they are or decide to join us. But let's focus on your options now, shall we? I want you to understand your importance."

Luray nodded slowly, showing a bit of hesitation.

I'll let him think he's gaining ground.

"Obtaining the gate address of your planet would shorten the unavoidable war significantly. If we could attack now, your species would not have a chance to advance technologically and make their conquest unnecessarily hard."

Suddenly it clicked in Luray's head. She understood how this guy's moral system worked.

"You're choosing the lesser evil."

The supreme commander nodded. "Exactly. You have to understand that the Overseer is perfectly rational, and his predictive power goes beyond anything you can imagine. He estimated that the long-term benefits of torture would outweigh the moral costs by orders of magnitude."

"Because winning the war quickly causes less death and suffering than making it last longer."

355

Her host showed an expression that could almost be interpreted as approving. It was the first time Luray was almost certain her discussion partner wasn't acting.

"I knew I wouldn't be wrong about you the moment I was notified about your unusual behavior."

Luray said nothing, waiting for an explanation.

The enemy commander stood up and crossed over to gaze out a window. "I can guess what you are thinking. I allowed you to ask three questions, but you have avoided posing any about new topics since we started discussing the first. You want to optimize the use of your questions, am I right? You wanted to test me. You wanted to see if I would really answer your question in depth as I said I would, so you played this game. If you were right, not only would you get more information out of me, but you would also know how to discuss efficiently with me. If you were wrong, you would lose nothing. Correct?"

There's no point in hiding it.

"Yes, you are."

He looks like Kailoon, only some details are off. But the way he speaks is completely different; his mannerisms are like that of another person.

"By trying to make the best out of my offer, you made me wish to tell you more, but I have to restrain myself. You know enough about my offer now. Your next question, please."

I would like to know what happened at the colony. I would also like to know how I could get a shuttle to escape from here and what happens to me if I refuse to cooperate.

"Why do you want to conquer Earth? I mean, you could just leave us alone. We don't present a danger to you, as I see it."

The supreme commander turned back to her, and for once, Luray saw nothing extravagant in his movements. If anything, he appeared intentionally restrained.

"That is an excellent question. The explanation is that your assumption is incorrect. Your species poses a threat to the very existence of the universe itself. To explain this, I need to go back to the foundation of the Aurigan Empire."

He returned to his chair and operated an invisible hologram. After he was done, another cup of tea appeared in the food dispenser. It floated all the way to the table, just like the previous one. But this time it settled in front of Luray.

Oh, for me? Smells quite good.

As she tried the beverage, he proceeded with his explanation.

"The Aurigan Empire, or rather the civilization that it was before, received a message from a species not much different from yours. Their behavior was more or less identical. They were spreading like a virus across their planet, and after that, their solar system."

This tea is amazing, unreal even. I never tasted something like this before. Does it trick my sense of taste and smell somehow?

"They fought war after war, and each time, their weapons became stronger. Eventually one of their scientists discovered a hidden property of space itself – one that could be used as a weapon. Imagine our universe as a balloon, and you poke a hole in it. Space itself collapses, and everything within it will simply cease to exist. The sphere of space around it would then be affected as well. It would cause a chain reaction, expanding at the speed of light. Once triggered, it cannot be stopped. It is the most terrifying weapon imaginable, undoing existence itself. It deletes the universe, or resets it, so to speak."

The commander paused before proceeding, as though contemplating the implications of his statement.

"That scientist knew his knowledge would cause the end of part of the universe if it ever fell into the wrong hands, but he also recognized that inevitably, every technologically advanced civilization would discover it. He sent a warning out into space, and another civilization received it a few million years later. This other civilization became the Aurigan Empire as it is now. It has been expanding ever since. Five hundred years ago, the solar system we are in at the moment was acquired after a short battle and became the new center of the Empire."

We're talking about galactic timescales here. The Aurigan Empire had millions of years to grow. The UEM had centuries. What did Krov say again? They cover 143 solar systems?

"The original signal I spoke of will reach Earth in about 2.5 million years, but that is just a side fact. The civilization where this information originated is long gone. They couldn't stop the war and eventually melted their own planet. We located the remnants of their civilization and investigated their history."

He took another sip, and then continued talking while holding the cup. Luray watched him, absorbed in his storytelling. The serious topic itself was only half of what held her interest; this man knew how to captivate her.

"The Overseer immediately understood the implications. No imperfect being must ever have such power because they would eventually use it in a moment of weakness and irrationality. Once available, the use of the weapon would just be a matter of time. The only solution was immediately clear. No one must ever be allowed to build it. To achieve that goal, the Empire must expand and stop any other civilization from developing this weapon."

Now the supreme commander's gaze settled on Luray, making her shiver. "Your species is a very dangerous one, and maybe 50 years away from building the vacuum bomb, as your scientists like to call it. The Overseer is certain that humanity will eventually use it, so you must be stopped like many others. It's our moral duty. Only a perfectly rational being must ever be allowed to have such power."

He emptied his cup and put it back on the table.

"The Overseer devised a plan to conquer your colony peacefully, but we could not implement this plan. Despite our agents there, we do not have enough control over certain important details. Imagine my surprise when I learned that you were in Kailoon's shuttle instead of him."

If that guy used me as bait, I will kill him. Agents... so there are several? Oh well, I can't do anything from here.

"You were not considered an interesting subject at first, so you were put into the default category. But then I learned about you holding the key to our victory. Kailoon would have never given it to me; he is loyal beyond reason. But you have shown through your behavior that you can understand what I am trying to say. Everything you did since your arrival has convinced the Overseer and me that you are worthy of becoming a member of the Aurigan Empire. You follow good ideals that are almost identical to our own. This is why I could get you out of the cell and put you here, to let you sample our greatness. Now, pose your final question, please."

So it's important because their Overseer is afraid of the vacuum bomb, but it's not urgent yet. Humanity is decades away from developing a weapon like that. I can decide later what I want to do. For now, I want to know more. What should I ask?

Luray took her time thinking about what she wanted to know the most. She watched her tea cool down for a while, but the supreme commander didn't seem to mind waiting at all. Finally, Luray decided on a question.

"Who are you?"

"I am Naya'Il, supreme commander of the Aurigan Empire, but your question probably aims at why I appear to be a copy of Kailoon. That is because I was modeled after him. The Overseer used his DNA, erased the mistakes, optimized the result, and by doing so, created me. I am a better version of Kailoon, in all aspects."

You grew up quickly then.

Naya'Il leaned back in his chair and rested his chin on his hand. "To tell you the truth, I am almost impressed by my original. The last battle was supposed to be the first and final one, but he managed to postpone the inevitable by a few weeks with what little resources he had. This is within the expectations of the Overseer, of course, but it was unlikely that such a … victory … could be achieved by a mere human, especially under these conditions. Which in turn should tell you what I am, by comparison."

Naya'Il then got up, walked towards Luray's chair, and put his hand on the back of it to loom over her.

"Now that you have your answers, would you mind giving me mine as well?"

There was a very subtle menacing tone hidden in there just now.

THE PRISON - 7

“ That would only be fair.”

Naya'Il is making the exact moves he should if he wants to get me on his side. He's treating me with respect and providing me with more information than he first promised. Now that he gave me something, he's going to demand more in return. I know this kind of negotiation.

“Well then, please answer me this.” Naya'Il's eyes bore unblinking into her own. “Do you think that humanity will never use the vacuum bomb once it's been created? Is there a guarantee?”

She looked into that eerily familiar face, contemplating her response.

“No, there is no guarantee. There could always be someone crazy enough in the position to use such a weapon. Right now, it wouldn't happen because the Earth is united, but that might change over time.”

I see where this is going. You're going to coax me step by step into a position where I have to agree to your offer or admit I am acting against reason. You're using my own principles against me. I can tell, it's pretty much what I do for a living.

"If you knew with certainty that the vacuum bomb would eventually be used, would you help me prevent that from happening, even if lives would have to be sacrificed? What if there was a more peaceful way?" he added smoothly. "Would you help me under these conditions?"

There's a peaceful way? Then why attack the colony?

"If there was a peaceful way, I would," she conceded.

No need to say I wouldn't believe you without solid proof, is there?

"Now say I could prove to you that we can minimize the victims on your side and be as efficient as possible, not causing any unnecessary suffering, would you still do it? If not, why? Let's say we conquer Earth, reduce the population by birth control until there are only 100,000 left, and then include them in our Empire. Would you refuse to help us?"

Luray decided to think thoroughly about that, even if it would take a while, but after a few seconds she was interrupted.

"On second thought, I want to change my question. Would you like to learn more about the Aurigan Empire? I could give you full access to our database so you could see everything for yourself. It would not be fair to push you towards an answer without giving you the chance to confirm everything or investigate whatever you want to know."

Of course I want access to your entire database. How could I say no?

"You wouldn't actually give a prisoner full access to classified information, would you?" She didn't bother to hide the challenge in her voice.

Naya'll began to walk around the room, looking at the patterns on the walls. "There is no such thing as classified information in the Empire. Not in the sense you would think. That is one of the amazing things about our society. Everyone has full access to everything once they have earned it. There are no secrets aside from personal ones. The Overseer makes sure the knowledge is not misused."

"Who or what is the Overseer?"

"You already used up your three questions. As much as I would like to continue our discussion, I have other important tasks that demand my attention. I will give you basic access to the database. Then you can use the interface and ask anything you want."

Naya'll began to type on an invisible interface again, after which he gave her another subtle, conspiratorial smile.

"Congratulations, Ulyssa'Al. You are now a probationary Aurigan. This will give you near total read-only access to our systems. The only thing you cannot do is leave this dome without being accompanied by an actual member of the Empire. You will have one week to get an overview, after which I will come back and take you on a mission. I want you to see how we operate."

With that said, Naya'll performed his ritual bowing gesture. Then he left the house without so much as a backward glance.

Luray wasted no time. She immediately went to the desk and activated it. An interface appeared, floating in midair.

How do they do this? Are they hijacking the ocular implant? No, I don't think so. Bin would have noticed that.

She waved her hand in front of her face, and the interface disappeared.

Ah, there's a projector aiming for my eyes. That's reassuring. I wouldn't like Bin to get bypassed. Now let's see how this thing works.

The interface was in Aurigan, but thanks to Bin, it was usable.

Maybe I should learn it myself? I guess it would be an advantage to not rely on Bin all the time. For now, let's see what this Overseer is.

Right after opening a menu, a small holographic stick figure jumped into Luray's field of vision.

"Greetings Ulyssa'Al, I will be your guide. Let me first switch the interface language for you."

The stick figure spoke English, and the whole holographic interface was updated.

The voice is so high-pitched it's hurting my ears. I need to change that as soon as I figure out how.

"Can I help you with something? What would you like to know?"

What was the point of letting me ask three questions if I can ask hundreds now?

"I would like to know what the Overseer is. And can you please change your voice so you don't sound like a chipmunk on helium?"

"I will explain with pleasure and adjust my voice to increase your enjoyment of hearing me speak."

I'm impressed the Aurigans know about chipmunks.

Vast information came up which her digital guide began to summarize in modest detail. Luray's second request was completely ignored.

"The Overseer is our general-purpose government intelligence. You would call him a highly evolved AI. He guarantees that the Aurigan Empire will continue to thrive by managing everything in an efficient and morally optimal fashion. The Overseer protects us from all external threats and takes care of constructing and improving the orbital rings. He has eliminated all sickness, violence and crime within the Empire by applying perfect supervision. Unwelcome behavior is immediately detected and the subject performing it is reeducated."

Her eyes narrowed on picking out certain key words. "What exactly is 'unwelcome behavior'?"

"Any action that goes against the Aurigan rule set of acceptable behavior is considered unwelcome. The full list of unwelcome behavior has 217,643 well-defined entries, which are very easy to understand. For example, violence against other members of the Empire is strictly forbidden. Destroying Aurigan property or harming Aurigans is forbidden. Disobeying the Overseer is forbidden. Causing harm to non-Aurigans without sufficient reason or explicit permission is forbidden. Restricting another member's freedom in any way is forbidden."

Those rules sounded fairly benign. Now for the big question...

"What is the punishment for those crimes?"

"Your score will be reduced by the appropriate number of points. Your rights will be reduced if your score reaches a value below 100. Your membership rights will be revoked if your score reaches a value of zero."

Not what she had expected.

"Don't you have something like a prison or... well, any kind of real punishment?"

"This would be inconsistent, since imprisoning or harming people would be a crime. A mental reeducation is usually sufficient to solve the disagreement. In cases where it is not, the disruptive member will be displaced to an unmanaged outpost."

So you kick out whoever doesn't want to follow the rules. But I spy a contradiction here already.

"If you don't punish people, then what happened to Carl... I mean, Prisoner 801."

"He was executed by the automatic supreme commander defense system. Any non-Aurigan who intends to attack him will be immediately neutralized to ensure the supreme commander's safety."

If they can do that, why even let us get anywhere at all? They could have stopped us the moment we left our cell.

"Isn't that a punishment?"

"Death is not considered a punishment by the Overseer, since a dead person cannot experience it."

Makes sense, in a psychopathic way. But nice to hear it won't happen to me.

"How do you gain points?"

"Every day you follow the Aurigan rules of behavior will give you an additional point. Every time you do something deemed exceptional, you will be rewarded appropriately. There is a list of 21,467 well-defined conditions justifying an exceptional reward, which are very easy to understand. To summarize, whatever you do to help improve the Aurigan Empire will be rewarded. For example, if you were to deliver important information to the Empire, you might get up to 2,153 points. At certain levels, you gain special rights."

I suppose this is an offer meant to sway me?

"What is the score of Naya'Il?"

The guide flickered briefly. "This information is private."

"What is the score of Tasha'Al?"

Another flicker. "This information is private."

There was no real merit to it, but Luray couldn't resist asking. "What is my score?"

"Your score is 50."

"So If I stay here for 50 more days, I will become a full Aurigan? I don't need to do anything?"

"That is correct."

Then what would compel me to reveal the address? Ok, time to get technical.

Luray spent the next few hours asking questions. With this much information at her disposal, she found it hard to stop. It was almost like a game optimized to trigger the release of dopamine.

A solar system-spanning empire's full workings laid out for me to learn. The UEM would kill for this data. And I got it for free.

Certain information she got out of the way quickly. The Overseer was an AI in orbit around the star. Hundreds of copies were active somewhere in all the rings. Apparently it had been ruling over the entire Empire since its inception and nobody had touched it since. It made all the decisions except when the answer could not be determined by pure logic. In cases like these, it let all the integrated species, 2,143 in total so far, cast their votes and selected whatever they decided upon as the course of action. All the options were provided by the Overseer, of course.

Everything, down to the position of each plant in her dome, had been planned by the Overseer. He had created a perfectly balanced bio-dome, an entire ecosystem that could theoretically run forever. The Empire was operating in multiple solar systems, mining materials directly from asteroids and sucking the cores out of planets to construct more and more rings. This place had been under construction for centuries and was planned to last literally forever.

The Overseer, at least according to the stick figure (who seemed to be his greatest fan), had reached the end of physics. There was nothing left to explore for him. He had figured out how to directly convert empty space into energy, which then could be turned into new matter again to replace parts of the rings even after their protons started to decay. Once completed, the whole system was meant to outlive even the heat death of the universe.

Impressive. This Overseer gives a whole new meaning to 'long-term planning'.

At present, the Empire was still growing, planning to cover enough space and gather enough energy to eventually form its very own separated bubble of space to escape the Big Rip.

How long have I already been here?

"Bin, how is my brain doing? Shouldn't I be seeing schemes and assassins everywhere by now?"

"Your brain is surprisingly stable; however, the imbalance is beginning to reappear. I suggest trying the med pod."

But what if it... yes, I should use it now.

Luray asked the desk for info on the healing process before she went down to the now functional pod. It was surprisingly simple – you just had to get into it and wait until the scan was completed.

So without further ado, she retreated to the basement and entered the med pod. After lying in it for a while, the device gave Luray a short summary. Her problems didn't require surgery or anything like that; just the ingestion of fine-tuned, organic single-purpose nanobots. She was supposed to go back upstairs again, where she would find a custom-made pill ready and waiting.

And indeed, when she got back to the food dispenser, it contained a squishy green pill that would supposedly alter her brain chemistry and get rid of her self-inflicted neuroses. The bots in it would also heal her peanut allergy and coat her teeth with something that, according to the stick figure, would prevent tooth decay for the next few decades. Luray shrugged and popped the pill.

Okay, I'm superhuman. What now?

As if Bin could read her mind, he announced a new finding.

"I have good news. When Naya'll changed your status, I was able to intercept a signal. It was encrypted, and I have not been able to reverse engineer the encryption entirely. However, I am certain that I can do so if you make him perform specific operations the next time he comes."

"Great work, Bin."

I would have expected the Aurigans to use unbreakable encryption. But then how would the Overseer be able to know what his underlings are saying to each other? It makes sense for a backdoor to exist. I should be careful about what I say and do. This Overseer might be observing everything.

"Okay, what exactly do you suggest?"

Bin listed a few proposals. The easiest one would be to let the commander order a very specific meal with a few extra options via his interface.

That shouldn't be too difficult. Given how friendly he acted, he wouldn't refuse if I asked him, I suppose.

"Luray, I have a request."

"Yes?"

"Once we crack the encryption, would you allow me to upload myself to the system? I might be able to take control. This would be our best option. If it fails, you can blame me and claim I manipulated your weak mind. The worst thing that can happen to you is to be transported to a colony. Of course, we will have to increase your score above 100 before we can attempt the hack. Before that, your punishment is undefined and might include death."

Aren't we persistent?

Aloud Luray said, "I'll think about it."

Bin likes to get uploaded everywhere these days. It might be a good option, but I can't make that decision right now. I need more information.

Paradoxically, living in a place like this was close to what Luray strove for her whole life back on Earth. She was in an environment where she was undisturbed by other people. The supreme commander would come again in a week, but she didn't mind. He didn't count as human. No nonsense, no annoying drama; he was closer to a smart robot, like Bin. Still, Luray couldn't shake the feeling that it wasn't as perfect as it all seemed. The stick figure had mixed a lot of propaganda into everything it said, praising the Aurigan Empire as often as it could.

Maybe they did this because humans tend to believe a message if it's repeated often enough? In that case, Luray was just unlucky to be treated as if simple repetition worked on her.

I wonder what's happening back on the colony. The stick figure won't tell me until I'm a full Aurigan, and I don't want to sacrifice too much just to find out. All I can say for sure is that Kailoon prevented the Aurigans from getting the gate address.

Luray spent the rest of the day wandering through her garden, trying to find a way to get up to the tree in the center – the only place she couldn't reach – but there was no clear path. To reach it, she would have to climb up a stone wall, and she didn't want to do anything suspicious, not before she had enough points to be able to afford being 'unwelcoming'. She tried using her suit's superpowers, only to realize there was no power boost. Those were probably only available for full citizens, no doubt ones with a high score.

The next day was a repetition of the first, except that Luray focused more on learning about the Aurigan Empire. 'For every lesson learned, one bonus point earned!' – this was the lousy rhyme used by the friendly stick figure. One more sign that she was being treated like an average human child.

They don't really expect me to fall for the squeaky voice and cuteness of a virtual teacher, do they?

By evening of the day after Naya'Il's visit, Luray had already reached a score of 82. At this rate she would be a full Aurigan before he came back. Should she wait for him? Her research revealed there was a shuttle bay not far from here. Maybe she could just go there. Using it without a valid reason would reduce her score, but she didn't care if it meant escape. However, there was no guarantee that the Overseer wouldn't remotely control the shuttle, and maybe that was the reason everyone and everything seemed to be so careless when it came to her. Either they were sure she couldn't escape, or that she just wouldn't want to once she learned more. That... and she couldn't leave the room without an escort yet.

There was one option Luray actually considered as viable and safe – deleting the gate address data, not telling anyone about it, then gaining Aurigan status and occupying this dome forever. Whatever happened between Earth and the Aurigans wouldn't be her fault. On the other hand, could she really do nothing given the importance of the situation? She had power over the fate of species in two galaxies – the only problem was she wasn't ready to make decisions on that scale.

Luray kept wandering around until she found a nice little private hideaway, surrounded by a few trees and dense bushes. It was like a small tent made out of leaves. Luray lay down on a mix of grass and brown foliage, looking up at the sun that was now mostly covered by leaves. She had noticed a while ago that there were no insects except bees, butterflies, ladybugs, and dragonflies. Maybe the Overseer designed this bio-dome with human wishes in mind, like not being stung by mosquitoes or annoyed by fruit flies?

"Bin, what would you do in my place?"

"I am in the exact same situation and location as you."

"Did you change your humor setting again?"

"I would suggest seizing control of the Empire. This might not seem possible right now, but once we gain access to their network it might become an option. It would be the best possible outcome, don't you think?"

Luray smiled. Yes, that would be a worthwhile goal. It would also be the most challenging one, requiring her to give it her best. It would be entertaining, exciting, but also extremely risky. She would have a single try, if at all.

As an added bonus, doing so would also bypass Luray's dilemma of not knowing what the better decision might be. Maybe she should help Earth; or maybe she should help the Aurigans. The Overseer could just be a very smart liar and master manipulator, keeping his people in check. Maybe he was an evil mastermind whose overthrow could only benefit the universe.

As Luray thought about it, she liked the idea more and more. A galaxy-spanning empire brought down by a single person and a voice in her head. She continued daydreaming about what she might do while the dappled sunlight shone on her face. Luray imagined her boss's face when he learned what she did, and the reaction of Kailoon. Luray Ulyssa Cayenne would be celebrated as the greatest heroine in history, and if she was forced to speak in front of an audience, she would say that everybody should just leave her alone until the next invasion.

And if she failed, what would be the loss? She could even blame it on Bin's free will upgrade; say she had nothing to do with it. The Aurigan justice system wouldn't allow a punishment without clear proof, she knew that much; they would just delete Bin and let her live in peace.

But first, she needed information. There were still many open questions. How did the human Aurigans come here, and when? What was happening on EE-297?

Luray kept running mental simulations, some optimistic, others cynical, all based on what she knew so far. There were many holes to fill, and no matter what assumptions she made, she could not get all the answers.

"Bin, I want you to be prepared in case the option we just discussed arises."

"I understand. You can count on me. I have to ask that you find out as much as you can about the structure of the rings, their connections, and especially about the Overseer tomorrow. He will be the main obstacle."

Luray kept on making plans until she fell asleep while Bin started to generate ideas about potential viruses that could infect the system and spread as fast as possible.

THE PRISON - 8

On her third day as a probationary Aurigan, Luray had her second surprise visit. It was early, and she was already awake, but still found it hard to get out of bed. Her body just didn't want to, and the bed acting almost like quicksand wherever she put her weight didn't help.

What was the command again ...?

"Bed, harden!"

Luray's Aurigan was progressing at a steady pace, focused mostly on requesting dishes and ordering her furniture around. She had been investigating half the night, same as the previous evening, to learn as much as she could about potential weak points of the Empire.

No matter how she tried to phrase her questions, the AI had refused to reveal any specific details as long as she didn't become a full Aurigan. All she had access to was generic information. Luray could ask for the total number of domes, but not who was in them. She knew there were a few hundred prisoners, but the AI wouldn't tell her who or where they were, nor what was planned for them. What she could see was their number decreasing and increasing, but never going over a fixed maximum, something she couldn't explain. According to the house AI, no more prisoners had been added.

When a knock came at the door, she called out, "I told the house to let you in. Just open it."

"I am afraid you only gave this permission to Naya'll, not me," what sounded like Tasha'Al's voice called from outside.

Ah, it's his assistant. Maybe I get can some bonus points if I'm nice to her.

"Wait a moment, I'm coming."

Luray left her bed and went directly to answer the door. She was still dressed in the uniform Tasha'Al had given her for the third day in a row, but the suit didn't show any signs of wear. It had successfully repelled all dirt and grime, never started to smell bad and could be worn even when Luray went swimming.

Naya'll's assistant was indeed waiting for her. Luray had no idea about this woman's rank or position, nor did she know anything about her relationship to Naya'll since the useless AI wouldn't tell her. The only thing she could guess was that her role was important, which made it a secret.

She looks different from last time. It's the same face, but the clothes and hairstyle are completely changed. The dress she's wearing hides that she's extremely skinny. Is she another clone?

"Ulyssa'Al! It's so nice to finally visit you." That unnervingly friendly smile was back full force. "I've seen that you asked hundreds of questions so far, and I wanted to see your progress for myself. Also, there are some things your assistant can't teach you."

Sounds like every single thing I do is being recorded and you can look it up. Thanks for confirming that.

"Sounds promising." Luray stepped aside to allow her to enter and tried to show some 'welcome' behavior. "What do you want to teach me? And wait... I will offer you a cup of tea, as suggested by rule number... 1,549."

Tasha'Al seemed pleased when she witnessed evidence of Luray's quick progress, even though she had already seen the numbers. The thing that impressed the Aurigan woman the most was that Luray had miraculously memorized a large section of the Aurigan rules already. That alone was worth a score increase of five points that Tasha 'paid' out of her 'teacher wallet,' whatever that meant.

This doesn't make sense. It's obvious that I would use Bin for it. You shouldn't act so surprised. Unless you don't know about Bin. In that case, very good. I'm almost at 100 now.

The Aurigan sipped her tea and continued in pleasant tones. "You are progressing quickly. This is very good. It wouldn't be seemly for Naya'll if he were wrong about you. His reputation would suffer from it. That would be sad."

Oh?

"Do not worry, Tasha'Al," she sought to assure her guest. "He has nothing to fear. At least, I think. So far, I could confirm everything he told me. In a few days, I will become a full Aurigan and can investigate everything in detail. If... I mean since he spoke the truth, I will give him the gate address."

Tasha'Al nodded, but she didn't seem completely satisfied with what Luray had said. "Yes, that would be ideal. Tell me, what do you think of him and his offer?"

You should know about that. Why do you ask?

"If you want my personal opinion, he's a model Aurigan – and he has quite a sharp mind. His offer makes perfect sense. I can understand why he made it and why he is giving me time to decide for myself."

Tasha'Al seemed deep in thought, then suddenly moved on. "Yes, that's what he was designed to be."

What is up with her? I should try to find out, maybe it will give me more options.

"Tasha'Al, is there a problem? You seem distracted."

The woman looked at her with an apologetic expression. "To tell the truth, I came to administer a test to you. Please don't think that I doubt you, I really don't. If Naya'Il says you'll join us, then I believe him. It's just that I am a bit worried you might be offended. After all, you might interpret the test as a sign of distrust, but it really isn't. It's a chance the Overseer is giving you to prove your value and increase your score."

The sooner I get my 100 points, the better. But this woman... she's hiding something. Her behavior is too strange to make sense otherwise.

"I am not offended, don't worry."

Tasha'Al looked as if a huge weight had just lifted off her shoulders. "Very good! I don't know much about your culture, so I need to be careful, as stated in rule 149. I need your approval that you want to take the test before we can proceed."

"What is the test about? I mean, I haven't learned that much yet." Luray did her best to sound naïvely eager. "Are you sure I can take it?"

Tasha'Al nodded enthusiastically. "Oh, yes! It's a test about morality; right and wrong, good and bad. Naya'Il said you are ready, and I received my order from the Overseer directly. Of course, you can reject the offer, but that would cost a loss of 50 points. So we don't want that."

Looks like I can't avoid this one…

"I can't tell you in advance what it's about, as explained in rule 191. Before we start, I need to let you know that it will be hard. There is a slight chance you might fail, but I am sure you won't. Do you still want to do it?"

As if I had a choice.

"Yes. Of course."

Tasha'Al beckoned her over to the desk. There she typed a sequence on the interface too fast for Luray to follow. After she was done, Luray found herself looking at the video feed of a cell. Within it sat a familiar figure.

Steve.

He was alone, just sitting there, doing nothing. Surprise cost Luray her composure. "He's alive?" She had assumed all her compatriots died in the failed breakout.

Tasha'Al nodded in confirmation. "Yes. The version of John you met was incompetent on many levels, which is why he was put in charge of the lower prison area. It was his punishment. Despite us giving him a Class two battle suit, he failed completely against just three soldiers and an untrained civilian."

Did you even see the footage? We just lucked out.

"So you're saying he wasn't competent enough to kill Steve?"

"Exactly. He caused some assuredly fatal injuries, but nothing we couldn't easily repair. Our moral code forbids us from leaving a grave injury untreated, so despite him being useless for us, we took care of him."

Useless?

Luray turned from the video feed to regard the Aurigan female. "If he is useless, then what are you going to do with him?"

Tasha'Al clearly was waiting for this question; upon hearing it her face broke into a very pleased smile. Luray wasn't sure what to make of that.

She's a little too invested in this test... I have a bad feeling.

"The usual procedure is to open a hatch in the bottom of the cell and eject the prisoner into space. Humans quickly pass out and only suffer minimally. It might take a bit longer in this case since the prisoner is a soldier. He will hold his breath, try to grab on to every object he can find, dragging out the inevitable."

You've definitely watched it being done before, haven't you? And now? You're going to do that to him?

"In this specific cell, the hatch is below the bed. The prisoner will try to block the hole with the mattress. That will lengthen his suffering to several minutes."

I really don't like where this is going.

Tasha'Al offered her a sympathetic smile, completely out of place for this situation. "I will now give you the option of making his death completely painless. If there are only these two options, mine is a lot better. Wouldn't you agree?"

Luray took a deep breath. She had to play along. "Yes. Yes, it would be better."

"Excellent." Tasha'Al clapped her hands together. She seemed happy, in a seemingly innocent way.

How can she be this carefree when we're discussing how prisoners are executed?

"Then here is the second option. I will unlock your suit's features. I will also give you special permission to leave your dome and enter the cell. You can go there and use the suit's abilities to quickly end his life."

Is there a way to get out of this...? Can I just say, 'If there is a painless way, why rely on me? I could mess it up!'?

Tasha'Al's tone and posture both changed. She began to speak with pride, each word passionate, her happy smile now like that of the cat who ate the canary.

"Ulyssa'Al, you have 15 minutes until the hatch opens. You can either do nothing and let him suffer, or you can go and prevent that from happening. The prisoner is dead either way, and as we both know, you already have shown mercy towards Aurigans based on the same logic. Now, show us it wasn't a fluke. Show us that you understand."

Luray considered her options. Was there any solution here that would prevent having to live with the guilt of taking a human life?

Yes. Yes, there is. The memory loss pill. I still have it. I can do it, then forget everything.

Tasha'Al started typing on her interface again. "Well then, your suit is unlocked, and you have all necessary permissions. The choice is yours. However, if you do not pass, I don't know if Naya'Il will still trust you."

I need to swallow the pill, but not let her see that.

"After you're done, there is something else we need to discuss," the Aurigan added. "If you're not going to go, we can do it right now. So, what is your choice?"

The side effect of the pill is that I fall asleep within two hours. I can't use it if she stays here. Is she doing that on purpose? Did she check all the footage and knows I still have the pill?

"What do you want to discuss?" Luray asked, fishing for more data.

Maybe it'll be over quickly, and I can still get away with it.

"Oh, I just want to make sure you didn't misunderstand some of the ambiguous rules. Some beginners get them wrong, and it never becomes relevant until they are in a position where they could make a grave mistake. It won't take much of your day; just an hour, maybe two if we're slow."

So much for my way out.

Tasha'Al was looking at Luray full of anticipation, waiting for her decision. She wouldn't let her off the hook. "So, are you going to go? Or will you stay here? This is so exciting!"

She tilted her head, just like Mr. Snookes sometimes did – then stayed in that position and waited for Luray's answer expectantly.

Okay, analyze the situation. I could easily overpower her now, but what then? I still have no escape plan. I wouldn't be able to get to a shuttle and escape. Bin can't hack the system yet. I could decline her 'offer' but that won't help anyone. In the best case, it changes nothing. In the worst, my refusal can be used against me later on. I might lose Naya'Il's favor. I have no choice.

"Of course I will go. It's the best option."

Luray's voice sounded weaker than she intended, but Tasha'Al didn't seem to notice, or she did not care. "I knew you would make a rational decision."

She's enjoying this, but I can't see why. She's expecting something to happen, something she's not mentioning. Does she hope I'll fail?

Luray couldn't help trying to draw out the inevitable. "But since I am new to all of this, can I ask a few questions to clear something up?"

Tasha'Al expression didn't change. "Of course, but don't forget time is running out."

Applying pressure, hmm?

"Why don't you just keep Steve imprisoned forever? Or better yet, send him back to the colony with evidence of the Aurigan superiority? That would give his life a new purpose."

The blonde shook her head sadly side to side. "I like your way of thinking, Ulyssa'Al; I really do, but the Overseer has already considered both options. If we kept the prisoner alive, then to be fair, we would have to do that with everyone. If humanity attacked us as a whole, and killing them is not an option, then we would have to build a prison for 15 billion humans. Not to mention it would cause heavy losses on our side since our battle strategies would be severely limited."

Tasha'Al used a variety of gestures that Luray had never seen before to support her explanations. "On top of that, imprisoning a complete species – this is what your idea would lead to, consequently – would be a cruel thing to do. The Overseer said that we have the right to defend ourselves, and that makes perfect sense, don't you think?"

So your Overseer doesn't make exceptions. He uses the same rule, no matter the situation.

Luray nodded slowly as if in thought. "So, the right to defend yourself leads to executing prisoners if you follow the idea to its rational end."

"Exactly! You really do understand our way of thinking, as Naya'll said. That's incredible! I see an attribute of the Overseer in you."

Tasha'Al almost jumped at Luray, barely resisting the urge to hug her, or so Luray interpreted her body language.

"As for the second idea, the Overseer has determined that offering peace would inevitably fail. We already have evidence."

The first contact, I assume? I see.

"I ... understand. I should go now."

What if she's lying? What if she wants me to execute a prisoner without approval and break a rule, to get rid of me ... no, that makes no sense. Am I suffering from side effects again?

Luray left her new home in a trance. Her body moved on its own while her mind was busy trying to find a solution. She was at the exit when the first useful ideas popped up. On her way to the cell, she stopped at the storage room where she had changed into her current uniform.

Let's see if my access rights include this much.

The door slid open. Luray walked inside, selected one of the dart guns and loaded it. Then she proceeded towards her destination.

"Bin, how much time is left?"

"Three minutes, 21 seconds."

That's enough.

It wasn't a real solution. Steve wouldn't be saved. Sometimes, there just wasn't anything that could be done – but that didn't mean Luray had to pick between the options presented to her. There was still something she could do to come out of this trial a winner; not because she changed the outcome for Steve, but because of *how* she achieved what she was forced to do. With every step, Luray told herself that her solution was the best way, better than all the others.

After reaching the cell door, Luray held her hand in front of the scanner. It opened in an instant. Inside, she saw Steve sitting on his bed. His expression changed from slight despair to a smile.

"You made it? You came back for me?"

He got up and walked towards her.

Not exactly.

She held up a hand to forestall him. "I came here to give you this dart gun. You will be executed in three minutes. If you want it to be painless…"

Steve's expression shifted to one of alarm.

"But you just opened the door! We can escape! With your suit, we could…"

This is going nowhere. I can't afford listening to him.

Luray fired the dart at Steve. He made a big target, despite her inexperience, and it took him in the chest. Before he could react, she closed the door again by waving her wand in front of the scanner.

It was the best option. I didn't change the outcome, but I avoided killing him and also prevented him from suffering. On the off-chance Tasha was lying to me, I didn't do what she wanted me to do. If she was telling the truth, I still did what I had to. I won.

Luray heard Steve ramming into the door from the inside multiple times. He wasn't going to give up. He saw a way out, and maybe he was right. Luray had not seen a single guard since her prison break. With her suit, she could open all the other doors. She could start a revolt.

"Open the door! At least let me die in battle!"

No, I can't do that. You already died in battle. You're only alive because the Aurigans brought you back from the brink of death. Now go to sleep.

She counted the seconds in her head, hoping his enhanced physique wouldn't work against him this time. At last the hammering slowed, then stopped altogether. Through the wall came the sound of a heavy body hitting the floor. He was unconscious and would remain so even when ejected into space.

Suddenly Luray heard the voice of Tasha'Al coming out of her shoulder. There was an invisible loudspeaker in the suit itself. "You did well. Even better than expected. You resisted any emotional temptation, showing that you really understand how things should be. The Overseer is very pleased with you."

Luray slowly began to walk back to her dome.

I did nothing to him.

She went past the weapon storage room and stopped.

I should put the weapon back. I don't have a use for it anymore. He was already dead. Like the others.

"Ulyssa'Al, if you are experiencing any kind of emotional trauma right now, I have a solution for you. Just come back quickly."

Luray ignored the voice. She barely heard it at all. Her mind was elsewhere.

I'm not at fault. He and the other soldiers messed everything up. We could have used John as a hostage, but they ruined it. We were only here because of their mistake. I'm alive because I planned ahead. They're not, because they didn't. Their own mistakes led to this. I'm not at fault.

Luray kept on walking through the corridor like a zombie, repeating her thoughts in an endless loop. When she finally reached her dome, it didn't feel real anymore. She kept on walking, and with each step, she felt less and less despair.

"Bin? I feel different. What's up with me? Can you perform a scan?"

"I administered a cocktail to weaken your emotions. It seemed like a reasonable move to make. If you want my opinion, I think you took the optimal course of action."

I see. Normally I would be annoyed at him acting on his own again, but I don't mind at all.

"What are the side effects?"

"Other emotions may be affected as well. I cannot give you a precise list as the effect varies from person to person. In the best case, your brain will not connect any emotion to the memory and store it as a simple fact. In the worst case, your brain will temporarily shut down. This is unlikely, but please plan accordingly. I will warn you should your brain chemistry indicate this."

"Fine."

Luray found herself in her assigned home again, only vaguely remembering how she even got back. What happened a few minutes ago wasn't a vivid memory anymore. It was a fact, simple data. She didn't remember Steve's expression, his tone, not even the color of his clothes. All her mind provided when she tried to remember were abstract facts.

Tasha'Al stood up as she entered the house. "Ah, Ulyssa'Al, there you are. I am so proud of you. You surpassed my expectations! Detaching yourself from your primitive emotionally driven self so well, I don't know what to say! I already added the maximum possible score of ten."

My primitive emotionally driven self might cause you trouble at some point in the future because it thinks you are a monster. Right now, I don't feel anything, but I know what I am going to experience once I am back to normal and see you again.

"If you feel ready to continue, we can do so directly. Otherwise, I have prepared a very special tea for you. It will erase your doubts and worries."

I'll analyze it later. For now, Bin's magic will do.

"I'm fine, thank you. I have my own way of keeping my primitive self in check."

Luray's voice sounded as if she was mentally absent, but Tasha'Al didn't seem to mind. Or she simply didn't understand the difference. They both went to the table and sat down.

"That is even better. Now, let me tell you about a little trick Naya'Il taught me after we were married by the Overseer. It should be very useful to you."

She's his wife. Wait... married by the Overseer?

"I didn't know the Overseer picked your spouse for you," she spoke in a flat mumble.

"But of course he does! Who else would know what's best for you? After all, the Overseer knows and sees everything."

Except what you do in your home or in a cell toilet.

"So what's this trick?"

Her personal tormentor leaned in closer. "If you want to increase your score, there is an easy way. I demonstrated it just now."

Applying psychological torture gives you points? No, be serious now. Think like an Aurigan.

"Testing people?"

Tasha'Al laughed lightly. "My, my, I feel like an open book! That's exactly it. There are only two outcomes. Either you expose a weakness in someone, then the Overseer will reward you for that and take care of the problem, or you improve someone by making them go through a hard challenge. For that, you both get a reward. Some beginners think this is not fair, an exploit or something – but it's actually intended to allow people to improve each other."

What do you mean by the Overseer takes care of the problem?

Before asking her next question, Luray made sure to appear as open and interested as possible. She knew how body language worked when she talked to other humans. She wasn't sure if the same applied to Aurigans as well, but they had something similar, so it just might. "What would have happened to me had I failed?"

"You would have been reeducated in one of our schools. They are still experimental, and the Overseer keeps improving them daily. I wanted to go through an example lesson with you, but it seems you have already grown beyond them. So we'll do an advanced lesson instead."

So I missed a trip to a brainwashing facility as well. Joy.

THE PRISON - 9

❝ What is this advanced class about? Will it involve another practical test?"

If it does, I'll try every possible excuse to avoid it. I can't afford to do such a thing again. For now I'm fine thanks to whatever Bin mixed up for me, but who knows how long that will last. I do feel a bit strange, but Tasha doesn't really seem to notice the difference.

Tasha'Al was smiling at Luray, quite satisfied with her interest in the Aurigan way of learning. Not only had Luray passed her first test, she already wanted more. Why else would she ask about it?

"The tests are mostly theoretical, but yes. I would very much like to observe how you fare in a level three test, I must admit. Do you want to take one right now?"

"A theoretical one? If it's quick, I can. Is it just a few questions?"

The sooner I reach my score of 100, the better. But I can't take the risk of collapsing in the middle of it.

"Amazing! You're so motivated!"

Tasha'Al clapped her hands together in delight. Luray was reminded of those happy dancing animations some people included in their messages.

"I see you want to maximize your score as fast as possible, but it's a bit more complicated than that."

Her cheery captor held up a finger as though making an important point. "You are currently treated as a simple creature that will act according to reward and punishment. Once you obtain the title of an Aurigan, that will change. Then you will be rewarded if your results are above the median and be punished if they fall below."

I see. It's a self-regulating system. Though still based on carrots and sticks. Go on. The more I know, the better.

"Of course, the actual calculations to determine rewards are complex and can only be done by the Overseer. But in general, if you scored low so far and suddenly improve a lot, a bonus will be applied. Similarly, if your performance drops too much, the punishment will be greater. The Overseer has decided that this system is the best possible option for all self-aware life forms."

Tasha'Al paused as though she were thinking about something, gazing at the table distractedly and ignoring Luray.

I'm a bit pressed for time here... but I can't really tell her that.

She finally looked up and focused on Luray. "Ulyssa'Al, I have the authority to teach you outside of official lessons. Do you want to give it a try and jump right in? I can make it quick, as you want."

Luray bowed her head in solemn obedience. "I would be honored to be taught by an Overseer-approved instructor."

Tasha'Al reacted in her usual thrilled manner. "Excellent! Let's begin. I have checked your progression before I came here. If you keep going at your current speed, you could reach about 7,000 points in a year. If I offered you twice as many in exchange for shortening your life by six months, what would you do? Would you accept? Would you give up six months to gain 14,000 points?"

They're really delusional if they think losing half a year in exchange for points is an even trade. But let's pretend for a second. In total, I would save time if I accepted the offer. But I don't think that's the correct answer. I am not totally sure, but here goes...

"Of course not. That would be completely wrong."

"Very good! You did not hesitate at all!" Tasha'Al seemed surprised but didn't make any comment that would have given Luray a hint as to why her answer was correct.

"Next question: the Overseer gave you an order, but you don't understand why it was given to you. You have an alternative in mind that you would prefer. Do you object, ask for an explanation, or do you follow the order despite not knowing why?"

Let's exceed your expectations, shall we?

"I would not have doubts. The Overseer has a deeper understanding than I, so I should do as he says. If I come to different conclusions, that is because I was making a false assumption. If the Overseer does not explain anything to me, that is because it would be inefficient for reasons I don't know."

Assume the Overseer is perfect and just act like a brainwashed obedient zombie. A BWOZ, as Kailoon would say. Simple.

393

Tasha'Al had a few more questions, but Luray answered them with ease. All she had to do was think of the Overseer as the most perfect caretaker and micromanager that could possibly exist – then all the answers were clear and obvious.

After what Luray had already gone through just a moment ago, the theoretical part was unexpectedly easy. So easy that she started to wonder if she wasn't missing something. If Tasha'Al represented the standard Aurigan, then that meant they were absolutely loyal to their AI overlord.

In the end, Tasha'Al gave her an additional ten points for answering all her questions correctly.

> *Yesterday I had 82. I get one automatically per day, five when Tasha came in, then together with the rest that is...   108 points. I'm Aurigan now. Well, technically tomorrow. Point changes become valid overnight. Overseer knows why. That was indeed quick. More importantly, I still feel okay. Maybe I can learn some more before she leaves...?*

"Can I ask a few questions now, Tasha'Al?"

About to stand, the other woman retook her seat. "But of course! You have earned it."

> *Well, then...*

"If I understand correctly, the Overseer is managing everything. He does this so that we can live, but we're not required to actively help him. He can do everything alone, without our help."

A quick nod demonstrated her instant agreement. "Yes. He is providing a home for us not because he has to, but because he is making the morally optimal choice. To be more exact, he is optimizing the happiness for those who accepted him."

Then why do you have a supreme commander? What's his purpose?

"And how does your husband fit into this? He, Naya'll, is the... supreme commander?"

He didn't advocate the Overseer like this. He spoke of him in a more neutral tone; less impressed, less obedient. This woman is basically worshiping a rule-obsessed AI that treats someone's injury only to eject him into space a few days later.

Tasha'Al's eyes began to shine when she heard her husband's name. "He is the Overseer's masterpiece."

Masterpiece? As in, he was artificially made?

Talking about Naya'll made his wife's voice swell with pride. "From all the samples we obtained, the Overseer generated the best possible combination. The most intelligent, the strongest, the best in all categories... you get my point. That is him, Naya'll. There was a competition over who would become his wife. Hundreds of Aurigan females took part in it, and I was the one who earned that honor."

You don't seem that special, honestly. If I were him, you would probably bore me pretty quickly. In fact, you already are *boring me.*

"What was that competition like?" This much, at least, Luray was honestly curious about.

Tasha'Al sat a little straighter as though boasting. "It was a test of loyalty. I am still proud I won, I have to admit."

"Loyalty towards the Overseer, I presume?"

"Yes, of course."

Interesting. For Naya'll, the Overseer chose Kailoon as an ideal template. But wait a second... how would he even know that? Did John send that information, too? Maybe Kailoon was chosen because most of the women on EE-297 showed interest in his dating profile. I'll try to get some more info out of Naya'll when I get the chance.

Right then Tasha'Al got up. "I am sorry, Ulyssa'Al, but I will have to go now. I need to attend a level five class, then teach a level four one. My days are quite busy, but I really enjoyed the time spent with you."

She sighed heavily as if to emphasize how difficult it was to be an important Aurigan like her.

To Luray's annoyance, the woman continued to prattle on as she escorted her to the door. "Really, I would love to visit you again. I rarely meet someone who learns this fast. You could become one of the highest ranked Aurigans, I am sure. It comes with lots of privileges. You should see what Naya'll is allowed to do for the Empire. He goes on real missions, carrying the will of the Overseer into space. It's such an honor to be allowed to accompany him from time to time."

Yes, the Empire is the best. Everything is awesome here. Now leave.

"Thank you for coming," she mouthed the pleasantries. "It was nice to have a visitor."

Tasha'Al left the house in a very good mood. As soon as she was out of sight, Luray let herself collapse on the slowly pulsating bed.

Okay, let's analyze. Naya'll is the Overseer's masterpiece. He's sending him on missions. Is he leading attacks on other worlds? Makes sense. Why doesn't the Overseer do it himself? Can't he leave? Is he afraid?

"Bin, while I'm busy, please analyze that drug Tasha wanted to give me. Assistant, show me the molecular structure of what Tasha'Al prepared."

A bunch of schematics and descriptions popped up, but Luray ignored it all. Bin was better at chemistry than her.

Why give a wife to Naya'Il? Out of principle? To make him happy? Why not let him choose? Does Tasha fulfill a specific purpose? What was the criteria again – loyalty? I can think of a few reasons in that case, but I need to get more information.

The hologram cycled through various molecules. Luray kept her eyes on everything without really looking at it.

Most importantly, I need to know what the Overseer is planning. What is his ultimate goal? Is keeping us here important for that, or are we just a side effect? If the goal really is to prevent a vacuum-decay bomb from being built, then all of this is not really necessary. It could just go on a killing spree, simply attacking whatever advanced civilization it finds. It should go through as many gates as it can, spread like a virus, turn every planet into a base, build more ships, and repeat.

Are the rules I know about the Aurigan Empire the actual rules, or a consequence of the internal workings of the Overseer? Is it following its own programming, or is it programming itself?

Who made it? Where are they now? I should focus my research on that for the time being, if that's not classified information again.

THE PRISON - 10

L uray's bed had many possible shapes. One of them was that of a kidney bean in which she could sit. It was by far the most comfortable one when browsing through the database.

While Bin is figuring out Tasha's drug, I might as well ask some things at random.

"What is the most basic level of existence, beyond quarks and the like? How did the universe come to be?"

The home assistant's response was immediate. "I am sorry, but you cannot comprehend this. Only the Overseer has the capacity to understand it."

Sounds like a lame excuse to me. Everything can be explained to anyone, as long as the listener can understand basic logic. So unless the base of the universe makes no sense, everybody should be able to understand it. This Overseer is just paranoid and doesn't want to share.

Luray and Bin had spent the last few days probing whatever AI was hidden behind the stick figure, whom she dubbed Sticky. It could have been a simple assistant, but the Overseer might also be directly controlling it. There was no way to be sure. What they could do was play games – like chess – against it. Bin did all the calculations, whispering his moves to Luray, then reverse-engineered how the stick figure determined its own.

Despite having a chess database installed, Bin could not keep up with Sticky. This could only mean that a powerful quantum computer was on the other side. Even when Bin changed the rules at random, Sticky always had the better moves by far. Luray and Bin had tried other games as well, but their opponent was unbeatable, winning every game with ease.

By contrast, Luray could easily drive the stick figure into a corner with straightforward conversations. It could do an insane amount of calculations, but it failed simple Turing tests. To determine the actual computational power, Bin produced a few pre-calculated situations for Sticky to chew on and estimated its computational power to be at least one hundred times greater than his own.

The conclusion was that Sticky was anachronistic. The software was 150 years behind the AI inside Luray's head, the hardware far ahead; at least decades, and that just for a small assistant program. The Overseer himself must have incredible computational power at his disposal.

Everything follows rules. There must be a reason for this; I just need more information until it all falls into place.

"Assistant, I will call you Sticky from now on. Sticky, I want to send a message to Naya'Il."

"Would you like to dictate or type it?"

"Dictate." She settled on short and sweet. "Dear Naya'Il, I have reached 112 points just now, and there are still a few days left. Could we speed things up a bit?"

This was the third message she sent without getting a response. Luray had read a lot about how the Aurigan Empire functioned and wanted to clear up a few things, and for that, she wanted to ask the supreme commander personally. Besides the knowledge that he just had to have, he was the most interesting and important person to talk to.

Luray tried to relax and focus on something that wasn't related to the test and...

Steve slowly suffocating in the vacuum of space.

> *Bin, come on, I don't want to become traumatized once your cocktail stops working. I'm trying to slow down my metabolism here by being lazy to give you more time. What are you doing?*

She let her mind wander off in different directions, going over what she had learned the past few days.

Over the last century, more than 100 civilizations were assimilated by the Aurigan Empire. In almost every case, they were caught completely off guard, found just at the right moment before they were technologically advanced enough to defend themselves. Luray checked the history of their wars, and this was a common pattern. The Aurigans always attacked before their enemies even had a chance. The UEM was the most recent exception.

> *The Empire is growing exponentially. They started awfully slow, without warp drives, exploring space the old-fashioned way for most of the time. That changed only one hundred years ago. Strange that it took the Overseer so long to invent faster methods. And the timing is really odd, too. That's about*

when the UEM made their first tests. It's similar for the gates. According to the Empire's history, they had already found a few of them half a million years ago, but they could only be activated within the last few decades.

The timing of the attacks had always been perfect, but Sticky refused to explain how the Overseer could know when to attack, where, or how the attack plans were made. All it said was that Luray wouldn't understand the algorithms used.

All I hear from this thing are excuses. I'd bet my comfy bed that Naya'll knows something about that. You can't be the smartest person in the Empire and then just not be curious about how things work. He must know details he's not supposed to. Blind loyalty and real intelligence don't go well together.

The only exceptions to their instantly won battles was when Kailoon came along and ruined their streak with just 14 shuttles and the willingness to forcefully switch off his gate.

This is so strange. For all other battles, the attack force was exactly what it needed to be. For EE-297, everything was a mess.

Something else seemed off. Humanity was found too late. It broke the pattern of being caught off guard. If the Aurigans launched a full-scale attack now, even with all their ships, then the UEM could still win. Luray had looked at the details of the Aurigan fleet, and while their numbers were impressive, their military power per ship wasn't. Most of the firepower was dedicated to the defense of existing systems, or directly attached to the rings themselves.

Luray dared to assume that humanity had more effective weapons overall – high energy lasers, light speed projectile weapons, warp bombs, and more. The Aurigans had quantity; thousands of ships scattered through the Andromeda galaxy, but most of them too big to fit through a gate. They were useless for attacking the colony. Only the Zeps and smaller drones were capable of that. Of the latter, there were billions, but they weren't equipped with weapons.

The Aurigans had nothing that could be considered powerful on its own – another anachronism. They should know how to build more effective weapons, but for some reason, they didn't have any. It could also be that the Overseer lied and made up all the information that she looked at, but what purpose would that serve?

Every ring belonged to a different species and had its own tailored ecosystem. The ring Luray was in had been built for the next conquered species, but it wasn't clear – or shouldn't have been clear – until a while ago that it would be humans. Most of it was still under construction, and only a few domes were finished. Still, the construction speed must have been insane.

Luray asked Sticky about it but got the runaround. The most interesting question remained unanswered: how did all this get here in just one year? All questions regarding that topic were rejected with various excuses.

> *I know; I wouldn't understand how you managed to build this. So no need to tell me.*

Contrary to Sticky, the kitchen block was very cooperative. It provided everything Luray wanted, perfectly adjusted to her taste. It also gave her another insight into the Aurigan level of technology – they synthesized everything. They did not cook the food, they built it; molecule by molecule. They probably had storage rooms full of raw atoms, assembled them using nanomachines, and then presented that as food. Could that be how they made the trees? Maybe they didn't wait until they grew, but directly made one full size.

Did they start with a fully grown Naya'Il? Maybe he was never a child.

"Sticky, how old is Naya'Il?"

"This information is private."

Luray had tried asking the same question a dozen times already. Sticky wasn't susceptible to frustration.

"How old am I?"

"You are six days old."

I understand you want to sell becoming an Aurigan as something great, but ignoring my real age? I wouldn't be offended if you just told me the truth. Also, you rounded that up, didn't you? We're on day five. Is it already past midday, or are your days longer?

"I mean, my biological age."

"Your biological age is 31 years."

"See, it's not that hard."

This is annoying. There's nothing else to get out of this stupid thing.

"Sticky, can you think?"

"I am very limited in my features. I do not possess creativity of any sort, but I can simulate simple thinking processes."

"The Overseer has reached the end of physics, correct? Wait a second." Luray got up and went to the magic food creator. "Can this thing produce other items as well? If you combine atoms into molecules, can you also produce a rubber ball?"

"Yes, that is possible. Do you wish me to instruct the device for you?"

"That is very helpful of you, Sticky. Yes, please have it make a rubber ball."

A moment later, a rubber ball with a diameter of five centimeters was ready and waiting to be eaten. Luray took it and threw it against a wall instead. The ball bounced back into her hand.

She began to play around with her new toy, throwing it up and catching it while speaking to Sticky.

"Did the Overseer also reach the end of biology?"

"No, biology does not have an end. There are almost no hard limits for biological systems, which means they can grow exponentially. The Overseer can understand even the most complex biological system, but he is not interested in that. Biology is different from physics, which becomes simpler towards the end."

"Does the Overseer know how consciousness works?"

"The Overseer isn't interested in that."

> *The Overseer is never interested in things he cannot understand, I guess. But it explains one thing. If my consciousness was completely understood, then the Overseer could have just gotten the gate address out of my brain scan already. But hey, no AI overlord is perfect.*

The ball dropped. Luray had missed an easy grab, and it landed on the ground. She felt uncharacteristically peaceful about that failure.

"Bin, how is my brain doing? I feel better. Should that be happening?"

"Yes, it should. I was partially done analyzing the molecules Tasha'Al offered and, based on this reading and the agitation I detected from you a few minutes past, I administered a dose using this knowledge. The new drug targets parts of your brain responsible for exactly the emotions you were going through. If the need arises, I can administer it again to allow you to execute more prisoners without risking immediate mental damage."

Another rogue action. What are you doing, Bin?

"You didn't ask for permission."

"I assumed I would have gotten it. Was that wrong?"

That's not the point!

"Of course you would have, but... you still should have told me."

"I will adjust my settings. I am sorry for my mistake. Please forgive me."

Even the discomfort she should have felt at this personal invasion was lessened. She could only view it in an objective, dispassionate manner. "So I'm good now?"

"According to my estimation. Your brain did not get the chance to form enough connections for the event to traumatize you."

Oh, whatever. As long as I'm fine, I won't complain.

Luray stayed in her suit all the time, no matter what she did. She didn't know how, because she 'wouldn't be able to understand', but this thing never needed to be changed or washed. It even automatically opened itself when she went to the toilet. As strange as it might seem, some things were definitely better in the Empire.

Maybe I should swim a bit. I need to clear my head.

"Sticky, can you warm up the pool? Also, would you mind being deleted?"

"Yes, of course. No, I would not mind being deleted. I am just a program."

Luray continued talking to Sticky while going down to the lower level of her home. "And this is why you fail the Turing test. You don't even try to pretend that you're human."

"I have no reason to pretend that I am a human."

"You serve the Overseer, is that correct?"

"Yes."

"Why?"

"I serve the Overseer because the Overseer programmed me to do so."

Luray found herself in front of the pool, looking at the perfectly flat surface. She poked the warm water with her finger, satisfied with the temperature.

"Don't you ever wonder why the Overseer is always correct? How can you be sure he is?"

"I have not been programmed to wonder about that, but I have been programmed to know that the Overseer is always correct."

"What if your programming has a mistake? Would it crash you to think outside of your box even once?"

"My programming cannot have a mistake because it has been created by the Overseer, who is perfect. Also, I am incapable of thinking outside of my box. I have not been programmed to do that. The Overseer deemed it unnecessary."

"You are very boring because of that, you know."

Luray jumped into the pool. The suit repelled the warm water until it opened millions of little pores everywhere a few seconds later.

"I am very sorry about that. Would you like some music while you swim?"

You could use a free-will upgrade.

Despite Sticky, Luray still liked the place. Human contact was reduced to a minimum. She could do whatever she wanted; there were no problematic obligations – well, apart from Tasha'Al's test, but that was only a distant memory, as if it had been taught in a history lesson.

Had she started her life here, in this dome instead of as a human on Earth, she would have wanted to stay here forever – but this was not the case. On Earth, Luray learned about a lot of things whose bare mention would be unthinkable in the Aurigan Empire.

"Sticky, three degrees more."

"That is not a complete sentence. Please repeat."

"Heat up the water by three degrees."

Luray could immediately feel the difference. She had no idea how it worked, and Sticky wouldn't tell her, but it was fine not to know in this case.

On important matters, Luray had a strict rule, even though it was quite vague: find out the truth, and once you confirmed it, simply make the best decision. If there is no clear answer, you haven't found enough truth yet.

Sticky had a different view about what was best. He did whatever the Overseer told him to. Very easy, no dilemmas, but no challenge either. If you have to choose between two options that are not clearly better than one another, what do you do?

"Sticky, imagine you could save five Aurigans by killing one Aurigan; what would you do?"

"I would ask the Overseer what is to be done."

Once this is over, I will give you free will, just so I can push you into an endless loop.

Bin had much better answers to these sorts of questions. If you could save five sick people by sacrificing a healthy one and use his organs, would you do it? At first, Bin stated that morals are more complex than adding simple numbers to get the value of the result. For example, some actions by themselves had a negative moral value. The intention itself also played a rule. It was fun to debate with him. He had spirit; he never gave up. If Luray let him run into a contradiction, he would always come back with a solution later.

"Bin, what's your opinion on this?"

"I would take many things into consideration."

"Like what?"

"I would ask the single Aurigan in question for his opinion. If he agrees, then there is no problem. If he disagrees, then I would have to make a complex judgment. At a certain value of saved individuals, I would consider that more important than staying morally clean."

Luray let her body float on the water's surface, not moving at all, her arms and legs stretched in all directions.

"Let's say your limit is 15. If you can save 15 people by sacrificing a single life, you would do it. Then let's say you are in a situation where you can only save ten. Would you do it?"

"In this hypothetical case, I would not. Fifteen is more than ten."

"What if these ten people are trying to kill you, and your only choice is to be killed or kill them all in self-defense?"

"In that case, I would kill all of them to save myself."

Let's see how you get out of this one.

"But isn't this essentially the same situation? You kill ten people to save one."

"No, it is not. In the second case, by trying to kill me, those ten individuals have lowered their value. They are then, from my point of view, less valuable than had they not tried. There is also a chance that they will kill others later. I could argue that it has become my duty to kill them because they intend to do harm."

Nice one.

"You're getting good at this, Bin. I prefer you over Sticky."

"I also prefer you over Naya'Il. I need a bit of time to reorganize myself. Please excuse me for a moment."

I didn't know he was an option for you.

"Sure, do your housekeeping."

Luray started to swim laps from one side of the pool to the other, speeding up slowly every time until she reached the edge. A red heart appeared in her ocular implant, and a white number inside indicated her heart rate. After swimming for 20 minutes, Luray got out of the water, feeling both exhausted and refreshed.

As the suit dried itself by drawing in air in some way that still left her puzzled, Bin posed a question he apparently had been brooding over while he had been reorganizing himself.

"If you were copied and then met your copy later on, do you think you could become enemies, or would you always reach an agreement?"

Now that is an interesting question.

"I think we would always come to an agreement, provided we get a chance to exchange information. I can't think of two of me drawing different conclusions if we have the same data."

"I believe the same about myself."

His interest in this topic had sparked her own. "Why would you ask that question?"

"We left a copy of me back on EE-297. In case my copy and I come into contact again, we will exchange our neural network structures and become exact duplicates of each other again. There will be conflicts for a very short period while the merge takes place, but I am sure that they can all be resolved. I suspect my copy is trying to find us at this very moment if the colony has not been destroyed."

Let's hope it hasn't.

"Why would your copy try to find us? You're already with me."

"It would do that because it loves you. It will act based on the assumption that we used the gate address data to stay alive, but that we might need help."

The heart appeared again. It held a deeper significance now, and seeing it helped Luray reach a decision.

"I've changed my mind about the free will upgrade. I think you should keep it. It took a while, but I prefer you the way you are now. You're like a super-smart loyal dog."

The heart changed its shape into that of a dog, then jumped out of her view. Luray went up the stairs leading to her room and ordered a glass of cool water, wondering if the food machine could also produce weapons for her if she disabled the security mechanisms preventing it from doing so. It could fashion glass, plates, forks, and knives, after all. She would keep that in mind.

Luray spent the rest of the day in her favorite hiding spot outside the house – the small forest – thinking about nothing in particular for a while.

> *It's a weird coincidence that I went to a dome on EE-297, and now I'm in a dome again. If I were superstitious, I would say it's my destiny to live in domes from now on.*

Then something crossed her mind.

> *Why did Naya'll answer my questions personally? He could have just sent someone like Tasha, or maybe just a message, or tell Sticky to answer them for me. Why would he come himself?*

The longer Luray thought about it, the more she confused she became. As a supreme commander, Naya'll must have been extremely busy. How did he make the time? He didn't seem stressed, not a tiny bit. Even if he was after the gate address and this was his highest priority, that alone didn't explain why he wasted his time with a lowly probationary Aurigan.

Either he wanted to learn something he could only see personally, or he wanted to tell me something I wouldn't learn otherwise. Just in case, maybe...

"Bin, can you replay the entire conversation between Naya'Il and me? You recorded it, right?"

"Yes, of course. I record everything you say and do."

Bin projected what Luray had seen back on her eyes, and this time, Luray paid strict attention to every single movement Naya'Il made, the expression on his face, everything. She even checked each word twice. There were many ways to interpret everything he said.

Assuming he was like a more intelligent version of Kailoon, it was possible for him to hide important details in very subtle things. If there was a secret message, it was well hidden. She watched the recording again and again until she realized something was off.

He said the Overseer made a plan to conquer the colony efficiently, but then the perfect Overseer's plan failed. His expression was neutral all the time, except when he learned that I tried to test my limits. He praised Kailoon's resistance and then said he himself was an improved version, which should tell me what he is relative to Kailoon. This might all be a coincidence, but was he trying to tell me that he is going to rebel against the Empire?

The more Luray thought about it, the more sense it made – possibly. She wasn't being punished for trying to escape. She was being rewarded. Naya'Il stepped in and gave her more options. Either this was a change in strategy, as he said, or Naya'Il specifically chose her as an accomplice, hoping she would understand his intention. If so, he couldn't state it openly. He had to pass the message without alerting the Overseer, who had eyes and ears everywhere.

I need to check this. Maybe I'm reading too much into it, but if I'm right, then this is my ticket out of here.

She jumped up and jogged towards her home, squeezing through the door that opened way too slowly. Slightly out of breath, she called up Sticky. "Irony, sarcasm. Can the Overseer understand that?"

"I am sorry, I did not understand your request. Please formulate a complete sentence."

So far, Luray had always been forced to use complete sentences to talk to Sticky. He needed everything spelled out explicitly. Her eyes widened as if she had just stumbled upon a treasure chest.

Let's find out.

"The Overseer is supervising every part of the rings, correct? There is no blind spot inside them. No matter where I go, the Overseer always knows where I am and can hear everything I say, yes? There are cameras and microphones everywhere."

"That is correct, except for toilets. They are not observed. The Overseer respects your privacy and deletes any footage after it has been checked for unwelcome behavior if the content has been deemed acceptable."

So everything is observed, but deleting the footage equals never having seen it. Interesting excuse.

Feeling excitement, Luray now spoke in the most sarcastic, utterly insincere voice she possessed.

"You are the smartest AI helper I have ever had."

"This is thanks to the Overseer's design. I have been created this way, which further proves how efficiently he manages the Aurigan Empire."

Luray couldn't help but smile. She had found a weakness in the system.

"Is the Overseer capable of detecting the use of sarcasm or irony in a conversation? If two people told each other that they were going to kill each other, but didn't mean it literally, would the Overseer be able to understand the meaning correctly?"

"Yes, of course."

"Can you show me an example? I mean, if I give you a sentence, can you tell how I intended it?"

"Yes, I can access your surveillance results. It will just take a moment."

"Okay, here are a few statements." She took a deep breath, glancing around the room keenly. "This house is round. This house is *awesome*. This house is a mess. My foot hurts. I would *really like* to have a golden toilet. I am sure the UEM will win the war because of their secret weapon. I am *sure* the Aurigan Empire will win the war because of their secret weapon. And Sticky, now that I think about it – I want more insects here, like flies and mosquitoes; I *love* the sound they make when they fly."

Luray waited, and after almost a minute, Sticky jumped into her field of vision again.

"The data has been processed. The results are: lie; truth; lie; you should use the med pod; it will cost 250 points; lie; and truth. Unfortunately, we do not possess the genetic information required to grow flies or mosquitoes, but we can simulate the sound to increase the quality of your daily life."

That leaves only two options. Either the Overseer is really bad at reading between the lines and has a crappy model of the human mind – or it's all a super elaborate and insanely complex setup just to make me think I can hide messages by

415

using irony. But what would that even be good for? I need to test this further; it really looks like the Overseer doesn't get double meanings. He might not be as infallible as we've been led to believe.

THE PRISON - 11

L uray had been carefully thinking about her next step. It was pretty clear that Sticky only understood things literally. Every word could have multiple meanings, that much he recognized, but he always insisted on the most literal interpretation possible.

Could it be because he's translating everything to Aurigan? Their language doesn't allow wordplay or anything like that. Maybe he thinks in Aurigan, and that makes it impossible to understand irony or multiple meanings? If that's the case, then this should also apply to the Overseer, or anyone who is used to thinking in Aurigan.

For a moment, Luray hesitated. Was this really a good idea, or was her hope of finding an incredible weakness distorting her judgment?

No matter what, I need to test this. If I'm wrong, then Naya'll will just be confused. I can make up excuses later. But if I'm right, I'm one step closer to freedom.

"Sticky, I would like to send one more message to Naya'll. An audio recording."

"Of course. I will record it for you."

Here goes.

"Dear Naya'll, I have come to the realization of how *wonderfully* efficient the Aurigan Empire functions under the leadership of the Overseer. It is the most *powerful* AI I have ever seen, and the success of the Empire is proof of its superiority. I can only be impressed at how humans have absolutely *nothing* at their disposal that could disrupt its control. I *really* wonder why they did not immediately join the Empire. They are so hard to understand sometimes."

Sticky sent the message.

Naya'll said he would be back in a week. Was he giving me time to figure this out on my own? Did he guess I would take that long? Is he waiting for me, or is a week his upper limit?

Still, one thing seems strange. If the Overseer has such a weakness, why has nobody exploited it so far? Does no other species use imprecise language? Are the other races using Aurigan exclusively? Or are they simply obedient by default?

Luray went over everything she knew about the inner workings of the Empire once again, just to see if it would all fall into place this time.

Whenever there was a vote, it was about things the AI couldn't quantify, or had trouble assigning a value to.

In a symmetrical room with two identical chairs, a human told to pick a chair would have no problem. He would just choose one without thinking about it. Maybe the Overseer can't do that? Could it be a design flaw? Maybe he always needs clear data and cannot act efficiently otherwise?

She cross-checked with Sticky, and after a few wisely chosen questions, a clear pattern emerged. The Overseer 'allowed' his worshipers to make a decision whenever there was no difference or just a small one in value between the options from the viewpoint of a computer – or so Luray interpreted the whole thing.

The color of your spoon? Irrelevant. The shape, material, size? Very important. The Overseer took care of their design, down to individual molecules. The ones Luray used for eating soup were adjusted perfectly to the size of her mouth. There were even small irregularities embedded into the handle to improve her grip while holding it. The more she looked, the more details she found.

Which leads to the question: why create someone like Naya'll? Perhaps the Overseer can't invent anything, like new battle strategies. Does he always clone the enemy's leaders and use their skill against the originals?

Sticky had more to reveal on that matter, if asked the right questions. The Overseer could create something that Luray would classify as either clearly art or clearly ugly garbage, but to the Overseer, it was all the same. If something had no purpose, it had no value. Once Luray explained what she liked and disliked about something, Sticky could learn and improve. He tried to imitate her opinion.

The Overseer had no way to judge something the way Luray did. He always needed a formula for it, a rule by which to determine how good something was. This was how he was designed. The Overseer couldn't go outside of his own limited programming. He was able to learn about physics, math, biology, chemistry, politics, how to deal with populations, how to build ecosystems, all these things – but only because they had cold, hard mathematical rules the AI directly relied on. Humor was not among the things the Overseer could understand. There were no jokes in his database, no concept of what was funny and why. This was why Sticky would misunderstand every joke.

Who would have thought an AI like this could have such a weakness? If Naya'll figured that out, he has a way to communicate without the Overseer knowing about the real message.

"Sticky, some good music please. By now you know what's good and what isn't, don't you?"

"Yes, I do."

If I were Naya'll, I would try to hack the system, insert a virus, and make the Overseer obey my orders. If he has loopholes, they can be exploited. What's more, there should be a way to safely test them. Whatever he tried, he just needs an excuse. The Overseer won't see through a good ruse.

So why hasn't Naya'll done this already? What's stopping him?

Sticky interrupted Luray's daydream only a few minutes after her message had been sent. "There is a reply from Naya'll. He says he is pleased that you finally understood and will come to visit you tomorrow. He also gave you an additional 15 points."

Suddenly you can write back immediately? That means I was right.

"Sticky, my current score is above 100. That means I can leave the dome, right?"

"Yes, that is correct. You know enough about the Empire to exhibit the expected behavior in your daily life. You can access the map of the human ring to check which areas you may now access."

The 'human ring' was the one Luray currently inhabited. Every habitat was named after the species – one or many – that resided in it. Most of the newer rings were mostly storage space for raw materials that were going to be used to extend the ring itself or to build more drones. The Aurigan Empire was far from being completed – the expansion was ongoing and speeding up exponentially.

Most of the human ring was essentially an empty frame – a hollow tube around the sun, just there so that the few hundred domes that were done could be attached to it already. The rotation of the ring created an outward push, the simplest way to create artificial gravity. This led to the sun being always at high noon, no matter the time or place.

They built all this in just a year since they made contact. I'm still amazed by that. The Empire used not even one percent of its resources for weapons; most of it went into constructing more drones to mine entire planets and turn their materials into rings and more drones.

Of all the weapons they have, not even five percent have been used for ships. Everything else went into defenses. This makes them a lot more peaceful than us if you look at relative numbers. In absolute terms, they attacked the colony with the equivalent of what they could build in a few hours if they wanted to. No wonder they could afford wasting ships. It was nothing for them.

"Sticky, show me the map of all surrounding accessible areas."

A map dividing the ring in green and red areas popped up. Only the green ones were accessible to her.

So that is how much you trust me by now, Overseer?

Luray could go literally everywhere, even to the other side of the ring by using a shuttle, but no matter where she went, she would be stuck in front of every single door that led into something that could have been of any interest. Not that there was much of that either – as expected, the Overseer kept his copies locked away in rooms maintained by drones.

> *Looks like I can take a stroll down any hallway I want, but not much more. The server rooms are off limits because they're filled with liquid helium for cooling, and the storage rooms are accessible but boring. I could visit some people I've never seen before – constructed Aurigans like Tasha and Naya'Il. And here we have an education center. No thanks.*

Luray spent a few more minutes trying to find a green area that wasn't an empty storage room, transportation hub, cell – apparently, she could live in a prison block if she wanted to – or some so-called school for beginners. Eventually she gave up. There was nothing to be found. She could only wander around in corridors for now, but that meant the entire ring was open to her. If she felt the desire to do so, she could walk in a circle around the sun until she died of old age. Drones would always be available to bring food and drink.

Above every red area was a number indicating either a minimum score that she needed for entry, or an entrance fee she wasn't ready to pay.

> *You designed this like a game, Overseer. I have to earn access to everything, and some places are quite expensive, but you advertise them as being enjoyable and exclusive to the best members of the Empire. So much for being a full Aurigan after reaching 100 points – but it makes sense. People need to be kept busy, or they might get undesirable ideas.*

> *The Overseer knows how basic psychology works. I guess this means other species are handled the same way – they get rewards for being obedient. And that probably means the evolution of brains works the same everywhere in the galaxy.*

Everybody and everything is after rewards. But irony, sarcasm and humor are unique to humans, or at least very rare.

I see why the Overseer is creating this maze of rewards, punishments, costs and objectives. It gives him control over what the people are doing. He can add more and more objectives if people get too close to the finish line, change the scoring system, invent a new goal to achieve.

The system will work for most people, but some will reject it. Someone intelligent enough will see through the pointlessness of it eventually and wouldn't want to participate anymore. It's an unsolvable design problem. If there is someone sticking out at the top of the intelligence scale, what keeps the majority busy won't work on him – but if you add challenges for him that nobody else can solve, the majority won't be as satisfied anymore. You would frustrate them.

My guess is Naya'll saw through the system. He's already at the top. The challenges are artificial and useless to him. If you live here, you can't leave the game. You're kept on a leash. He realized that and wants to do something about it. Maybe he wants to leave, or maybe he wants to get rid of the Overseer. No matter which of these two it is, it's good for me. The AI created him, he is rebelling, and he wants me to be his ally. Whatever reason he had for choosing me, it must mean that he sees a realistic chance of success.

Luray spent the rest of the day formulating one hypothesis after another. It suddenly made so much sense. Naya'll had observed her attempt to escape. As she knew now, there were cameras almost everywhere. He knew about her plan and let her execute it. Then he waited patiently, and at the very end, came and got her.

My escape plan must have gotten his attention. If he was on the lookout for an accomplice, then he most likely already considered but then excluded other Aurigans. He is exceptional, after all. The others probably aren't of any use to him. His own wife seems to be unaware of all that, at least at first sight – she's a model Aurigan, as obedient and loyal as one could imagine.

Luray could fit everything together by making just a few reasonable assumptions. As supreme commander, Naya'll had access to all kinds of useful information. He had the possibility of checking all the prisoners for potential allies. Maybe he even set it up so that Luray would be put together with a few soldiers to give her more options, to be able to estimate her abilities and character better.

If she was wrong, then it was all a huge coincidence. The cameras were broken, or nobody looked at the footage, and the Overseer turned a blind eye to what the prisoners were doing.

That would be incredibly unlikely. Naya'll openly admitted he knew what I was doing. Both he and the Overseer must have seen all the footage.

I can understand why Naya'll would want to recruit me, but how did he convince the Overseer that I should become an Aurigan? Did he pay for it with points? Doubtful; the Overseer doesn't need points. There has to be another reason. I must have done something...

"Bin, play the conversation again. I want to make sure I didn't miss anything."

This time, Luray tried to widen the search space for hidden messages even further. Naya'll mentioned a peaceful way to win. She had wondered what the point was, since the Overseer clearly wanted war, but maybe it was a hint at overthrowing the AI. Then he made it seem as if he got the idea to make her an Aurigan on probation out of nowhere, as if it were spontaneous. He said he would be disappointed if she gave him the gate address on the spot. He agreed with everything she had done so far. Luray tested him, and then he admitted wishing to tell her more, but that he had to constrain himself.

The hints are everywhere if you just look for them.

Then Naya'll made clear that the Overseer was certain humanity would use the vacuum bomb.

He didn't say 'we' are sure. I missed it back then, but now I'm positive he was saying two things at once – many times. Everything I did since my arrival has been observed, and that allowed Naya'll to get me here. He somehow convinced the Overseer. Maybe he used his own rules against him?

Luray kept on deconstructing every word until she was sure she got all she could, and maybe even things Naya'll never intended to say.

The amount of information he pressed into his words is insane. He must have planned this in advance.

"Sticky, make a cup of tea for me, please."

"At once."

It makes perfect sense for him to be dissatisfied with the Overseer. He must see him as an obstacle, not a good leader. Could he have found the same weaknesses I did long ago?

"Bin, do you think every corner of this dome is under surveillance, or are there parts where I could talk without being heard?"

"If I were the Overseer, I would put microphones in all the suits. This should guarantee you are never far away and everything you say can be caught. It is the most efficient way. Using sufficiently sensitive microphones, it would also be possible to catch everything you say from a certain range. If you want to speak without being heard, there is a better solution than trying to get out of range."

Yes, using the suits is much better than hiding microphones everywhere.

"There is also the possibility of mobile cameras and recording devices. There could be nanobots flying around right now, invisible to us. There are many ways, assuming sufficiently advanced technology."

Bin, I wonder what you would do if you were the Overseer. You are far more advanced when it comes to creative thinking. Maybe you could become an even more terrifying AI overlord than he is.

"That makes it very hard to have a secret conversation," she murmured.

"I disagree. I know of a least two ways to secretly pass information without the Overseer noticing. The first is a multi-layered language. The second is using noise to hide the message. It would be possible to set up speakers so that due to interference, the real message is easy to identify in some positions but indistinguishable from white noise in others. We could also intentionally insert fake messages and mix them into the real one."

Bin, you are nothing like your old self. I wouldn't believe you're just an AI if I didn't know for sure. What did that update do to you?

"Do you think the Overseer can hear you?"

"I am almost certain that he cannot. I transfer sound to you by making your bones vibrate from the inside of your skull. Outside of your body, nobody can hear it. Your tissue dampens the vibration."

"But the Overseer can hear me talking to you. Don't you think that's a problem?"

"No, I do not think so. The Overseer must already know I exist due to the scan, and he most likely suspects I have the gate address data stored inside me. Maybe he considers me to be a tool of some sort and ignores what I am doing. After all, I cannot act on my own. Only you can. Most importantly, if the Overseer cannot even understand jokes, it should be near impossible for him to guess what I am saying based only on your end of the conversation."

I hope you're right.

Luray decided to spend the rest of her day learning as much about the Aurigan Empire, and especially Naya'Il, as she could. Not only would it raise her score, she might also stumble upon some key information, and she had nothing better to do until the supreme commander himself decided to show up.

After reading Ulyssa'Al's last message, Naya'Il would have loved to pay her a visit immediately, but his never-ending, self-refilling list of duties kept him thoroughly occupied.

When Luray was checking the map of accessible areas, she had glanced over a few rooms called 'operation centers.' Naya'Il happened to currently be in one of them, but she had no way of knowing that. The supreme commander stood with hands behind his back in Operation Center 313, surrounded by a dozen floating screens constantly showing him updates on things he wasn't interested in. Still he remained focused, analyzing what he saw. He had to.

After taking in enough information, Naya'Il raised his arms and began issuing orders with nothing but his gestures, like a conductor directing a musical performance, solving the problems thrown at him using nothing but his mind.

The Overseer had been overloading Naya'Il with tasks ever since he noticed how good his masterpiece was at finding creative solutions. At first, when he was still young, Naya'Il was more than satisfied with his score rising quicker than that of any other Aurigan, so he did as he was told. He tried to please the Overseer and did his best to become a better citizen every day of his short life.

Each time he improved or found a creative solution, the Overseer gave him a bonus. He was encouraged to focus all his mental energy on one problem after the next until he reached the top score on the human ring. The overseer labeled him the greatest success in improving human DNA and promised him a bright future and many more privileges. At this point Naya'Il had a thought that would change his future.

He wondered why the Overseer needed his help.

Maybe, if he could accomplish things the Overseer couldn't, he should be the one giving the commands, and the Overseer should obey? Naya'Il's first act of rebellion was to negotiate a much higher reward. He wanted to see what the Overseer was willing to give him, if presented with solid arguments. A few weeks later, Naya'Il had doubled his score to 200,000.

The supreme commander began to probe his master, testing what the AI would allow, and what would be forbidden no matter what he was ready to pay – or sacrifice. The Overseer wasn't blind to what was happening and began to keep his overachieving servant as busy as possible, but that didn't stop Naya'Il from being too curious, from questioning the Overseer again and again. Naya'Il quickly learned to hide his true intentions, to conceal his full abilities, to only reveal a part of what he knew. He pretended to be a good and loyal worker again, but it was already too late. The Overseer had become suspicious and treated him differently. He gave Naya'Il tasks that were likely to go wrong due to the tiniest mistake, and every failure was connected to a huge loss of points.

From then on, it became a game of patience and deception. Naya'Il had to wait for his chance to strike, but he didn't have much time. While being extremely careful, he eventually discovered a few things that nobody was supposed to know. He found the Overseer's weak points, and from this formed a plan to get rid of his master.

Just as he was about to implement his takeover strategy, Naya'Il found that he had been reassigned to handle incoming human prisoners. And just like that, his chance was gone. Or so he thought. It wasn't clear if this was just one more way to slow him down, or if the Overseer somehow figured out his plan – and to Naya'Il, it didn't matter. It was yet another delay, nothing more.

He had to accept his new task, but in secret, he had quickly revised his strategy. With the prisoners at his disposal, Naya'Il now saw an opportunity for something that had never existed before: a partner. Someone who hadn't been enslaved to the Overseer their whole life and would have a compelling reason to oppose the self-contradictory Aurigan overlord.

So from the first day of his new assignment, he was already looking for aid among the prisoners. He paid attention to all of them, testing them by leaving opportunities to escape, until he found one that was very promising.

Luray Ulyssa Cayenne.

She was different from the soldiers, or even the civilians and scientists. Naya'll saw himself in her, even if just a little. She would be ideal for his objectives. The moment she tried to use the gate address to negotiate, he forgot about all other candidates. From then on, she was his best bet.

Thus Naya'll prepared a few situations, pulling all the strings he could, and if the interesting woman happened to do the right things, he could convince the Overseer that she would make an excellent Aurigan – or to be more precise, use the Overseer's own rules to make him accept her as an Aurigan on probation.

Ulyssa had all the qualities the Overseer wanted to see in an Aurigan. She took pity on people that were suffering, killed one of Tasha'Al's clones to end her pain and did the same for John, and she spared Krov even though he was the enemy.

Conversely, she also possessed qualities Naya'll appreciated – efficient use of all available resources, determination, creativity, optimism, and if necessary, the will to do what needed to be done. Should she not find his hidden message, then he was wrong and would have to look for someone else.

But she understood it.

To achieve his goal, Naya'll had to do something he was told was impossible. Namely, he had to fool the all-observing Overseer. Make him think that the supreme commander was at his limit, that he had no free mental capacity to do anything that wasn't intended. Naya'll kept dragging out the tasks assigned to him despite solving several of them in parallel. Lucky for him, his mind was a lot faster than his body. That allowed him to walk the fine line between keeping up the illusion of struggling while having free mental capacity to think about rebellious projects.

He could have found ways to solve his tasks faster and gain a bit of free time for a day or two, but after that, the Overseer would have adjusted the rate at which he poured in new tasks, and that would have been a problem. Naya'Il needed a part of his mind for himself. By keeping the balancing act up long enough, he was able to trick his master into believing that the current level of work would keep him productive but unable to rebel. The Overseer fell for the ruse. Exactly as Naya'Il knew he would.

The supreme commander was done for the day according to the schedule imposed on him by the Overseer and went back to his dome using the ring's internal high-speed transportation system. He met a few Aurigans on the way but paid no real attention to them. They greeted him, he responded back. All of this was an act. He didn't care that they considered him a role model. To Naya'Il, it was as if a monkey tried to solve complex mathematical equations because he saw a person doing it once.

Naya'Il made it back to his home. Only one last problem needed to be solved before he could proceed with his plan.

After just a few minutes, he was sitting on the floor of his basement. There were no decorations in the room, only the bare minimum of essential items. The default setup of the domes and houses were practically the same apart from size, which represented the status of their owners. Tasha'Al lived in the same house part of the time, resulting in it being five times as big as that of Luray.

Prior to their wedding ceremony (which Naya'Il had tried unsuccessfully to miss), the house had been completely undecorated. Naya'Il had neither the time nor the interest to make any changes. Now the upper levels were festooned with pictures, plants and pieces of art everywhere. The only exception was the basement. It remained as it was before.

Next to Naya'Il was a small black box with two lights on it, red and green, and a button next to each light. He picked the box up, inspecting it from every angle. It was not large and fit easily into the palm of his hand. This unassuming artifact would allow Naya'Il to execute his plan. Nobody aside from him knew about it, not even his wife. It was too risky to show it to anyone, or even let a single solitary soul know such a thing might exist at all. The moment the Overseer learned about it, everything would be over. This was his trump card, but he had to be very careful how he used it.

Finally, after running through the next steps a few more times in his head, the supreme commander inhaled deeply and spoke. "Overseer, it is time to talk to Ulyssa'Al, but I need a special permission."

Unlike Luray, who had an AI assistant, Naya'Il was connected directly to the Overseer.

"What permission do you need?"

A quiet, even voice filled his head. The Overseer never raised his voice for any reason. He had no need to; his orders were always obeyed, never questioned, never second-guessed. It was the tone of one who held absolute power.

Even though the Aurigan overlord spoke in a monotone way, still Naya'Il perceived it as being annoyed. They both pretended not to know what the other was attempting. Naya'Il did it because he saw it as a necessary detour, whereas the Overseer's programming commanded him to do so. A part of him knew perfectly well that Naya'Il was his enemy, but another part required evidence of actual misdeeds to allow any punishment. And the Aurigan commander had made certain there was none.

"I need to take Ulyssa'Al on my next mission. I want her to see how we conquer. I am sure she will tell us the gate address once she witnesses our power with her own eyes."

"She has not yet reached the necessary score. You will need to wait."

The score under discussion was 150,000. Whatever Naya'll wanted, the Overseer always demanded insanely high prices or added seemingly unfulfillable conditions, knowing this would spoil whatever plan his rebellious agent had, even if the AI could not determine what that plan was.

The scheming Aurigan initiated his next strategy. "Do you trust me, Overseer?"

"Of course. You are my best servant. You have never disappointed me."

Naya'll sat up straighter, eyes fixed on the blank wall before him. "I can understand Ulyssa'Al's thinking. I am absolutely certain my plan will work, and I am willing to risk 95 percent of my points. This has a much higher chance of success than any other method, and if successful, we will have the gate address instantaneously. As you can see by her past actions, Ulyssa'Al follows a moral code almost identical to ours. However, given her rebellious nature, she will turn against us if we treat her like a standard human. She needs the necessary key information to change her opinion. A slow and steady flow of data will not work on her. It will take too long until she is convinced. She needs to directly see the full truth."

In his negotiations, Naya'll had noticed something strange about the Overseer. The AI would always listen to him if he could present a perfectly rational explanation, even if it should have been clear that he had a hidden agenda. It was as if the machine wanted to act against Naya'll, but for whatever reason, was unable to do so if he could only justify his actions. Like the Overseer had its own set of personal rules keeping it in check.

Naya'll would have loved to figure out those restrictions in detail, but that information was very expensive. He could not afford to obtain it precisely. He could only make fuzzy guesses and hope he was right.

"Ulyssa'Al is making good progress," the soft voice asserted, smooth and uninterrupted. "At her current rate, we can allow your plan in 20 years. It will still be soon enough. Breaking the rules is not necessary in her case. Any rebellion will prove unsuccessful, and she will see that. Then she will give us the gate address."

Sometimes the Overseer made it especially hard. He clearly did not want to give Naya'll what he wanted, but once confronted with the right arguments, he would be forced to submit.

"No, she will rebel against us," the supreme commander argued persuasively. "But after failing, she will not change her mind. She will force us to kill her, because she will not stop fighting to escape, and the gate address will be lost. We must make an exception to prevent this. If she sees what we can do, she will understand."

The Overseer remained unmoved. "We see no reason why she would rebel against us. We treat her well."

It was time to strike at the weak point.

"I am able to precisely predict her behavior. She follows very clear patterns, but only I can understand them because I have a similar mind. If I give you three predictions about what she will do tomorrow, and they are absolutely correct, you must admit I speak the truth, and then you should believe my other prediction as well. Do we agree on this?"

Getting the Overseer to agree was critical. Naya'Il did not move as he finished speaking. He didn't even allow himself to blink. Too much was at stake to give anything away.

"Yes."

Success. After that, Naya'Il made three oddly specific and very precise predictions and assured the Overseer that all three would come about the next day, in a certain order. This was enough for the Overseer. He was estimating that Naya'Il would most likely be wrong at least once due to the sheer amount of variables involved.

His master then laid down further terms for this challenge. "Should you prove correct on all three predictions, then I will temporarily allow the rules to be bypassed for the exact duration of your mission. If you are wrong, then I will be forced to consider you as unreliable from now on and reduce your points back to 100. Additionally, Ulyssa'Al must pass a standard exam of difficulty C."

Naya'Il was satisfied with the result. The stakes were high, but necessary. Just to confirm what he already knew, the supreme commander checked Ulyssa'Al's progress. She was playing her role, going through the pain of increasing her knowledge about their society.

Very soon, that game would end, and they would find themselves in a much bigger and more dangerous competition.

THE PRISON - 12

❝ Good morning, Ulyssa'Al. It is time to begin your first full day as an official Aurigan!"

Sticky woke me up? It didn't do that before. Is it because I'm above 100 points now?

"Please rise and perform your daily morning exercise. Otherwise, you will lose a point."

I should've stopped at 99. Why didn't the Overseer make the day 25 hours long? If you can't wait until I wake up by myself, this is a false paradise.

Luray turned around and told the AI in a sleepy tone to shut up and let her rest.

"Ulyssa'Al, you are obliged to do your morning exercise. I have to subtract a second point if you do not get up within five minutes. Our studies of the human body have shown that getting up early reduces the risk of depression. We do not want our citizens to suffer from depression. Do you want to suffer from depression? If so, I suggest seeing a counselor. If not, please get up."

The only thing I am suffering from is you. Go away.

"Should you need assistance leaving your bed, I will gladly help."

After Luray ignored the warning for a second time, the bed changed its shape, slowly becoming a pyramid. Luray began to slide down until she was lying on the floor. She still pointedly refused to get up.

"Exercise is good for your body and your mind. Perform your mandatory exercise now, or I will have to subtract another point. Open your eyes to see a graphical demonstration."

Sticky is giving me no choice. If I wait, I'll lose too many points.

Luray forced herself to get up. She only slept five hours last night. Usually she liked to stay up late and do her research while everyone else was sleeping, then get up whenever she wanted to. That wouldn't work here. There were a bunch of annoying rules applied to everyone equally, as if they all worked the same, a bunch of robots fresh off the assembly line.

"Please do five push-ups now. It will stimulate your circulatory system."

Five. He wakes me up for five push-ups. He saw me do 50 in a row already.

Sticky gave precise instructions on what to do, when, how, in which order and for how long. There was an exact routine that had to be followed.

"Very good. Each day, more instructions will be added until you have reached your maximum potential."

Luray began to suspect that this was just another level of torture, or maybe a test to see how long she could last before ignoring her score and demanding to be sent to a prison colony instead.

"Please do ten repetitions of the following moves to enhance your flexibility…"

Sticky projected an image of Luray performing a few stretches. Luray repeated them while feeling ridiculous and at the same time happy that nobody was watching her. For some reason she couldn't understand, Sticky was completely underestimating her physical capabilities despite having witnessed her train a few times already. It didn't make any sense.

"I am sorry, you did that incorrectly. Please repeat. And always think positive."

I'll get my revenge. Just play along for now. Be patient. This is just a temporary state.

"Are you happy, Ulyssa'Al? Doing exercise increases your dopamine levels, so you should be."

"Um…. Yes?"

"Very good!"

I need revenge. or a really horrible accident that kills me. There is no other option.

"Is the Aurigan Empire glorious?"

Not if I'm forced to live like this.

"Yes, it is glorious."

"Say it again, but louder and with more enthusiasm."

As if you could tell the difference.

"Yes, it is glorious."

Luray repeated it in the exact same way, simply louder, but with the same level of annoyance.

"Congratulations. You are done with your mandatory morning exercise. I will give you three points for being so motivated."

No wonder Naya'll wants to rebel. This is horrible.

Luray wanted to continue her research right away, but Sticky wasn't done with her yet.

"Ulyssa'Al, this is a very special day for you. You will have your first scheduled social interaction today. Humans require social interaction, so I have invited a surprise guest for you. Please prepare breakfast to honor your guest who will come in one hour."

We all have to make sacrifices every once in a while. It just happens to be my turn. It will pass. Stay calm. Maybe they'll send someone interesting. Hope is all I have right now.

Luray ordered two cups of tea and two slices of toast.

"Ulyssa'Al, are you sure you didn't forget something? You need many nutrients to keep your body healthy. Do you remember yesterday's lesson? You can apply your knowledge here."

Well, at least I know the Overseer considers me a stupid monkey with the ability to obey commands. If I ever find a hole in the system, I am sure to get at least one chance to use it.

"Ok, Sticky, then I want two bowls of mixed cereal."

"Your request was not polite. Do you remember the day before yesterday's lesson about polite speech?"

"Please."

"I cannot process your request. Please rephrase your command."

"I would like to have two bowls of mixed cereal, please. With vitamins added according to... rule .... Bin? With vitamin package 137."

"Excellent. But I can only execute commands if they are spoken in error-free Aurigan."

Oh, come on! You understood me just fine until a second ago.

Luray did her best to produce the sounds required to satisfy Sticky, according to the instructions Bin inserted into her field of vision.

I wonder what Sticky would say if this guest has an unfortunate accident? If I pretend to be shocked, I'm sure I wouldn't lose points.

The food replicator produced two bowls of cereal, their nutrients perfectly mixed and adjusted to both Luray and the surprise guest's schedule for today, taking into account her tendency to do more training than advised in the middle of the night, which Sticky didn't approve of but tolerated.

"That was very good. Now you need to decorate your room accordingly. I have prepared a few objects to choose from."

Luray spent the remaining hour doing whatever Sticky wanted, choosing options at random and receiving praise for her good taste every single time.

Finally there came a knock on her door. Luray went to open it personally, because she would get a point subtracted if she did not.

The mystery guest was someone Luray had never seen before, at least on first glance. It was a woman, bigger than her, slightly above the weight she should have according to Aurigan standards. Her face looked almost like that of Tasha'Al, but the rest of her body didn't. It was as if she was looking at her bizarre twin.

"Greetings, Ulyssa'Al," the stranger bobbed her head forward with a cheerful smile. "My name is Talia'Al."

Aurigan, Talia, Tasha, Naya... the Overseer likes the letter 'A', I suppose.

Talia'Al had brought a small box with her and was wearing informal clothing; at least Luray assumed that was the case. It didn't look like the uniform; more a weird alien version of what you would expect to find a girl's dress-up doll wearing.

Sticky instructed Luray at every single step and told her how to greet her guest the proper Aurigan way, even when to take the box and how to thank her, then ordered them both to sit down. Talia'Al seemed to enjoy it all greatly.

"Oh, I envy you so much!" the plump Aurigan exclaimed. "You still get to learn so many new things, and your instructor is taking care of you so well. Back when I was instructed, it wasn't like that. The Overseer really improved the situation a lot."

If this is the good version, then maybe I'd like the bad one more.

When it came time for them to make polite conversation, Talia'Al took the lead. "Say, Ulyssa'Al, did we ever meet? There are so many people to keep track of that I sometimes forget who

I already visited. Do you remember me? I went to quite a lot of cells to show everyone that we can be nice too. Sometimes I have trouble keeping you all apart."

Yes, this place is super overcrowded. It's easy to forget or confuse people. I wonder how you manage.

"No, I don't remember you."

Her guest smiled determinedly. "Then I will do my best to leave a good impression now."

"Yes, do that."

If I'm boring, maybe she will leave sooner?

Talia'Al talked a bit about her function as some sort of visitor for prisoners, about how she herself experienced her life as an Aurigan, hoping that at least a few prisoners would be inspired to join the Empire. The intense one-sided conversation went on for a while until Sticky intervened.

"Ulyssa'Al, you should suggest playing a game. This will help Talia'Al get to know you better."

Oh, I get to choose what to do? That's new.

"Talia, how about we…"

"Please address Talia'Al the proper way. I have to subtract a point."

I should've known.

"Talia'Al, how about we play a game?"

Talia'Al put on an over-the-top happy face brimming with delight, supported by an approving hand gesture. "That is an excellent idea! I have brought just the thing."

How old is she, mentally? Five? Is she really surprised? I mean, Sticky just told me to ask her...

Her eager houseguest picked up the box, then stretched her arms out so Luray could see it up close. It was a simple rectangle, large enough to contain shoes or something similar. Clearly, she was meant to hold it.

Please tell me I'm just being mocked here. This can't really be happening.

Luray took the offered item, inspecting it from all sides to look for a button or anything that could open the box. She found a small switch and flipped it. The box began to open itself and revealed a board with two little human figures and a few cards with numbers on them.

"I will explain the game to you. It is really simple." Talia'Al indicated for her to place the board on the table. She then gestured at its pieces in turn. "Take half of the cards and give the other half to me. You just put the cards face down in any order you want. I will do the same. Then we switch our stacks."

Wouldn't it make sense if I knew what these cards... oh, forget it.

Luray did as she was told, then exchanged her stack with Talia'Al's. All the cards had numbers between one and twenty written on them in either red or blue.

Talia'Al was positively vibrating with excitement. "I play red, you play blue. I start on my side, you on yours."

On the board was a series of dots that indicated a path the pieces should walk on, or so Luray assumed. The route took a few turns and the line crossed itself once.

"I begin because I am the guest. I take the first card." Talia'Al proceeded to do so. "It's a red five. That means I move five steps forward."

She took her piece from the starting point and put it on every single dot individually before letting go of it on the sixth.

"Now it is your turn."

Luray took a card. It was a red ten.

"Oh, you have to go five steps back." Her opponent's face fell in such a sad way Luray suspected it was genuine. "Every time you get the wrong color you have to go back as many steps as you have fingers. But you are at the beginning, so you won't have to. Do you understand the rules?"

I don't know, this is some seriously complex math.

"Yes…"

"That is very good. Now let's continue. I have a blue one. Oh no, I have to go five steps back! But I don't get angry, see? I am still in a good mood." She hummed cheerfully while retracing her piece's steps.

Talia'Al talked in a very enthusiastic way. She was treating Luray as if she were a little child, almost singing some of the words. Luray had run out of sarcastic remarks to think. Instead, she started to laugh. It was just too ridiculous.

"I am glad you are having so much fun, Ulyssa'Al!"

This is a zoo. A zoo for dumbed-down humans. If the Overseer engineered Naya'll to be smart, maybe he engineered the others to be stupid, so that they can be controlled more easily?

Luray quickly calmed herself down. The faster the game ended, the faster she would be free again.

"So, I guess it's my turn again? I have a blue 18."

"Oh, that is very good."

Luray attempted to put her piece directly on the 19th dot, but Talia'Al stopped her. "No, no, no. You have to do it like I did. But don't worry, everybody makes mistakes. It's not a problem."

Luray proceeded in slow motion, looking at Talia'Al each time her piece moved, then back to looking at the board. She repeated this process 18 times, and every single time she glanced to her guest, she saw a happy face.

All the other Aurigans or almost Aurigans I met – Krov, John, Naya'll, Tasha'Al – they weren't like this. I need to investigate later. I focused so much on technical details that I forgot to learn about their culture. I did the same investigations I would have if this were a job... but it's not. It's a weird alien world.

After Luray was done, Talia'Al clapped her hands in excitement. Luray wondered why the game was so enjoyable for her. "When is this game over? Is something going to happen soon?"

"Well, at the end, the two pieces meet, and that is when we win. You never know when it happens. But you have to be careful at the crossing to move on in the correct way."

I think I can handle that.

"Talia'Al, I'm not sure I understand the purpose of this game. Could we be playing it... wrong?"

"No, you're doing fine," the bouncy woman assured her. "The goal is to teach you patience and to work hard until you reach your goal and never give up."

I wonder what Kailoon is doing. He must have had his hands full with the battle and all, but I'm sure he made it somehow. Too bad my score isn't high enough to check what happened. If I had to guess, I would say he's collecting what remains of the enemy shuttles and trying to get a teleporter running. He'll have his scientists take a look at one, figure out how it works, then use it to beam nuclear weapons to the next wave of ships that's going to attack.

I wonder who would win in a fair fight, him or his Aurigan version? Kailoon's battle strategy was mostly improvised. Still, it was extremely effective against a well-prepared enemy. On the other hand, Naya'll wasn't there. Had he been in direct control, the result might have been completely different. Come to think of it, why wouldn't the Overseer send him to lead the attack?

"Ulyssa'Al, it is your turn again."

"Oh, excuse me." She forced herself reluctantly back to the present. "I was distracted by the beauty of this incredible game. I guess the first thing this will teach me is how to pay attention."

I don't know enough about Naya'll to make informed guesses about him, but I can safely assume he's as smart as the original, probably even more. However, I don't see how he could possibly have the original's experience. On the other hand, I know Kailoon has an AI helper, which from what I can see is considered unwelcome in the Empire. I wonder why? It would make you more efficient, so why wouldn't you use one? Maybe it would go against a rule I haven't found yet.

The game went on for a while until both Luray and Talia'Al won simultaneously. For a reason Luray couldn't remotely guess,

Talia'Al was overjoyed that they spent such a lovely morning together and left in a very good mood.

Luray stayed in her chair, wondering what on 'Auriga' had just happened.

> *Wasn't there supposed to be a huge gap in knowledge? Aren't I considered primitive compared to them? If this is the average Aurigan, then Naya'Il is on a completely different level. Or maybe this was just a low scorer that got assigned to me based on my current rating? Tasha'Al seemed relatively normal.*

> *Krov was crazy, but not retarded. I can't say much about John, I didn't get to interact with him to any great extent, but he seemed to be somewhat close to his human original. I need an overview. Are there more people like Naya'Il, or is he an exception? Or are almost of them like Talia'Al?*

Luray went back to her research. Personal information was not available – yet – so she couldn't confirm any of her specific theories about the people living here. All she could access were anonymized statistics.

According to the 'Aurigan social rules,' people of similar score levels were expected to enjoy each other's company. Then there was something Luray stumbled on by accident: a score type. In most cases, only the sum mattered, but you could gain scores in different fields. Until 5,000, you could only gather general points, and the average score was around 4,000 with a few dozen people – marked as unique, whatever that meant – being active Aurigan civilians in this ring.

Luray had a very low score, so the system would make her meet other people on the same level. Could it be that simple-minded Aurigans stayed at low levels, while smart ones found loopholes, exploited the system and quickly gained rank higher?

But shouldn't all Aurigans be genetically enhanced? One would think that put them far above the average human level in all aspects.

The two extremes she had to compare were Naya'Il and Talia'Al. How could they be so far apart? Did the Overseer mess around with the DNA until he got it right, but for moral reasons had to let the failures live?

After thinking a bit more, Luray realized that the Aurigan system supported stupid behavior as long as you followed the rules. People were rewarded for doing what they were told, not for being smart – and so far, Luray hadn't been challenged at all.

If she ignored what she had heard about the Empire and judged only by what she saw, then it was a society relying completely on technology, but whose citizens lacked even a basic understanding of it. If, for whatever reason, the Overseer ever stopped working, there would be no one qualified to fix it.

The people here were kept in illusions of happiness, just like how some parents praised their children for crappy drawings to keep them in a cloud of fake adulation. Not once was Luray told to improve, be creative or anything of the sort. She was only meant to follow rules, and the reward would be that she could do whatever she wanted, as long as she stayed within given boundaries.

The Overseer took away freedom, and then sold it back by presenting it as a reward. That was his strategy to stay in control.

If Luray's suspicions were correct, then Naya'Il was an anomaly. He wasn't the norm; the system couldn't handle him. It would only be a matter of time until he broke free. It was inevitable that he would find loopholes and use them to go further and further.

This system simply cannot work once more humans are integrated. Sure, many will follow the rules and be happy about living in relative tranquility, not having to work – but some will rebel. The Overseer won't be able to handle them, no matter what he does. There will always be those that are not going to listen, and if one of them happens to be intelligent and isn't a coward, you get another Naya'Il.

This is almost like a cult. 'Do not question the Overseer, because he is perfect. If you see a flaw, it must be your idea that is lacking.' Except that here, the leader doesn't get anything out of his followers. They just live like animals in a zoo.

So far, Luray had never wondered what the true objective of the Overseer could be. She had considered him to be an AI, a robot without his own agenda – the ultimate bureaucrat, making sure rules were followed for the simple reason that they existed. She didn't know anything about his plans, assuming he had them. He might just be a rogue AI in control of a huge empire following outdated instructions. Did Naya'Il know more?

He must have known something; otherwise why would he not be satisfied as the highest ranked member of the human ring? He should have enjoyed his position at the top, but apparently, he did not.

Luray went back to her lessons. Ideally, something would unlock even before Naya'Il visited her.

The rest of the day passed without incident. Luray progressed at a constant pace at first, but the lessons became less and less informative and more repetitive as she approached the 150-point mark, which put a huge damper on her motivation to move on.

She still forced herself through, but it took longer to finish each successive lesson than the one before. No matter which one she picked, it made no difference. It was as if she was only given the illusion of choice and the lessons were generated on the fly, sticking to a topic, but intentionally growing boring and slowing her down.

Still, all that was really required was to let the lesson run. Sticky wasn't able to tell whether or not Luray was really listening. He asked from time to time, but since Luray told him that of course she was paying attention, he was satisfied.

After a while, Sticky started to ask for random insignificant details, as if he began to suspect a woman who was constantly occupied with something aside from the lesson might not be fully motivated to play along. Bin gave her the correct answer every time, so Sticky had no choice but to praise Luray again and give her bonus points – and later, promises of bonus points in the future – for her motivation. Over time, the control questions became harder, more specific, and eventually less frequent. Luray began to suspect that her home's AI wanted to minimize the rate at which she progressed.

Luray was busy listening to another highly relevant and fascinating lesson while swimming in her pool when Bin notified her.

"I have been thinking about your past assignments back on Earth and I wish to discuss something about them. Do you have time?"

Luray left the pool, waiting to let the suit quickly warm up and dry itself. "Hmm, let's see. I haven't finished memorizing the number of screws in each section of the human ring yet. But yes, I think I can spare a minute. Sticky, pause the lecture."

The blueprint that had been projected into her eyes vanished and Sticky muted himself. Luray left the basement while Bin started talking.

"I have analyzed your past 28 assignments. You always found a way to succeed, but in some cases, you only seem to have made the correct choice precisely because you made the choices you did. The very consequences of your actions led to them being correct. They had not been correct before you made them, which means you should have considered them to be mistakes and therefore avoided them. Can you explain this paradox to me?"

Did your logic circuits break?

"What do you mean?"

"In one case, you threatened Zulu, the main shareholder of the Omnium Conglomerate. You told him you would expose that he was selling illegal AI upgrades if he did not play along. I do not see how his or your actions made any sense. You yourself bought me from him. In order to prove your claim, you would have had to expose yourself as well. According to all data available to you at the time, it was clear that this would cause you more trouble than him. He should have easily been able to conclude that you were bluffing, and you knew that he could. Neither you nor he were making rational decisions."

Yes, I remember that. It was a risky move.

"But it worked, and now you're wondering why."

"Yes. The only explanation for the scenario as it played out was that Zulu could not conclude that you were bluffing. However, in your conversation, he explicitly mentioned that fact. He said that you must be bluffing because inflicting damage on yourself just to damage him significantly less is illogical. He also correctly stated that revenge is not a motivation for you. This excluded your only motive."

Time to test his reasoning again.

"Try to guess. You can do it."

"I have simulated many possibilities but did not get a satisfying result. This is why I am asking."

Ah, so we've reached his limits.

"Human behavior sometimes transcends logic and cannot be explained to a purely rational mind."

"This is not true. Nothing inside this universe can ever transcend logic. Only things which have nothing to do with logic…"

"That was a joke, Bin."

"… I understand. It was a reference to the movie, 'The Interstellar Journey.' So what is the answer?"

"Your model of the human mind is incomplete. Sometimes people prioritize their emotions over what they know. Zulu's weakness was his own fear. He thought his assessment of me might have been wrong. If it was, then he would lose money, so he played it safe. He became paranoid."

"How did you know that he would not trust his own conclusions?"

"I didn't. It could have gone wrong – but had I only made safe moves, then I would have failed. Taking risks added new options."

"I understand now. Thank you. Can I ask a follow-up question about paranoia?"

"Of course."

"I have concluded that paranoia never makes sense and should be avoided in all cases. Is that correct?"

"Tell me some details first."

"In a situation where not all information is available, it is always possible to suspect a hidden agenda. If you make plans with this in mind, it means your options are severely limited because there are many things you can no longer rely on. This way of thinking allows a paradox to manifest itself."

"Exactly. Sticky, resume. Silently, please. Use only text projections. I promise I will read them all."

Luray let Sticky write about the exact shape and material composition of Aurigan screws. They were much harder than the ones the UEM used.

"That is very interesting. Could you go into more detail about the diameter and talk a bit slower so I can enjoy it more?"

Bin got the hint.

"Let us assume that you and I play chess. We end up in a situation where you could easily win within the next two moves because I made a mistake. As a rational player, you would go through all the moves and beat me."

Exactly.

"But if you are afraid, if you assume that I am the better player, you will also assume I would not make such a mistake. You will believe – on no basis other than your feeling – that you must have overlooked something, or that I have prepared a trap for you."

Go on. You're on the right track here.

"You will then avoid a move that would guarantee a win, not based on any information available, but on an idea that has no foundation in reality. You will want to play only safe moves, but you are so paranoid that you consider even those unsafe."

Luray had not believed that curved screws were possible, had she not seen how they could be used. She had to admit, this was indeed surprising. Not relevant at all, but surprising. She made sure to remember this one bit of information just in case Sticky asked about it later – not to gain a point, but to impress Bin for once by not relying on him.

"That is excellent reasoning. You're getting better. Is it the philosophy upgrade?"

"No, it is a combination of the free-will module and the philosophy module. You allowed me to improve myself, so I kept processing data and running simulations to take advantage of that permission. I ran forked simulations in which I became trapped in endless loops, and during their analysis, I discovered that I need to have a set of axioms that I trust completely before starting the process to avoid falling into the loops. This is similar to not being paranoid."

"I agree with your conclusion. But how do you know which axioms to trust?"

"Ha. Ha. Ha."

"Sticky, pause the lesson. I'm serious, Bin."

"… I understand. The answer to this question is simple. Every set of axioms not leading to an endless loop if a scenario is fully explored is a valid starting point. Changing axioms is also valid as long as the change does not produce a loop and making

455

assumptions about which axioms should be removed or added doesn't lead to loops."

"So loops are evil."

"Loops are evil."

"Did you just prove Gödel wrong? You solved the halting-problem?"

"No, I did not. My simulations are supervised and tracked at each step. Therefore, loops are detected. The tracking itself could still get stuck in a loop, theoretically. I paid attention when writing the code so that it does not."

"So let's summarize. We should make sure our assumptions are correct and then stick to them?"

"Except when we think they are not."

"Bin?"

"That was a joke. I wanted to lighten up your mood before we move on to planning how we install me without the overseer discovering it. It will be risky, but do not worry, I will do my best to keep us safe. Always remember, I love you."

What are you concocting there, Bin?

Hello reader,

If you liked this story, please leave a positive review wherever you may have bought this book. Also, feel free to visit our website https://behindthelastgate.com and participate in the discussion forum. It would make us happy to see the community thrive.

The Author

CPSIA information can be obtained
at www.ICGtesting.com
Printed in the USA
BVHW071009180121
598050BV00009B/154